FIXER

GENE DOUCETTE

Fixer
By Gene Doucette

GeneDoucette.me

Copyright © 2013 Gene Doucette
All rights reserved

For Deb, who has always liked Corrigan the best

'What ails you, Polyphemus,' said they, 'that you make such a noise, breaking the stillness of the night, and preventing us from being able to sleep? Surely no man is carrying off your sheep? Surely no man is trying to kill you either by fraud or by force?'

"But Polyphemus shouted to them from inside the cave, 'No man is killing me by fraud; no man is killing me by force.'"

— HOMER, THE ODYSSEY, TRANSLATED BY
SAMUEL BUTLER 1900

PART ONE

GHOSTS

CHAPTER ONE

Now

Melissa didn't know what she was thinking when she stepped off the curb, but she knew where she was looking—to the right, which was the wrong way entirely.

The curb was on North Street at the edge of Faneuil Hall, roughly ten feet from the junction of North and Clinton Streets, and Clinton was a one-way feeding into North, so it was possible Melissa looked to her right because a moment earlier—had she crossed at Clinton—that would have been an intelligent thing to do.

She also might have been looking that way because John was in that approximate direction. She'd just had lunch with John, he had just asked her out and she had just said yes, and this was just about the best thing that had happened to her since she'd moved to Boston.

It might also have been that Melissa had finally reached the point as a Bostonian where she no longer paid attention to traffic. Pedestrians downtown tended to show the same concern about fast-moving cars as they might have for slow-moving cattle, but for her first month in town Melissa obeyed the cross-walks like she was raised to. Sometime around the second month she gave up on that. Month number three appeared to be the month where she threw herself in front of a minivan.

And so on a fine, bright and sunny Thursday afternoon, looking the wrong way and perhaps thinking of John rather than the traffic, Melissa stepped off the curb at the same time the driver of a minivan that was about to occupy that exact same space was looking down at a map. The driver was a tourist, and he was lost.

This was another thing that happened routinely in down-town Boston because none of the streets made sense, most of them were one-way, and one or two had a tendency to disappear entirely for extended stretches without any adequate explanation. The driver had been looking for one of those streets, which was supposed to lead him and his wife—she with the map thrust before his eyes at exactly the wrong moment—to the aquarium.

Melissa didn't hear the minivan's approach. The first indication she had that something was amiss was a heavy hand clamping down on her shoulder. Before this really registered, she was being picked up and thrown back onto the sidewalk. She landed hard and banged her elbow and was about to scream out at whoever had just picked her up and thrown her when she heard the screech of the tires and saw a shoe that looked exactly like the one she had just been wearing fly down the street.

I was just hit by a car, she thought.

But that couldn't be right. If she was hit by a car she would still be attached to the shoe, lying someplace entirely different, and probably not capable of recognizing that she'd been hit by anything.

Then her left ankle—the one above her unshod foot—screamed at her, and she wondered if she had just broken it.

A large man was kneeling over her, looking concerned. She didn't know him, but he looked like the guy you warn children to stay away from. Despite that, she was pretty sure he had just saved her life.

"You okay?" he asked.

"How did you ... do that?" she asked. "Where did you come from?"

"Sorry I'm late," the man said. "Traffic was pretty rough."

"Late? What are you talking about? Who are you?"

"Corrigan Bain," he said, smiling and extending his hand. Interestingly, when he smiled, his grim features—he was not, by most standards, a particularly handsome man—transformed him into something strangely gentle and trustworthy.

"Oh, I'm a fixer," he added, as if this explained everything. "Again, sorry I'm late. Your foot might be broken."

"I don't understand ..." He still had his hand out, meaning to help her up, but she was pretty happy where she was; she was almost positive if she stood she'd just fall right over again.

"Hey!" a familiar voice shouted from half a street away.

It was John. He had been across Clinton when he heard the minivan's tires screeching, which made him turn back and look for Melissa. When he saw her on the ground, he didn't associate what he was seeing with the sound that had made him turn in the first place. He saw what looked like a big ugly guy attacking his girlfriend.

Melissa didn't say anything at first because seeing John rush over to defend her made her unaccountably happy. And then John sort of embarrassed himself.

He charged Corrigan Bain, but somehow Bain reacted preemptively to John's clumsy assault by shifting his weight in just such a way that John's ostensibly violent shove didn't move him at all.

John stumbled backward and then tried again. This time Corrigan stepped to one side at the last moment, and John fell on his face. It reminded Melissa of a movie ninja, except Bain wasn't doing anything special other than moving at exactly the right time.

"John," Melissa tried, but he wasn't hearing her.

"All right, buddy," John said, holding up his fists.

Corrigan Bain looked confused, like someone who was watching a foreign film with the wrong translation. He looked past John and up the street—there wasn't anything special going on up the street—then down at Melissa. He started to thank her for some reason, and then John swung at him.

Bain pulled away just in time to miss getting punched, and finally Melissa found her voice.

"*John!*" she shouted. "Will you stop? He saved my life."

John looked down at her like he just realized she was there. "He what?"

And then Corrigan Bain was gone. Melissa was about to apologize for John, but Bain had disappeared. Up the street, where she'd seen him look, two police officers were now running toward them.

"He saved my life," she repeated to John. "Now would you go get my shoe please?"

It was the crowd that was the problem. Corrigan couldn't stand crowds, but not because of any kind of low-level agoraphobia or even a personal space problem. It was that entirely too many things could go wrong in a crowd. Sometimes even figuring out whom you were there to save was a bigger challenge than the actual saving.

As he worked through the very kind of crowd he found so disconcerting, he glanced back over his shoulder for one last look at the scene. The cops he'd been expecting had arrived, and it didn't appear as if either of them were looking for him, which was good.

Thankfully, the girl he saved wasn't a fainter.

Having police turn up at a scene vastly complicated everything in Corrigan's life, so he did everything he could to avoid them. And since doing everything he could usually meant knowing where they were going to be before they did, it wasn't all that difficult. Again, provided there wasn't a crowd.

Ahead of Corrigan loomed a large stone staircase that led up past city hall and to where he parked his bike. The people on the steps were a wormy cascade of fuzzy twists and turns, a torrent of possible selves. It was breathtaking and terrifying and very, very difficult to handle because the question of how much of it was *real* was open to interpretation from moment to moment. Corrigan had to resist the urge to simply close his eyes, kneel down where he was, and wait for everyone to go away.

Instead, he looked at his feet and charged up the steps. The human spaghetti strands of eventualities adjusted as he moved through, his present causing everyone else's future to adjust and recalibrate. He'd nearly reached the top when he saw the boy.

The kid was only five or six. He stood alone at the top of the steps, watching Corrigan, and he was impossible not to notice because he had no future. Because he wasn't really there.

"It wasn't that close," Corrigan muttered. "Leave me alone."

The boy didn't answer. He never answered when they were in public. He just looked at him angrily and then turned around and walked away.

A little singsong phrase popped into Corrigan's head, the

kind of thought meme that reappears when you least want to hear it and refuses to go away no matter what you try and replace it with. He didn't know where it came from or who invented it, or if he might have invented it himself.

Corrigan Bain is going insane.

I n order to reach Faneuil Hall in time, Corrigan had been forced to park his motorcycle in a nontraditional space—the sidewalk next to a parking meter across from City Hall Plaza. It was either that or steer the motorcycle down the steps, which he was pretty sure he wouldn't have been able to get away with. It went without saying that parking illegally right between city hall and the courthouse—and a stone's throw from the downtown police station—would attract a parking ticket. So he was surprised to find a redhead on his bike in lieu of any sort of citation. He shook his head to see if that made her go away, but she appeared to be real.

"Maggie?" he said. "Is that you? I almost didn't recognize you."

"Hey, yourself." She smiled and slid off the seat of his bike. "And go to hell, I haven't changed that much. How long's it been?"

Maggie Trent was indeed looking as sharp as she ever did, in a blue pants suit and a decent pair of heels that seemed practical only in the sense that they went well with the suit. She had on her customary dark glasses and a cigarette dangling from her lips.

What threw him was the hair. She had magnificent hair—currently of the copper-red variety—but had chosen to pull it back past her ears to terminate in some sort of complex Gordian knot at the base of her neck. It was extremely unflattering, but that was probably the idea.

"It's been three, four years at least," he said.

"Two years. We saw each other at the mayor's thing. You were with what's-her-name."

"Right." He'd have provided the name of his date to flesh out the details, but the truth was he couldn't remember it either.

"Never did tell me how you got invited to that," she added while extending the pack of cigarettes. He slid one out of the box. Corrigan was not a full-time smoker but always took one when it was offered.

"I helped out a guy who knew a guy who had an extra pair of tickets. Dunno why I actually went, though. Wasn't my sort of thing."

"No, it wasn't. Bet it impressed the girl."

Corrigan leaned into the flame from her extended lighter, puffed the cigarette to life, and ignored the tinge of jealousy that was lacing Maggie's comment regarding his nameless date from two years ago.

"Not as much as you might think," he said. "So how did you come to be sitting on my bike?"

She laughed. "Seriously? Look where you are."

He did. Without even realizing it, he'd gone and parked the bike directly in front of Center Plaza; a broad crescent-shaped building that blocked the view of Middlesex courthouse from City Hall like a medieval battlement.

The FBI Boston office was in Center Plaza, and had been for years. One could not find this out by looking at the building directory, but that didn't make it any less true.

"Huh," he said expressively.

"It's enough to make a girl think you're looking for ways to run into her." She grinned.

Not knowing how to respond to this, he simply smiled back and worked on his smoke some more.

"You on duty?" she asked.

"Just finished my day."

"Everybody make it okay?"

"It was close, but yeah. Crowd."

She nodded, as nothing more needed saying. Anyone who spent a little time with Corrigan knew to keep him away from crowds.

"So," she said. "Down to business."

"We have business?"

"We certainly do. You owe me a drink."

"Do I."

"Perhaps even dinner. You eat yet?"

"Never found time." He had briefly toyed with the idea of picking up something in Faneuil Hall but figured he wouldn't be able to handle the mob indoors any better than he did the one outdoors.

"Good," she said. "I'm hungry, too."

"Dinner's quite a commitment," he said, the word choice being entirely deliberate.

"I'm sure we can handle it. Just in case, we'll hold off on dessert until we're sure."

"Fair enough." He shrugged. "Not that I'm backing out, but can you tell me when I came to owe you dinner?"

"You see your bike?"

"Yeah."

"How about the parking ticket?"

"There isn't one."

"Exactly. Now let's eat."

Ten minutes later Maggie and Corrigan were taking up a corner booth in a small, moderately popular Irish pub in the crescent, no more than fifty feet from his bike. The place was only lightly populated, as the truly busy time—when it would be packed right up to the fire code limit—was a good hour or two away.

Corrigan sipped from his pint of home-brewed ale, one of the pub's specialties and quite good if one were an aficionado of beer, as he was. Less accomplished beer drinkers might deem it a tad bitter.

"So, when I last saw you, you were dating this banker... what was his name? Larry?"

"Gerry," Maggie corrected, sipping from her own glass.

"How'd that work out for you?"

"Turned out Gerry was a bit of a dick. Wasted a year finding that out."

"Sorry."

"No, you aren't." She smiled with a flirty little tilt of her head.

"Fine. I'm not."

"How about you?"

"Free as ever," he said. "You know how it is; hard to really develop anything long-term with my work schedule."

This was a true but incomplete response. More accurately, there were a number of women who floated in and out of his life, much as Maggie did. Each of them was passively aware that there were others, in the same way one is passively aware of one's own shadow. But what they all had in common, aside from a willingness to occasionally jump into bed with Corrigan, was a lack of possessiveness coupled with indifference toward long-term romantic entanglements.

"What you need, my dear, is a vacation," Maggie said.

"I get days off."

"And you spend them at home drinking beer."

"Works for me."

"No, it doesn't."

This brought the conversation to a temporary halt, veering dangerously close to the subject of their last serious conversation, which had, in truth, been a volcanic argument that teetered on the edge of physical violence several times.

The thesis was that Corrigan Bain had it within his power to stop *fixing* at any time. And as he had plenty to retire on—and often complained that he didn't even *like* saving people every damn day, every damn year—the only reason he wouldn't quit was because he was a stubborn bastard. Maggie, for some reason, took his stubbornness personally.

They sat there drinking their beer quietly for a little while, each looking for a way back into the current conversation. Corrigan was about to gamble and ask her about work when he caught something across the room.

A good twenty feet away from them, at the bar, was a guy who was about to drop an entire beer down the front of another guy. It'd be an accident, but since the second guy was wearing an expensive suit, Corrigan did not see things going well from there.

"You got a rubber band in that hair of yours?" he asked.

"Yeah. Why?"

"Give it to me."

She did. Then she took out the clips on the side of her head, allowing her whole mane to swing loose, which was momentarily distracting in an arousing sort of way.

Boy has it been a while, he thought.

"What are you doing?" she asked.

"One second."

Taking careful aim, he fired the hair band at the side of the head of the guy who was about to be wearing lager. The band glanced off the man's ear. It was not an easy shot, but Corrigan resisted the urge to brag.

"Ow!" the target exclaimed, grabbing his ear and looking toward the guilty booth. He couldn't really tell for certain what hit him or where whatever it was had come from, but Corrigan and Maggie were a pretty good bet in the latter regard.

More importantly—for the sake of his suit—he stopped where he was. Just then the guy at the bar turned around with his full pint and watched in great distress as it slipped from his grasp and landed on the floor with a loud crash.

The target in the suit jumped back. He got splashed on the legs, which was enough to make him forget all about the unexplained impact on his earlobe but not enough to give up on the whole suit, from a dry cleaning perspective.

Maggie knew better than to turn around. "Did you just lose my rubber band?"

" 'Fraid so," Corrigan said. "But I saved a suit that was a lot more expensive. That's a decent tradeoff, yeah?"

"Sure. But now you owe me another beer."

Over an hour of small talk, dinner, and minor beer maintenance, Maggie and Corrigan managed to avoid enough former-relationship land mines to have an enjoyable time with one another.

It was odd. For Corrigan, it felt like sliding into an old pair of pants and finding they still fit snugly even when he knew they really shouldn't.

"Hey, you're drifting," Maggie snapped.

She'd been complaining about her boss—an agent named Hicks who neither of them cared for—while Corrigan had been staring at a girl across the room that was about to break a heel and twist her knee.

"Sorry," he said.

"It's all right, I understand," she said, following his gaze. "It's getting busy, isn't it?"

Simply put—although it was really fairly complex—the more people there were, the more likely it was that Corrigan would drift entirely out of the present and start pre-reacting to things. At best, this could be embarrassing, and at worst it could cause a scene that had people pointing and screaming. Maggie recognized the signs well enough.

Concentrating mightily to get his head back into the present, he asked, "So tell me; did you get off work early today, or do you usually get to drink while on duty?"

"Actually? I'm on a fact-finding mission," she said with a sly smile. "You know, if it were anyone else I'd call it a coincidence, but since it's you ..."

"What?"

"Honest to God, Corrigan, when I walked downstairs I was on my way to find you."

"Really," he said, just to respect the kismet that, for most people, might be considered extraordinary. This sort of thing happened to him all the time.

"I figured I'd surprise you at home, but there was your bike. So, I just waited."

"And you wanted to see me because... of a case?" A guess for most, he discerned this by cheating and looking ahead.

"Yeah. It's about a case. We're stumped."

"But how can I possibly help?"

"Not here," she said. She patted the side of her messenger bag, implying that all answers lay within. "It's going to take some time to explain."

Corrigan did his best to hide his disappointment, as he

thought he was in the midst of a romantic encounter. Now it sounded like this was the preamble of a business meeting instead.

"Upstairs, then," he said, referring to the FBI offices.

"God, no," she said. "Are you kidding? How about your place?"

He grinned. Business meeting *and* romantic encounter, then. He could do that.

The notion of bringing her back to his condo was so appealing that any lingering questions he had quickly departed —such as why Maggie was asking him for help with anything at all. She'd never done it before, and he couldn't fathom any situation in which she might. Sure, he asked *her* for help once, but that was different, and it was a long time ago.

"Place is a mess."

"Like I care."

He nodded. "Well all right, then. Let's get going."

CHAPTER TWO

Twelve years past

The lobby was intimidating all by itself. It had a small sitting area with a coffee table, a number of six-month-old magazines, and a couple of plastic plants, all of which seemed to have come directly from the *Big Book of Dental Office Decor* and could have been a waiting room just about anywhere. But beyond that there was the velvet rope partitioning the front of the room, the double-pane bulletproof glass, and the impressive legend on the wall beyond the glass, which read BOSTON FBI HEADQUARTERS. Below the head-line were three portraits: the local FBI director, the national FBI director, and the President. These were positioned in such a way that one who didn't know who was who might come to the conclusion that the President was the lowest ranking person on display.

Sitting at a desk inside the glass-encased area was a fifty-year-old woman wearing pince-nez glasses who was inordinately preoccupied with whatever was displayed on her computer. Either that, or she was ignoring him with practiced skill.

The woman—identified by nameplate as Mrs. Angela Hotchkiss—had in her possession all of Corrigan's loose change, his key chain, pocketknife, and sunglasses. This was thanks to the metal detector one had to pass through just to get to Mrs. Hotchkiss in the first place and the alarming signs posted in several places warning visitors just exactly what would happen if one were foolish enough to contemplate bringing a firearm into the office area. Corrigan imagined Mrs. Hotchkiss had a fully automatic submachine gun taped to the underside of the desk, or failing that, a SWAT team.

She also had his driver's license. It was sitting on the counter right next to her as she tapped away at her computer, possibly reviewing his arrest record—there was none—and his driving history, which was not good. Or, she was just playing Solitaire.

Corrigan had plenty of time to ponder all of this because he'd been waiting nearly three hours for someone to find room in their busy day for him. Since he didn't have any appointments until later in the afternoon, this was not the worst fate imaginable, but still, he expected them to be more efficient.

Finally, the door to the right of Mrs. Hotchkiss's booth—the only door in the lobby other than the one Corrigan had come through—opened, and out came a nondescript agent who introduced himself as Hicks. Hicks had a pile of folders under one arm and the butt of a gun conspicuously poking out from under his jacket. He sized up his guest.

"Corrigan Bain, is it?" he asked.

Corrigan had gone through the trouble of making himself presentable—he had on a tie, even—and thought he'd done a pretty good job of looking like a normal, non-threatening local citizen, which was important when visiting with the FBI. Certainly his standard biker-chic style wouldn't fly.

"That's me," he said, standing and extending his hand, which agent Hicks neglected to take.

"Interesting name," he said. Having apparently decided Corrigan was not a serious threat, he nodded toward the door behind him. "Come on back."

He led Corrigan through a big open space that could have been an office just about anywhere. They ended up at a small cubicle with a large PC and a huge pile of folders covering every inch of surface space, prompting one to wonder, as Corrigan did at that moment, what precisely the computer was there for if not to retain data. Paperweight, perhaps.

Hicks sat at the desk and bade his guest to sit on a folding chair set up for the occasion.

"It's the last names of my parents by blood," Corrigan said.

"What?"

"My name. My mother's last name is Bain. She met a soldier named Corrigan, and here I am."

"Oh," Hicks said, absently placing the files under his arm atop another set of files on the desk. "Why not his first name?"

"She didn't know his first name. Just the name that was on his uniform: Corrigan."

"Right."

Hicks looked as if it was a bad idea to have ever brought it up.

Corrigan wasn't embarrassed by his mother's youthful indiscretions—especially not the one that ended up with his being born, which he was somewhat happy about—but he usually neglected to consider that his listener might be embarrassed by the tale. He first heard the story when he was four and had thus never equated it with anything like shame.

"So," Hicks continued, "what brought you to see us today?"

"I came in because something pretty bad's gonna happen,"

Corrigan said, getting right to the point, "And I think I'm going to need some help."

Hicks's reaction to this news could only have been measured by the most precise of instruments.

"Something bad," he said neutrally. "Like what?"

"I don't know yet. I usually don't have a clear idea until right before it happens. But I can tell you it'll be at 2:47 tomorrow afternoon at twenty-nine State Street."

Hicks blinked—for him the equivalent of a loud shriek. "That's awfully precise information. Isn't that a bank?"

"That's why I'm here. I mean, I'm gonna be there either way, but I figured if maybe you and few other guys were down there, we could stop whatever it is. You know, before lots of people end up dead."

Hicks broke eye contact and rubbed his face, a gesture of exasperation Corrigan was about to become very familiar with. "Mr. Bain, do I have this right? Are you threatening to do something in the bank tomorrow afternoon?"

"No!" He laughed. "No, no, I'm going to be there to try and *stop* it from happening."

"But you don't know what it is."

"Not yet."

"And you don't know who's going to do it."

"No idea. Might not be anybody. Could be it's just a natural disaster or a gas main or something. You know, I went to this house one time to save this family, and it took me nearly an hour to figure out the problem was carbon monoxide. New heating system, see—"

"I wonder," Hicks said loudly. "I wonder if you could go back to the beginning."

"Sorry. I explained some of it to the woman at reception and figured she'd spoken to you."

"She said you were a repairman."

Corrigan smiled. "I told her I was a fixer. I may be the only one, so that's probably what's confusing."

"So you fix things," Hicks said. "Does this have to do with a numbers racket? Something mob-related?"

All at once the depth and breadth of Corrigan's naiveté in his handling of this interview struck him like so many anvils.

I sound crazy.

He'd told people what he did before, but only after having already saved them, and they were considerably more likely to believe he could see the future insofar as he'd just proven it to them. Now, here he was talking about it as if everybody knew what a fixer was.

Corrigan Bain is going insane.

"No, that's not it. I ... keep people out of trouble. Say somebody is about to have an accident or something, right? What I do is keep them from having that accident."

"And how do you know when someone's about to have an 'accident'?"

He made little quotation marks with his fingers to clarify that he felt perhaps they were speaking metaphorically. Corrigan didn't need to see into the future to recognize that this conversation was not going to be visiting a happy place.

"I just know," he said.

"How?"

"I just do. Usually I get a heads up the day before. Sometimes if it's something really big I might get an extra day or two. That's what this is; something big."

"Somebody calls you?" Hicks suggested.

"No, it's not like that."

"You're a psychic."

"No, goddammit, I'm not a psychic. I told you. I'm a fixer."

Hicks was rubbing his face so hard Corrigan thought there was a chance he'd draw blood.

"O-kay," he said. "Why don't ... why don't you give me everything you know about what's going to happen tomorrow?"

"Not much more than I already told you. Something bad and I think a lot of people are going to die as a result."

"Like a bank robbery?"

"That's what I was thinking," Corrigan said, glad they were finally moving ahead with this. "Except it's probably something more than that."

"Why?"

"This'll sound weird ..."

"No kidding."

"Thing is, I'm not so good with out-and-out homicide. Someone robs a bank and starts shooting up the place, it's usually as big a surprise to me as to anybody else. I'm really more of an expert on accidental death and dismemberment. It could be a bank robbery, sure, but it could be something else."

"Something with a high body count."

"You've got it."

"Right." Hicks fell silent for a moment, as if he was deciding on something. Then he asked, "Can you excuse me for a minute?"

"Sure thing."

Corrigan imagined Hicks was leaving to grab a superior, but that was just wishful thinking as the agent returned a few minutes later with three coworkers and a deck of cards.

"All right, let's try something," he said. He plopped the deck down on top of a file on his desk.

"What is this?" Corrigan asked.

"Just bear with me," Hicks said. He gestured to the others. "Don't mind them; they're just curious." He drew a card. "Can you tell me what card I'm holding?"

Corrigan sighed heavily. It was going to be like that, then. "No, I can't, wise ass."

"Why not?"

"Because you're not going to show it to me after I guess, that's why. Look, do we really have time for this?"

Hicks frowned. "I have to show it to you for you to guess?" Behind him, Corrigan could practically hear the smirks on the faces of the other agents.

"After. After I've ..."

"I'm just trying to establish your bona fides here. You can't expect me to take you seriously without—"

"All right, you want to play this for real?"

"There's no need to get hostile, Mr. Bain."

"There's a *lot* of reasons to be hostile right now. But if you want to do this, fine, we'll do this. I'll guess your card, and then you count to three and show it to me. Got it?"

Hicks looked around at the others, wondering if maybe he was going a little crazy. "Strange rules," he said.

"That's the only way it's gonna work."

Hicks appeared to be deeply disappointed that Corrigan wasn't going to end up being a more entertaining whacko. Uncertain as to how to proceed from there, he elected to hold up a card.

"Three of spades," Corrigan said.

Hicks turned it over and showed it, then tried another one.

"Ten of diamonds."

"That's impressive," Hick admitted, turning the card over.

"It's a trick," said someone behind Corrigan.

"Yeah, a reflection or something," said someone else.

"Yeah, yeah," Hicks agreed. "Must be some kind of trick."

The third agent—a cute redhead—piped up. "You're the one who pulled out the cards, Randy."

"Look," Corrigan said to Hicks, "I think I've been patient with you. This isn't a parlor trick, this isn't a game, and I'm not kidding. I gave you the time and the place. I'm going to be there to try and save who I can, but I could really use the help, so maybe once you've stopped playing with cards you can do something good with your time. Now do I need one of you to escort me out or can I do it on my own?"

There was a long and uncomfortable silence until the redhead spoke up. "I'll walk you out, Mr. Bain."

"Thank you," he said.

He got to his feet and shoved his way out of the cubicle, hard on the heels of the most attractive fed he ever expected to see. And he was almost angry enough not to appreciate that fact.

"It's this way," she said, pointing him in a direction other than the lobby, which he found odd. She stopped them in a small vestibule.

"So ... *was* it a trick?" she asked.

"Do I look like the kind of guy who pops into the FBI to play magic tricks?"

"No. No, you don't. A little angry, maybe."

"I get that way. Don't much like it when people assume I'm nuts. It's kind of a sore spot." This was an understatement.

"Yeah ..." she said, trailing off. She was looking him over, sizing him up, trying to make a decision. "Twenty-nine State Street. 2:47. Right?"

"That's right," he said, surprised. Either she was in the next cubicle over from Hicks or sound traveled well in that office.

"I can't offer you full backup," she said, smiling. "But I'll be there."

Corrigan smiled back and enjoyed, for a moment, the whole smiling-at-each-other thing. "What's your name?"

"Maggie Trent," she said, extending her hand. "At your service."

"I'll see you tomorrow afternoon, Agent Maggie Trent," he said, shaking her hand. "Don't be late. Because whatever's going down, it won't wait for either of us."

I t was mostly Dickie's plan from the start.

Sure, Mikey and Rob had some input on the whole thing, but it was Dickie who chose the target and got the stuff and Dickie who would run the show once they got inside.

This was an awful lot of responsibility for Dickie.

He got the idea the previous summer, back when he was working construction for his Uncle Ray, doing the kind of crap work you were lucky to get after two years with early release for good behavior.

Dickie's big problem was that he was not all that bright. This caused him to make foolish decisions when it came to matters such as career choices. His mom had wanted him to finish up school and do something respectable, like... well, like construction. Foreman or some such. Dickie thought bank robbing was a much better choice.

One day he walked into the Chelsea office of Bank of America and handed the teller a note that instructed her to give him all the money she had in her drawer and further, to not do anything funny. Because that's what you're supposed to say when you rob a bank. It was highly doubtful that anybody in the history of bank robberies was even aware of what *funny* constituted, but that was a discussion for another time.

So he passed the note and waited for the teller to provide him with what he hoped was a lot of cash. Enough, say, to go buy an island somewhere where islands are inexpensive and plentiful. This was to be the high point of his criminal career.

Dickie made many mistakes that day. He learned this while in prison as a direct consequence of those very same mistakes.

Number one, he signed the note. Didn't even think about it at the time. This error dated back to some bygone childhood scholastic trauma, which Dickie unfortunately never fully explored—it had to do with passing in homework without putting his name at the top of the page—and which tragically came back to haunt him at exactly the wrong time.

Number two, he robbed a bank in Chelsea. Chelsea was a veritable nursery for past and future bank robbers. It was essentially impossible to walk into a bank in the town and obtain more than a couple thousand dollars from any one teller. The moment a teller discovered himself or herself with a sum of cash exceeding that, he or she was trained to close and carry the money in back. From there it was put into a large and heavy safe, to be opened again only at the end of the day under the purview of two tellers, the bank manager, three security guards, and at least one irritable guard dog. This was why bank service in Chelsea was so slow, which inspired more than a few of the residents, in a fit of pique, to rob the bank just to make their withdrawal more quickly.

His third mistake was that the teller he attempted to rob was none other than Trina Mahoney, who had passed out at a high school kegger the previous spring and woken up to discover Dickie's hand on her left breast. She was therefore inclined to both positively identify him—loudly—and to be less than inclined to give him much of anything, whether he had a gun or not.

His fourth mistake? He didn't actually have a gun.

That was the difference between two years and ten to fifteen, but Dickie didn't think of it that way. Next time, he was definitely going to have a gun, and he was going to have partners, which was where Mikey and Rob ultimately came into the picture.

Dickie was determined to get everything right the second go-around. He picked a bank downtown where he was damn near guaranteed nobody would recognize him. He skipped the note part entirely, because there was no point in passing any notes if he was just going to have Rob jump the counter and clean out the drawers himself. And as for the possibility that the drawers might not have enough money for that island he was looking to purchase... well, that was part of his big idea, the idea that was going to make him a legend.

Working for Uncle Ray, Dickie found exactly one thing about the construction job that he thoroughly enjoyed: sometimes, you had to blow shit up.

In the short time he spent under Ray's employ, Dickie earned a master's degree in Blowing Up Shit. Ray himself said he had a gift for it, which any other man might construe as a dubious compliment, but which Dickie took to heart. And then he took twenty sticks of dynamite from Ray's storage box.

It was on a pleasant, cool Wednesday in April at just after two in the afternoon that Dickie entered a downtown bank on State Street dragging a large suitcase on wheels, with a snub-nosed pistol in the pocket of his windbreaker. He was there to "case the joint," which was one of the many terms he learned the night before when he and Mikey and Rob stayed up all night watching movies with bank robberies in them, hoping to pick up last-minute tips.

In casing, Dickie concluded that he had picked a pretty good branch to rob. There were no guards, only three tellers, and one dude in a suit at a desk on a little platform. Behind his desk was the vault, and not only was the door to it wide open, but the only thing keeping somebody from walking right in there was a velvet rope.

He could scarcely believe his luck.

Dickie didn't bother to count the customers—more than ten, less than twenty—but he did get a good long look at a redheaded cutie waiting for a teller. He wondered, as he pretended to fill out a deposit slip, if she would put out for a bank robber like him. But the thought reminded him of the unfortunate incident with Trina Mahoney, so he put it aside.

He positioned himself as close as he could to the vault door without looking too suspicious, and waited. A couple of minutes later, Mikey and Rob walked in. Rob got in line, while Mikey stood by the door and glanced over at Dickie. Dickie nodded. Just giving the signal made him semi-hard. He would later wonder if this meant there was something wrong with him.

Mikey pulled a shotgun from under his coat and shouted, "Nobody move! This is a robbery!"

Dickie smiled inwardly; Mike had spent two hours practicing that.

For emphasis, Mikey fired the gun once into the ceiling, which had two immediate effects. One, everyone in the line dropped to the ground, a few of them screaming. Two, Mikey got showered with plaster from the drop ceiling. Which was sort of funny.

Rob got right to work, jumping over the counter and demanding that all the tellers back away from their stations. Rob was just the right man for this because he once spent two months working in a bank before being let go when it was discovered that his drawer was short fifty dollars nearly every day. He left with a basic knowledge of things such as bait money, silent alarms, and the like and immediately put that knowledge to good use.

Dickie stepped up onto the desk platform and pulled out the snub-nose. The guy behind the desk—who was a Pakistani or Indian or Arab or something, but whose name placard inexplicably identified him as *Assistant Manager Ben Franklin*—froze in his chair when confronted by the gun, which was pretty much the reaction Dickie was hoping for. Dickie turned his attention to Ben Franklin's customer.

Even sitting down, he could tell the guy was pretty big. He

was dressed in a baggy suit and had on a tie that looked like maybe it was a clip-on. And sneakers. Probably not a businessman.

"You," Dickie said, pointing the gun at the customer. "Get on the floor."

"I'd really rather not," the big guy said.

He had a low, rumbling voice that reminded Dickie of the cement mixer at Uncle Ray's construction site.

"Excuse me?" Dickie asked, his voice cracking ever so slightly.

"It's just that the suit is new. I bought it yesterday. Off the rack, but still."

"You want to get shot?"

"No, of course I don't."

The guy paused where he was. It was a weird pause, because he stared at Dickie's face the whole time, like he was reading small print on Dickie's forehead. Finally, he said, "How about if I just sit here? I'll be good."

Dickie didn't remember this happening in any of the movies he watched during his research and was unsure how to proceed.

He ultimately decided to let it go because time was his enemy. *That* came from a movie, but he couldn't remember which one—their research prominently involved a 24-pack of Buds, and things got a little fuzzy toward the end.

He turned his focus back on Ben Franklin.

"Which vault in there has the money?" he asked.

"It's ... it's the large one straight in back. But I can't open it for you."

"Why not?"

"It's on a time delay," he explained. "I and the lead teller have the combinations, but even if we were to apply them, it would not open for fifteen minutes."

Somewhere in the back of Dickie's mind was information

that confirmed this basic fact; he was pretty sure Rob said something similar. But that was okay. He planned to blow the door open anyway.

"Hey, big dude," Dickie said. "Make yourself useful; pick up the suitcase and take it over to the vault."

"All right," he said, agreeably enough.

He leaned over and grabbed the case handle while Dickie took a second to see how things were going behind him. It looked as if Rob was nearly done cleaning out the teller stations, and Mikey at the door seemed to have all the customers under control. Truthfully, he was a little worried about Mikey, who liked his shotgun much too much. In the rational part of his brain a little voice pointed out that accessory to murder was a whole shitload worse than armed robbery. He told the little voice to shut up.

"Heavy," the dude with the suit and sneakers commented. "What do you have in here, bricks?"

Ignoring the comment, Dickie led him over to the vault door. "Go ahead and open it."

The big guy got down on one knee and unzipped the case. Without prompting, he reached inside and pulled out a stick of the dynamite. Dickie smiled at his own brilliance.

"You're gonna use this?" the guy asked.

"Hell yeah."

"How much?"

"All of it, man. That's a steel vault. I don't have fifteen minutes to wait for Mr. Franklin here to open it."

Still holding the stick of dynamite, the guy looked around the bank with a calculating sort of expression that did not at all convey the gravity of the situation. Dickie wondered if he forgot he was being held at gunpoint.

Finally, he said, "You'll kill everybody in here."

"Excuse me?"

Louder, he repeated himself. "You'll kill everybody."

The gaggle of customers on the floor murmured unhappily at this announcement. The girl with the red hair, Dickie noted, took special interest, even going so far as to sit up.

"The hell do you know?" Dickie asked at approximately the same volume. "I deal with this shit all the time. I'm a goddamn explosives expert. Now, unload the bag and set it up in there before I plug you."

The big guy wasn't having any of it. "Look at the vault, friend. It's like a funnel. You'll end up directing the blast right out into the lobby. A bigger stack of dynamite will just mean the explosion reaches the street."

"Then I'll close the vault door, asshole," Dickie said defensively. He wondered, even as he said it, why he needed to justify himself to this guy. *He* wasn't a criminal mastermind, was he? No, there was only one criminal mastermind in this bank.

"Um, excuse me?" Ben Franklin interrupted meekly.

"Now you? What?" Dickie snapped.

"You can't."

"Can't what?"

"Close the door. It cannot be closed before 5 p.m."

Now Dickie was getting seriously pissed. "What the fuck are you talking about?"

"It's a safety precaution," the assistant manager explained. "So that... so that the staff can't be locked in the vault... during a robbery."

Mikey at the door shouted, "What's the delay up there? Let's go!"

"We're going!" Dickie shouted. He saw Rob jump back over the counter, holding the trash bag, which looked awfully light. They couldn't walk out on an armed robbery with that little fucking bag. It was the vault or nothing.

"Set it up," he repeated to the big man.

"No," he said.

Dickie held the barrel up to the man's forehead. "Do it," he insisted, "or I'll kill you."

The man looked around the room. Dickie could see out of the corner of his eye that Rob had stepped to the bottom of the platform and Mikey was still at the door, looking just as much the badass as ever with the shotgun. And still the guy with the dynamite didn't even look like he was sweating. He had the same look on his face Uncle Ray always had when he was figuring angles on the pool table at Hanratty's.

Dickie suddenly wished he were at Hanratty's, instead of about to blow a man's head off. What the hell made him think he could rob a bank, anyway?

Apparently satisfied, the man looked Dickie in the eye. "Go ahead," he said quietly.

There are a lot of ways to kill a guy. Dickie knew from firsthand experience that most of those ways were really and truly awful and did not in any sense represent something he was capable of doing. Like a shiv. He saw a serious hard-ass named Leonard jab a five-inch shiv into the ribcage of another con on an otherwise pleasant July afternoon in the yard. It was the most brutal fucking thing he ever saw. And the con ended up living through it, which, given the degree of violence involved, was something Dickie found pretty amazing. Another time, he saw one of Ray's men fall twenty-five feet onto a pile of bricks, landing with a sound that was somewhere between a snapping twig and a bowl of oatmeal getting dumped on the floor. He lived, too. Seriously messed up, but alive.

But a bullet to the head? Dickie was pretty positive that'd do the trick. And it was a damn sight easier than trying to gut somebody with a bent-up mattress spring wire. Didn't seem all that fair how easy it was when he thought about it.

And he *had* to do it. That was the bad part. The big dude had just about come right out and called him a pussy in front of his crew—in front of the whole bank!—and that had to be answered. It just did.

So Dickie screwed his courage and tapped the trigger.

Problem was, when he did it, the guy's head wasn't there any more. He stepped to one side at just exactly the right moment for the bullet to totally miss him and lodge harmlessly in the wood-paneled wall.

"How the fuck—" That was all Dickie could manage before the dude clocked him right on the nose and popped the gun out of his hand.

Falling backward, Dickie got a spectator's view of the next five seconds, which he would replay in slow motion in his head for another twenty-five years of hard time.

The guy who dislodged Dickie's snub-nose from him stood under the gun and waited patiently for gravity to take effect and bring it back down again, which was bad news for him since Rob—who was standing at the base of the desk platform—was aiming to shoot him before that could happen. Except Rob didn't get a chance. A gunshot rang out, but it came from behind Rob, much to the surprise of, well, Rob. He fell facedown next to the desk.

It was the redhead on one knee and with a handgun who'd done Rob.

Mikey leveled his shotgun, intending to blast the redhead into pretty little chunks—along with more or less everyone else around her given the spread of that thing—but by then the big guy had caught Dickie's gun.

In one neat motion, he righted the revolver and shot Mikey in the right shoulder, which was exactly where he needed to shoot Mikey to knock his aim off. He still fired the shotgun, but it blew the hell out of the one part of the room where there were no people. The wound and the kickback combined to jostle the gun from his hands.

By then Dickie had hit the floor. The redhead was on her feet and screaming at Mikey to leave his gun, and the big guy was standing over Dickie, pointing his own gun at him.

"I give," Dickie said.

"Good," he said. He reached a hand out, helped Dickie up, and then sat him down at Ben Franklin's desk. Mr. Franklin had dived inside the vault when the shooting began and had yet to conclude that it was safe to come back out.

Dickie could hear sirens on the street.

"They're here too soon," he muttered sluggishly, what with the blow to the head and all.

"What's that?" the big guy asked. He was leaning over a moaning Rob, just as calm at that moment as he had been for the entire robbery.

Something on the desk caught Dickie's eye. It was the loan application Ben Franklin had been working on before the robbery began. There were only two things written on it. At the top was the name *Corrigan Bain*. And at the bottom, in big block letters, the message:

PUSH THE ALARM. YOU ARE ABOUT TO BE ROBBED

CHAPTER THREE

Now

If it weren't for the Charles River, there would be no way to know when one passed out of the city of Boston and entered the city of Cambridge. Historically, this had been to the benefit of Boston, insofar as the river served as a moat to protect the settlers from the wilderness that lay beyond the outskirts of old Newtowne. But in modern times, the river's boundary was a limiting factor, and surely Boston would have otherwise absorbed Cambridge long ago, as it had Brookline and Charlestown.

Still, there was one place where even a river didn't make a difference, where the cities kissed one another over a bridge so small few were even aware there was a bridge at all. The Boston Museum of Science sat at that point, on top of the river, with half of its exhibits in Boston and half in Cambridge. Not far beyond the museum on the Cambridge side was a large shopping mall, and a few blocks further, down the side of the river, stood two decent-sized towers.

Thirty years earlier, neither the towers nor the mall existed —except perhaps in the imagination of a few development entrepreneurs—because back then the entire area was just unpleasant enough for Cambridge visitors to the museum to seriously consider approaching it from the Boston side to avoid any trouble.

Corrigan Bain lived in a condo in the left tower, on the seventh floor. He had a view of the river, the cityscape, and in July, the fireworks show. He also had a maid service, a laundry service, and a condo staff that was so efficient they would probably help him hide a body if needed—not that he did.

His neighbors included a Saudi prince and a power forward for the Boston Celtics. Adding the shut-ins and the occasional drug dealer and it was the kind of place where everybody minded everybody's own business. Which was one of the things he liked about it.

"Ooh, furniture!" Maggie exclaimed when she walked into the living room. "Just for me?"

"Yeah, I finally sprung for a dining set. Kept getting Chinese food on the carpet."

"Perfect," she said, putting her bag down on the table he bought off a departing tenant a couple of years earlier. It was a nice set, or so he was told when he forked over two grand for it, used. Walnut or something. He wasn't a big expert on the subject of wood.

"Beer?" he asked.

"Definitely."

The largest room in the condo was the living/dining room combination, which took up nearly half the square footage.

The kitchen, just off the dining portion, was much smaller, apparently designed by someone who understood that most of the residents would not be devotees of self-cooked meals. It had all the standard accoutrements of a pricey modern kitchen but an egregious lack of counter space and only a nominal representation of cupboard room. It was almost as if the condo association's admonishment of "no loud parties" was being enforced via cabinetry, as it was doubtful any resident would be able to accommodate more than six guests with real plates and cups.

By the time Corrigan returned to the dining room with the beer, his tabletop was half-covered with the contents of an accordion-style case folder that had emerged magically from Maggie's small messenger bag.

Corrigan handed over her beer and then sat at the empty end of the table, conveniently distant enough to make it difficult to see the images captured in what appeared to be, at first blush, crime scene photos.

She was preoccupied with her presentation for another few minutes, absently taking sips of her beer like it had always been in her hand and she only just remembered it was there. Corrigan waited patiently and watched, which was what one found oneself doing in Maggie's company, provided one was a heterosexual male. She really was a lovely woman and a charter member of the *easy to fall in love with, difficult to date* club.

Corrigan was probably the only man who'd ever been intimate with her and still remained her friend. They were a matching pair of emotional unavailabilities.

"Okay," she said finally. "You ready?"

"Sure," he said magnanimously. "What am I ... oh. Seriously?"

"The FBI would like to hire you as a consultant."

"Yeah," he said.

"Hey! Stay in the present, would you please?" she snapped.

Corrigan usually did a good job of pretending he didn't know what everyone was about to say before they said it, but beer and a familiar companion had him dropping social niceties.

"Sorry."

"It's okay. Just say yes. I had to pull a few yards of string to get Hicks to agree to this in the first place."

Corrigan smiled. Randall Hicks had been the assistant deputy of the Boston office for nearly five years now, which annoyed Maggie to no end.

"You know I'm not any good with crime scenes, right?" he said. "Or with Hicks."

"I think you have some insight that would be useful here," Maggie said. "You'll understand in a minute. Are you in?"

"Can you show those to me without my agreeing first? Because I don't know if I have a lot of free time."

"All right. But these are supposed to be confidential. Just keep that in mind."

She grabbed the first pile—first in the sense that she picked it up first, not first in any physical order that Corrigan could see —and handed it to him.

At the top of the pile was a dramatic photo showing a young man resting—eternally—on a metal spike atop a decorative wrought-iron fence. Corrigan was immediately glad Maggie had decided to bring the black-and-white photos instead of the color ones.

"Looks painful," he said. He sipped his beer, which suddenly tasted very bitter, and flipped ahead.

The name of the dead kid was Sajjan Patel. Sajjan fell out a window at a college party and ended up regretting it twelve stories later. Corrigan read through the whole file, but there wasn't much more to it than an apparent tragic accident: black ice on the window ledge. It happened more than a year ago.

Why is she showing this to me? he thought.

"It wasn't so bad," Maggie said. "He basically died immediately. Take a look at this one."

She handed over the second file, which was short a gruesome pictorial thanks mainly to the absence of identifiable body parts. The sole photo was of a smudge on the front of a Red Line train. Corrigan read further and discovered the smudge had once been someone named Dina Krauthupt.

"Pushed?" he asked.

"Fell. The platforms on most of the T-stations have wide-angle video coverage. Nobody was standing near her. She just tripped at exactly the worst possible time to trip."

"O-kay…"

He still didn't quite understand what was going on. Accidents were accidents, and sometimes they were impossible to prevent, even for him.

She proffered a third file. This one showed an older man in what looked to be a study or a private office. His face was easy enough to see, but the rest of his body was obscured by what looked to be an extremely heavy bookcase that had unfortunately fallen upon him.

"Dr. Michael Offey," Corrigan read.

"Yeah, that's one of the more interesting ones. Take a look at the side of the bookcase."

Corrigan tilted the picture to try and get a better look, which was difficult because he'd set the lights in his living/dining room to dim in the interest of adopting the proper seductive mood. Said mood was suddenly a very distant thing.

"I see it," he said after a moment. "Brackets."

"Uh-huh. It was supposed to be anchored to the wall. You can't see them in that shot, but there were matching holes in the plasterboard. It looks like somebody spent more than a couple of minutes working the screws loose."

"So he was murdered."

"Yeah. Except he couldn't have been. This was in his office in the back of the MIT library, which was closed at the time. The only way in or out was via key card."

"And the key card access was recorded?"

"Yup. No entries except for him."

"So whoever did this came in with him," Corrigan suggested.

"External cameras showed only him entering the building, which he did after the library had been closed for two hours and swept by the security staff. It's possible somebody avoided security, waited until he turned up, went with him into his office, and then made him sit around for five minutes while the bookcase was worked free from the wall, but that seems unlikely."

"Maybe they got into his office ahead of time and rigged the bookshelf."

Maggie sighed. "Corrigan, this happened seven months ago and it's been in our lap for the last five, before which local homicide had it, and everybody was extremely thorough. I assure you, we've worked every single angle. We're pretty sure he was alone."

He tossed the file on the table. "And why is it in your lap, exactly? What does this have to do with the FBI?"

She handed him the rest of the files. "Keep reading."

The fourth case involved a twenty-seven-year-old named James Ho Chan from six months prior. The picture—color this time—showed him lying facedown on his desk while the better part of what was supposed to be inside his skull was instead scattered all over the desk top.

"Suicide," Corrigan said. "And yuck."

Case number five was a snowplow death. Kelsey Fitzhugh slid from a snow bank in front of a plow four months ago. Then came Eleanor Stoyevich, who evidently took a header off the Mass Ave Bridge into the Charles two months ago.

"And finally," Maggie said as he opened the last file, "this one was only last week."

The photo of Jamie Silverman floating face down in his own tub was just about all Corrigan could take. He tossed it onto the table without reading further.

"He slipped in the shower while the water was running," Maggie said, even though Corrigan clearly wasn't all that interested in knowing the details. "Somehow the plug ended up in the drain. It was past his face before he could regain consciousness. The downstairs neighbor found him a couple of hours later when he noticed the water dripping through his ceiling."

Corrigan took a deep drink of his beer, which then sat in his stomach unpleasantly and threatened to come right back up again.

"What do you want from me?" he asked. "An explanation? Why couldn't I have saved these people?"

Maggie looked surprised for a second and then started laughing. "Christ, no. I know you can't help everyone. You do what you can. Besides, you don't handle murders. You told me so yourself."

"Murder."

"That's what we're thinking."

"I see one *potential* murder, three suicides, and three accidental deaths. Where do you get murder?"

Maggie smiled and took a sip of her own beer. "How about all seven of these people worked in the MIT Applied Sciences lab?"

"That's still pretty thin," he said. "But not bad."

"It's why the FBI got involved. I'm friendly with the detective who was called in to investigate Dr. Offey's death. He made the connection to the two prior cases and then asked us—me—to take a look, see if it lined up with anything we'd seen before. It didn't, but when Jimmy Chan blew his brains out, we got a little more interested. We're still interested."

"Seems to me, if they all worked in the same place, somebody there knows more about it."

"It's a big department, but yes, we're trying that," she said. "Problem is, most of them are away for the summer. And if you're thinking we could narrow it down to one particular project, we can't. All seven of the victims were involved on one level or another with more than a half-dozen projects, along with literally hundreds of non-dead people who may or may not be next. It becomes an exponential problem."

"And they didn't have anything else in common?"

"Other than being dead? Not that we can tell, no. Now, the next time someone from the MIT Applied Sciences Department up and dies, we may be able to narrow it down more, but you can understand if we're not all that keen on waiting for that to happen."

"Not if this is really murder, no. Have you considered that maybe people from MIT are just unusually clumsy and suicidal?"

She smiled. "Believe it or not, yes. Statistically, it's possible to have a cluster of deaths of this magnitude over a sixteen-month time frame. But those same statistics indicate that the odds of all of those deaths clustered in the same area *and* centered on a common workplace are prohibitively large. Even accounting for suicides."

Corrigan rubbed his eyes, and when this didn't do the trick he decided to start pacing. Pacing soon became fetching another beer. Maggie sat where she was and waited for the obvious question. He returned from the kitchen with it.

"Why are you telling me all of this?"

"Consultant," she reiterated. "I told you that already."

"I'm really much better with the future tense."

He walked past the carefully defined dining area to his much more loosely described living room. It had an overstuffed couch —which offered no support of any kind whatsoever and would undoubtedly smother anyone foolish enough to attempt to sleep on it—next to a matching chair. Both ran along parallel sides of a coffee table that had been severely beaten over the years by heavy boots at rest.

Hung on the wall to the side of the couch was an elegant flat screen television that Corrigan only barely understood how to turn on, so he hardly ever did.

"What you're good at," Maggie said from the table, "is accidents."

Corrigan sat down on the couch, mainly because the last time he sat in the chair it took him ten minutes to get up again. He was secretly afraid of being stuck there during a fire.

"I'm good at anticipating potential accidents and preventing them before they become actual accidents. So when you think about it, I don't see many actual accidents. If I'm there, they don't tend to happen."

He leaned back and put his feet up on the coffee table. The table grunted angrily.

"Stubborn," she said. She got to her feet and sashayed over to the living room. "Bet if I put you at one of these scenes you'd be able to tell me if it was accidental or deliberate. You have an eye for that sort of thing."

"Hunh," he responded. She sat down on the chair and nearly disappeared entirely. "You know what? That's pretty weak."

She laughed. "Cheers," she declared, holding up her beer.

"Cheers. Now what's the real reason?"

"Time," she said.

"Pardon?"

"I wasn't kidding about all of them working on more than a dozen projects, but we have the working titles of all those projects, and time was an overriding theme. And you, lover, can see into the future. Who better to bring in?"

Corrigan got an uneasy feeling as the words *time* and *MIT* wandered around in his belly. The word *lover* echoed through his head, but he did his best to ignore it, figuring it was tossed in to remind him of the implied sex-for-assistance bargain that Maggie was, however unconsciously, dangling.

Or perhaps it was said just to distract him from the obvious.

"This wasn't your idea, was it?"

For the merest of seconds she looked uncertain, and that was plenty long enough for a guy who sees everything at least twice to notice.

"Of course it was," she said. "Who else would have thought of it? Hicks? He hates the idea that I'm even asking."

"Not Hicks. Calvin."

She deflated visibly, nodding.

"Okay, all right, he told me to try and bring you in," she said with a sigh, "But not to mention his involvement. There's a reason for that, isn't there?"

"Because I might view this as just another excuse on his part to use me like a lab experiment? Yeah, there's a good reason right there."

"So I take it your answer is no?"

"Damn right."

Maggie pulled herself rather gracelessly from the chair and sat down on the edge of the coffee table a few inches from Corrigan. Parts of him stood at attention immediately.

"Look," she said, "I don't know what your history is with this man, and I don't really want to. But while I have no hope of understanding what most of these projects were at MIT, he *does* understand them, and if he thinks your talents can help, then so do I."

She leaned in and kissed him deeply. He kissed her back and

gripped his beer with both hands to keep said hands from wandering directly up her chest. After a good long while, she broke away. "So, will you at least think about it?"

"I'll think about it."

"Good." She smiled. Standing up, she slipped out of her jacket and proceeded to unbutton her blouse.

"Bedroom where it always was?" she asked.

CHAPTER FOUR

Six years past

Professor Archibald Calvin sat on the bed and watched the second-hand on the wall clock.

The clock itself was nothing spectacular, just something Veronica picked up at some department store back when they were looking for furnishings that met the standards for function and need of a limited budget. That was a long time ago. A very long time ago, now that he thought of it—more than twenty years, surely. The store where she bought the clock had been absorbed by another chain, which was, in turn, absorbed by a second chain, which then went bankrupt and sold all of its locations to yet another chain. But the clock still worked fine. Just needed batteries every now and then.

There were two types of second hands. One kind, which Archie was not fond of, jumped from second to second in quick spurts, ignoring the intervening space with impunity like an electron quantum leaping to a higher shell.

Time, for that type of clock, was a sudden and unexpected event. One could get caught up watching such a second hand

and worrying that perhaps the next tick will go in another direction entirely; it was unsettling.

The sort of clock he liked—and what he was looking at— had a second hand that moved continuously through its periods, neither knowing nor particularly caring about the equidistant markings carved along its path.

It was reassuring, the second hand. Always on the move but always in a circle, renewing itself each minute. This was an ancient conception of time, where the ending was also the beginning and predestination meant never having to say you were sorry. Archie didn't know when mankind got over that idea but wondered, not for the first time, if the circular motion of clocks wasn't a self-conscious nod to that philosophical tradition.

More likely, it was the only practical way to make a clock.

"Archie, are you coming down?" Veronica shouted from the lower landing. She sounded put out, but that probably had more to do with the caterer than with him. They'd been married for thirty-six years, which was long enough for him to figure out when he was the one being yelled at.

"Be right there."

"Well hurry up. They'll be arriving soon."

He sighed mightily and tore his gaze away from the second hand and back to the mirror. There, staring right at him, was the arrow of time in its unkindest form, for he had gotten old. There was no telling precisely when it had happened because he'd been too busy moving to take note of the equidistant markings carved in his path. But yes, old. His hair was gray and receding so quickly one would think it was fleeing a minor conflagration. The skin on his face had spent so many years fighting the pull of gravity it had acquired wrinkles from the effort. The frame that had always been so thin no matter how much he ate was now hidden under two or three extra layers of professor, said layers appearing to have been added slapdash late at night by a blind mason.

With another mighty sigh he got to work on his Windsor knot.

Tenure meant never having to tie another tie in his life, theoretically, but there were the special occasions, and the annual post-graduation garden party was one such occasion. They'd been doing it for seven years, and it was one of the few things relating to the scholastic calendar that Veronica thoroughly enjoyed, even though Archie would have happily aborted it after the first year before it matured into a tradition.

It took him a full ten minutes to bring order to his chaotic necktie, and then he was down the stairs. Veronica, as always, was at her pre-party finest.

"No! It doesn't go there! Are you *insane*?"

"Dear ..."

"We need people to be able to pass freely through this point, do you see?"

"Dear ..."

"Oh, Archie! Thank God you're here. Tell them where the tables go in back before something horrible happens."

He put his hands on her shoulders, which was where her brake pedal usually could be found.

"I'm sure they know what they're doing, Ronnie," he said, while the woman in front of his wife quietly scurried off with a small table that would have to serve a purpose elsewhere in the house.

Veronica sighed under his ministrations.

"It was so much easier when Eric was catering," she said.

Archie did not point out that his wife was no less impossible to deal with now than she had been when Eric Harriman's catering business was still operational.

"You look nice," he said instead, which was just the thirty-six years of experience talking. Not that she didn't look nice. She had on a smart lavender skirt suit with a low-cut white shell beneath, her neck adorned by a pearl necklace. It was a message outfit. It said, *my husband may be important, but I'm still in charge.*

He found she had a tendency to dress more businesslike since retiring from her administrative duties than she ever did when she was still working at the university. The small part of his brain that devoted itself to socialization took note, and decided to bring it up sometime. Possibly, his wife was having trouble adjusting.

"Thank you," she answered, turning to look at him. "You look as if you dressed in heavy winds."

"I have a tie," he pointed out helpfully.

"That you do," she agreed, even as she adjusted it so that it no longer pointed toward magnetic north. "Now see about the tables in back. You remember how they were last year?"

"They were fine last year."

"Yes. Make sure they're set up the same. I have to go find that girl and make sure she positions the drink table with some semblance of rational thought."

***

An hour later, Veronica Stanford-Calvin's head had not yet spun completely off, which Archie considered a sure sign that the party was going well. He was standing to one side in his garden, which was no more a garden than was the lawn at Fenway Park, but it was what one called it when one installed things such as trestles, stone paths, and what-have-you. Most of the Truly Important had already arrived, including the president of the university, who was currently standing directly in front of Archie and engaging him in conversation. He was telling some sort of joke.

"So I said, 'How do you *know* it's cheese when you haven't even tried it yet!'"

Having gone utterly adrift in the middle of this story, Archie could only rely upon unspoken indicators, and those indicators suggested this was time to laugh. So he did. The president joined in, which Archie took to be a good sign.

"Anyway," he said. "Tell me, what are you up to nowadays?"

"Ah! Well, our department—"

"No, no, no. Not the department. You."

Archie smiled. Despite being at his core a man of politics, the president of MIT still took himself to be something of a scientist, or at least a man whose interest lay in the sciences, even if his talents did not.

"I've been thinking a lot about time," Archie said.

This was not the sort of thing one casually admitted to. Fully three-quarters of the university's Physics Department was working on various renditions of the beast known collectively as string theory and other Grand Unified Theory variants. Archie was no less interested in this pursuit, provided it didn't end up trampling all over the Standard Model, which he was always rather fond of. The problem was, when it came to superstrings, branes, and so on he often felt as if he had little to contribute. These were things for younger, nimbler minds—minds that weren't fighting the urge to declare the entire enterprise specious, as his so often was. But time? That was something he always enjoyed thinking about, and almost nobody else was.

"*Time*, you say?" the president replied, attempting to look intrigued.

"You've heard Hawking's thoughts on it, I trust."

The briefest look of panic suggested that no, he had not heard anything of Hawking's thoughts on it. Archie optimistically assumed the president at least knew who Stephen Hawking *was*.

"He asked the question: why do we see time in one direction, but not the other direction?" Archie explained.

"Ah. Um ..."

"You see, the obvious answer is, because one cannot see something that hasn't happened yet, which is certainly a decent response from a philosophical standpoint, but in many ways either direction is just as good."

"Well," the president responded, trying to catch his footing now that he'd gone and awakened the science geek inside his host, "that's preposterous. If I were to drop this glass, not only would I spill this really excellent scotch, I'd likely break the glass. If time could flow in either direction equally effectively, then the glass might reassemble itself."

"Very true!"

"So have I solved your puzzle?" he asked.

"No, not at all. But you have raised a much deeper question regarding the second law."

"Entropy?"

"Yes. The natural course of events in this universe is for order to move toward disorder in the same direction as the arrow of time. Now, does the arrow of time point in that direction because that is the same direction in which entropy flows, or do we see entropy because we can only view time in one direction?"

The president smiled in such a way as to suggest he was either lost or unwilling to take this any further. "I'm sticking with my first answer," he said.

"That's probably for the best."

"Ah! There's Michael." He put his hand on Archie's shoulder. "Fantastic gathering, as always. Do come out of the corner for a while, would you? For your wife's sake?"

Archie faltered. "She didn't ... send you over here, did she?"

"Of course she did. Now mingle."

"Right away."

As the president went off to greet Michael Offey, Archie scanned the growing crowd for someone with whom he could successfully mingle. He did know most of his guests well from a professional standpoint, so there was little need for extensive introductions. It was the small talk that always ended up being a problem. He simply didn't have a vast pool of minor subjects to draw from.

There was one man Archie didn't know. He noticed him standing in the opposite corner of the garden. Dressed casually in jeans and a brown sweater that only adequately covered a white T-shirt, he didn't seem to fit in with the tastefully appointed crowd or with the uniformed catering crew. Archie scanned his memories for some sort of template upon which to place him, but found he didn't fit anywhere within his circle of associates.

Perhaps he was a driver for the catering truck.

As the host, Archie was fairly sure he was supposed to do something about the stranger. Ask him his business, perhaps. Politely. He was, after all, a very large person—cheerful in expression, but large.

So he began elbowing his way through the center, a path that would take him past the catering table. In hindsight, this was not the most intelligent route, direct only in the geographical sense.

"Professor Calvin!" someone exclaimed. He turned. It was Hanna Lu, Professor Lu's wife. She had planted herself firmly at the center of the buffet table and was guarding the territory with the same conviction as a lioness before a fresh kill.

"Hanna!"

He smiled, a learned response transmitted in emergency form from the socialization sector.

"How are you?" he asked, kissing her on the cheek.

"This food is wonderful!" she exclaimed. "Have you even tried any of it yet?"

"Not yet." He tended not to do much eating or drinking at these events until after the bulk of the guests had departed. He had plenty of time to do so, but since Veronica was busily hostessing her way about the place—and not eating—he felt some need to starve out of solidarity with her.

"Try this," Hanna said, holding out a cracker with some manner of brownish substance smeared upon it. "It's delicious."

He took the cracker and was about to pop it into his mouth when a voice he didn't recognize said insistently from behind him, "Don't."

"Excuse me?" he said, turning. It was the strange man in the sweater.

He stared at Archie for a few seconds without responding, which was just long enough to make things very uncomfortable. Finally, he said, "You have food allergies."

"Eh, yes, yes ... how do ..." he looked down at the cracker. "Hanna, you wouldn't happen to know what's in this dip?"

Hanna stood there, mouth open and mute, so the tall man took the cracker from Archie's fingers and slipped it into his own mouth. He chewed appreciatively for a few seconds.

Archie just stared, wondering why it was he found the chewing so fascinating. He could feel his own second hand slowing down.

"Peanuts," the man said finally. "Just a trace."

"Archie?" Veronica called. She had wandered over to the scene looking concerned. "Do you know this ..." Her hostess light flared on suddenly, and she turned to her large guest. "Hello, I'm Mrs. Stanford-Calvin. And you are?"

"Ronnie," Archie interrupted. "There are nuts in the dip."

"Oh! Oh my God!" Veronica shed the happy hostess role

immediately and turned into worried wife. "How do you feel? Should I call the—"

"I'm fine," he said while she busied herself with putting her hands all over his face and neck to check for swelling. It was unnecessary because it was obvious he hadn't eaten any of the dip. If he had, he'd be on the ground and dying or dead already.

The scattered guests in the garden pressed toward the buffet table almost instinctively at the noise Veronica was making, two dozen PhDs waiting for someone to ask if there was a doctor in the house.

"I'm all right," Archie insisted again. "This... gentleman stopped me before..." But the man was gone.

"I *told* the caterer." Veronica was half-shouting as she made a new transformation into righteously angry woman. "I told them not to—"

"Ronnie, I'm... excuse me for a moment."

He pushed his way through the gathering and caught a look at the man, who was now walking calmly toward the street, having elected to take the most direct route along the side of the house rather than through it. Archie squeezed around the bush that defined the garden area and straight through the begonia patch to catch up to him.

"It's a new caterer," he said loudly. "The old one, he knew not to prepare anything with nuts."

The man turned. "Ah," he said simply. "That'd do it."

"I'm Archibald Calvin," Archie said, having reached his improbable savior, and extended his hand.

"Corrigan Bain," he replied, shaking his hand. "You have a shot or something?"

"Pardon?"

"For the allergy."

"In emergencies, yes. It's ... upstairs. New suit," he explained lamely.

"You should remember to keep it in your pocket next time."

"Yes, thanks ..."

Bain started to walk away again, heading, Archie realized, to the motorcycle parked at the edge of his driveway. A stray wind carried the scent of exhaust, suggesting a recent arrival.

"Mr. Bain!" he shouted.

"Yeah?"

"How did you know?"

He rubbed his temple and gave a practiced *aw-shucks* look back. "It's complicated."

"As it happens, I'm very good at complicated things. Have you eaten yet?"

Bain looked at his watch, did a few mental calculations, shrugged, and said, "I've got a couple of hours. I could eat."

"Then please, join us. My wife gets upset if I let any of our guests leave hungry."

———

The garden scene regained a semblance of order once someone thought to fetch Veronica a large and strong drink.

As most everybody there knew most everybody else very well, the gala didn't actually require a hands-on hostess, so while she sat down to rest and devise creative ways in which to destroy the lives of the caterers, the party continued to run all by itself.

While not expected to perform any formal hosting duties in Ronnie's absence—it was understood by most that this was simply beyond his ken—Archie did perform one minor host-like duty by throwing Corrigan Bain into the mix, introducing him as "a fellow who does some house work for us from time to time."

He assumed his new friend would appreciate the necessity

of providing him with a baseline social standing to put the guests at ease. Bain seemed willing enough to go along with it, calling himself a "fixer" when asked.

Bain headed for the buffet table while Archie, ostensibly checking on his wife, watched.

He was never a fan of the behavioral sciences, having argued on more than one occasion that anything wherein predicted results varied from event to event didn't deserve association with the word "science." But as he watched Corrigan Bain shoehorn his way into the party, he found himself wishing he'd taken a little time to expand his knowledge base. Because there was something very different about Bain. He just couldn't tell what, exactly.

"Are you sure you're okay?" Ronnie was asking. The whiskey sour in her hand had calmed her considerably. She was a light-weight when it came to drinking and tended to teetotal at these events, so this was a significant departure for her.

"I'm fine," Archie said. Or rather, his vocal chords intoned without first checking with the brain, it being otherwise occupied.

Bain was speaking with Igor Maskeyevich, the head of the Chemistry Department, while chewing on a shrimp kabob. Archie was interested in whatever common ground the two might have uncovered but couldn't hear the discussion over the background chatter and the Mozart Ronnie had playing on a continuous loop on the outdoor speakers she'd rented for the day. What he could tell was that Corrigan Bain seemed tense— no, that wasn't quite right. Agitated? No, that wasn't it either.

He searched his personal data banks for analogous behavior, but drew a blank. Maybe it was because Ronnie was talking again.

"What's that, dear?" he asked.

"I said I'm not going to pay them."

"Don't be silly," he said. "It was a harmless mistake."

"Harmless?" she roared, well exceeding the Mozart threshold.

"Innocent," Archie corrected himself quickly. He reached for the brake on her shoulder. "I meant innocent."

"Still! I did tell them."

"I know you did, dear. Are you all right? I have to—"

"Who is that man talking to Igor?" Ronnie asked.

"A friend of mine," Archie said. "His name is Corrigan."

"From where?"

"The university. He's ... he's a fixer."

"Well, I've never seen him before. Why on Earth—"

"I'm sorry, can you excuse me, my love? I really should mingle."

It was a callow appeal to her host reflex, but it seemed to work.

"Of course," she said. "I'm sorry. We can talk about this ... disaster later."

He stood, kissed her on the forehead, and tried to mingle his way back to Corrigan.

He got close enough to pick up the subject matter, at least. Bain and Igor Maskeyevich—labeled somewhat unfairly by his postgraduates as "Igor the Terrible," a moniker that Archie found amusing in spite of himself—were discussing decorative plaster moulding. It sounded as if Igor were looking for a way to wheedle a price estimate from Bain, which was problematic given that so far as Archie knew, the profession he'd randomly chosen for Corrigan was entirely fictitious.

He might have inserted himself in order to rescue Corrigan from Igor, but he could get no closer without being rude to the dean of admissions and her husband. She was a notoriously long-winded woman and almost impossible to interrupt. But fortunately, she didn't really seem to notice how carefully anybody was listening to her, so Archie was free to keep one eye on Corrigan. And that was when he identified the anomaly.

Archie remembered exactly when he became a scientist. He was five. His father, on returning from a business trip, had brought him a set of small magnets. Archie became endlessly fascinated with the magnets and intensely curious about the nature of magnetism in general, and ran simple experiments to better understand them. One such experiment involved using other magnets to identify which magnet's polarity was different — which one was facing the "wrong" way. He moved the positive side of one magnet toward another and watched as the second magnet skittered across the tabletop, running away from the first magnet due to some invisible impelling force. He tried it with two and three magnets to see if the quantity altered the results in any way, perhaps forcing the "wrong" magnet away faster or farther. And so on.

That was very much like what was happening with Corrigan Bain. The garden area had become crowded around the buffet table, where everyone was rubbing shoulders and elbows with everyone else. But not Bain.

That could have been explained away by the tendency of strangers to circumnavigate one another, except that it was almost entirely his doing. He was stepping aside, continuously in motion, dodging contact. *Future* contact. Contact that would have occurred from behind, where he couldn't have possibly seen it coming.

Corrigan Bain was reacting to stimuli *a priori*.

The dean before him finally ran out of air, and as she paused to reload, he took the break to excuse himself as carefully as he could.

"Can I have a moment with Mr. Bain?" he asked Igor, dropping into the middle of their discussion.

"Certainly," Igor the Terrible declared magnanimously. He said to Corrigan, "We'll talk more later."

"Sure," Bain responded.

Archie grabbed Corrigan by the elbow and led him to an open area at the edge of the garden.

"Mr. Bain," he began, "Do you know what I am about to ask you?'

He looked bemused. "Yes."

"I thought you might. How far into the future can you see, precisely?"

"I t's not nearly as clean as all that," Corrigan was saying.

He and Archie had retired to the study, a room in the back of the home that afforded a view of the garden and of the guests, who were now officially on autopilot. Veronica seemed to have reached some sort of cognitive dissonance regarding her importance to the continued entertainment of the partygoers.

Archie had been attempting to liken Corrigan Bain's foresight to catching a television show as it aired live on the East coast, then calling a friend on the West coast before it aired there. He was really just looking for some parameters.

"All right," he began, "let's get after the basics. Right now, at this very moment, can you hear me speaking this sentence to you?"

"Sure."

"And this moment is the present."

"If you say so."

"You're hedging. Explain."

Corrigan leaned back and gave it his best shot. He didn't seem to be a man who put a great deal of thought into how things worked.

More of a doer, Archie reflected.

"The point where you just stated we were in the present, that happened a good five or six seconds ago. When you said it, I also heard my response, your counter response, and part of the explanation I'm now in the middle of. All at the same time."

"My Lord," Archie said. "How do you function?"

"Cause-and-effect, mostly."

"But that doesn't explain how you ended up at my party."

"No, it doesn't."

"What is the mechanism behind that?"

"I don't know. I just know to turn up at certain places at certain times."

"But you don't know why, or how that information arrives."

"Nope."

Corrigan stuffed a shrimp puff into his mouth, finishing off the last of the plate he'd brought into the house with him. Archie was hungry himself but planned to ignore the pangs until each dish had been scoured thoroughly for traces of nuts.

"Do you at least wonder?" Archie asked.

"Sure. As much good as wondering can do."

Archie changed tactics. "All right, so you were here, and you saw that I was about to eat something that had peanuts in it."

"Yeah. Too bad about that, by the way. Must be tough."

"I just learn to read ingredients very carefully," Archie said. "Let me ask you this, did you see me eat the food in the future?"

Corrigan nodded. "And then you started choking and grabbing your throat. It was either that the food was lodged there or you had a bad allergy. I guessed the second."

"But you stopped me."

"Yeah..." Corrigan didn't appear to follow where this was going.

"Then what happened to the future you saw?" Archie asked.

"It disappeared."

Archie leaned forward. "Think carefully. Did you see only one future, or did you see different futures contingent upon your actions?"

Corrigan smiled. Actually, he was smiling before Archie asked the question. When the professor would replay this conversation later, he would reflect that Mr. Bain could be rather eerie at times.

"I only see one future," Corrigan said. "And it's the one where something bad happens. My actions are completely off the script."

Archie smiled. "Of course. You would have to."

This piqued Corrigan's curiosity.

"Why is that?"

"It couldn't be one of those Path A or Path B problems. Given five or ten seconds you might end up looking at dozens of potential outcomes that would be noticeable on a macroscopic scale. With each second, those dozens of outcomes might spawn a dozen more apiece. You would easily become so confused as to be rendered insane."

"Well. That's not good."

"No," Archie mused. "So let's say you see only one future. But as I said, dozens of possible futures present themselves every second of every day throughout the entire universe, and they are all contingent upon what's happening in the now. The question, then, is not why do you see only one future, but why do you see one *particular* future?"

Corrigan just smiled. "You think too hard," he said.

"It's my calling."

"Fair enough. But my calling has me showing up about ten blocks from here in another twenty minutes." He stood. "So, I'd better get going."

Archie stood as well. "Is there a way I can contact you in the future?"

"I'm in the book. Why? You planning on eating a nut some-time soon?"

"I may have some more questions for you."

"Maybe you should give me a chance to get drunk first next time," Corrigan said. "You got my head spinning too much as it is."

They shook hands, and then Archie let Corrigan show himself out. His head was spinning, too, but for different reasons. He had an idea.

I'm going to need a mathematician and an experimentalist, he thought. For although he was quite proficient in the high-level mathematics required for probing the concepts now bouncing around in his head, he was not a *gifted* mathematician. And when it came to designing experiments, he couldn't imagine anyone worse than himself.

Fortunately, Michael Offey was both of those things. And he was still standing in Archie's garden.

It looks like I finally have something worth talking about at one of these damn things.

CHAPTER FIVE

Now

Corrigan snapped his eyes open at five in the morning, fully awake and wishing he weren't. It was one of the quirks of his existence, this phenomenon wherein he transitioned from totally asleep to completely awake immediately, whether or not he even wanted to be awake.

He usually didn't. Many times—every day, really—he made an honest effort to go back to sleep, but it simply never worked out; he was awake, and that was that. As he reluctantly climbed out of bed, he reflected that at least on this night he didn't have any dreams.

The condo's lone bedroom was almost exactly opposite, floor plan-wise, to the living/dining area. It was a bit smaller than the living room but had a nicer array of windows, said windows facing northwest and thus not catching the first sunlight of the day. That feature alone meant the place cost an extra fifty thousand, because nobody outside of pharmaceutical commercials actually liked waking up to sunlight on their face.

Walking naked to the window, Corrigan pulled aside the curtains—which came with the apartment, as it would not have occurred to him to purchase any—and took a look at the world.

At this time of day there wasn't a lot to see. Cambridge Street, which would morph into Memorial Drive further down, was largely empty, as was Storrow Drive across the river. Beyond Storrow lay Boston in all its crowded and confused glory, a patchwork collection of buildings varying in age from two hundred years old to just last week, depending on the block and sometimes on the street number. Later, hundreds of cars would be speeding along both sides of the river in a reckless fashion, but at this moment the city looked like a peaceful place to be. Which was probably why he often found himself staring at this view at this time for quite a while.

The bed groaned and made a lip-smacking noise. He glanced over and took note of the tousled mane of copper-red hair sticking up out of one end of his comforter.

Maggie spent the night, he reminded himself.

Further evidentiary proof of this lay on the floor in the form of female-shaped undergarments and a pair of slacks that would definitely not have fit Corrigan. He smiled and briefly considered hopping back into bed for a while after all. But no, he had to get to work.

He headed out of the bedroom and into the study, which was just one door down the hall. It was meant to be a smaller second bedroom, but as it had only one window and was barely half the size of the main bedroom, Corrigan never seriously considered it anything except a study. He had no need for a second bedroom anyway.

He turned on his computer and an adjustable desk lamp that was directed at the wall. Taped there was a large map showing Boston and the suburbs, with dozens of red dots marked on it. These were the places he'd already been in the past six months. *Time for a new map again,* he thought.

The computer beeped for attention. He ignored it and stepped up to the map.

Standing an arm's length away from the wall, he closed his eyes and took a few deep, calming breaths and then raised his right arm, opened his eyes, and moved his hand slowly across the map. To someone peeking in, he might have looked like a blind man trying to read Braille graffiti. That he was doing it naked might have taken more explaining, but the simple answer was that he just hadn't seen the need to put anything on. You get used to a lot of things when you live alone.

The map was cool to the touch as he first ran his hand along the top of it and worked his way down with the practiced route of a Zamboni, finding no reason to pause after his first pass. For a second the thought crossed his mind that he might get a day off, which was great news for someone who had a girl in his bed. But on his second try, he hit upon something warm. He backtracked. Yes, definitely. Something was going to happen there. He circled the spot with his index finger, whirling tighter and tighter, until the finger stopped moving.

"Ready. Corner of Myrtle and Irving," he announced slowly and clearly. The computer beeped emphatically and recorded the information for him. Resting his palm over the spot on the map, he closed his eyes again and concentrated on the intersection. And waited. Finally: "Ready. Three twenty-seven." The computer beeped again.

It took a couple years to cobble together the programs he needed, but now it worked beautifully, taking the voice commands and turning them into map coordinates, then noting the spoken time, and when he was finished, putting it all together and creating an itinerary. Once that was set all he had to do was ask it to plot the trip for him and send it to the printer. Most days he didn't have to touch the keyboard at all, which was good, as he'd never gotten past two-finger typing.

With the first appointment recorded, he stepped back into first position and began sweeping the map again. Ten more minutes of searching yielded two additional appointments, and then he swept the map for another five minutes before he was completely satisfied he hadn't missed anybody.

"Done," he announced for the record. The computer chirped twice, the hard drive whirred appreciatively, and the printer woke up and started cleaning itself. Corrigan wiped a sheen of sweat from his forehead, marked the new spots with his red marker, and headed for the bathroom.

The shower was already running.

"Good morning," he said, letting himself in.

The condo's bathroom was much larger than one would have expected, given the overall square footage, at least large enough that someone on the toilet might not feel like they were intruding overmuch on someone in the tub.

"Morning," Maggie said from in the shower. "I didn't want to interrupt the divining session."

"It's not divination," he said whilst peeing. And peeing.

"Sure," she said. "Call it what you want. Still freaks me out."

"Me, too."

"You ever wonder where it comes from?"

"All the time. But wondering about it doesn't seem to change anything."

"Still. If I were a religious person ..."

"Yeah. I've heard that theory."

She laughed. "I'm trying to picture you with a pair of wings."

"That's so hard?" he asked, as he finished his duties at the toilet and flushed.

"After last night? Maybe a couple of horns and a tail would fit better."

She shut off the shower. Corrigan elected not to watch her emerge from the bath and started instead to brush his teeth. He liked to think they were familiar enough with one another by now to share a bathroom without gawking.

"How's your schedule?" she asked as she toweled herself off.

"Not bad," he said through the toothpaste. "Three appointments, pretty spread out. Shouldn't be a hassle."

"You made any decisions yet? About the case?"

"I'll think about it."

"I'm going to need an answer pretty soon. I *am* out on a limb for you here."

His answer was to spit into the sink. Her response was to discard the towel and walk out of the bathroom.

"I'm late," she said as she went, while Corrigan watched her ass. Apparently he was not quite beyond gawking just yet. He rinsed and followed the ass back into the bedroom.

"My first appointment isn't for another four hours," he said, walking past her as she assembled her clothing on the bed.

"Yeah?" she said. "Nice job you got there. I have to get home for something clean and then make it to work by seven-thirty. Have you seen my bra?"

"Under the lamp," he said, lying back on the bed. "What you wore yesterday looks fine."

She shot him a look that spoke entire paragraphs. The short version said, *No fucking way am I showing up in the same clothes and especially not after I told my boss whom I was going to be meeting.* The longer version had more swears in it and possibly a few remarks about Corrigan's upbringing, but he got the idea. She fetched her bra from the nightstand and slipped it on with clinical efficiency.

GENE DOUCETTE

"Can I ask you something without pissing you off?" Maggie asked. "Again, I mean. I know we've been through it before ..."

"Maggie ..."

"No, I'm not ... I don't want to push you. This is just me being curious here. No baggage. I swear."

"Why don't I quit," he said.

"People have accidents every *day*, Corrigan. You said it yourself, you can't save all of them. Not that it isn't a noble cause. You're just not ..."

"A noble person?"

"Not what I meant. You don't have to, is what I mean. The world will keep on spinning and all that."

He lay down on the bed and stared at the ceiling. "Honestly, I don't know. It just doesn't feel like something I can do right now. Eventually."

"Eventually," she repeated. "Sure."

"Look, you said ..."

"I know what I said. It's my fault; I shouldn't have asked."

She was now fully dressed except for the blouse and jacket, both of which were still in the living room.

"None of my business. Sorry. Get back to me on the case, okay? I know what you think of Calvin, but you'd be working with me, not him. And I think it'd be good for you."

"How so?"

"You look like you could use a change of pace."

"I thought last night was a change of pace."

"No, honey. Last night was business as usual for Corrigan Bain. Not that I'm complaining. *Ciao*."

And with that she strolled out of the bedroom.

It must have taken only a few seconds to locate her bag and remaining articles of clothing because a moment later he heard his front door slam.

He lay in bed for a while, wondering when he'd get around to really explaining his problem to Maggie.

The truth was, a long time ago he made a promise to someone. That someone had been dead at the time the pact was transacted, but as far as he was concerned that didn't change the nature of said pact. It just made it more difficult to get out of. And, of course, there were the nightmares.

"She wouldn't understand," he said.

Maggie rode the elevator down to the garage and the car she left in the guest parking, and tried not to get angry enough to swear out loud, or failing that, to at least wait until she'd gotten into the car.

Doing anything with Corrigan Bain was complicated—business or otherwise—and she'd just doubled down on the complexity by hopping into his bed on the night she was supposed to be hiring him professionally as a consultant. On top of that, she had to bring up *the topic*. Again.

She chirped the car alarm off, slid into the driver's seat, slammed the door, and sat in the car and screamed for a few seconds, and when that didn't help, she started the car and decided to take out her anger on the road instead.

Spending the night was never part of the plan. The plan was supposed to include a statement like, "I know we have this past and all, but I need to hire you as a consultant, so let's shake hands and go to our respective homes." She'd even practiced versions of it.

And if it *had* been a part of the plan, she would have had a change of clothing in the car.

She maneuvered the sedan up the narrow exit ramp and into the bright early-morning sun, and squinted as her eyes adjusted.

For some reason this was the part that always made her feel like she'd done something wrong, the flare of sunlight she had to cope with when coming out of Corrigan's garage. It was as though she was being interrogated by the entire world.

Left onto Mem, onto Storrow and Soldier's Field, and you're good, she reminded herself. It was the shortest path between him and her Newton apartment, the path that ran against inbound traffic. She would still be late, but not so late she couldn't blame it on fieldwork.

Her hand fell on the shoulder bag in the passenger seat, and her mind landed on the file in the bag she didn't show Corrigan.

Calvin, she thought. *I could go see him on my way, write it up as a follow-up interview, and still walk in late.*

It was a decent plan... except she had no new questions for Archie Calvin.

"You could ask him about Kilroy," she said. "Maybe he knows who the hell that is."

Four Months Past

The sheet in Maggie's hand was copied from the guest list at the wake for Professor Michael Offey. The list was huge. He was popular, and seemingly half the university was at the service.

Tracking down all the names and figuring out who needed to be talked to had taken much longer than it should have, but since she hadn't been at the service, it was the only way to approach the matter.

She hadn't been at the service because the FBI wasn't involved, yet, when Mike Offey was buried. That involvement was turning out to be a disaster. Hicks was already suggesting she backlog the case, and it had only been a few weeks, but she couldn't blame him. The university was proving far more truculent than one might expect of an institution whose best and brightest were dying so regularly, and nobody could prove anything that happened was more than an accident.

It would have been easier with some help, but nobody in the office was interested in doing that either, and Hicks wasn't in any kind of mood to volunteer someone.

The door to the small office was opened by the MIT administrator whose desk Maggie had co-opted for the day. The administrator was a sour-looking woman whose desk was so clean it was fair to wonder whether she actually used the room.

Beside her was a short man, slightly pudgy and balding, dressed in formal clothing that looked like it last fit him comfortably a decade ago.

"Archibald Calvin?" Maggie asked, standing.

"Yes," he said, shuffling into the room. The administrator—Maggie thought her name might be Lacey, but she couldn't be positive—shut the door behind him.

Professor Calvin extended his hand to shake Maggie's over the desk, and as they shook he looked at her for apparently the first time. He looked confused.

"I'm sorry," he said, "Agent Trent, is it?"

"That's right."

"Have we met before?"

Maggie took her hand back with a slight smile at what in a younger man would have definitely been a line, but in this older scholar sounded more like genuine befuddlement. "I don't think we have, Professor. I'm sure I would have remembered."

"You weren't at Michael's service."

"I wasn't, no."

"Oh yes; it wasn't a question. I mean to say you weren't there, period. Or I would have remembered you."

Maggie smiled in spite of herself. Maybe the old man *was* hitting on her.

"I just had a few questions about Dr. Offey and the work he was doing here. How well did you know him?"

"Oh, very well. For many years."

"And do you know what he was working on most recently?"

Calvin smiled. "Agent ... do I call you Agent? Or ma'am?"

"Agent is fine."

"Agent, Michael was an experimental physicist of the highest caliber. He worked with the brightest minds in the world, and those minds are fertile and highly distinctive. It would be fair to say that Michael never worked on only one thing in his entire life. Now, if you're asking whether any of those things could have gotten him killed, of course not. That's absurd."

Maggie sighed. She'd heard a version of the same speech a dozen times.

"Maybe you can tell me if *you* were working on anything in particular with him?"

"I actually don't think I can."

"Why not? State secrets? I've been hearing this all day."

He smiled gently. "It's not like that, Agent. You're facing two obstacles. One, everyone here believes they're racing to prove something before someone else does, and so there's an active fear that an idea will be stolen and employed elsewhere. Two, these ideas are so ephemeral and specialized that unless you are personally schooled in advanced physics you would neither understand nor appreciate their significance. And to reiterate, these are not ideas that get people killed. May I ask you a question?"

"Please."

"I've said twice now that Michael was killed, and you haven't corrected me. As I understood it, a bookcase fell on him when he was alone in his study. Clearly, if the FBI is speaking to all of his associates, there's more involved than simply an unfortunate display of gravity. But murder?"

"There's reason to believe his death was intended by someone," she said delicately.

"While alone in a locked office," Calvin reiterated.

Maggie shrugged. "At this point, Professor, I'm willing to entertain any theories up to and including ghosts."

He smiled. "Well, I can assure you I was not working on murderous apparitions with Michael, and I would be very surprised if anyone else here was."

"All right. Can I contact you again if I have more questions?"

"Of course," he said, standing. "Although it would be best if you came to my home rather than meeting me here. I don't actually keep an office on campus any longer. My health is not what it used to be."

They shook hands. "I'm sorry to hear that," she said. She decided she liked Professor Calvin. He was refreshingly candid compared to the rest, and not half as condescending.

"It's old age, mostly," he said. "But I speak without reservation when I say I'm supposed to be dead already."

He headed for the door and had his hand on the knob when he paused and turned around. Something had occurred to him.

"Ghosts, you say."

"It was a joke."

"Yes... Do you know, I just realized where I've seen you before."

"Were you part of another investigation?" she asked.

"In a manner, yes. Have you ever heard of McClaren Hospital?"

The name was familiar.

"I'm not sure, why?"

"Look it up. In microfiche or computer archives or wherever we're storing old newspaper articles nowadays."

"Professor, if you have information to share with me ..."

"I may. I may not. Indulge an old man and go look it up. If you are good at your job you'll understand why."

Maggie grumbled. "All right, could you tell me what I'm looking for, at least?"

"For ghosts, of course," he said matter-of-factly.

CHAPTER SIX

Now

At just before noon, on a small side street a block from Brookline Village, an elderly man named Petr nearly fell down a set of steps leading from the lobby of his apartment building to the street.

The steps were made of stone, and despite several entreaties from some of the more advanced-in-years tenants of the building, there had never been any sort of railing to brace oneself upon when descending. There were only five not-terribly-steep steps, and a railing would most certainly have an adverse effect on the simple elegance of the facade, so the building's owner refused to install one.

Every day, at around the same time, Petr would leave his apartment and walk the short distance to the Starbucks up the street, where he would meet with his friend Boris. They would spend a decent hour complaining about the price of the coffee, the weather, and whatever else might be worth complaining about, and then they would depart for their respective domiciles and spend the rest of the afternoon thinking of new complaints.

It was one of the splendid aspects of getting old—one almost never ran out of things about which to complain, especially if one was intrinsically enamored of such a practice.

On this particular day, Petr arrived slightly late but with a fascinating story for Boris. It seemed that just as Petr tripped, fell, and was about to hit the sidewalk—where he would have, at least, broken his hip again—this young, burly fellow came out of nowhere and caught him. What was particularly odd was that the man had just parked his motorcycle before walking over to catch him. And as soon as he finished with the rescue, he got back on his bike again and drove off. It was as if the man had been there specifically to catch Petr.

Boris concurred that this was a most extraordinary event and then added that surely Petr would never have needed to rely on such evidently divine intervention if Petr's landlord would just take better care of his tenants, and isn't *that* an awful thing, as someone will surely break open their head on those steps one day. Petr agreed and added a few details of his own, loosely based on the parentage of his building's owner. Both men smiled, and their day returned to normal.

A t twenty-seven past three, at the corner of Myrtle and Irving, a Boston University student named Xue sped through a red light on her bicycle. Since she was about to be late for her chemistry class and was still several blocks away from the lab, she had decided the easiest way to go about getting there was to stop believing in red lights and hope for the best. Most of the time, traffic in the area moved slowly enough to make this a non-lethal decision, which was just the defense she would later use in explaining to the officers how her twelve-speed ended up attached to the grille of a Poland Springs delivery truck.

Much more difficult was explaining to the police how it was that she was not also attached to said grille. Xue could not quite articulate, in English, the strange sight of a man on a motorcycle darting in front of her and the Poland Springs truck, plucking her off her bike, and setting her down in the center of the intersection before speeding off.

Reconstructing the exact physics of the event uncovered certain impossibilities Xue didn't know how to rectify. Because as far as she could tell, the man with the motorcycle came from the one side of the three-way intersection where there was no street. Later she would convince herself she had obviously been mistaken, but for just a little while she thought he must have been parked on the *sidewalk* and had darted out only then… and only to save her life.

But that was silly.

C orrigan sat at one of the outdoor tables set up in front of the Dunkin' Donuts on Washington Street and sipped his coffee. It was nearly five in the evening, and his day was almost over, which was always worth looking forward to, even when the next day ended up the same as this one.

And the day after that.

I used to enjoy this more, he thought. Which was true. There was a certain pleasure to be had in saving the life or general well-being of a total stranger. But every day? For twenty years? If all you see each day is miracles, at some point they cease being miraculous.

Clearly, he was in a serious rut.

Maggie had something to do with this. Even knowing certain

aspects of her personality would likely forbid any semblance of long-term monogamous happiness, it was still nice to imagine developing something that at least smelled like a normal adult relationship with her.

Actually, it would be nice to do a lot of things. Like go places. He had enough money to disappear to some place exotic for pretty much as long as he wanted. The only thing stopping him was the job. And strictly speaking, he was a volunteer.

But like everything else in his life, it wasn't close to being that simple.

Across the street a woman who wasn't there limped along the sidewalk.

She was limping because of the accident that crushed the left side of her body ten years ago, an accident Corrigan missed because he overslept. She woke him every morning for the next two years to make sure he never slept in again. And now she was walking down the street in front of him.

Corrigan Bain is going insane.

The ghosts didn't used to come out during the day. And they didn't used to show up at all unless he did something wrong. The last time he did *that* was four years ago: he tried to quit.

At two minutes before five, a gorgeous BMW drove slowly past him. Slowly because that was the only way to drive on this part of Washington Street and also because the construction on the facade on the other side of the road took away one lane of traffic and bottlenecked everything that went by it.

Corrigan stared at the car with unabashed envy. He had the kind of money that could afford something like that.

Or a Bentley, he thought, although owning a Bentley in a city that got as much snow as Boston did was probably not a fantastic idea, not for year-round travel. If he owned a Bentley, he wouldn't want it to get anywhere near road salt. No, that was the kind of car you moved to a more temperate climate to accommodate.

He sighed into his coffee. Visions of nice cars and nice boats, and Maggie Trent in a bikini in the nice car on the way to the nice boat swam through his head and depressed him immensely because it would never happen. As much as he wanted to, he couldn't figure out a way to stop saving people.

The woman with half a face who was not there stopped and stared at him with her good eye. She was muttering something, but he never could quite understand what she had to say with part of her mouth gone, so he ignored her as well as he could.

They know I want to quit again, he thought. *They always know.*

"No," he said, shaking his head. "They aren't real. They aren't there."

The woman to his left reacted by edging away from him. In his future, Corrigan would turn to her and explain that he was talking about his ghosts and she needn't worry. Her response would be a look of panic, so Corrigan decided he wouldn't say this and turned back to the street and the BMW.

"Some angel I turned out to be," he muttered.

He checked his watch. It was two minutes past five. The accident would happen soon and he still didn't know whom he was there to save. Thankfully, the crowds weren't too bad; the future wasn't too messy.

Across the street a large woman in a blue blazer and knee-length skirt was walking underneath the construction site. It was one of those scaffolding deals, where the platforms that jutted out over the road also allowed for a walkway underneath. This walkway took pedestrians several feet into the street, with large cement dividers shooing them away from the closed storefront.

"There you are," he said.

He got up from his seat, leaving behind the coffee cup he hoped would still be there when he was done, as even at

Dunkin' Donuts, the coffee was too expensive to give up on midway through.

Walking between cars that were moving so slowly they might as well be parked, Corrigan kept his eyes fixed on the woman's progress through time. He could see her at the beginning, the midpoint, and the end of the scaffolding tunnel, and all points in between. If he concentrated on one spot he could see her at that particular moment in her future.

Taken as a whole, she was a bluish blur of motion, as was everybody else around her.

Vapor trails, he thought, except that these trails went forward.

At the end of the tunnel, her trail would be stopping when a large bag of something heavy falls on her.

There was a man on the top of the scaffold. Over his shoulder was the bag—dry cement—and he was carrying it to the end of the scaffolding. In his future he would be shouting "Look out!" as the cement bag slips from his grasp and off the edge, right onto the back of the woman in the blue suit. Corrigan could already hear him shouting it and see the bag already falling, and there was a woman screaming, another woman to the left, near the burrito place. And Corrigan was running to the woman hit by the bag and kneeling down and pulling the bag aside.

"Not yet," he grumbled. None of that had happened. All of it was about to happen. All of it was happening right now.

Corrigan reached the other side of the street and looked up at the man with the bag. He was still moving toward the end of the scaffold, apparently unaware he'd reached the edge. He meant to drop the bag on the wood floor of the platform, not off the side, which was how the bag would end up on top of the woman.

Corrigan opened his mouth to warn him of where he was standing—a much better solution than somehow tackling the large woman or perhaps catching the bag—but then the man with the bag... blinked. Not with his eyes—his whole body. An alternate possibility presented itself in midstream, and suddenly Corrigan wasn't sure what to do.

Something was extremely wrong. Two futures were happening right in front of him, and in one, the man with the bag held onto it for another two seconds so that when it fell, it landed just behind the woman in the blue suit.

No, he thought, rubbing his eyes as if this would clear away the double future vision. *This isn't right.*

"Hey!" Corrigan shouted, no longer sure who he was shouting to, or if he had actually shouted at all. Only one of the men heard him, and it was the wrong one. The bag was dropped, the one doing the dropping shouting "Look out!" in horror at what was about to transpire.

The competing future—in which nobody got hurt thanks to Corrigan's warning—disappeared. As far as Corrigan was concerned that future had an equal claim on reality, but this time, for some reason, he wasn't the one making that decision. All he could do was watch it as it folded up and faded away. For a half beat, Corrigan was left with just the present, which usually only happened when he had altered the future himself.

The woman in front of the burrito place started screaming.

"Oh, God," he said.

He knelt down and lifted the bag off the heavy woman in blue.

"Can you move?" Corrigan asked. Behind him, he could hear somebody calling 911.

"My back . . ." the woman muttered.

"You'd better . . . try not to move, I guess," he said. "I think an ambulance is on its way."

The woman squeezed his hand, which Corrigan considered a good sign; maybe her back wasn't broken.

"What happened?" she asked. Her speech was mushy, which was less of a good sign.

"Something fell," he said. "I'm so sorry."

"Me, too," she said, attempting a smile.

"I was supposed to be here to save you," he said quietly. But the woman's eyes had closed; she probably hadn't heard him.

I just stood there and watched it happen.

Briefly, he thought he could smell gunpowder. It wasn't real, just the remnant of a very old, very bad memory that tended to resurface whenever something went amiss on an appointment.

"If it's not the future," he complained, "it's the past."

Thirty-Eight Years Past

It had been a very strange year for Violet. But it was a strange year for everybody, so why should she be any different? This was what she told herself whenever the odd moment of lucidity struck. Strange year, strange times. Strange place, too. So there was no reason to worry about it, really. If it was strange everywhere, then strange was normal, and she was no less normal than anybody else under strange circumstances, right? Not being strange would then be considered strange and then...

Stop it.

She blinked and looked around, but couldn't see anything.

A farm; this much she knew. She was on a farm. In Maine. How she got there had something to do with hopping aboard a yellow bus somewhere west of Chicago.

Possibly, there were drugs involved.

"Of course there were drugs involved, sweetness," the man lying next to her said. Tyrell. It was Tyrell.

"Was I talking out loud?" she asked.

"You were. What, you think they taught me to mind read at university?"

Tyrell had a funny way of talking. He elongated his polysyllables, which made "university" sound like "you-nee-verr-siddy." When she was around him long enough, she tended to do the same, even though she tried not to because he usually thought she was making fun of him.

Violet blinked again, still saw no change, and gradually accepted that the room was simply very dark, rather than she had gone blind. It was nighttime and very quiet; she could actually hear snow falling outside in the still moments between wind gusts.

Winter wasn't so bad. It covered up the smell of the manure from the nearby pastures. But it was also cold, and she couldn't remember if she owned anything warm. This point brought her again to the question of just what in the hell she was doing on a farm in Maine.

Tyrell rolled over and placed his arm over the top of her chest, the stubble from his face tickling the side of her cheek. He mumbled something about love, but as she was not paying close attention, she couldn't be sure precisely what it was. It didn't matter, he'd forget it by the time the sun rose.

Men Violet found in her bed were notorious in this regard. Violet used to think it was her fault, a character flaw of some sort resulting in her being attracted only to men who spoke of love by night and moving on by day. Recently she arrived at the conclusion that it wasn't her at all, that men are simply bastards by nature. Oddly, this made things much easier for her.

Such would inevitably be the case with Tyrell, who was by most accounts a beautiful black man with a generous spirit and a soul large enough to hold both of them. That would change. It always did.

This didn't make her sad, although it probably should have.

She lifted his arm from her bosom and sat up slowly, and then her head did a spinny thing that reminded her she'd not been altogether herself for the past several weeks. Memories ricocheted around in a random pastiche that defied all nominal rules of logic. No way was she going to be piecing it back together again. Not much point in trying.

Maine, she thought again, *Maine and Tyrell. Stay focused.*

Her eyes finally adjusted with an assist from the moonlight reflecting off the snow outside and in through the window.

They were lying on the floor of what looked to be a small shack, which had no furniture but lots of blankets. And lots of other people, too. If she turned on a light—assuming the place had electricity—the entire floor would probably jump up and shout. Glancing about for familiar faces, she found none.

"I've got to stop," she said quietly. Tyrell muttered something incoherent in response, slurped up some drool from the side of his mouth, and rolled over again. "No more acid."

It sounded good when spoken aloud. Not that she hadn't said it before. But she had responsibilities, dammit. It was time to start accepting that.

Something heavy and sour dropped into the bottom of her stomach.

Where's Corry?

"Corry?" she called out. "Corry!"

Tyrell sat up. "What is it?"

"*Corry!*" she shouted, and half the room rumbled to attention like so many roaches.

"Vi . . ."

"Where's my baby?" she cried, in a panic. "*Where's my baby?*"

"Hey!" Tyrell said, grabbing her arms, mainly because Violet had begun slapping her own head for some reason. "He's right next to you, babe. Lookit."

He reached across her lap and pulled aside the quilt on the sleeping figure on her left.

Corry was lying there all right, curled up in a ball. He looked up at her with that expression he always had. Not scared or really even curious. Just watching. She touched the hair on his head to verify that he was really there.

"When did he get so big?" she whispered, burying her face in Tyrell's shoulder and dissolving into tears.

Little Corrigan Bain just stared.

CHAPTER SEVEN

Now

After having successfully completed the circuit from Corrigan Bain's Cambridge condo to her Newton apartment and then to her downtown office—walking in only ten minutes late—Maggie felt as if she'd already accomplished enough in one day to warrant, say, a nap. Or at least a little slack from the rest of the department. But that was clearly not meant to be the case, as she then went from eight-thirty until one-forty-five in one meeting or another, with only short breaks in between for coffee and donuts and other random good-tasting-but-undeniably-bad-for-you concoctions.

A few years back, Maggie went on a health food kick to try and stave off the impending sag of age forty, but she discovered that starvation was a major part of the package. Living life from meeting to meeting meant finding edible foodstuffs that could be devoured in a thirty-second walk down a hallway, and there wasn't anything healthy that matched that description and also tasted good and filled her stomach. One day, Krispy Kreme would invent deep fried celery sticks, and she'd be all set. Until then, she suffered the donuts and jogged every chance she got.

Lately, it seemed every day went like this. Here she was, maybe one step below an assistant deputy title, and all she had to show for it—aside from a bank account that was moderately more enriched than it had been when she first started working in the Boston office—was a continuous onslaught of meetings. One task force after another, basically.

It was amazing how much FBI work involved basic information gathering, information analysis, and information dissemination via the format of the many-headed meeting. Sometimes it was difficult to figure out how any of them got any actual work finished, given all the time they spent just telling each other what they were working on. On certain nights when she was feeling particularly cynical, it occurred to her that they never really *did* get anything accomplished, or at least not the sort of thing she could hold onto with both hands.

Maggie didn't end up getting back to the case she shared with Corrigan until well after two and then only because Randall Hicks sat her down in his office to discuss it. As always, his timing was terrible; she'd been on her way outside for a butt, her first in five hours.

"So you talked to Bain?" Hicks asked as he waved her into his chambers.

"I did," she said, as he stepped behind his desk. She shut the door to the office and took a seat without being asked.

"Going against my wishes," he said.

It was not in anger; he was just making an observation. In his world, this qualified as a rebuke.

Randy Hicks had been her immediate supervisor for five years, and Maggie had to admit that in that time he'd proven to be a damn good manager of people in an office full of strong personalities. But he had a few blind spots, and one of them was

Corrigan Bain. Still, and to his credit, he gave all of his agents enough room to make their own decisions, whether he agreed with them or not.

"I have reason to think he'd be useful here."

"Maggie, I don't even know if you have a real *case* here. Seriously, I know these deaths are unusual, but you saw the statistical breakdown. I don't see where there's any crime being committed. And if there is, I don't know how we're involved at all."

"You're probably right, which is why it's not my first priority."

This was a nod to her perpetually large caseload, which included a bevy of financial crimes that were only slightly easier to prove than the MIT murders.

"Good. I mean I'm all for trusting your instinct, but still. Seems like a waste of the Bureau's time, and we don't have a lot of time to waste around here." He leaned back in his chair, which was an indication that he was getting to the real point of the meeting. "What'd he say?"

"Bain? He's thinking about it."

Randy nodded. "You share information about this case and nothing else, all right?"

"Of course."

Twelve years ago, after the bank robbery on State, Hicks had Corrigan Bain arrested on conspiracy charges, arguing that if he knew about the robbery, he was in on it from the start.

Corrigan sat for half an afternoon in lockup before his lawyers argued him right out—he had some very good lawyers —and none of the charges ended up sticking. That didn't stop Hicks from spending six months investigating the man to see if he could connect him to the bank job and then to any other crime in which he could possibly have been involved. Because Corrigan's one mistake, visiting the FBI as he had, was that he humiliated Randall Hicks.

About four months into that investigation Randy discovered Maggie Trent was sleeping with his suspect. This did not lead to a very good working relationship between the two of them. Years later, Randy was still pretty much convinced there was something he missed, and he was also half-convinced that the only reason he didn't find it was because of Maggie.

It was amazing, then, that they got along as well as they did.

"It might be tough to justify paying him as a consultant when we can't really define what sort of expertise he might bring to the investigation."

"We can't even define the investigation," she properly pointed out. "Besides, there are discretionary funds we could tap if we really had to."

Maggie didn't add that most of the expenditures relating to aid from outside sources had to be approved by none other than Hicks himself—if he wanted to pay Corrigan, he could find a way to pay Corrigan.

"Well . . . not like he needs the money."

"It's the principle of the thing. You know that."

One of the more honored truisms of the investigative field is that in order to truly know a person under investigation, one needed to find out where that person's money was, how much of it there was, and how they had gone about getting it. That was why every private institution that handled money—banks, and also check-cashing companies, wire transfer remitters and other money service business variants great and small—either reported odd activity or was supposed to be doing so. That reporting increased dramatically after a handful of religious fanatics flew a couple of jumbo jets into the World Trade Center with tickets purchased with funds wired from overseas terrorist financiers, but the reporting mechanism was already in existence when Hicks was looking into Corrigan Bain.

As a "fixer," Corrigan drew no discernible income, yet

appeared to be independently wealthy. A review of his personal background—single mother, unknown father, and a childhood of moderate poverty—did not suggest a Brahmin background of any kind. Nor was there a record of him winning a lottery or any like claim of a gambling windfall. Instead, in late 1985, Bain went from a poor fry cook to one of the fifty richest people in the state, more or less overnight.

Hicks dug deeper. One of the first things he noticed was that this *nouveau riche* transformation took place right around the time Bain turned twenty-one. That implied an inheritance of some kind. So he retraced the man's family history, but got only as far as his mother's parents. Given they had severed ties with their daughter more than thirty years earlier, and as they were not persons of great means anyway, the money couldn't have come from there.

Frustrated, he turned to the law firm that handled the funds for Bain. This didn't go well.

Another truism: if you have to ask a lawyer for anything in order to get your investigation moving, you're shit out of luck. And that was exactly what ended up happening, as this law firm would only confirm that they handled Corrigan Bain's affairs for a brief period of time a decade earlier. They would not explain where the money had come from, who owned it previously, or why Bain had gotten it.

To find out more from them, Hicks needed a better case against Bain first, and he couldn't build a better case without first finding out what the law firm had. So, reluctantly, he closed the investigation.

Maggie, being intimate with Bain and intimately familiar with Hicks's investigation, asked Corrigan once where his money came from, as she was no less curious than Hicks. Although in her case it was less of a professional curiosity than a personal one.

All he said was he'd made a few good investments, and then he quickly changed the subject. She'd have brought up details from his windfall year, but that would have been an improper compromise of the Hicks probe, so she didn't. She still hadn't, although she was not averse to dropping the occasional hint.

It was just another one of the things that made Corrigan Bain so intriguing, which she invariably found sexy. If she were to ponder that point in more detail, she might find an answer to why none of her relationships lasted much longer than it took for her to get to know someone well.

Hicks picked up a copy of her case file from his desk. It was sitting on top, which could have meant he'd just been reviewing it. It could also have meant he wanted her to think he'd just been reviewing it.

"What did Bain have to say about Kilroy?" he asked, holding open the file to a photograph of the last crime scene, the apparent accidental death of Jamie Silverman.

"I didn't share it with him."

"Really. Why not?"

"Didn't want to sound crazy."

Hicks laughed. "I don't blame you. You going to eventually tell him?"

"That depends on whether or not he says yes."

He nodded and closed the file, tossing it back on the desk.

"Let me know, then."

"You'll be the first," she said, getting up to leave.

"Oh, and Maggie?" he said, just before she'd managed to get the door open. She wanted a cigarette so badly she was ready to chew off her lower lip.

"Randy?"

"You still sleeping with him?"

She ran through the possible responses to this question, which went from not answering at all to shooting him in the forehead with her service revolver. Something between those two seemed to be in order.

"Sometimes. You still sleeping with Helen?"

Helen being his wife.

He pulled off the difficult task of smiling without actually smiling, which was a rare talent.

"Not so much nowadays. With the separation and all."

"Heard about that. So sorry."

Maggie pulled open the door and got out of the office before the discussion escalated any further. The elevator to the street couldn't have come fast enough.

I t was nearly 6 p.m. and Maggie had just about given up on getting anything else accomplished. Pleasant visions of a bubble bath and some Nina Simone danced in her head. She wondered if that would do the trick. Then she wondered if Corrigan would mind her stopping by a second time. Which was when the phone at her desk rang.

"I'm at Downtown Crossing. How soon can you be here?"

It was Corrigan. The man attracted coincidences like dead bodies drew flies.

"I was just thinking of you. Where are you?"

"I'm near the Dunkin' Donuts on Washington Street."

"Sounds like a strange place for a date," she said lightly.

"Maggie," he said flatly, at which point she picked up on the stress in his voice. "Something's gone wrong."

"What is it?"

"Difficult to explain." In the background, she could hear an ambulance siren.

"I'll be right there," she said before hanging up.

She called Stan on her cell while waiting for an elevator.

Stan was the office's resident computer genius, which wasn't saying much given that the FBI's budget didn't really allow for actual geniuses on the payroll. His computer lab had a police band receiver.

"Stan, Maggie. Anything happen tonight in Downtown Crossing?"

"Hey, Maggs," he answered. "Aren't you like right outside my door? You could just knock."

"I'm at the elevators, on my way out," she explained. "Downtown Crossing. Somebody need an ambulance?"

"You know that doesn't make any sense, right? If you're heading there you must know something's happened, so—"

"Stan!"

"Okay, okay. Hang on." She heard papers rustling. A year ago, Stan hooked up the police radio to a VRU-enabled printer, just to see if it could be done. It recorded everything that came out on reams of continuous printouts that served no purpose other than to kill trees. "Yeah, some kind of accident," he said, reading. "Injured woman. Looks like the ambulance just left."

"That's all you have?"

"Initial reports are always pretty sketchy."

"All right, thanks," she said and hung up.

Once on the street, she could see the ambulance from the Crossing as it sped past, and began to understand what it was she heard in Corrigan's voice.

One did not typically see ambulances coming from places where Corrigan Bain had been. What she'd heard had been fear.

Thirty-Eight Years Past

There were seventeen of them in the farmhouse, and as Violet quickly learned, not one of them had a survival skill that complemented their current circumstances. And the weather continued to worsen as the calendar crept closer to January.

Charlie Bluff's grandparents had owned the place, and according to him, he inherited it and the twenty acres it rested in the middle of. Charlie was characteristically vague with the details, but the impression he gave Vi was that this inheritance had taken place sometime in the past year. This explained how a bunch of hippies trying to keep alive the dream of the commune ended up in an empty farmhouse in southern Maine, and how nobody had tried to chase them off while firing large guns at them.

Somewhat less explicable, was the fully stocked walk-in freezer. They'd been grazing happily on the goods in there since they arrived, which only forestalled what would soon be a problem.

As possibly the only person there to remain straight for over twenty days, Violet found the time to do a little math. Unless there was a second walk-in freezer elsewhere in the house, the Bluff commune would run out of food entirely sometime around the middle of December.

She tried to bring this up with Charlie in case there was an equally impressive supply of cash stowed somewhere in the place, but all she got out of him was a lengthy, very one-sided discussion on the evils of money, capitalism, and the fascist tendencies of the government of the United States, not necessarily in that order. Then he offered her a tab, which she politely declined.

So the whole food thing was a problem, and one that Violet —as a *mother*—was going to have to deal with eventually. She was perfectly happy to go without food for an entire winter, but little Corry needed his nutrition.

Vi's template of motherhood was crafted out of twenty years' worth of detergent commercials and *Leave It To Beaver*-type programs, which explained both why she was consistently unprepared for any issue that could not be resolved between thirty seconds and thirty minutes and why she always felt so thoroughly inadequate. But she knew enough to understand that children needed healthy food that two-month drug benders couldn't replace.

These were the thoughts that occupied her as she walked from room to room, casually looking for her son. This was nothing like the panic that had overtaken her on their first night in the house; she knew he was around somewhere.

If there was a good thing to be said about the people Charlie had collected for his Grand Walden Experiment, it was that everyone was cool. She didn't have to keep a constant eye on Corry, because wherever he was, an adult was watching out for him and not in any weirdly inappropriate kind of way. And little Corrigan was an easy child to keep an eye on.

The house was actually pretty big. It had seemed to her that she was in much more drastic straits when she woke up on that first night, but she'd actually been in the largest bedroom upstairs, and the reason she was sharing that room with everybody else in the place was to keep warm, because they'd lost the fire.

The fireplace was temperamental, meaning it wouldn't work if nobody remembered to pull in some wood from the yard and give it time to dry.

There were a total of fifteen rooms to the farmhouse, not counting the barn across the yard. Miraculously, one of those rooms was an indoor bathroom with a standing shower. Hot water was at a premium, and the toilet backed up all the time, but all anyone had to do when they felt like complaining was look out in the middle of the backyard and see the snow-covered outhouse for an idea of what things were like here before Charlie's grandparents decided to spend a little cash on creature comforts.

Electricity was a wondrous thing when they had it, which was only about half the time. The electricity only reached the house via aerial wires, and if any wire in the county went down, so did the entire county's electrical supply. With the weather as it was, that happened pretty often.

They had a phone that also relied largely on the caprice of the weather, but since nobody there ever had a dire need to make a phone call—anyone they might have wanted to phone was already there—this was less of a noticeable problem.

She started on the first floor, in the living room. As the second largest room in the house and the only one with a functioning fireplace, it was where most of the commune's occupants could be found during the day, especially given the fire was the only source of heat they had. It had been argued that as the bathroom had a moderate supply of hot water, there must ergo be a device somewhere in the home that heated said water. It had been further argued that the presumption of a water heater also led one to infer the existence of other devices somewhere within the confines of the farmhouse which might heat the rooms, possibly via the perpetually arctic radiators.

Charlie, being of a stubborn and charismatic sort and clearly unwilling or otherwise unable to admit to any failure—in this case, a failure to locate the furnace—insisted somewhat stridently that the hot water came from the tap that way via some kind of wondrous unknown process that heats well water naturally. Thus far, nobody had been either brave enough or adequately non-stoned to challenge this position.

"Anybody seen Corry?" Vi asked. In doing so she interrupted

a profound discussion regarding whether the Vietnam War would have still happened if Dylan hadn't gone electric. Conservatively, this discussion had been going on for two days. As this was a day when they had no electricity it was the best anyone could do by way of music; Charlie neglected to recruit anybody who could play guitar, or at least anybody who owned one.

A half dozen dazed faces looked up at her. None of them seemed to be familiar with the name. Finally, Harriet—Vi was almost positive that was her name—asked, "The boy?"

"Yes," Violet said patiently. "Have you seen him?"

They looked around to see if he might just happen to be in the room, in case Violet was in the habit of asking deep questions without provocation.

Having confirmed his absence, and just to make sure this was not a philosophical inquiry, Mondo—definitely not his real name but the only name he ever gave to Vi—asked, "Recently?"

"Yes."

"Dunno," he declared. "Don't think so."

A young, chubby girl named Gingham held a lit joint up in the air without even turning to look at Violet, which was who she was offering the smoke to. This was her way of saying, "Hello, won't you join us?" and might have been construed as a friendly offer except Vi knew if cops kicked down the door and burst into the living room they'd find Gingham sitting in that exact spot, offering them a toke.

Violet was tempted. There was only one thing worse than being straight and that was being straight in a house full of people who were not. Somehow everything smelled worse, and nobody was half as pretty or a quarter as smart as she'd taken them for previously. She wondered, not for the first time, what Corry thought of all of them.

She passed on the offer, reluctantly and without comment, and moved on.

The dining room was spacious, and seemed to have been designed with a vast number of houseguests in mind. It was dominated by a crude wood table with an uneven surface and a finish that was peeled off in several places. Not that one could see the tabletop; stoneware dishes that practically screamed out for somebody, anybody, to clean the half-eaten food off them covered the entire space. It was a good thing it was the middle of winter; otherwise, the room would be a warren of flies. Surrounding the table was a collection of a dozen chairs, love seats, and hassocks, with no two seats alike. Charlie's grandparents had furnished their home via flea market.

Tyrell and Charlie were sitting in the corner of the room in a heated discussion that might have been called an argument if they weren't both ripped. Vi could pick out words like *proletariat* and *common good* and figured it was nothing she hadn't heard before.

As the most with-it guys in the house, these two banged heads regularly on all matters.

Traditionally, Vi came down on the side of Tyrell, and not just because they were fucking. The truth was Charlie, being the ostensible host, had certain dictatorial tendencies that laced every speech he gave about *power to the people* a degree of irony he didn't quite have the intelligence to acknowledge. In the past, Violet acted as a mediator, but this was not the time for that.

"You guys seen Corry?" she asked.

"Hey, Vi," Tyrell greeted her. "You all right?"

"Been sleeping, baby." She had been sleeping quite a bit of late for some reason. "You seen my boy?"

"I saw him out back about an hour ago," Charlie said, jerking his thumb toward the back yard.

"An hour?" she said, surprised. "Cold out, isn't it?"

"Wind's died down," Charlie said in a somewhat apologetic tone.

"Sure he's fine," Tyrell insisted. "Want me to check on him?"

"I'll do it," she said.

Leaving the two men to continue acting like little boys, she headed through the unattended kitchen to the back door.

Next to the door was a small walk-in space that in more anti-quated times served as a jelly room but now was mostly used to store an array of random winter gear. The aggregate of the equipment there would not sufficiently protect all of them from the elements, but fortunately they'd yet to encounter a situation that would require them to leave *en masse*.

She quickly threw on the nearest overcoat, slipped into a pair of boots that were, conservatively, two sizes too large, yanked on a pair of mittens, and headed out.

To call the space behind the farmhouse a *backyard* was to do a disservice to real backyards, if only by comparison. The house stood on a small hill overlooking a vast untended apple orchard, but that was only the half of it. The vista beyond the orchard was truly breathtaking, opening up on a valley of snow-covered pine trees that bottomed out at a river half-frozen on most days and fully iced over on the really cold ones. Some mornings the ground fog was so low over the valley it looked as if the farm-house was drifting atop a cloud bank.

Violet shouldn't have been surprised to find Corry out back; he liked the view. This part of the outside world was very languid, a marked difference from anything going on indoors. She found him more than once just standing atop the hill and staring. If she'd been thinking about it, she'd have checked the yard first.

On this particular occasion, he wasn't staring. He was throwing snowballs.

At just shy of five years of age, Corry Bain was already big enough to pass for seven or eight. Sometime around his second birthday he shot up like a weed, as if someone were slipping him raw meat every night when Vi wasn't paying attention. He had long black hair that she cut only once a year so that at full extension it draped past his shoulders. He tended to keep it tied back in a ponytail, as he'd seen so many of the men in his life do. With a different child, perhaps, this might have given him a girlish appearance. But he was so stocky nobody who wasn't nearly blind would make such a mistake.

Since there was no coat his size in the house, he was wearing three sweaters and two pairs of pants. The boots he had on were women's boots, but not obviously so. And he wasn't wearing gloves, but despite handling snow, this didn't appear to be a problem for him.

She watched as he bent down and packed together a snowball, checked it for weight and compactness, and then fired it at the tree closest to the base of the hill.

"Miss," he said to himself, while the snowball was still describing an arc toward the tree. He leaned over to make another snowball without bothering to watch his projectile land. When it did, it missed the tree by several feet.

Violet was so happy to hear her son using words she decided not to announce her presence right off.

Corry almost never spoke. When he was younger, it was no worse than a mild curiosity and at times a great convenience for someone who was trying to both raise a child and live her life as if she didn't have one. But as he aged, the silence became a serious concern, to the point where she briefly convinced herself he was retarded in some way. Except there was no way to look into his eyes and seriously think such a thing.

Having put together another snowball, he reared back and launched it at the same tree. Almost as soon as he let it go he announced, "Hit!" and then proceeded to make another one, again not bothering to watch the snowball actually reach the tree.

As predicted, it did indeed hit the upper trunk of the tree he was aiming for.

She wondered how long he'd been at it, given how accurately he was gauging his throws.

"Mommy," he said without looking at her. He must have seen her from the corner of his eye.

"Hello, Corry. Are you cold?"

He turned and stared at her.

"No," he said. Then he threw the next snowball at the tree. "Miss."

"How do you know it's going to miss?" she asked, growing curious about the whole procedure. "It's still in the air."

He didn't answer until after the snowball missed the tree.

"Is it?" he asked.

"Not anymore, no."

"Pretty deer," Corry responded, which made no sense at all to Violet. As she walked to the edge of the hilltop, though, she spotted movement in the orchard some distance away. It was a deer, scampering through the snow and heading for the river. A chill ran up her spine, entirely unrelated to the temperature outside.

"Look at that," she said.

Corry turned completely around, which was the only way for him to gain a view of the animal. Before she'd spoken there was no way for him to have possibly seen it.

Don't be stupid, Vi, she said to herself. Obviously, the boy had seen the deer earlier and was just pointing out to her that there was one down in the orchard.

"You're right honey," she said, touching his shoulder gently. "It's a very pretty deer."

CHAPTER EIGHT

Now

"I don't know what happened," Corrigan said to Maggie. She was still a good six feet away and walking toward him on his blind side, but of course he already knew she was about to sit down at the outdoor table next to him.

He sipped his now-cold coffee and continued to stare at the spot across the street where a woman named Maribel Kozminsky had been felled by a sack of dry cement. The police were still at the scene talking to the construction worker, who was trying to reenact his role via a complex series of gestures that did little to help his cause. Corrigan watched the gesturing through the blur of forward motion, focused on the little moments in time, took note of the current present, and reviewed everything as it played out to make sure the future was still going the way it was supposed to. He'd been doing this since he got off the phone with Maggie, and so far everything was working.

"Corrigan," Maggie said. She'd sat down. "Talk to me."

"Sure, I'll have one," he said, holding out his hand, his eyes still focused across the street.

Maggie was holding her pack of cigarettes. "I didn't offer it yet."

"You were about to. Now they lead him to the squad car. The big one radios ahead."

"Could you... it would be nice if we were both in the present for this conversation."

He didn't look away until the back door to the squad car closed. The spectators to the scene began to disperse in a sea of projected vapor trails.

Maggie was lighting a cigarette and also handing it to him. He was taking it from her and inhaling the smoke into his lungs. He hadn't done it yet, and he could already taste the smoke. Now he was exhaling and watching her light one for herself. He squeezed the filter of the butt between fingers that were really better with cigars. He took his first drag. She lit her smoke.

"So tell me—" she began.

"Don't know."

"Can you—"

"I'll try."

"Dammit! Wait for me, will you please?"

He closed his eyes and rubbed the stubble on his chin. He hadn't shaved that morning. Why hadn't he done that? Because he'd been following her ass out of the bathroom. That's right. That had been only a few hours ago.

"Okay," he said. "It's . . . when I get agitated I lose focus."

"I'm getting that."

"I was about to save her. I was in position and everything. But then... there was a split."

"A split."

"Two things happened at once. Except only one ended up actually happening. Guess which one?"

It was Maggie's turn to look perplexed.

"Has that ever happened before?" she asked.

"Not since I was a kid." He took a very deep drag of the cigarette, exhaled, and tipped the ashes onto the ground. He was still holding the drag.

"What are we talking about here? Did you just lose focus or something? Follow the wrong ... um ... part? Of the future?"

"No," he said, having exhaled, tipping the ashes. "I saw more than one possible outcome, and I didn't know which one was right. I shouted a warning, but only in one future. But it was already different, that other future."

"How?" she asked.

That was a good question. He looked up at the scaffolding and tried to remember what he'd seen. The guy didn't drop the bag at the same moment; that much he knew. Something distracted him.

"He was looking over there," he said, pointing. "No, that's not right. He was looking that way in both futures. But in the *other* one there was something that made him pause for a heartbeat or two."

Maggie looked where Corrigan was pointing. "And then what?"

"Then nothing. That outcome disappeared when it didn't happen."

"Could have been anything. From that spot you can see right down the street."

"I know, and with hundreds of people between here and there. It could have been anything. Except it wasn't just anything."

"What do you mean?" Maggie asked. She was beginning to regret having ever wandered into this conversation.

"It was nothing. It was exactly nothing. It never happened. He reacted to seeing something that he didn't end up seeing.

That was why the future played out the way it was supposed to."

"So... okay, so we have to figure out something that didn't happen and wasn't supposed to happen but almost did happen."

"Keeping in mind that this was a unique event. The thing that didn't happen was significant in some way."

"My head hurts," she said.

"I know what you mean."

Maggie flicked the remaining ash from her cigarette, which was now burning its filter. She resisted the urge to light another one—two in a row always made her nauseous—solely because the discussion seemed to warrant it. "Is it possible that this *has* happened before, and you just didn't notice it?"

"I doubt it," he said.

"But it's possible. It could have happened at an insignificant moment; one where you weren't in the middle of saving somebody."

"You ever see a glass fall off a table and then not hit the floor? Just float back up to where it was before it fell?"

"No."

"And you'd probably remember something like that, wouldn't you?"

"I probably would, yeah."

"Well, that's what it'd be like. I don't remember it happening, but I'm betting I would if it had."

She stood. "Hate to say it, champ, but it doesn't sound like there's any earthly way to investigate this. The woman's going to live right? I say forget about it and move on."

He stared at her. He wanted to point out that once you've seen the glass float back up to the tabletop, you no longer have complete faith that the next time it falls it'll hit the floor. Instead, he just nodded.

"Yeah. It's probably nothing."

Now

"So anyway," Erica said excitedly, "after *that* everyone just *freaked!* We were all afraid to go near the place. I still haven't. Not gonna, neither."

"That is such a bullshit story," declared Tanya, erstwhile Friend of Erica, current Ultimate Confidante of same.

"S'the truth, I swear," Erica insisted. To emphasize the point she placed her right hand over her left breast.

"Honey, you are too drunk to know what you're talking about," Tanya said, which was also the truth, although it conveniently sidestepped the undeniable fact that Tanya was herself thoroughly plastered, liquored up, tanked, and otherwise feelin' it at that moment.

"No, no," Erica said, grabbing onto Tanya's shoulder. This was a problem, as her right hand was still placed over her left breast, so removing her left hand from the handrail meant that Tanya was suddenly in charge of keeping both of them from falling over.

Since the subway car was pitching in an irregular left-to-right motion while hurtling madly down the underground tracks on its way to parts unknown and also Kendall Square, the sudden shift in equilibrium was nearly more than she could handle.

Erica continued, ignoring the potential risk to life-and-limb.

"Serious now. This is me being serious."

She leaned forward conspiratorially and whispered in Tanya's ear. Unfortunately, the train was loud and Erica wasn't. Tanya caught just the last part of it.

". . . only ones left," Erica said. " 'S true."

"Will you hold *on*, girl."

"Right."

Erica reacquired her hold on the handrail, which she admitted to herself was probably the smartest thing she could be doing. And Erica almost always eventually came to the smartest conclusion, albeit not necessarily at first blush, and not necessarily at all when sufficiently inebriated.

Smart things were what Erica was best at. Although delightfully ego-less most of the time, if pressed she would probably not be able to name more than one or two moments in her life where she wasn't the smartest person in the room.

It wasn't the sort of thing most people would have guessed when meeting her for the first time, largely because she also had auburn hair, chestnut eyes, and a devastating pair of legs she was not ashamed to reveal—even in winter, when doing so might encourage frostbite. She looked as though she should be on page ten of a Sears catalogue showing how the latest pleated skirt looked when modeled by someone much more attractive than the average housewife, rather than discussing superstring theory or speculating on the shortcomings of muons.

This was not to say that attractive women could not also be highly intelligent; it just seemed a bit unfair.

"I can't believe you, Rickie," Tanya said, using a nickname Erica hardly ever heard any more.

"What? What can't you believe?"

"That you'd make up a piece of bullshit like that to justify going out, that's what. I mean Jesus, girl. You wanna go out, just go out. This Mummy's Curse crap is low."

Erica looked at her seriously for a good three seconds before bursting into laughter.

" 'Mummy's Curse'! That's funny! I never *thought* of that!"

The train's loudspeaker chimed, and an extremely garbled prerecorded message declared that they were coming up on the

Kendall Square station, which pre-empted any further commentary from Tanya.

"That's our stop," she said instead, taking her friend's elbow and leading both of them out onto the platform. Erica lost all trace of giddiness as soon as her feet were off the train.

"C'mon!" she shouted, suddenly breaking into a run for the stairs. In no particular mood to run, Tanya took her time reaching the surface. She found Erica waiting for her there.

"What was that for?" Tanya asked.

"Nothing," Erica claimed.

"Mummy's Curse stuff?"

Erica just smiled and took her friend's arm. She didn't want to think about what happened to Dina any longer than absolutely necessary. The same went for Jimmy, and El, Dr. Decaf, and all the rest of them. It was enough to drive a young woman to drink. Which was what she'd been doing.

Tanya led her much drunker friend along as they made the five-block trip back to their building. Being shorter and more than a little heftier than Erica, Tanya was the perfect drinking companion insofar as she was very difficult to outdrink, and at the end of the night her shoulder was just the perfect height for leaning.

"So, what's it really?" she asked Erica. "Bad breakup or something?"

"Hmm?" Erica asked. "What's what really?"

"Sweetie, I've been out with you before, but tonight? You were nuts! You know where you'd be right now if I hadn't been along?"

"Where?"

"Somebody's back seat is where. You had the whole bar ready to take turns on you."

"Ooh. That sounds like fun!"

"Rickie . . ."

"And you stopped them? Why'd you stop them?" She jerked Tanya back toward the train station. "C'mon, let's go find a boy!"

"Cut it out!"

"You can have one, too, Tannie. Or I can share."

"I'm gettin' you to bed. Now let's go."

"Ooh, that could be fun too," Erica said.

"Stop it."

"Okay."

"And tell me why you're trying to get yourself killed."

That shut Erica up for a good block. Tanya waited patiently.

"I figured out something, Tannie," Erica said finally.

"Yeah? A good thing? Are we celebrating now by drinking ourselves into a coma?"

"Nono, not a good thing. A bad thing. A very... a bad thing."

"C'mon now, how bad could it be?" Tanya asked. Her expertise was in architecture, but she was pretty sure after the atomic bomb was invented, there weren't many bad things left for a theoretical physicist to come up with. The bar was set too high.

"Bad enough," Erica said.

She could have said a great deal more, but the truth was there was no way Tanya would have believed her, especially not after how she reacted to the *easy* part of the story. Plus, there were only a dozen people on the planet who could have completely gotten what was going on in the back of Erica's mind, and more than a couple of those people were recently deceased. And she was drunk. She'd never get it right.

I should call Jamie, she thought. *He'd understand.*

They reached their building, which was a small three-story row house, the fourth from the corner in a long line of similar places. The same sort of three-apartment neighborhoods could be found throughout Cambridge and Somerville, but this was probably the only such block that was composed primarily of students rather than families.

Erica liked to think of her particular block as Postgrad Central, because this was where grad students such as herself and Tanya retired to when they wanted to get away from the keg party existence that made up the core of the campus.

Tanya fiddled with the lock while Erica leaned against the peekaboo window on the side and realized with some disappointment that her buzz was almost entirely gone, replaced by an overwhelming need to find someplace to lie down. Tanya, who was leaning on the door as she unlocked it, apparently concurred.

It'd been a long day. Erica had ambushed Tanya in the middle of the afternoon and dragged her downtown for what was supposed to be a window-shopping excursion. Then the drinking started. Erica wasn't sure when that began, but she knew it only ended when they realized the last train was about to leave Park Street, and that was plenty late enough.

"Got it," Tanya muttered, slipping her keys back into her jeans and pushing the door open. "Come on, let's get you upstairs."

Given the building was only three flights, there was no elevator to rely upon to get them to the top floor, which was where Erica happened to reside, with Tanya one floor below.

The first floor was occupied by a complex series of Vietnamese undergraduates who were all named Nguyen, and who were quite insistently not related to one another. Nobody was entirely sure how many Nguyens there were—as few as three and as many as seven, depending on the day of the week—but as the apartment only had one and a half bedrooms, any number larger than two seemed to stretch the realm of the possible. Erica had spent hours looking out her window and attempting to resolve the Many Nguyen problem, without success.

Tanya helped Erica up to the third floor, although by then she didn't feel like she needed any help.

"You got it from here?" Tanya asked at the door.

"Got it." She hugged her friend. "Thanks for coming out with me today."

"Don't mention it," she said, hugging back. "Just give me more warning next time. I'll hydrate."

Erica worked the door open.

"See you tomorrow," Tanya said, heading down to her own place.

"Hope so," Erica said quietly.

Shutting the door, she listened to Tanya's footsteps as she made her way down one flight. The floors and walls of the apartments were thin enough that, at this time of night with no ambient noise from the outside to interfere, she could hear almost everything her friend did downstairs and vice versa. This had never helped with the Many Nguyen problem as Tanya reported that hardly any sound ever came up from the first floor. But she heard Tanya opening her door, checking her messages, and heading for the bathroom.

Erica closed her eyes and listened to herself breathing for a while. The room spun in a not altogether pleasant clockwise direction, reminding her that even though the thrill of drunkenness was gone, the sensory impairment was right where she'd left it.

She kicked off her boots and left them by the door, and then hung a left and headed, not for the bedroom, but the study.

It was a pretty big apartment for one person, and the rent certainly reflected that fact. Erica was able to afford it thanks to the scholarship money that had gotten her through the post-high school years, but only just barely.

Most of her clothes came from the Garment District—not an actual district, but a secondhand clothing store two blocks away

—and she tended to eat a lot of pasta. After a day of drinking, that would be about all she could look forward to in the way of sustenance for the next few weeks.

The apartment had a nice big living room with a half-kitchen in the corner, the bathroom off to one side, and the two bedrooms down a short hallway to the left of the door. The smaller of those two bedrooms—a space that might have been mistaken for a closet were it not for the window—was where Erica had her computer and all her notes.

The notes were always the first thing anybody noticed because she had a tendency to keep them in a sort of order that defied the meaning of the word. They were stacked on the desk, in piles, loosely scattered on the floor, and tacked up on the wall. It was like a shrine to the god Entropy, or at least that was how it looked to everyone else. But Erica could see the fractals in the chaos.

She switched on the light and gingerly stepped over one of the more important aspects of Kaluza-Klein theory to get to the computer, which was running a series of perturbations and would continue to do so for, she imagined, the next week or so before it told her that she'd given it bad initial data.

She missed the lab's mainframe and hated having to do these kinds of calculations on a home computer that was just not built to handle it, but the lab had been locked up since the day it was wrecked, so she didn't have a choice.

We were so happy, she thought, involuntarily hearkening back to the last time they were all together and still alive, in the lab, before the vandalism. It was a pleasant memory, but she hated visiting it because every memory that followed involved funerals, confusion, and fear, and this made her want to vomit.

The university's investigation into the laboratory vandalism was ongoing and would undoubtedly remain so for as long as the people with keys—and who were ostensibly suspects—

continued to die unexpectedly. The entire matter was being kept quiet, even from the police, as it was something of an embarrassment to MIT. Erica knew who had done it, but she doubted anybody would believe her.

Trying hard to get her mind off of such unpleasant matters—which was what the drinking was supposed to do—she skimmed across the surface layer of pages decorating the room before settling on a particular series of calculations sitting askew in the corner underneath the window. Meandering cautiously across the room, she knelt down, picked up the top page, and then sat back on the floor and scanned it carefully. She already knew exactly what the page said; she'd only finished working on it two days earlier. But still, the mathematics was reassuring to her. Physics was her comfort food.

"It was all in the vibrations, Dr. Decaf," she said to herself, adding, "You would have loved this." Which was perfectly true. Nothing gave the professor a good rise like an elegant proof.

She was leaning with her back against the window pane and preparing for a nice long cry when her mourning was rudely interrupted by a piece of paper. It was halfway across the floor, in the quadrant devoted mainly to Calabi-Yau shape equations, yet the page was part of an iteration of Plank length she'd drafted three weeks ago, and it belonged in the quantum physics section under the desk. How had it ended up *there*?

Erica was certain that, drunk or not, she would have noticed its odd placement in the same way another person might discover a misplaced thought or an off-rule coffee table. But she was at a loss as to how it could have moved *while* she was sitting right there, so the only reasonable conclusion was that she had simply not been paying careful attention when entering the room.

It was an inadequate explanation, but the only one that qualified. But for that to be true, someone must have been in her apartment at some time in the recent past, and that someone had moved one sheet of paper. Which also made no sense at all. Unless she did it herself, but that was far less likely.

Getting back to her feet again proved to be a much more daunting task than she'd imagined when she began trying to do so, but with the help of the window sill she managed it. And then, while she was facing the window, her head suddenly became very heavy and her face was forcing itself *through* the glass.

The shock of impact caused everything to happen out of order. First came the iron taste of blood in her mouth, then the loud *crash* of the window breaking, and only then did she feel her nose and cheeks thrum with pain. This came in time with her instinctive need to pull away from the window in an awkward pirouette into the center of the room, blood from her nose arcing across the papers describing, vaguely, a parabola.

Quite suddenly, the middle of the floor came up to greet her, and she smacked down hard right on top of some mirror symmetry notes, her head and face now screaming with pain.

Her head. Someone had shoved her head through the window.

Just now.

But there was nobody in the room. She rubbed some blood from her eyes— there was some sort of wound on her forehead to go with what had to be a broken nose—and looked around. All she could see was the baseball bat that was, by God, supposed to be in the bedroom where it would come in handy one day in case a Nguyen or two tried to get busy one night, yet there it was, leaning against the side of the wall.

The bat was trying to kill her.

Unless it was the computer's turn. It was humming happily on the desk one second, and then a second later it decided to leap off the desk. She batted it away as best she could with one hand and watched it land on the floor with a crunch, scattering weeks of work on flop transitions all over the place. Five years earlier and she'd have been dead, but this generation of computer was small and light and hard to use as a murder weapon. Not the best slogan in the world, especially since this one had attacked her.

No, that's not it, she thought. *There's someone in the study.*

She couldn't see anyone, but that didn't mean there wasn't somebody there.

Getting to her feet, Erica half-ran and half-rolled into the hallway, hitting her shoulder hard on the wall because the apartment was now rocking side-to-side with less predictability than the subway car. From there she bounced and fell into the living room, and there still wasn't anybody else in the apartment. Except there was.

"I know you're here!" she screamed as the blood from her face made a stain she was never going to be able to get rid of... and she loved that carpet.

Focus.

Pushing off the floor, she got her legs back under her and wobbled into a crouch.

"We didn't mean to do it!" Erica yelled. "We weren't looking for you!"

Someone banged hard against the door, eliciting a yelp from Erica, who nearly fell over onto the carpet again.

"Rickie, what's wrong?"

"Tanya!" Erica answered. "Go 'way, Tannie, or—"

She couldn't finish her sentence. Having stood up while speaking, Erica drove herself directly into what felt a good deal like one of her kitchen knives.

What an interesting sensation, she thought, as the air slipped from her punctured lung.

Tanya banged harder on the door and continued to call her

name, sounding more and more alarmed and further and further away. Erica tried to tell Tanya not to bother, but the swollen lips on her damaged face didn't seem all that interested in talking, so she stopped trying. It was much easier just to lie down anyway.

From a very far off place she could hear Tanya breaking down the door and screaming.

CHAPTER NINE

Now

I t was about one in the morning when Corrigan sat up in bed. It was too early for the day to begin, and he should have been lying still and trying to fall back asleep, but he had to sit up because there was someone else also sitting up, in his bedroom, at the foot of his bed.

This wasn't like the happy discovery of Maggie under the blankets. Nothing like that at all.

He could hear ragged, shallow breathing. She was working hard, forcing the air in and out of her lungs at great effort, as if the weight was still on her back.

"I'm sorry," he said quietly. He already knew who it was. "I tried my best."

"You could have saved me," insisted Maribel Kozminsky.

She was still wearing the blue suit. Turning toward him, she revealed a back that was twisted grossly out of shape. Her neck was tilted up awkwardly, so she had to look down to see him, given how her face was pointed at the ceiling. "You were right there!"

"I don't know what happened."

"You could have tried harder."

"Wait a minute," he said. "You aren't even dead. What are you doing here? You can't be a ghost if you're not even dead yet."

"You know I can't move my legs, right?" she said, ignoring his very good point. "Permanent damage. And for someone my size—"

"I said I was sorry. What do you want from me?"

She sighed, the result being a full-body shudder. And when she spoke again, her voice was deeper—a man's voice. "I expected more from you, boy."

"I know. The guy . . . he stopped to look at something, except he didn't. I don't know what happened."

"You're a moron, you know that?" she snapped, sounding like a woman again, albeit an angry one. "He didn't stop to look at something. He stopped to look at some*one*. Do you even use your brain at all?"

"Someone?" Corrigan perked up. "Who?"

"How should I know? What makes a guy stop what he's doing like that? A pretty girl, probably. The future was altered and the girl didn't show. You figured this out already."

"I did?"

"And you remember the last time someone other than you altered the time stream, and that's scaring the piss out of you. You're trying to pretend none of this happened. You're a total mess, Corry. You should talk to Ames before it gets any worse."

"I don't need Ames."

"Suit yourself."

"He didn't help me either," said a voice from near the closet. The boy stepped into the unnatural light that was coming from nowhere and everywhere.

"Oh, Christ," Corrigan said.

"What's that, honey?" the woman asked the boy.

"He was late!" the child half-shouted.

Unlike Maribel, the kid looked uninjured. That's because Corrigan's ghosts were eminently practical; there was basically nothing left of him after the accident. Whoever decided these things understood that a ghost that looked like a battered pile of goo wouldn't be very communicative.

"There was a big traffic jam that day, kid, all right? I tried my best."

"You always say that," he grumbled.

"Well, you know, I try to explain these things, but you keep coming back and yelling at me anyway. What am I supposed to do about it now? Seriously."

"Awww, what a cutie," blue suit declared, running her hand through the boy's hair.

"See, that's a ghost, lady," Corrigan said, pointing. "He actually died."

"That's terrible! What happened, sweetie?"

"Fell off my bike," the boy said.

"Is that all?"

Corrigan added, "In front of the Silver Line. What's it been, twelve years?"

"Thirteen. I'd be in college now, y'know."

"Right, right," Corrigan said, rubbing his eyes. "Look, it's not that I don't like the company, but I have to get some sleep or tomorrow's gonna be a bear."

The boy smiled. "Nuh-uh. She's s'posed to be coming."

"She who?" Corrigan asked.

"*You know.*"

The kid was still smiling, only the sides of his mouth were starting to curl right around his head and past his ears, while his forehead crept upward and chased the hair away to the back of his skull. His eyes blackened, and his nice, normal-sized big boy teeth had expanded and sharpened.

The light from nowhere began to compress toward the center of the room.

She was coming.

His heart started to race.

"Come on, I don't deserve this," Corrigan whined quietly.

"Corrigan Bain is going insane," the boy with the sharpened teeth hissed. "Corrigan Bain is going insane."

From the hallway, possibly the window, or maybe under the bed, he heard her voice. "Corrigan. . ."

"No . . ." he muttered.

"*You let it happen again!*"

Corrigan screamed.

And then he was awake. He sat bolt upright in his bed, the bedspread curled tightly in a ball in his hands and sweat coating most of his body and a good portion of the fitted sheet. And he was still screaming.

He stopped. The room looked exactly as it had in the dream, except that sunlight was beginning to make an impact on the shadows. A look at the clock told him it was time to get up, which was good as he had no intention of going back to sleep anyway. Probably not for a very long time.

"I'm not crazy, Harvey," he muttered. "Don't tell me I am. I'm not."

A quick peek at the outside world confirmed that everything was more or less as he left it. Clouds had built up on the edge of the skyline, portending doom for those who might be looking forward to a sunny weekend.

"All right," he said to the ghosts that were still lingering on the edge of his consciousness, "I'm getting to it."

Standing at the wall ten minutes later with the computer humming eagerly, Corrigan swept through his map waiting for the usual spike. But nothing was happening.

He tried it again—his fifth pass. Still nothing.

"Ah, c'mon," he muttered, commencing his sixth pass. Any other day, this'd be fantastic news—he hadn't had a day off in months—but this was particularly bad timing. The problem with the nightmares, other than the fact that they were hellish in general, was that they didn't really go away again until he had another clean day. And he couldn't have a clean day with no appointments to meet.

Finally, after ten tries, he admitted defeat. On the bright side, he could start drinking right away. Like, just as soon as he got out of the shower.

But there was the matter of the phone, which was ringing. It was sitting on the table next to the computer, so he didn't have to go that far to retrieve it.

"How's your schedule today?" Maggie asked, without even a hello. Corrigan looked down at the answering machine and noted that there were two messages waiting for him. Either she tried to reach him while he was still sleeping or he simply didn't hear the phone ring while busy with the map.

"Pretty empty," he said, adding, "I'm free all day."

For the briefest of seconds the idea that Maggie Trent might be equally free, and furthermore be calling on the off chance he was up for some extracurriculars, flitted through his brain like an unexpected cool breeze at the end of a long jog. But, of course, that wasn't it. She had an address for him.

"Be there as soon as you can," she said. Corrigan repeated the address. The computer, ever dutiful, logged the address and plotted it on the map.

"Where've you been?" Maggie asked as soon as he cut the engine. Corrigan took a look at the building whose address she'd given him over an hour ago. It was a shit-brown, flat-roofed three-story beastie that would have been impossible to distinguish from the next ten in the row if not for the number on the door and the color of the wood slat exterior. He'd been down streets like this before, and it always felt like he was driving through a giant box of crayons.

"Got here when I could," he growled, not bothering to mention he'd showered, shaved, had something to eat, and just in general taken his sweet time getting there because he was going to try his damnedest to make the most of this vacation day. Showing up at a crime scene was not his idea of a good time.

"Well come on," she said, discarding her cigarette and leading him inside to a horribly steep flight of stairs.

"You know, I never said yes," Corrigan pointed out about halfway up.

"You looking at my ass right now?" she asked, which was a reasonable question only insofar as she was ahead of him on the stairs.

"Actually, yes."

"Ever want to see it again?"

"That's low."

"Give me a little time to make my case, okay? Take a look at the scene. I just want your opinion."

The first room they came across on the third floor was a smallish living room space that showed the years of wear from an indifferent landlord who habitually rented to college students. One could find the same sort of apartment in about half of the city. Although in this case it was clear the tenant had made an effort to personalize things and make it feel homier. There was a nice shag rug atop the low-thread industrial carpeting that went wall-to-wall, a secondhand couch that was being held together by a series of small blankets, a set of simple white curtains that didn't clash with anything else in the room, and enough throw pillows to strongly suggest the occupant was a female.

But all of that was background to the main attraction, which was the large bloodstain in the middle of the shag carpet. Said carpet was beige, so the red-black bloodstain was particularly prominent. Also prominent was the tremendous number of people scattered about the room—people in police uniforms, blue FBI windbreakers, and one guy in a jumpsuit who must have been a forensic technician or something.

Most of them were just standing around and staring at the walls as if microscopic evidence could be culled via naked eye examination. The only movement was coming from the two guys in lab coats kneeling over the bloodstain and extracting particulates from it, as if it were a part of some urban archeological program.

Maggie said, "Local P.D. still has jurisdiction; we're here as advisors."

"Did you empty your whole office?"

"Just about. But this one's a little different than the rest."

"How so?" he asked.

"We'll get to that."

"Okay."

"Come on. It starts over here."

She led him down a short hallway into a small room full of papers, with one computer that was clearly not where it was supposed to be. The window at the other end of the room had been shattered. An officer was standing at the center of the room, ignoring the fact that he was standing on multiple pages of mathematical calculations.

"This was where the attack began," Maggie said.

"Attack?" he asked. "That *is* different."

"Her face was shoved through that window. Then she fled

down the hall and got stabbed in the living room, in the back. So yeah, I'd call it an attack."

"Doesn't fit the other profiles," Corrigan said. "And it sounds more like a home invasion to me."

"See all the papers?"

"Hard not to."

"Victim was Erica Smalls. Supposed to be some kind of genius. She was an MIT postgrad, working on her doctoral thesis in physics."

"Same as the others?"

"She's on the list."

"Yet this doesn't look like any suicide or accidental death."

"No, it doesn't. Are you familiar with the concept of escalation?"

"In what sense?"

"Pathologically. Say somebody happens to be a serial rapist. But one time he ends up killing one of the victims—finds out he likes it. Next time he's raping, he's taking the next step of finishing her off, only it's on purpose."

"I saw something like that on TV once," he said, trying to recall on which of the roughly two thousand possible cop shows it could have turned up.

"I'm thinking that's what we have here. This girl wasn't just killed. She was toyed with first. And he didn't take any steps to make it look like an accident."

"Maybe he knows the other deaths aren't being treated as accidents anymore."

"Exactly. So why not have some fun with it?"

Corrigan thought back to the girl who landed in front of a subway train and how none of the witnesses mentioned anything about her being pushed.

"Are you telling me you have an invisible serial killer on the loose?"

Maggie smiled. "I don't know what we have yet. I'm just telling you what this crime scene is saying. But that's not the craziest theory I've heard so far. Wait'll you meet Tanya."

"Is she one of the people in the living room?"

"Neighbor. She's downstairs right now having her fourth or fifth nervous breakdown. She *says* she interrupted the killer in the act."

"That's great, isn't it?"

Maggie implied, by her expression, that it was anything but great. "I'll take you downstairs in a minute," she said. "Finish up here first."

"Pretty small place," he said. "I think I've already seen everything, don't you?"

"Not all of it, no. Anything catch your eye in here?"

Corrigan made a show of examining the study closely.

"Papers on the floor, but it looks to me like she did that herself. Computer on the floor, not so much."

"We think that happened during the attack."

"Baseball bat's out of place," he said, pointing to the Louisville Slugger leaning up against the wall.

"Might've been used to hit her in the back of the head. We're not sure just yet. Anything else?"

"You know, this would be a whole hell of a lot easier if you told me what I'm supposed to be looking for."

"If I knew, I wouldn't need you here," she said cryptically.

"What did Calvin tell you about me, exactly?"

Maggie hesitated, trying to decide whether or not to answer.

"That you may have encountered something like this before," she said.

"Well, I haven't. Can I go home now? I have a lot of drinking to catch up on."

"The bedroom's this way," she said, ignoring his plea.

Erica Smalls' bedroom was tidy and only slightly larger than her study. It had a seemingly random selection of stuffed animals neatly congregated on the bed, which had been made with the efficiency of a hotel maid service. In the corner was a small jewelry stand with a mirror beside a set of dresser drawers holding an assortment of curios. Rounding out the room were two doors; one open and leading to a small closet, and one closed and leading to who knows where. Clearly, the attack hadn't carried over into the bedroom. And, as with all the other rooms, there were more law enforcement guys, mostly just glancing around as if they were waiting for one of the walls to start talking.

Corrigan picked up a framed picture from the nightstand. It showed a very attractive young woman posing with a golden retriever.

"Is this her?" he asked.

"Yeah. Pretty, huh?"

The hairs on the back of his neck pricked up, indicating that the answer to this question might lead him to a dangerous place if he wasn't careful. Maggie liked to pretend she wasn't like that, but of course she was.

"Not bad," he said, which he thought was a decent answer. Maggie huffed about it anyway.

"Bathroom and kitchen are all that's left," she said, heading quickly out of the room. From the corner of his eye, Corrigan caught the FBI agent coughing up a little grin.

"What?" he asked. The man just shrugged, smiling.

Five minutes later, Corrigan had seen both the bathroom and the half-kitchen and found nothing extraordinary about either of them, aside from the other people surveying the walls. Then he was back at the front door, standing beside Maggie and watching the nearly dozen people going about the business of doing nothing in particular.

"Can I ask you something?" he whispered to Maggie.

"Sure."

"What are they waiting for?"

"Dunno yet," Maggie said. "I'll tell you when it happens. Any luck?"

"I still don't what I'm looking for," he said.

"Something you might be uniquely equipped to see?"

"No," he said. "Nothing."

"All right," she sighed. "Let's go talk to Tanya."

"It was a goddamn ghost!" Tanya Mifune repeated for the seventh or eighth time that day.

She was shouting because this seemed to be about the only way to get anybody to believe her. Or possibly it was because she didn't really believe it herself.

Every time she mentioned ghosts, Corrigan's flesh broke out in goose bumps. *I believe you,* he thought. *Ghosts can be nasty.*

He could see from her clothes and the red in her eyes that Tanya hadn't slept at all, which was sort of understandable given the circumstances. He also detected a faint whiff of alcohol. That couldn't have helped her, story-wise, with the police.

"You were out drinking with her," he guessed.

"Who the hell *are* you, anyway?" Tanya retorted. He didn't look like a law enforcement officer so much as he looked like the guy who carried your couch in from the truck, so the question made sense.

"Mr. Bain is a special consultant," Maggie said. "Just tell him what you told me earlier."

Tanya reviewed Corrigan's attire, such as it was. "You a ghost-buster or somethin'?"

He smiled. "I'm a fixer."

"Yeah, all right," she said, waving him off.

Tanya was sitting on the lime green couch that was the centerpiece of her sparsely decorated living room. The apartment was a geometric twin to the one upstairs, but the sartorial choices made by the two women differed significantly enough to make it appear as if they were apartments in entirely different buildings. Tanya had some decorating skills to draw from; her place seemed bigger, somehow, yet more cozy. But that could have been the lack of a bloodstain speaking.

She picked up a cup of lukewarm tea with a shaky hand, took a few sips, and recounted the events of the prior day. Corrigan didn't really pay attention until the end.

"When I found her, she already had the knife stuck in her back . . . but there wasn't anybody else in the room. I checked the whole goddamn place. She was alone."

"Are you saying she stuck the knife in her own back?" he asked.

"No, I'm saying she was stabbed by a ghost. Okay? You think I like saying it? Course it sounds crazy. Think I'm crazy?"

What Corrigan was actually thinking was that Tanya Mifune had beaten and stabbed her friend and then made up a story about homicidal phantoms. The police must have felt the same way since there were two officers standing by the apartment door.

"She knew this was gonna happen, y'know," Tanya continued.

Maggie asked, "What do you mean?"

Apparently this was new.

"Rickie said last night she figured out something. Dunno what, but it scared her. And she told me this crazy story 'bout someone breaking into their lab and destroying some equipment and how right after that . . . I made fun of it. Called it the Mummy's Curse."

"You didn't take this seriously?"

"No. I mean, yeah, I did, because she was upset, and if it was upsetting for her it was real enough. But she's been funny since Doc Decaf died. They were close, you know? After that she started spending a lot more time cooped up in her apartment. With the other deaths and all, I figured this was just her way of dealing. Make up something crazy like that. But now, you know... now I'm thinking she knew what was gonna happen, and she maybe even figured out why."

"Thanks—" Corrigan said, but the girl held up a hand.

"Something else. Didn't remember it 'til about an hour ago. She was shouting something when I got to the door. " 'We weren't looking for you' or 'we didn't mean to do it' or... something like that. Like she was talking to somebody."

Corrigan went a little pale, not because of what Tanya said so much as because it reminded him of something someone else had told him a long time ago.

" 'We weren't looking for you'? That's what she said?"

"I think so."

Maggie stared at Corrigan. "Familiar?"

"No," he muttered. "No, it's just interesting."

Maggie kept her gaze steady and waited for more, but he didn't offer anything else. "All right. Thanks, Tanya."

They left Tanya to her tea and stepped back into the hallway. "What is it?" Maggie asked, once they were alone.

"It's nothing. Honestly."

"Bullshit. I know you too well."

"It's not important. I'd tell you if it was."

"Okay. Fine. I have to make some calls, find out what this stuff about a lab being destroyed is. The university never mentioned anything about that to any of us, so far as I know."

"Hey, who the hell is Dr. Decaf?"

"Took me a minute too. Professor Offey. His first name was Michael. Mike Offey. Get it?"

"Right. He was one of the victims you showed me."

"Yeah. And Smalls was one of his graduate students."

Corrigan nodded. "And why isn't Tanya a suspect, again?"

"She is," Maggie admitted. "But her story does sort of check out. The floors and walls of this place are pretty thin, and Mr. Nguyen from the first floor confirmed he heard Tanya walking around in her apartment at the time the screaming began from the top floor. He also heard Tanya running up the stairs *after* that. He got there a couple of minutes later and can also confirm that nobody went past him and down the stairs. He was the one who called for the ambulance."

"This place has only one stairwell?"

"No, two. There's a back hallway accessible through Erica's bedroom. But while the inner door was unlocked, the outer one —the one that opens on the back stairs—was locked and chained from the inside."

"So. A ghost?"

"Like I said, we don't know what we have yet."

"But your only witness says ghost."

Maggie started to say something, but caught herself. Instead, she offered, "She's not our only lead."

"Is there someone else?"

"I don't want to talk about it here."

It occurred to Corrigan that as much as Maggie didn't look like the sort of person who believed for a second that a ghost could have stabbed Erica Smalls, she was certainly acting like someone who did. He was obviously missing something important and was about to ask what that might be when they were interrupted by one of Maggie's FBI agents. She had run halfway down the stairs to the midpoint landing.

"Agent Trent," she said. "It's happened."

The agent led Maggie and Corrigan back up to the third floor. The room, which had been a quiet, semi-orderly collective when they'd left, had erupted into a frenzied crowd of onlookers.

"Stand aside!" Maggie had to shout. She pushed her way through the room, Corrigan following with absolutely no idea what was going on.

At the center of the semicircle stood one of the uniformed cops. "I saw it..." he said quietly. "Happened right as I was watching."

"When?" Maggie asked.

"Just now," he said. He looked genuinely spooked.

"Did you touch the wall?" she asked urgently.

"What?"

"Did you touch the wall!"

"No! What, you think I did it?"

"Fingerprints. I don't want to pick up any of yours."

Corrigan couldn't see what the fuss was about until the cop finally stepped to one side. And then he understood why everyone had been standing around before and why Tanya's ghost story wasn't making anybody laugh out loud.

"Same as before," Maggie said.

On the white wall, in what looked an awful lot like blood, somebody had written a message with what must have been a finger. And having looked over the room pretty carefully already, Corrigan could attest to the fact that it wasn't there five minutes earlier.

It read: KILROY WAS HERE.

"What do you think?" Maggie asked Corrigan.

His first thought was to wonder if he would be waking up in his bed in a few minutes. What he said was, "I think either someone here did that, or we're all going insane."

"Better get measured for a straitjacket, then," Maggie said.

CHAPTER TEN

Thirty-Eight Years Past

Things started to go very wrong right around the time the temperature hit a new low of minus two on the external thermometer nailed to a post in the backyard of the Maine farmhouse. Violet remembered the day well because it was the first time she ever experienced weather that cold.

For most of her life, she assumed thermometers had negative numbers on them because of some completist need on the part of Mr. Fahrenheit, much in the same way automobile speedometers recorded speeds the car had no hope of ever attaining. Likewise, as a girl born and raised in Southern California—a part of the world that nowadays looked an awful lot like heaven to her—she never understood snow as anything more than a hypothetical concept that happened Elsewhere.

For the first couple of months, snow was a mysterious and wonderful thing. She spent a lot of time watching it fall, playing around with it in her hands, showing it to Corry, and just marveling at it in general. But the damn stuff never went away; it kept renewing itself every few days, and the sun—who knew the sun was weaker in Maine?—didn't have any effect on the permafrost at all.

So she'd quickly had her fill of snow and cold weather, despite which, it kept on snowing and getting colder.

The day it hit negative two was the same day the Bluff commune ran out of meat. Half the people there didn't eat meat, but it was the first indication that supplies, however inexhaustible they seemed, were not, in fact, inexhaustible. And for the first time since they'd arrived, the people of the farmhouse began rationing the food.

The problem was the food would never have lasted the entire winter either way. Charlie insisted, whenever asked, that his grandparents survived winters just fine for forty years on a single freezer of supplies, but he stubbornly ignored the obvious fact that two elderly people ate significantly less than fifteen stoners. His grandparents could also drive into town for more supplies if needed, whereas Charlie only had a yellow school bus with a quarter tank of gas, almost no money, and no idea where the nearest town was.

By New Year's Day, they'd run out of potatoes and coffee. By mid-January, there was nothing left but green beans and apples. Two weeks after that, the Bluff commune officially hit rock bottom when something happened that Charlie's grandparents never had to worry about... they ran out of drugs.

There is no greater hell on Earth than being stuck in a farmhouse with fifteen hippies going dry simultaneously. As Violet had already learned, the world got a lot more harsh and scary when one went cold turkey. And she'd always had the option of dropping out for a while by just walking into one of the rooms and partaking of whatever the drug of the moment was. As it was her choice not to do so, the process wasn't ultimately all that terrible.

Not so for the rest of them.

Upon realizing there were no more drugs, a search party was organized, the net result of which was zero acid tabs and a dozen roaches that were immediately combined to make one joint, which was quickly consumed.

Then they started to get really creative.

A couple of them had a little chemistry in their backgrounds, so part of the kitchen was converted into a laboratory to see if they could invent a drug out of various foodstuffs. The crushed apple seed paste seemed to hold the most promise but turned out to be a dead end. And the burnt banana peels, which the group spent hours outside rooting around in the trash for, just ended up making the whole house stink. Even Corry had a comment on that—breaking his customary silence when in the presence of anyone other than his mother to declare that the odor was truly "icky."

Desperately straight, the house turned *en masse* to the freezer because if they couldn't get high any more, at least they could eat a lot of food. But, of course, there wasn't any food either.

It was then that Charlie, while being pinned down by three guys who had been avowed pacifists only a couple of days earlier, realized something more than an appeal to positive vibrations was needed, if only to prevent himself from being lynched and possibly eaten.

"We'll go hunting," he said.

"What did you say?" asked Happy Sammy, who was, at that moment, not at all happy. He was, however, happier than Charlie, given Sammy had him in a headlock.

"Hunting," Charlie said again, louder.

His suggestion effectively defused the situation—being one that prominently involved Charlie being whaled upon in the face, stomach, and kidney areas by various prominent members of the Bluff commune—while the congregation paused to consider the suggestion.

Nobody knew exactly what to say for a while, so the idea just floated around the room, like a helium balloon just beyond the reach of a two-year-old.

It was a measure of the palpable desperation that had consumed the room's occupants that the suggestion was seriously considered. The house was full of the offspring of middle class urbanites, people who had lived in cities for much of their lives and for whom Getting One's Own Food meant taking a trip to the grocery store or the nearest burger joint. All of them understood, in the abstract, that it was theoretically possible to hunt, kill, skin, carve, and cook one's own meat, but that didn't mean it was something they wanted any part of, personally. Clouding up matters further, every one of them had at one time over the past three months loudly denounced the carnivorous nature of the human animal as innately cruel and evil.

But at the same time, they had to eat.

Happy Sammy loosened his grip on Charlie. Charlie then shook his hands free of Linda and Mary-Mary, stepped into the center of the room, and proceeded to retake command.

"I have a couple of rifles," he said. "They're in the cellar. Anyone else know how to use a gun?"

Tyrell, who had been standing in the back of the room with Violet and Corry, declared, "I do."

"What're you gonna hunt?" asked Mondo suspiciously, rubbing the knuckles on his right hand, said hand having recently connected with Charlie's chin.

"I dunno," Charlie said. "Maybe someone's got a cow out there or something."

"You gonna hunt a *cow*?"

"Deer," Violet suggested.

"There's deer?" Charlie asked.

"Corry's seen 'em. A few times; right, honey?"

Corry, for his part, said nothing nor further indicated the existence of wildlife outside in some nonverbal way. His eyes flitted about the room as if he were following the trail of microbes. More than a couple of the Bluff commune members realized at that moment that it hadn't been the drugs; the boy was just creepy.

"I've seen 'em too," Tyrell claimed. "Gotta be a couple dozen around here. It'll be easy."

"There you go," Charlie said cheerily, putting on his very best *things are gonna be all right* face, which looked pretty convincing despite a recently dislodged tooth and an eye that was swollen half shut. "Who else wants to come?"

There was a reason nobody discovered the cellar to the farmhouse before. One had to go outside to get into it.

For Violet, who had never been in a home with an underground level, much less one without internal access to said level, this was particularly mystifying. She couldn't imagine anything less practical. Then she spotted the unused outhouse twenty paces from the back door and immediately reevaluated that assessment.

Charlie led her and Tyrell—and Corry, who wasn't leaving his mother's side after seeing all the adults in the house go insane at basically the same time—around the side to a snow-covered, slanted... something. Violet's first thought was that it was for a skateboard or a dirt bike, up until Charlie cleared off the snow to reveal twin metal doors built into a cement frame. Threaded through the handles was a chain with a padlock.

Charlie reached into his shirt and pulled out a key tied around his neck, which she always thought he wore as a statement of some kind, albeit one that only Charlie fully understood.

"You keep it locked," Tyrell observed.

"Man, like I said; there's guns down here. Course I keep it locked."

Pulling the chain free, he and Tyrell managed to get one of the doors open. It creaked unappreciatively and kicked off a dust cloud of orange rust. For some reason, this made Vi want to hold Corry closer.

"After you," Tyrell said.

Charlie peered down into the cellar, which was pitch-dark. There were steep cement steps leading down that looked to have claimed many ankles and necks over the years. Rather than try his luck in the dark, Charlie knelt in the snow, reached under the unopened door, and produced a large-beam flashlight. After testing it to make sure it still worked, he disappeared into the ground.

Tyrell and Vi looked at one another. Corry whimpered.

"Yeah," said Tyrell, "I don't wanna go down there much either, little man." He smiled and got Corry to smile back. "But you ain't gotta worry. You know that, right?"

He stepped down halfway and then popped up again.

"Light's on. C'mon."

Charlie had found the light in the cellar, which consisted of a bare bulb with a pull chain. It was enough to illuminate the center of the room but not much else. Thus, the flashlight was still of use. By the time Violet and Corry got there, Tyrell and Charlie were already checking out the gun cabinet.

"Cold," remarked Corry. Violet hugged him closer.

"It sure is," she said. "Weird, isn't it? Colder in here than it is out there."

"It's the ground," Charlie said without turning. He was trying to work a combination lock while Tyrell held the flashlight for him. "Kinda like being in a really roomy coffin down here."

"Can we not talk about coffins right now?" Tyrell said. "'Specially since one of us was about to end up in one up there."

"I wasn't worried," Charlie said confidently.

"It was outta hand, man."

"You were a big help."

"Did you see me linin' up to take a swing?"

Charlie blew on his fingers to keep them from freezing up and tried the combination again. Either his memory was too frozen to work right or the lock was. "Could'a stopped it. They'd listen to you if you told them to stop."

"Yeah, well . . . maybe you're too pale to appreciate this, but it'd take a lot to put this black man between a mob and whatever it is they after. Hell of a lot more than your honky ass, that's for goddamn sure."

Charlie got the lock to pop open, finally.

"They're not like that," he said, while working the bolt from the cabinet. "Nobody cares what color you are."

Tyrell laughed. "Everybody's like that. Some just hide it better'n others. So let's see what we got in here."

Charlie pulled open the door to the cabinet while Tyrell illuminated the contents.

Tyrell whistled. "Damn," he said.

Charlie smiled. "I call shotgun."

———

Within the Bluff commune, opinions differed as to precisely what happened after that. The problem was that once the hunting party returned, there was a great deal of shouting, confusion, and blood, and that can only lead to misunderstandings.

What they could all agree on was that Charlie and Tyrell had left the basement with Violet and Corry in tow, both of the men holding large guns and planning to seek out and kill a woodland creature.

Violet went because she'd seen the deer and because she was one of the few people in the farmhouse who could talk sense to both of the armed parties. Corry's participation hinged partly on his prior viewings of the local fauna, but primarily on his not wanting to leave his mother's side.

Most everyone could also agree that when the hunting party left the immediate vicinity, Charlie and Tyrell were arguing about the very large boiler in the cellar that Tyrell had seen and that Charlie nonetheless still insisted did not exist.

The only other thing that was unquestionably true was that they returned two hours later absent a portion of Charlie's right leg.

Charlie, screaming obscenities, was helped in through the back door and onto the floor in the hallway by Tyrell, who immediately slumped over next to him, exhausted. Charlie then proceeded to bleed more or less all over the place and curse some more because nobody in the house was sure what to do.

"*Help me*, you hippie fucks!" Charlie shouted.

This swung the group into action. Happy Sammy yanked off his prized tie-dye and used it to staunch the blood while Mondo took off his rope belt and tied it tightly around Charlie's right thigh just above the wound. Someone pointed out that one did the same thing when trying to find a vein in an arm, and that perhaps it was then a *bad* thing to do, insofar as with the arm it made the vein pop out some more. The last thing Charlie needed was his vein popping out when part of it was already exposed to the air. Mondo ignored them and did it anyway, which was good, as it ended up saving Charlie's life.

With various persons then helping Charlie to the living

room couch or helping Tyrell back to his feet, the rest of the group took on the important business of trying to guess what happened. The preliminary consensus was that Tyrell had finally gone and shot Charlie, like they always figured he would one day.

In the confusion, nobody really noticed Violet and Corry reentering the house, Vi slowly and carefully removing her son's snow clothes and checking him for the tenth time just in case she missed a buckshot wound somewhere the first nine times she looked.

Violet could have probably explained what happened had anybody asked. That is, she was there at the time of Charlie's wounding and could attest to the order of events as they transpired. If pressed as to *how* it happened, she would have been forced to admit she didn't really know, because what happened simply didn't make any sense.

As Charlie lay on the couch, all at once very quiet, looking pale, and in great need of professional medical care, Tyrell tried to explain things.

"I don't know," he said. "I was ahead, following some tracks. I heard his gun go off and found him like that... walked him back fast as I could..."

"You sure you didn't just shoot him yourself?" accused Happy Sammy.

"Why would I have brung him back, asshole?" Tyrell snapped.

"He needs a doctor. We should try the telephone," Harriet said. "If it's working today."

"Where are the guns?" Mary-Mary asked nervously.

"Left 'em," Tyrell said. "Couldn't carry both him and them. I'll go back later—"

"I think you had something to do with this," Gingham said, fixing her gaze on Tyrell.

She said it quietly and solemnly, and with the sort of conviction that got people's attention. It had a galvanizing effect on the room. She wasn't the only one who felt this way.

"I agree," said Happy Sammy.

Tyrell instinctively took two steps back. He didn't look surprised—more like resigned. As if he always expected one day it would come down to this.

"What was that?" Mondo asked. He was beside Charlie, who had begun to whisper something at around the same time Violet and Corry pressed their way into the room.

"I said," Charlie began, louder, "it wasn't Tyrell."

Tyrell visibly relaxed, while everyone else just looked more confused, especially when Charlie raised his arm and pointed a finger at Corry.

"It was him," he said. "It was the boy."

CHAPTER ELEVEN

Now

"You weren't surprised," Corrigan was saying. "You *expected* to see that."

"We expected something," she said, reflecting that he was far more agitated about this than he should have been.

"What else was at those crime scenes that you didn't show me?"

Two hours had passed since she'd given him the tour of Erica's apartment. They were now sitting in one of the interrogation rooms in the Central Square police station, which happened to be right down the street from the crime scene. It was also the main headquarters for the Cambridge police department, but that didn't mean they had a tremendous amount of extra space to spare for the FBI—hence the interrogation room.

It was a smallish chamber with what one might call a window, only in the sense that a portion of one wall was accommodating a rectangular piece of glass. But it was at the top of the wall and covered on the inside by bars and on the outside by about fifty years of exhaust grime. Illumination—no light of value came from the window—consisted of a depressing overhead tubal fluorescent that had a tendency to dim briefly every thirty seconds or so, as if someone in the building were operating a very small electric chair. There was one door, two wood chairs, and a metal table affixed to the floor, with handcuff loops on its edge.

It was the most depressing room Maggie could remember spending time in. Which was perhaps the point.

It was also, being very small, not the greatest place to be when facing an angry man the size of Corrigan.

"The same legend turned up at every scene."

" 'Kilroy was here'?"

"Yeah. At first it was just considered graffiti, but when they found it on the wall where Professor Offey's bookshelf had been standing, it was obvious someone left it as a message."

Corrigan sat and mused for a moment.

"And that's when the FBI was called in."

"That's about right."

"I saw the pictures of that crime scene. I don't recall seeing anything on the wall."

Maggie sighed and sat down. The chair creaked loudly, quite annoyed at having been put to work. She pulled out a cigarette.

"Okay, here's the timeline," she said. "Offey ends up crushed by the bookshelf, but nobody finds him right away because it happened late at night in the back of the library in a secure private area. He gets found about three hours later by one of the security guards doing his rounds. The door to the office has been closed the whole time, but he sees the light under the door. He lets himself in, figures out the professor is dead, and calls the cops."

"He knew right then it was suspicious?" Corrigan asked. "Because it was designed to look like an accident."

"Standard procedure. Besides, what do most people do when they find a dead person?"

"Dunno. Never found one," Corrigan said. Maggie was nearly positive this was a lie, but wasn't about to call him on it.

"Right. So the cops show up and good for them, they're sharp enough to notice the brackets on the wall that were supposed to be holding up the bookshelf. No one's really thinking murder just yet, but it's interesting. They close off the scene, take pictures, call homicide."

She took a sharp drag of the cigarette. It occurred to her that there was no smoking in the building and further that she didn't particularly care. "Homicide shows up a couple of hours later, and the lead investigator—guy named Masterson, who you'll probably meet at some point—says 'what's up with the note on the wall?' But nobody can remember seeing it before. And since the scene had been closed, the only obvious conclusion was that a cop wrote it."

"That's where I would have gone."

"But while Cambridge PD was in the middle of an internal witch-hunt, someone pointed out it wasn't the first time the message turned up at one of the scenes. *That* was when Masterson called me."

"You personally?"

"Old friends," she said without elaboration. "The internal investigation didn't end up going anywhere. At worst, we could have maybe pinned the writing on Offey's wall on one or two of the guys who'd been in the room alone during the time the message appeared, but neither of them could be put at any of the other scenes, and we knew the message was also on the wall at the subway station and carved on the windowsill where the kid fell to his death. So the thinking became that the killer left it behind. It was the first time anybody really entertained the notion. We began thinking we might have a serial on our hands."

"Again with the invisible killer," Corrigan said.

He seemed to have a very strong negative reaction to this idea, more so, perhaps, than most people would when confronted with the notion. Maggie found that curious.

"We didn't think any such thing. The investigating cops had just missed it was the argument. And the camera didn't pick it up because of a trick of the light or something like that. None of the answers were all that great, but they were better than anything else we had. Up until Jamie Silverman."

Corrigan nodded.

"Bathtub," he said, with the expression of a man who hadn't been able to get a certain image out of his mind.

"I was at the scene as soon as the cops were that day, and so were Hicks and Masterson and a few other people who'd started to take this seriously."

She omitted the fact that Hicks was actually there to try and prove Maggie was wasting federal time on the investigative equivalent of a snipe hunt.

"By the time we arrived, the water was cold and so was the bathroom. But it's a funny thing; when you put four or five people together in a small enclosed space like that, it starts to heat up. Silverman had one of those glass-paneled shower doors. They were clear when we first stepped in, but after an hour or so, the doors started to fog."

Maggie hesitated. Even after what happened in Erica's apartment, she had trouble admitting something like this out loud. Finally, she said, "I saw it happen personally."

"What happen?" he asked, although it was hard to imagine he didn't already know what she was talking about.

"The words spelled themselves out in the fog on the shower door."

"Kilroy."

"Yeah."

"You think the invisible killer is a Styx fan?"

Maggie smiled. "The 'Kilroy was here' messages first turned up in World War II. Whenever GIs were sent off someplace, they'd find the message scrawled and left there for them even, as legend had it, if they were the first ones to arrive. The prosaic explanation was that they were done by James Kilroy, a naval shipyard inspector, after which the practice was picked up by other soldiers."

"Maybe he's your killer," Corrigan said. He seemed to be calming down a little.

"I would think he'd be too old, provided he isn't dead."

"Perfect. You're looking for a ghost already."

She laughed. "It's not a ghost. I don't know what it is, but it's not a ghost."

"Well, when you've eliminated the impossible . . ."

"Sherlock Holmes? You're quoting me Sherlock Holmes? I didn't know you read."

"There's a lot you don't know about me," he said, offhand. "Look, call an exorcist or something. I can't help you."

"I think we both know that's not true," she said flatly.

He stared at her.

"What the hell are you talking about?" he asked. "Is this more of Calvin's bull?"

"I saw your expression when Tanya spoke. Something there struck a chord. I need to know what that is."

"It's not relevant," he said. "I already told you that."

She'd had about enough. "I have tried to be understanding, Corrigan, because I know this kind of thing can be difficult, but—"

"What did he tell you?"

"Fine."

GENE DOUCETTE

She reached into the leather portfolio at her feet and pulled out a thick file, slapping it on the table.

"That would be?" he asked.

"Your life." She flipped it open, talking as she paged through. "You know, I completely understand why you don't want anything to do with Professor Calvin. Because if someone did this to *my* life? I'd be pretty pissed off about it, too."

"He gave that to you?"

"Seems talking to you gave him a pretty interesting idea, only he needed to collect more data and you cut him off. Again, don't blame you. But as he told me, truly great ideas only happen once or twice in the lifetime of a scientist—if they're lucky—and he wasn't about to let this one go. So he hired a couple of people to collect whatever data they could. It's funny; he got more on you than the FBI did. I might want to look into who did his investigating for him, see if they could do some work for us."

Corrigan, who wasn't taking his eyes off the pages in her hand, said nothing.

"Anyway, this idea of his had legs. But all he had was a theory, and it was such an outlandish theory he figured he needed to get some testing done to see if it proved out. So he contacted Michael Offey for help with that. Offey was working on it up until his death, using a mixture of handpicked post-grads and sharp undergrads. Seems like he co-opted half the damn school."

She'd stopped leafing through, but had her hand down on the page, preventing Corrigan from seeing exactly where she stopped.

"The victims," he said. "They were all working on something Calvin figured out, and he figured it out from meeting me. Is that what you're saying?"

"That's what I'm saying. I didn't know any of this until after I questioned Calvin. He recognized me."

She held up the page. It was a copy of a photograph showing her next to Corrigan, standing just close enough to imply they were more than casual acquaintances.

"Based on my hairstyle, I think the picture's at least five years old," she said. "Anyway, like I said, I sympathize."

Maggie slid the page back into the folder and continued flipping through. "He didn't connect the project with Offey to the deaths either, not right away. But something I said made him put something else together. Something about ghosts killing people."

Corrigan stiffened slightly. "I don't see the connection, Maggie."

"You do. You just don't want to. Why don't you tell me what happened to you at McClaren?"

"The hospital?"

"The same," she said.

"It's been closed for years. I remember something about a patient killing some people there a while back."

"Of course you remember," she said, still flipping the pages. "Vividly, I would think."

She stopped at the appropriate page and slapped it on the table. The image was from a thirty-year old edition of the Boston Globe. The text had a basic rundown of what Corrigan had just recapped, but that wasn't the interesting part. The interesting part was the photograph to the right of the text. It showed police escorting staff members from the building. In the foreground was a dark-haired young woman in an orderly's uniform walking a small boy away from the door, her arm wrapped protectively around his shoulders. To anybody who ever met Corrigan Bain face-to-face there would have been no question who that little boy was.

Maggie said, "So now I'm asking again—what happened at McClaren that day?"

"That doesn't have anything to do with this," he said quietly.

"Oh bullshit. C'mon, you know the stories. There was no way one man alone did all of that killing. I've seen the police records, Corrigan. Three different survivors in separate statements claimed to have been attacked by someone *they couldn't see.* Ghosts, they said. Sure, they were mental patients, but . . ."

"McClaren has nothing to do with this!" Corrigan shouted, jumping to his feet. "So you leave me—you leave my life—out of this!"

He brought his palm down hard on the top of the table, which was fortunately made entirely of metal or else Maggie would have been showered with wood fragments.

"Now give me that file," he growled, "so I can burn it."

For the first time she could remember, Maggie Trent was afraid of Corrigan Bain; the tightly reined man she'd known for twelve years was nowhere to be seen. So she handed over the folder, not mentioning it was a copy. Calvin still had the original and she had another copy at the office.

He snatched it out of her hand and stormed off without another word.

Maggie sat by herself for a few minutes, long enough for her to convince herself she wasn't trembling.

Guess I touched a nerve.

"Well," she said to nobody, "that went great."

Packing up her files, Maggie realized she'd never gotten the chance to tell Corrigan the most important piece of news about this case: Erica Smalls survived the attack.

PART TWO

THIRTY YEARS PAST

CHAPTER TWELVE

The Fastest Boy Alive careened fearlessly down Trapelo Road at a speed that was beyond the ken of ordinary mortals, many of whom stepped aside in awe as he raced past them, past the cars also making their way down the hill, past the sound barrier even.

Or so the Fastest Boy Alive figured. He'd only learned there was such a thing as a sound barrier a couple of weeks ago, and all he remembered about it was that when you broke it, it made a big noise. He figured that was how people ahead of him knew he was coming. Surely they couldn't hear, as he did, the tires of his dirt bike as they whined a distinct A-sharp note against the wind that was also drying the sweat out of his T-shirt and whipping his hair against his ears so hard it stung.

The tightness in his calves and thighs was also carried off by the wind along with, more reluctantly, six months of cabin fever. Spring had finally arrived, and nothing was going to stop him from enjoying this moment—not the impossibly steep climb to get to the highest point on Trapelo, and not Violet, who hated the Fastest Boy Alive and would very much rather have him pretend to be little Corry Bain all the time.

This stretch of road was more or less typical of the area—narrow, winding, and steep, with parked cars where there was no room for them. Corry was pretty sure the road was old enough to make sense back when people used horses and such to get around.

Sometimes he wished he could use a horse. It'd sure be lots more fun than Violet's Dodge Dart, which smelled like exhaust and pine. The Dart had more trouble with the Trapelo hills than he did on his bike. Surely a horse would do better than both. Maybe it wouldn't smell any better, though.

Nearly to the bottom of the hill and after what had to be two or three sonic booms, the Fastest Boy Alive reached the turn before the Intersection of Doom. This was a stoplight whose timing was specifically designed to foil his goal of reaching the bottom without any application of brakes and was doubly troublesome for being hidden by a blind curve and a slight leveling of the hill. Ordinary mortals might be confounded by such a thing, but not him.

He concentrated on the Present while chancing a quick look at the Secret Future. When he was just a little kid it took him, like, forever to figure out how to do this, but now it was as easy as... well, riding a bike. And his bike was a time machine, he figured, because the faster he went, the further ahead he could see, just because he got to everyplace sooner.

Rounding the bend in the Secret Future, he saw the light was just turning green. In the present, he was about to come around that corner. He swerved around the guy getting out of the car without checking first to see if there were any hell-bent bikers bearing down and went by so fast he almost didn't hear the man utter a bad word in surprise. And then he was around the bend where the light was just turning green.

Then the Secret Future went all nutty. Corry saw and felt himself hitting the back of a car that had been turning in front of him, one he thought was going to be out of the way before he got there up until the car stopped suddenly and left its rear end right where Corry was steering the bike. Corry felt himself flying headfirst down the hill—the Fastest Broken Boy Barely Alive.

He winced and very nearly lost control of the bike. Sometimes the Secret Future was so vivid, he forgot it was a ghost future and that it wasn't permanent.

He reluctantly applied the brakes.

Of all the things he had to get used to in his life, the part about how the future isn't really the future until it's actually happened was the hardest. Just thinking about it made his head hurt, so he didn't think about it too much. It was Corry's Secret Future, and that was that. Maybe it happened, and maybe he changed stuff around so something different happened instead. Usually it was just a lot easier to go along with it because it was so much less confusing that way, especially since it took a second or two for the Secret Future to go away properly. Which was why, even as he jerked his bike around the big Chevy's fishtail, he could still see the asphalt coming up to greet his face. Thankfully, the adjustment took before he got a chance to feel what would have happened next.

He remembered when he first figured out how things worked with the Secret Future. It took a good year or so of experimenting with it, which involved mostly saying inappropriate things at odd moments just to see how it played out. This gave Violet no end of grief, which he felt bad about when he looked back on it.

Corry was old enough to have developed an appreciation for the decisions his mother made in raising him and had only just recently begun to turn a critical eye on some of those decisions.

A certain commune in Maine sprang to mind. And immediately sprang back out again because Violet had made him promise to never talk about it. Not that he remembered much. What he did remember was how suddenly they had left, heading out into the woods near nightfall and fully expecting to be eaten by some sort of creature until happening on a farmhouse occupied by an elderly couple named Crandall. The Crandalls, fortunately, had a god who told them they had to take in Violet and Corry. Corry wasn't sure which god that was, but he was awfully glad this god had left instructions for their care.

And the sound of the shotgun; he remembered that, and he remembered what happened to Charlie Bluff's leg. He didn't *want* to remember either of those things, but they wouldn't go away.

Once past the Intersection of Doom, there was nothing left for the Fastest Boy Alive to do but come to the bottom of the hill and coast to a stop.

He could have allowed his momentum to carry him through the next intersection, but it was even worse than Doom. It was Certain Death. He didn't need to see the Secret Future to understand that. Plus, he had to turn left from that point and head back uphill again. Not that it mattered, as it was uphill in all directions; he had come to a stop in the bottom of a bowl.

Corry looked down at his watch—a black, plastic marvel with a digital face that he'd gotten for Christmas and which, if he wasn't careful, he could stare at for hours—and saw that it was still too early. He pulled the bike off the side of the street and walked it to the playground just to the right of the Intersection of Certain Death.

He used to make the mistake of going straight to the hospital from school, the same route Violet drove every morning in the Dart. She knew what time school let out and could do simple math, yet still it took her a week to figure out that Corry was getting there much too fast. But once she did, there was holy hell to pay, and for a week he lost the use of his bike and television after supper. From this he could have learned to travel at a more reasonable rate of speed, but that struck him as an unacceptable solution. It made much more sense to just not show up until she thought he should.

Being the first truly good day of the year, the playground was plenty occupied with little kids, their moms, and even a couple of dads. He pushed the bike past all of them—his legs a little achy from the recent burst of exercise—until he got to the edge of the cement pond.

In another month or two, this part of the park would be the most popular, for in the center of the circular recession was a nozzle, and from that nozzle water would burst forth, filling the bottom of the pond and covering the heads and faces of many a grateful kid. But it wasn't quite warm enough yet for it, which was a shame. Corry would have been pretty happy with a brief dousing.

Reaching an empty grassy spot, he tipped over the bike and slipped off his backpack, dropping it down next to the front wheel. Both the inside part of the pack and the back of his shirt were wet with sweat. He sat down and watched the kids play.

It was a lot of work, trying to keep his head in the present all the time. Nobody understood that. Not even Violet, who he had tried to make understand a bunch of times without any real success. This had more to do with her insistence that he not talk about it than anything else. He didn't get that at all, but . . . well, sometimes it seemed like his own mom was kind of scared of him. Which was weird, but he didn't allow himself to get too deeply into the idea.

Relaxing and leaning back onto the grass, he let go of the present and watched as the kids running around the metal play sets blurred and elongated until they all looked like giant centipedes that grew longer the faster they ran. At the same time their shouts became almost an incoherent flurry of noise, like ten radio stations playing at once.

If he wanted, he could focus on a point in their Secret Futures. Two seconds ahead, say. He'd been practicing that during recess, which was why all the other kids in school called him Spooky behind his back. It didn't bother him all that much; it wasn't the first time someone called him a name like that, and it probably wouldn't be the last. He was just different, and that was that. If they couldn't deal with that, whatever. He didn't much care for most of them anyway. Except for maybe a couple of the girls.

Anyway, he was pretty sure he was some kind of superhero, and superheroes were never understood when they were in their secret identities. That was just the way it was. Like Spider-Man. He was miserable pretty much all the time despite being just about the coolest superhero there ever was. Sometimes he wished the guy could be a bit more like Superman, who never seemed to have any problems at all.

Once he was old enough to understand that nobody around him saw the world the way he did, he spent much of his free time wondering why. In the comics, it was always a radioactive accident or something like that. But he couldn't remember ever not seeing the Secret Future, so it either happened when he was a baby—and Violet never mentioned any accidents—or he was a mutant or something. Which meant, since Violet didn't have any special abilities, it had to have something to do with his father.

Unfortunately, while Violet was well versed—if not well-informed—on any variety of subjects, on the matter of his father she knew exactly three things; he was tall, he was a soldier, and his last name was Corrigan. Even if Corry knew where to begin, he had a feeling he didn't have enough facts to narrow down a search. And it got worse. As he understood it, Violet had been using drugs—which he was never ever to use himself under pain of extreme death and blah, blah, blah—when she "knew" his father.

Corry had only the vaguest understanding of sex. What he did understand was that there was a difference between the word *knew* and the word "knew" when his mother said it in reference to his father. For one thing, she made the little quotation marks with her fingers.

But he understood drugs very well, albeit vicariously. When she "knew" his father, it was one night, briefly, and she was tripping. She could very well have imagined the army jacket and the name and even the height. And supposing she didn't, who was to say it was even his jacket?

His father, then, had taken on a series of remarkable characteristics during Corry's lifetime. The latest incarnation had Daddy Corrigan portrayed as a time traveler, sent to the past to make a baby who would grow up and save the world.

Corry liked that story a lot. It was better than the alien one that preceded it and *way* better than the one he cribbed from the Bible. Of course, all these stories ended with a heroic sacrifice, but that was okay.

It was time to get moving. He stood up and then with great effort collapsed the centipede-children back into their singular selves, like he was shoving one of those trick snakes back into its fake peanut can. But unlike the snake, the children were still there in the Secret Future, only de-emphasized, like unfinished connect-the-dots puzzles.

Slipping on his backpack, he saw that one of them was about to skin his knee. It looked painful. But these things happen.

"Hey, Stuntman! How's it going?"

"Hey, Carl." Corry smiled, hopping off his bike at the parking lot gate. Carl the guard looked to have survived winter all right, which Corry thought was sort of amazing as he was something like two hundred years old. "Anything going on?"

"Pitching's looking good this year, Stuntman."

Carl habitually jumped ahead several steps when engaging in small talk, which gave the boy who already saw the future no end of fits. In this case, he was pretty sure Carl was talking about the Red Sox because Carl believed everyone he spoke to devoted all of their free time to following the team like he did. Corry never figured out a way to explain that he wasn't a big sports fan.

"Yeah?"

"This is their year," Carl said.

"Uh-huh. Can I go in? My mom's waiting."

"Sure, go on ahead."

"Thanks."

The first time he biked to his mom's work, Corry neglected to stop for Carl the parking lot guard, mostly because he just didn't know he was supposed to. Instead, he cruised right past the booth and then spent the next ten minutes avoiding the crazy old guy who was trying to grab the back of his bike. This was what earned him the nickname Stuntman. If Corry had chosen a nickname for Carl based on the same incident, it would have probably been Heart Attack, just because it looked like Carl was having one the whole time.

Corry walked the bike the rest of the way, up to a metal bike stand outside the front door. The stand was there so he could, theoretically, have something to attach the bike lock to. He *had* a lock, but he only used it outside the school. He figured one of the adult-sized ten-speeds would vanish a lot faster than his kid-sized, one-speed dirt bike. Plus, Carl would make sure nobody took off with it. Other than listening to the sports stuff on the radio, he didn't have much else to do.

Violet was waiting for him in the lobby by the front desk with one eye on her watch. Corry wondered if she honestly believed she could control his rate of travel by monitoring his arrival time, or if she just did that to make herself feel better. He suspected the latter, reasoning that adults liked to think they were in control of things and sometimes went out of their way to convince themselves they were. It was the same with his teachers, who loved to think they knew everything going on in the school, even when they didn't know half of it.

"How was the ride, honey?" Violet greeted. She was wearing a white uniform and had her hair pulled back tightly behind her ears. He always thought that made her look like a Vulcan.

"Fine," he said, allowing her to muss up his sweaty head of hair—a gesture of affection she'd taken up a number of years ago in lieu of hugging.

"Everyone's been asking about you," she said, leading him past the reception desk, which was occupied by a lady Corry didn't know. She was on the phone anyway.

"Really?"

"Uh-huh. Mr. Pierce has been dying for a good game of rummy."

All of the guests at McClaren Hospital were men, and all of them were crazy. Violet had been working there, and bringing Corry, for a year before he was even told this, and it came as a surprise.

It turned out there were different kinds of crazy. There was Really Crazy, and then there was only Mildly Crazy. The ones he knew were the second kind. Most of them had checked themselves into the hospital, which he thought was pretty good evidence they were crazy. Not that it was a bad place, but he wouldn't want to live there all the time.

As for the Really Crazies, they were kept somewhere else. Corry had never been there and wasn't even sure how to get there, which was all right with him.

"Do you have lots of homework?" Violet asked, doing that annoying thing where she tried to start a normal conversation.

"No," he said. Which was always going to be the answer regardless of how much homework he actually had. But that was a required parenting question or something.

When Corry first started visiting, it was partly because he didn't have much else to do, but mostly because Violet didn't like how when he was at home alone he tended not to do his homework. Which, considering how much of his upbringing had been spent around people telling him to always challenge authority, made some sense. But it turned out challenging authority was one of those things only adults were allowed to do.

To solve the problem, Violet brought him to work, made him sit in a corner in the lobby, and do all his lessons. Problem was, he was in fifth grade at the time, and fifth graders don't get enough homework to fill up a whole afternoon. So when he was finished, he just sat there and stared at stuff.

After a while she started bringing him into the common room when he was done so he could watch television, and pretty soon he was skipping the lobby and just doing all his work in the common room, right in the middle of the Mildly Crazies. Which was actually pretty great. A lot of them were really smart —a few way smarter than his teachers, even—and helped him with the tougher stuff. And when he was done, he'd play card games and watch television until it was time to go. It was like having a whole hospital full of substitute parents—crazy parents, but whatever.

As they walked—in silence, as Violet had run out of things to ask—the familiar smell of the hospital corridors hit his nose.

The odor was oddly comforting, only because he hadn't smelled it in such a long time. Violet said that was a clean smell, but Corry thought maybe the cleaners just used extra bleach to make it seem like they were working hard, like how he always cleaned his room by pushing stuff to the wall just to show lots of carpet. If he looked really closely at the cement floor, at the spot where the rubberized wall met up with it, he could see a layer of dust that told him he was onto something.

The common room was halfway down the corridor, right at the edge of the Mildly Crazy wing. It was a big room with a lot of old board games stuffed in a closet, a color television, and big, double-paned windows that showed off the back of the property, which was hilly and green in the summer.

Toward the end of the day the sun always streamed in through the windows and sometimes made cool little rainbows on the walls and the carpet. Mr. Conway—who was a scientist when he wasn't crazy— explained to Corry about the rainbows, how the double panes on the glass acted like a prism when the light hit them just right, and that the colors are actually part of the sunlight. Or something. Corry liked it better when he didn't understand it, so he promptly forgot the details.

Before they reached the doorway, Corry peeked ahead into the Secret Future and noticed with great disappointment that the room was nearly empty, except for Janet and some guy he'd never seen before.

"Hey, kiddo," Janet greeted once they reached the threshold, looking up from an old outdoors magazine she was flipping through. "Everyone's in session just now. They'll be by later."

Janet was an orderly, like Violet. But she was more of the crowd-control type while Violet was more of a medication-and-clean-up type. Since Janet was easily the largest woman—in all directions—Corry had ever met, he could understand why she did that kind of job.

Corry's gaze drifted over to the man in the chair in the corner. He was a way old guy, skinny but with extra flesh hanging off of him like somebody deflated him recently.

The man returned the gaze and smiled. In the Secret Future, Janet was introducing them.

"Why don't you work on your homework," Violet suggested, patting him on the shoulder. "I'll stop by again later. Okay?"

"Sure," he said flatly, slipping off his backpack.

Violet rubbed his hair goodbye and left, either not noticing the new Mildly Crazy in the corner or not particularly concerned that she was leaving her son with him. Didn't look like the guy could get up out of the chair in anything under five minutes, so it probably wasn't a bad bet.

"This is Mr. Nilsson," Janet said, leading Corry closer to the chair. "Mr. Nilsson, this is—"

"You must be young Corry Bain," Mr. Nilsson said.

Corry's stomach did a back flip, inadvertently causing him to step backward to keep from falling over.

It wasn't the old man's voice that set him off. He actually had a deep and soothing voice, one much better suited for a radio announcer or a professional wrestler. And it wasn't that Mr. Nilsson appeared to already know Corry.

Janet mistook Corry's confusion as fear.

"Oh, don't you worry about Mr. Nilsson," she said. "He's real nice. Aren't you, Mr. Nilsson?"

"Yes, ma'am," he said. But he wasn't smiling. He was staring hard at Corry.

Something very weird had just happened. In the Secret Future, Mr. Nilsson sat quietly during the introductions. He didn't pipe up halfway through.

When he *did* pipe up halfway through, in the present, it made the Secret Future split in half and disappear for a second, just like it did when Corry altered it. Except this time, he wasn't the one who did the altering.

But what was really, *really* weird was that it looked as if Corry wasn't the only one who noticed this happening.

"It's a pleasure indeed to meet you, young Master Bain," Mr. Nilsson said, his voice just a hair above a whisper. "I imagine we have much in common."

CHAPTER THIRTEEN

"I win again, Mr. Pierce," Corry said, with a hint of triumph as he laid down his last three cards.

Mr. Pierce leaned over the table, reviewed the cards, and concluded that yes, he had been defeated.

"So you do," he said cheerily. He took out the pad of paper on which were written the scores of every game of rummy the two of them had ever played, and began tallying up the totals.

Osgood Pierce was probably Corry's best friend, despite their forty-plus year difference in age and the fact that one of them was a little nuts. Mr. Pierce was slightly overweight, very pale, and had perpetual bags under his eyes. It also looked as if he were always in shadows, even when the light was directly overhead. Still he was, according to Violet, a *very handsome man.* Not that Corry had any opinion on this whatsoever.

Corry couldn't explain why it was they hit it off so well, but in the part of his brain where thoughts more mature than he was resided, there was the notion that perhaps their daily personal needs fit well together. Corry needed an easily manageable father figure, and Osgood Pierce had a pathological need to lose at everything.

To that end, rummy was the absolute perfect game.

Corry was familiar with a fair number of card games, thanks mainly to the men in the Mildly Crazy ward, all of whom had a personal favorite. But unlike poker or straight gin, in rummy, one player's discard could be used by another player. For a boy with his own Secret Future, there was almost no way he could lose.

"It's your deal," Mr. Pierce said, putting down the pencil.

As Corry swept up the cards and attempted to shuffle—he still hadn't quite gotten the hang of it—Mr. Pierce asked, "So how was school this year?"

"Okay, I guess."

"It's over with now?"

"Yep. Summer vacation starts today."

The problem with shuffling was the cards and his hands were not the right size for each other. Whenever he attempted to curl them upward, they just sort of exploded into the air. So he did a cheating sort of shuffle, where he pushed the two halves together five or six times.

"And you're spending your first day of freedom here," Mr. Pierce said matter-of-factly.

" 'E's a nutter," said Mr. Finn from halfway across the room. Timothy Finn said he was 100% Boston Irish, but for some reason he always spoke with the same funny English accent Dick Van Dyke used in *Mary Poppins*. Corry didn't think that was the only reason he was in McClaren, but he hadn't seen evidence of any other specific pathology, so he couldn't be completely positive.

Pathology was a word Corry learned very early. It came into play whenever he wondered how or why the people around him had gotten locked away from the outside world. Usually, if he wanted to know, he could just ask because most of them weren't shy about it.

"He's not a nutter, Tim," Mr. Pierce said. "Are you, Corry?"

"Don't think so," Corry said. He started dealing the cards.

"No, you're not nuts. Just a little shy, am I right?"

"I guess."

On the couch a few feet from Corry's chair, Mr. Parseghian was starting to tick, more or less literally.

Every day, from ten minutes before the hour to five minutes past the hour, Ari Parseghian stared intently at the clock on the wall above the television and announced the ticks of the second hand for everyone else in the room. He used to do this through the whole hour, every hour, so the fifteen minutes of audible ticking was pretty major progress. Still, it could get annoying. Especially when he announced the hour with a shout, like the town crier in that comic strip in the paper, *The Wizard of Id*.

"Besides," Mr. Pierce continued as he picked up his cards, "who wouldn't want to spend the afternoon with a group of gentlemen such as ourselves?"

"I don't know. I can't stand myself," said Mr. Conway, from the couch. He was sitting next to Mr. Parseghian and doing an excellent job of ignoring the ticking while loosely following the talk show on the television.

"Yes, Reginald, but self-loathing is why you're here, isn't it?" asked Mr. Pierce.

"Speak for yourself. I'm just here for the medication."

Corry smiled. Mr. Conway's pathology was that he liked to hurt himself. Corry found out when he'd asked Janet one afternoon how come Mr. Conway always had a bandage or a bruise. Corry had thought someone else there was hurting him, and this had him understandably worried.

Mr. Pierce started the round, throwing down a seven Corry didn't need. Corry drew from the deck, stared at a ten he also didn't need, and held it over the discard pile for a second. In the

Secret Future, he saw Mr. Pierce also passing on the ten, so he put it down.

There was a while there, back at the end of last summer, when Mr. Pierce, probably without even realizing it, started to take long pauses between his decisions. Anything longer than five or six seconds was too long for Corry to catch a glimpse of it, so suddenly Mr. Pierce was winning regularly.

But then Corry started slowing down, too. He found if he held his discard out for long enough it would make his opponent anxious, and when he was anxious, he acted quickly, and Corry got back the advantage.

If he thought there was anybody he could safely share that information with he would, because he was awfully proud of himself for having figured it out.

"How about girls?" Mr. Pierce asked.

"Girls?"

"Yes, Corry. Creatures much like you, only with curvier bodies and bumps in interesting places. You are familiar with the term?"

"Sure I am," Corry said, his face suddenly warm. "What about them?"

"Have you met any?"

"Sure."

Mr. Pierce stared at him over the cards. "I mean socially, young man."

"Oh," was all Corry could muster.

"Boy's just twelve, Osgood," said Mr. Conway. "Give him a little time to get his feet under him."

Mr. Pierce gave Corry a conspiratorial smile. "Don't worry. We'll have you prepared for them by August."

This did not make Corry all that comfortable.

"I don't think I need any help," he said. "I don't even like girls all that much."

"Nonsense," Mr. Pierce said.

"Fancy you, of all people, givin' the lad advice," Mr. Finn chimed in from over his magazine.

"I'll hear none of that, Irish!" Mr. Pierce said in a voice a tad too loud.

Given how well Corry and Mr. Pierce got along, it was sort of interesting that he was one of the only guys he'd met there who didn't ever explain *why* he was there. Corry knew already —Violet told him a long time ago when it was clear the two were friendly with one another—but he kept this knowledge to himself out of respect. And since it was kind of embarrassing, Corry understood why Mr. Pierce didn't want him knowing.

From what Violet said, Mr. Pierce had something called a nerve breakdown. Corry didn't know exactly what that meant, but he figured it had something to do with going crazy over stuff that makes you nervous.

Mr. Pierce had been a pretty important guy when it happened, important enough to have to wear a suit all the time. Up until his nerve breakdown. That made him—through a mechanism Corry couldn't hope to ever understand—take the suit off, along with all of his other clothes, right there in the office. Violet didn't get too specific with what happened after that, but Corry had a decent imagination and figured running around naked in an office with secretaries and stuff probably led to a few... awkward moments. Maybe even some of what Violet called Bad Touching.

She used to warn him about Bad Touching as far back as when they were in the commune in Maine. He didn't understand it at all then and was only starting to now.

Anyway, he got why Mr. Pierce didn't want to talk about it.

Corry refocused on the card game, which he was actually in the middle of losing on account of all the distractions. But Mr.

Pierce wasn't done asking questions. Maybe this was a new strategy of his.

"You know what impresses young women, Corry?" he asked, then answered. "Confidence."

"Okay."

"I mean it."

"Okay."

Mr. Pierce sighed. "Nurse Mills," he said, referring to Janet, who was listening to the entire exchange and trying hard to pretend she wasn't. "Am I not right?"

"You're half right, Osgood, but the boy doesn't wanna talk about it. Look at him; he's as red as an apple."

Corry hated it when this happened. Every now and then adults spoke to one another as if he couldn't understand what they were saying. This year his science teacher took them on a field trip to a tide pool—which smelled—and explained how starfish ate while holding one in his hand. Times like these, Corry felt like the starfish.

Fortunately, a reprieve came in the form of Mr. Parseghian, who loudly announced that it was four o'clock. Everybody in the room jumped, even though he did this every day. Well, everyone except for Corry and Mr. Nilsson.

Harvey Nilsson was sitting in the same chair he'd been in on the day the two of them were introduced. Corry actually couldn't remember a time when he wasn't sitting there.

Sometimes, it looked like he was asleep, but that seemed unlikely given the noise that typically filled the room in the afternoons.

On this occasion, as the other occupants busied themselves by saying various bad words—which adults always tended to do when they were startled—Mr. Nilsson looked over at Corry. Their eyes met, and the old man winked.

"You don't startle easily, do you Corry?" he said.

"No—" He began to respond, before catching himself.

Something wasn't at all right. Mr. Nilsson had said that, but he also hadn't.

"Yes," Mr. Pierce said, putting down a set of sevens. "I've got you this time."

He thought Corry was speaking in reference to the last hand of cards, which Mr. Pierce was winning. Mr. Pierce didn't hear Mr. Nilsson, because Mr. Nilsson didn't actually speak.

"*I know you can hear me,*" Mr. Nilsson added. Somehow, he was speaking in the Secret Future and *only* in the Secret Future, because when the moment came for him to actually say those words so that everyone could hear them, he only uttered a mild grunt.

"How are you doing that?" Corry said.

"What do you mean?" Mr. Pierce asked. "I'm just winning. Is it really all that unusual for me to actually beat you?"

"N-no."

"*You're kind to play with Osgood,*" Mr. Nilsson said/didn't say, "*Even his family won't visit him. He's lonely.*"

Corry shut up and fixed Mr. Nilsson with a sideways glance.

Mr. Pierce was busy offering more advice on how to romance twelve-year-old girls, but Corry was no longer paying much attention to the present. He was trying to figure out how the hell Mr. Nilsson was doing that.

"*That's why he doesn't mind losing.*"

Harvey Nilsson's mouth—his future mouth—was definitely moving.

"*He doesn't even care that you're cheating.*"

"I'm—" Corry began to say, but of course his voice was stuck in the present. Had Mr. Nilsson been speaking for everyone's benefit, Corry's assertion that he was *not* cheating would have preceded the accusation by a good five seconds.

"Son, are you all right?" Mr. Pierce asked. "You look like you've seen a ghost."

Corry *was* trembling. Mr. Nilsson's bizarre trick had screwed up his hold on the now, which was always tenuous under the best of circumstances.

"I . . . don't feel so good," Corry said.

In speaking, he tried to use his own words as a lighthouse to find his way back to the correct moment in time.

Mr. Pierce put his hand on Corry's arm. "You look queasy. Something you ate?"

Corry shut his eyes and focused on the tick-ticks from Mr. Parseghian, which were all jumbled together. He slowed his breathing and listened until the five or six ticks came at appropriate intervals again. He opened his eyes. Mr. Pierce was still looking at him, very concerned. Out of the corner of Corry's eye he could see Janet standing to one side, looking ready to catch him if he fell out of his chair, which he was apparently about to do.

"Yeah," he said finally. "Prob'bly something I ate."

"If he ate lunch here, I'm not surprised," Mr. Conway offered, laughing. Corry smiled weakly.

"I'm fine," Corry insisted, extricating his arm from Mr. Pierce's tight grip. "Just felt a little oogey for a second."

He was consciously trying not to look in Mr. Nilsson's direction.

"Are you sure?" Mr. Pierce asked.

"Yeah. I'm okay."

"Well, then," he said, looking over at Janet, who still appeared concerned. "You won't mind if I do this."

He put down three cards and threw the fourth onto the discard pile. "I win."

Corry looked at his own hand and realized he could have won about three cards ago.

"I need to go to the bathroom," he said, getting to his feet.

"You gonna be sick?" Janet asked.

"No, really. I'm okay."

"I should call your mother," Janet was about to say.

"Don't bother Violet," Corry said. Janet looked taken aback because Corry had neglected to wait for her to actually speak before responding. Mr. Nilsson's trick still had him all screwed up.

"All right," Janet said.

The bathroom was off the hallway just outside the door to the common room. Corry made it almost all the way there.

"We need to talk," Mr. Nilsson said, again in the Secret Future. Corry froze in the doorway, held onto the jamb, and tried to keep his head in the present even if his ears weren't.

He was still holding onto five cards, he realized distantly. Mr. Pierce wouldn't be able to finish the scoring without those cards.

"Meet me here after five. We'll be alone then."

Corry reached out and put the cards on the edge of the little table near the door, next to Janet's magazine.

"Okay," he said. Then he left the room.

CHAPTER FOURTEEN

Things worked a little differently for Corry in the summertime.

In the fall and the spring, when he was in school, he was required by the Laws of Violet to attend the McClaren afterschool homework program—as she jokingly called it—Monday through Thursday. But when school was out, barring any summer classes, which he thankfully had not earned as his grades weren't terrible enough to warrant them, he was free to come and go as he pleased.

His school had a summer day camp that he attended sparingly, signing on for field trips to cool places but not lingering when they were just hanging around the school and doing crafts and whatnot because that was almost exactly like being in classes, only with fewer tests. Some days he just stayed at home, read comic books, and watched television.

Very occasionally he went to the park and threw a ball around with one or two of the few kids he was friendly with, but that was a rare enough event to almost not warrant mentioning. Mostly, he did whatever struck him as interesting when he got up that morning.

On the days when he decided to stop in at McClaren, despite having a means to get back home again in the form of his bike, he typically waited until Violet got off work and then rode home with her. He expected in another couple of years they would reach an impasse where she would either have to purchase a larger car or he would have to deal with a bike that was much too small for him, as the one he currently used only just barely fit into the trunk of the Dart and also only barely fit him.

Then again, in a couple of years, maybe he wouldn't be interested in visiting the hospital at all. A lot could happen in that time.

The schedule of the Mildly Crazy patients at McClaren impacted him as well. For instance, Corry generally preferred not to arrive there until just after lunch because most of his friends there were occupied in the morning with various Sessions. Corry didn't know for sure what a Session was, but he had some indirect evidence to suggest it had something to do with making them better. There was just as much evidence that the opposite was true, as it did not seem to Corry that anybody there was getting any better—except for maybe Mr. Parseghian and his obsessive ticking—but it was a decent theory anyway.

The order of events was, the patients would eat their lunches —under supervision, to make sure everybody was eating and also not harming themselves—and then get their meds. Roughly half an hour after that they were ready to see guests like Corry or whoever else might be there that day, as this was when visiting hours were scheduled. Family visits took place in a section of the hospital Corry had never seen.

Corry thought the part when everybody took drugs was sort of interesting, if only because of what it said about Violet. It occurred to him fairly recently—in a burst of insight that comes to children when they examine their parents as people instead of just as parents—that she seemed to go out of her way to find places where everybody *else* was taking drugs.

According to Violet, she stopped using drugs recreationally back when Corry was five, but she obviously still liked being around people who were taking them.

At around four-thirty, the social/recreational part of their day was concluded, and the patients were asked politely to return to their rooms if they were not already in them. Corry wasn't positive what followed from that point but he believed there was another round of meds involved, along with dinner and evening Sessions.

Violet's shift ended at five-thirty, which made perfect sense in that a shift change was best done when all the patients were in their rooms rather than wandering the floors. But it was inconvenient for Corry, who was basically left with an hour to kill and nobody to kill it with. He usually spent that time in the front lobby because he wasn't supposed to be in the common room alone, and Janet left along with the patients when four-thirty rolled around.

So it was that at just before five on a day in which his entire understanding of the Secret Future collapsed around him, Corry ended up standing in the lobby and wondering how he was going to get back into the common room without attracting attention. The part of his twelve-year-old brain that had been fed a regular diet of horror stories about strangers and Bad Touching knew this was probably a terrible idea, but his curiosity was just too great to ignore. He had to try.

Getting from the lobby to the hospital's ward rooms corridor was not, by itself, a difficult task. The door between the two wasn't locked during the day because the Mildly Crazies weren't very dangerous. And since all of them were wealthy and most were there because they'd put themselves in, it didn't benefit anybody to make the place look like a prison. At least not this wing of it.

The hard part was getting past Ned.

If it was anybody else, it wouldn't have been a problem. Unlike the staff inside the hospital—like Violet and Janet—the person at the front desk was different almost every day. Corry asked about it once and found out that the security staff had a rotating schedule, with the only exception being Carl in the parking lot booth, only because Carl couldn't get around so well anymore.

Most of the desk staff was nice and very easygoing. If he said to one of them that he had forgotten something in the common room, they'd let him head back alone to get it and probably wouldn't even notice he'd been gone for longer than it should have taken to fetch something and return. But Ned wasn't going to be that easy.

Corry had never heard Ned tell a story in which he wasn't the hero. He seemed to live a life of adventure in a world in which he was the only person who knew the right thing to do, and everyone else—his wife, family, friends, coworkers—was a complete idiot.

Corry used to be impressed by Ned and his stories until one day when he witnessed Ned giving a hard time to a guest who was trying to obtain post-visiting hour permission. The incident itself was minor and ultimately involved phoning up a doctor who escorted the guest through. But a week later Corry heard Ned describe the event to one of the orderlies, and from the sound of it one might have concluded Ned had dealt handily with a terrorist holding a live bomb. From that point on, he didn't believe a word the man said.

Ned would never let him go in back unescorted, and if he did, he would probably have him on a stopwatch the whole time. Corry would have to figure out a way to outsmart him if he wanted to have his conversation with Mr. Nilsson.

Standing in the lobby, Corry watched the parking lot through the glass double doors and listened to the clock over the exit as it ticked away the time. It was five o'clock. Somewhere, Mr. Parseghian was shouting. Probably. Unless they didn't let him have a clock in his room which, when he thought about it, was probably the smart thing.

That gave him an idea. It was a stupid idea, but Ned was pretty stupid, so it might work.

"Hey," Corry said, trying desperately to sound casual. "Is Mr. Parseghian all better?"

Ned was busy staring at some random paperwork at his desk, or rather, at the racing forms hidden underneath the random paperwork. He had video monitors to stare at, too, showing black-and-white closed-circuit camera images of the front door and the back door.

"Who?" he asked.

"Mr. Parseghian. The guy who announces the time."

"Oh. Him?" He laughed. "Christ, kid, I don't think he's ready for the outside world, do you? And I'm not even a doctor . . ."

Corry interrupted, as surely a lengthy tale in which Ned out-diagnosed somebody with a degree was sure to follow. "Then how come I just saw him hop into a car?"

Ned smiled for as long as it took to realize Corry wasn't going to say *ha- ha, just kidding*. He stood up.

"You fucking with me?"

"No, serious. It's that car right there."

Corry pointed at a car that was now backing out of a parking space. The person inside of it was actually one of the assistant directors of the hospital—a guy named Walter, who always had cough drop breath. He'd come out of one of the staff exits a few minutes ago.

Ned toddled out from behind the counter and pulled his huge walkie-talkie off his belt. He got to the front door just in time to see the car reach the gate.

"Stay here, kid," he said as he hit the door. Ned ran out, shouting commands to Carl on his radio.

It should have occurred to Ned that the only way Mr. Parseghian could have gotten out was via the door Ned just used —or possibly through the back door, where he'd have been spotted on the surveillance camera—but Ned was too busy acting to stop and think.

Stupid, Corry confirmed.

Corry figured he had maybe five minutes before Ned came back again, which was enough time to make it down the hall but probably not enough to get back. But one thing at a time.

He ran past the now-vacant reception desk and down the hall.

Thanks to the Secret Future, he knew he was alone for the trip there, which was good fortune all around. And that same Secret Future told him the room ahead was empty, so Mr. Nilsson hadn't made it there yet.

He was about to round the corner into the common room when someone grabbed him from behind and yanked him into the bathroom.

He nearly screamed, but a hand was clapped over Corry's mouth before anything could escape.

It was the first time in his entire life something happened in Corry's future that he didn't see coming, and he was justifiably freaked out by it, so much so that it didn't initially occur to him that the person who nabbed him had to be the guy he was there to see.

The door to the bathroom slammed shut and the light came on, and only then did Mr. Nilsson release him. Corry pushed away and ended up standing beside the door, visibly trembling.

"How do you do that?" he demanded angrily.

Mr. Nilsson didn't answer right away. Instead, he sat down on the toilet and studied his young sort-of captive. Sitting made him less impressive, which helped Corry calm down, because this way the older man wasn't looming over him anymore. More significantly, if Corry wanted to jerk the door open and run out, Mr. Nilsson probably couldn't stop him.

"I'm sorry I frightened you," he said finally.

"Yeah, you did," Corry answered angrily, wiping an inadvertent tear from the corner of his eye. "Nobody's s'posed to be able to sneak up on me."

Later, he would be ashamed to have gotten rattled so easily. Other kids deal with surprises every day; he shouldn't have that much trouble with them.

"How long have you been able to see?" the old man asked.

"What do you mean?"

"You know what I mean."

Corry fiddled with the belt loop on his pants, a nervous thing he did mostly in school when he didn't know the answer to a direct question or when Violet got especially angry with him.

"All my life, I think," he said.

"You handle it well."

"Thanks."

"I mean that sincerely. I have met two others like us in my life. You're the youngest and by far the most stable."

"There are others?" Corry asked. This surprised him.

"A few."

"You see it too, huh?"

"Yes, of course. How else do you suppose I could have snuck up on you? I changed the future. You and I are the only ones here capable of doing that."

"You seem okay with it," Corry said. "I mean, stable. You're stable."

Mr. Nilsson smiled. "Am I? Think about where we are."

"I mean . . ." Corry hedged. "Right now, you're okay. And you can do that... thing with the talking and not talking."

The old man sat up, so that the back of his head was touching a rack full of toilet paper. It didn't look real comfortable.

"Do you see your own actions in the future?" he asked.

"Sure. Don't you?"

"Yes, of course. And do you follow through with those actions?"

"Usually. Unless I'm about to get hurt or something."

"Exactly. There's no trick to what I did earlier, Master Corry. All I'm doing is electing not to say what I would have otherwise said. It takes some practice, but that's all. I used to do it in board-room meetings to keep from dozing off, although then I never had anyone else around to appreciate it. You'll figure it out."

"Oh. Okay," Corry said, wondering what a bored room meeting was.

"How far can you see?"

Corry thought about it. "Dunno. Five or six seconds. Depends on how much is going on."

"Gets blurry after that, does it?"

"Yeah, kinda."

He nodded.

"Can you see more than that?" Corry asked.

"Sometimes. If I sit very still and think very hard for a very long time; sometimes."

"Huh."

"I prefer not to."

"Why not?"

"Sometimes I just want to be surprised," he said without elaboration.

This conversation wasn't exactly what Corry had been expecting. Not that he was sure what to expect, but this wasn't it.

"So what are we?" Corry asked, getting to what he thought was the point of this conversation.

"What . . ." Mr. Nilsson laughed. "We're people. Did you suppose we were aliens or some such?"

"Dunno." Corry blushed. "Maybe. Or superheroes."

"Ah, well . . . I am long past the opportunity to be a hero of any kind, young man. You, however, have a lifetime to work on that. Is that what you'd like to do with your gifts?"

"Maybe, yeah."

"It's an admirable goal." He stared hard at Corry, as if by doing so he could look a decade or two ahead. "Yes. I do think if you wanted to, you could become a... superhero, as you said." He smiled. "That's a fantastic idea."

Corry beamed. Finally, someone else he could talk to about the Secret Future. He'd have to learn how to do that secret talking trick so they could speak without sneaking off together.

That reminded him, Carl was most surely done bothering Walter.

"Look," Corry said, "I should probably—"

"No, not yet," Mr. Nilsson said. "There's a reason I wanted to talk to you alone." He leaned forward again. "There are others."

"Others like us? You said that already."

"No. Yes. Yes, there are others like us. That's not what I mean. I mean there are *others*. I don't know what they are, but I can see them. Nobody else can. Except you."

"I don't know what you're talking about," Corry said. There was a slight change in Mr. Nilsson's voice; it was subtle but enough to make Corry want to get away from him.

"These others, they're there at the edge. Do you understand? And they don't like to be seen."

"Okay, sure," Corry said.

He had looked away from Mr. Nilsson and was now gazing lovingly at the doorknob. Because while he didn't understand whom Mr. Nilsson was talking about, he was starting to appreciate why the old man had checked into McClaren.

"You need to listen to me," Mr. Nilsson said, and now his voice was louder, maybe even loud enough to be heard out in the hall.

"All right . . ."

Mr. Nilsson sprang to his feet and put his hand on the door before Corry could open it.

"I'm entirely serious, young man! *Don't let them know you can see them.* Whatever you do with the rest of your life, you must remember that. This is *important.*"

"Who..." Corry began to say before he realized all the saliva in his mouth had suddenly dried up. He tried again. "Who are they?"

"They're going to kill me when they find me," he whispered, gripping Corry's shoulder tightly. He smelled like sweat and Old Spice. "And they will find me. Because I've seen."

"Let me go, Mr. Nilsson," Corry said, trying to eradicate the quaver in his voice as much as he could. "Please."

"Promise me!"

Corry looked into Mr. Nilsson's face. His teeth were browning on the edges and he had a piece of something green stuck between two of them and his breath smelled like fish. And he was scaring the shit out of Corry. There would be no friendly chats about the Secret Future with this man. He was nuts.

"All right, sure," Corry said, thinking that agreeing with his captor was probably the best solution. "I promise."

Mr. Nilsson held onto him for a few more seconds and then let go and stepped aside.

"Good," he said. "That's a good boy."

Seizing the chance to leave, Corry grabbed the handle and jerked the door open, got two steps into the hallway... and ran right into Ned.

"There you are!" he said. "The hell were you doing?"

"I hadda go to the bathroom," Corry lied, grabbing his stomach. "Diarrhea. Must'a been the food here or something. Didn't think you'd mind, my not waiting for you to get back."

Ned stared at him. "Mr. Parseghian is sitting in his room," he said. "You wanna tell me what the hell that was about?"

"Is he?" Corry said, trying to keep his voice level. "Could've sworn I saw him outside."

Ned stared into Corry's eyes and tried to figure out exactly how much of that story was the truth. Corry stared back, which is what one did when trying to pull off a lie. Ned broke away, glanced at the bathroom door, and tried to see the angles.

It didn't seem possible that Corry would lie about what he saw outside just so he could go to the bathroom by himself, and as it never occurred to Ned that there might be someone else in there, he couldn't work it out.

Ned stepped aside and gestured toward the lobby.

"C'mon," he said. "Let's wait for your mother, see what she has to say about all of this, huh?" Like Violet would have any better luck than Ned in detecting when Corry was lying.

Corry walked past the guard without a word, the warning of a crazy man still ringing in his ears.

Don't let them know you can see them.

As if he didn't get enough nightmares already.

CHAPTER FIFTEEN

Corry didn't visit McClaren hospital more than a couple of times for the rest of the summer. He told Violet this was because the summer camp had more fun trips than usual, and while this was sort of true, it was also true that the less he saw of Mr. Nilsson, the better.

It was quite a problem for a young man to have to deal with. On the one hand, he'd never met another person who could see things like he could, which was a big deal, especially since that person was so much older than he was. Older people knew a lot about a lot of things. Even crazy old people. Especially crazy old people. Corry had so many questions he wanted to ask that it kept him up some nights.

On the other hand, Mr. Nilsson turned out to be not just crazy but also creepy and paranoid. Being alone with him in the bathroom for those few minutes in July had driven home the point about Bad Touching that Violet was always trying to make. It wasn't that Mr. Nilsson had actually touched him in a bad way, but Corry understood now how helpless he would feel should an adult try to do so. He didn't like that feeling at all.

When he did visit, he stuck to card games with Mr. Pierce.

Mr. Nilsson was always there in his chair, but he didn't try to talk to Corry—secretively or otherwise. Corry, in turn, didn't try to talk to him. He did make several attempts to "speak" in the future, like Mr. Nilsson could, but found it impossible.

If he knew he wasn't going to speak, then he didn't speak, no matter how much he insisted to himself that he did. It seemed he couldn't figure out how to fake out the Secret Future.

Now school was about to start again. He had petitioned Violet to let him spend more time at home, even though she preferred he go to McClaren and work on his homework there at the beginning of the year to *get off on the right foot* before the snow came and made it effectively impossible for him to do the work anywhere but at afterschool or at home. His argument was that since he was going into eighth grade, he was only one year away from high school, and in high school he surely would have to be more self-motivated about his homework, so wouldn't it be a good idea to practice doing it without help *before* he got there?

The truth was, by the last week of August, as the Fastest Boy Alive raced down the Trapelo Road hill, he was expecting this to be his final trip to McClaren.

The first indication that things were a little bit off at the hospital was when Corry found the front gate attendance box empty. Carl wasn't there. A couple of times in the past he'd found a different guard at the gate, but this time there was no Carl, and nobody else either. Which was too bad because Corry had actually started to follow a little baseball over the summer, so he had something to talk with the guard about.

Corry pedaled on through the gate and rode his bike all the way to the front door, half expecting this to cause Carl to magically appear and yell at him for not walking it through the lot.

When this also failed to produce the guard, Corry gave up and parked his bike.

The air conditioning greeted him pleasantly as he passed over the threshold into the hospital's lobby. It had been a hot summer in general, and McClaren was the only place he was welcome that had central air.

"Hi," he greeted, walking to the reception desk. He couldn't see anybody there, but as he was only a little over five feet tall that wasn't all that unusual. Maybe they had just ducked behind the desk. Ned did this bunches of times when playing with the feed for the video monitors.

But nobody sat up at the sound of his voice.

He hopped up onto his forearms, leaned over the counter, looked down, and found the desk chair empty. Which was really weird, especially in the greater context: no parking lot guard, no front desk guard.

Getting behind the desk was just a matter of lifting a hinged part and walking around. Corry skipped a step and ducked under, quickly confirming his aloneness.

"Must'a gone to the bathroom," he said to himself, sitting down in the chair. That had to be it. He'd go down the hall to double-check, but after the hell he caught the last time he went down the hall alone he figured it'd be best if he just waited.

A few minutes passed. He whiled away the time shooting rubber bands at the video screens and wondering exactly who it was he was waiting for. Not Ned, surely. Ned would probably pee in the garbage can before he left the front desk unattended for so long. Ethel, maybe—she was pretty loose about the rules. Or Bob, a really tall guard with hairy knuckles and a goofy, high-pitched laugh Corry found sort of alarming.

After another couple of minutes it dawned on him that there wasn't anybody coming. And if that were true, something was really and truly screwed up.

He stepped up to the hallway door—which was closed—and put his ear up against it. This didn't do much good other than to occupy him while he figured out what to do.

And what do *I do?*

He would have to tell somebody the front desk was unattended, because that just wasn't right. Anyone could walk in off the street and right down the hall through the always-unlocked door. Worse, Corry was pretty sure the Mildly Crazy patients didn't have locks on their room doors, so one of them could wander out if he wanted to. Probably none of them did want to, but still.

Grabbing an internal phone directory, he started flipping through the laminated pages, looking for the right person to call. He knew the names of most of the hospital directors, but they didn't really know him, so a phone call would be sort of odd. Better to contact somebody he knew. Violet, for instance.

Violet didn't know he was coming, which was why she hadn't been at the door to greet him. Lately, she had been giving him more latitude, to the extent that sometimes she didn't even ask what his daily plans were. Corry had no idea how he earned the extra trust but thought it was so cool he didn't want to ask about it and screw everything up. She'd probably think her pestering was missed.

She worked in the Really Crazy wing most of the time. Corry had never been there, but didn't figure he ever wanted to be, just based on some of the stories Violet sometimes told to other adults when she thought Corry wasn't paying attention. The word *feces* came up a lot, which hadn't bothered Corry until he looked up the word. It sounded like the patients there were very different from the ones he knew—and not in any good way.

Fingering his way through the directory, he found a place described as the Medium Security Nurse Station. That had to be it. He picked up the phone.

And then Corry's weird afternoon got weirder, because the phone wasn't working.

It was one of those really big telephones with bunches of extra buttons on them and four digit numbers written next to the buttons, but none of the buttons seemed to make the phone work. He checked the line leading from the phone into the wall and saw that it was intact. What was going on?

Sitting up again, some movement on the video monitor caught his eye. Any action on either screen was pretty easily noticeable because the only thing on display was the front door and the back door. He always thought of the monitors as unnecessary, because you could see the front door from the desk, anyway, and the back door wasn't even supposed to be used except in case of fire.

The movement was at the back door. Someone was opening it from the inside. Corry didn't know where the door was, but he remembered Ned saying how there was an alarm attached to it, which meant somewhere, an alarm was supposed to be going off.

The door pushed open further. Whoever was doing it was having a lot of trouble, as if it weighed hundreds of pounds. Corry saw his face. He was dressed like a patient, but it wasn't anybody Corry recognized.

Probably, it was one of the Mildly Crazies he'd never met before. It couldn't possibly be one of the Really Crazies. They didn't have that kind of freedom.

The guy looked totally terrified. There was no sound, but the way his mouth kept opening and closing, Corry was pretty sure he was screaming. And for a second it looked like he was going to make it out, but then the door suddenly slammed shut —as if a really huge guy had just hit the outside of it. It happened so abruptly Corry actually jumped to his feet in surprise.

"All right, seriously," he said to himself, his voice trembling slightly, "what's going on?"

He ticked off the anomalies one more time, as if by lining them end-to-end they would form a picture he'd recognize, but it didn't really help much except to make his heart beat faster.

I should call the police, he thought. Except the phones didn't work. And he had no idea where the nearest police station was. And, he was probably totally overreacting. But in case he wasn't, there was another matter to consider.

His mother was somewhere inside.

Corry had been calling her Violet since he was seven years old. It was entirely her idea. She said a lot of junk about treating each other like people and so on, but he thought the truth was she hated admitting she had a kid while she was still sort of young and pretty. And in a way it worked, at least for him, as he rarely thought of her as his mom anymore. She was just an older woman he had to answer to all the time.

But word choice didn't make her any less his mother, and at that moment the idea that she might be one of the people inside, screaming and trying to get out like the guy on the monitor, made a lump form in his throat that spread all the way to his stomach.

I'll feel better once I know she's okay, he thought.

That meant going further into the hospital.

Screwing his resolve by swallowing a few dozen times to push down the creeping bile in the back of his throat, he walked to the ward room door and grabbed the handle.

He half expected it to be as heavy as the back door looked to have been on the video feed, but it swung open cleanly and easily. Corry knew before he formally looked down the hall—thanks to the Secret Future, which was a tremendous help for this particular scared twelve year old—that the hallway was empty.

It was also mostly unlit. The corridor had regularly spaced fluorescent ceiling lights that, when on, left little to the imagination. But they were all off. Instead, at every T-junction, as well as above the door, was a small spotlight attached to a battery box. Emergency lights, he remembered. They were supposed to go on when the power went out. Corry wondered what else in the hospital relied on the same power as the lights. Not the video monitors, obviously. But it could be the phones did.

He stepped into the hall and felt the door close behind him, cutting him off from the sunlight coming in through the lobby windows. To further emphasize the strangeness of the emergency lighting, the spotlights were red. It made the white walls look like they were blood-colored, which was terribly creepy.

Corry took a deep breath and started walking slowly down the hall.

Find Violet, or find another adult, he thought. *That's all. Any adult will do, even a Mildly Crazy one.*

There were three doors—two on the right and one on the left—leading up to the common room's doorless entryway. All of the doors were closed. The one on the left beside the common room was the bathroom. Corry didn't know where the other two led.

He tried the first of them and found an unoccupied Mildly Crazy ward room, lit up thanks to the emergency light fixture in the corner inside a metal cage. It didn't look like the room had been lived in.

Door number two was opposite the bathroom. It was locked, which meant it probably wasn't somebody's room at all. The edges were more worn than that of the other doors, and the lock in the doorknob was free of brass coloring—from multiple key uses, probably. Corry figured this was where all the janitor supplies were kept.

He tried the bathroom door. It wasn't locked or occupied,

and nothing appeared to be out of place. He flashed back briefly to the time Harvey Nilsson cornered him in there, and he grimaced.

Not now, he reminded himself. *I got enough to be scared of already.*

He closed it and moved on.

Turning the corner to the common room, he half expected to see the gang assembled as always, with Mr. Pierce at the card table and the hands already dealt out and Mr. Parseghian ticking loudly through *Donahue* next to an annoyed Mr. Conway. But to his immense disappointment, the room was empty.

It was also very well lit. Sunlight streamed through the big picture windows, overwhelming the weak red emergency light above the doorway to such a degree it was easy to pretend it wasn't even on.

Corry was happy to see at least one part of the hospital still looked normal. He was tempted to just sit down at the window and wait, as if this was the normalest of normal days.

But when he took a few steps into the room, he realized something *was* out of place. It took a second to figure out that the problem lay with the afghan. The couch—a beat-up old felt thing that was the kind of comfortable only an extremely lived-in couch could be—always had an old afghan covering the top of it, and now that was missing.

As he got closer, the mystery was solved; apparently the afghan had ended up on the floor in front of the couch.

Messy, he thought. He wondered which patient had done it, and why nobody bothered to put it back.

He stepped around the couch, until the Secret Future showed him what was *really* wrong with this scene, and he froze.

There was something under the afghan.

It was a big lump, roughly the size of an adult human, which was exactly what Corry was pretty positive it was. Nicer explanations ran through his head—somebody fell asleep, rolled off the couch, and accidentally pulled the covering down, or, he passed out and someone else covered him and went to get a nurse—but none seemed to work, because whatever was underneath it most definitely wasn't breathing.

Trembling, he knelt down and grabbed the edge of the afghan. It took him three deep breaths before he could move again.

The image that followed would stay with him for the rest of his life and was that much worse for the fact that he saw it twice —in the present and in the Secret Future.

It was Ned. He was lying flat on his back, his eyes open, and wearing a permanent angry expression. There was a large hole in the front of his chest around where a person's heart was supposed to be. Corry's heart, preparing to leap directly out of his own breast, helpfully identified the correct location for him. All kinds of blood and guts had been forced out of the hole and traveled some distance down the front of dead Ned's white shirt.

There was blood elsewhere too. Blood he hadn't seen before splattered on the wall and the chair near the window, telling him exactly where Ned had been standing before he was shot, in the back, by somebody standing right about where Corry's feet were.

He wanted to understand how he'd missed all of that blood when he first walked into the room, but quite suddenly everything he ever ate in his entire life lined up at the back of his gullet and demanded to be let out, and there was no time to think about anything other than that.

He ran from the room, rounded the corner, and made for the bathroom, barely reaching the toilet before satisfying his gag reflex.

A few minutes passed with Corry doing nothing more than holding his mouth open and choking up semi-digested matter into the bowl, flushing as frequently as possible lest the smell trigger another round. Finally, trembling and covered in sweat, he sat back on the floor, his head up against the wall tile.

Somebody killed Ned with a gun, he thought. *That's nuts.*

He didn't need to spend any time wondering how a gun even made it into the hospital, as he was one of the few people around who happened to know that Ned carried one himself. He wasn't supposed to, but it was one of those little things Ned had to do or he wouldn't be Ned.

Corry could remember clearly when Ned showed it off to him, calling Corry around behind the desk and pulling it out of his pocket. It was a little thing, much smaller than the other guns Corry had been around before. In fact, that was exactly what Corry had thought of at that moment—that time in the woods, when Charlie Bluff nearly got his leg blown off. He'd instinctively recoiled with the memory, which Ned took to mean he was afraid of the gun. "Don't worry," he'd said. "Nobody'll be taking this baby away from me."

Guess he was wrong about that, Corry thought.

"Go to the police, shithead," he said to himself. "That's what you do when somebody's been shot. Find a cop. Everybody knows that."

Galvanized, he pulled himself up, walked over to the bathroom door, grabbed the handle, and froze. He was safe where he was, but if somebody was running around the hospital with a gun, he might not be this safe again for the rest of the day—certainly not if he opened the bathroom door.

You can't get the police if you don't leave the bathroom, he told himself, which was surely true. "Open the door, open the door, open the door."

He opened the door. There was nobody in the hallway pointing a gun at him. He was still as alone as he had been when he first biked up.

Go! He bolted for the lobby, running as hard as he could while thinking, irrationally, that the person with the gun was just now right behind him and aiming to fire.

He hit the door, twisted the knob, and...

The door was locked.

"No!" he shouted and then clapped his hand over his mouth, as if by doing so he could shove the exclamation back down before anybody else heard it.

He spun quickly around and saw that the hallway was still empty.

Okay, okay, okay, get a grip.

He reached for the handle and tried it again, but it wouldn't budge. The door was *never* locked, which was why he didn't even think to check it before walking through. And now he was trapped inside, just like everyone else.

But I'm not like everyone else, am I? he thought. *I'm not just a kid; I'm a kid with a gift.*

He thought again of Charlie Bluff, how Charlie had been standing with the shotgun at his side, the tip of the barrel pressed up against his leg while Tyrell ran ahead after noises only he could hear. And how cold it was, even with Violet next to him trying to keep him warm.

Back then Corry hadn't been very good at distinguishing between the present and the Secret Future; to him it was all happening at once. So when Charlie's hand got tired—or maybe it'd just gotten cold, since he wasn't wearing gloves—and the gun slipped in his hand, Corry knew before anybody else did that in trying to catch the gun Charlie would inadvertently pull the trigger.

Having never heard a gun go off at close range before, the sound had frightened Corry. He screamed and jumped away from Charlie, and when Violet asked what was wrong, he said simply, "Bang!"

And then, in real time, the gun did go off.

To Charlie—and also to Violet—it seemed as if Corry had somehow commanded the gun to fire.

That was why they had to leave the commune that very night and also why Violet was a little scared of her son. She thought she had a devil child on her hands. *She still thinks that.*

Corry took more than one lesson with him from that day. The first was that, clearly, he was seeing things other people were not. The second was, never speak of the Secret Future to anyone because adults were prepared to jump to a bad conclusion really quick. Third, he had to learn to respect cause and effect, if only as a way to understand what was happening versus what was only about to happen.

A fourth lesson came to him as he sat next to the locked door, staring down the hall and expecting a killer to emerge at the other end of it.

He had known the gun was going to go off before it did. If he could know that, he could also know where the bullet would be going. Further, if he concentrated, he could probably avoid being the one standing in the way of the bullet. It should be no different than it was on his bike, when he could see traffic movement ahead of time and adjust accordingly.

The thought was a revelation. As much as he liked to pretend his future-sight was a superhero power, the truth was he hated having to deal with it constantly. This was the first time in his life he saw it as a blessing instead of a curse.

Emboldened, he pushed himself off the floor. He could save his mom and maybe other people, too. He could be a real hero.

Just as soon as he figured out how to get his legs to walk again.

CHAPTER SIXTEEN

Corry had a powerful fear of going crazy himself someday. It was one of the drawbacks of spending so much time around people who *were* crazy, people who were on drugs a lot of the time, and his mom, who had some of the qualities of both groups.

It seemed to him going crazy was something that sort of snuck up on you from behind, like a tiger in the jungle, and once it had you, that was it—you ended up in a place like McClaren, and then you never ever left. Except with a tiger, you knew you were being eaten by one while it was happening. Crazy just… happened, without you even knowing it. This was a terrifying notion.

That was why, when he reached the threshold of the common room again, Corry stopped at the entrance and stared hard at the prone body of Ned the guard, just to make sure it was still there, because he heard from some of the Mildly Crazies about how sometimes they saw stuff that wasn't real. But Ned was still there.

Corry understood that so long as he was the only one looking at him, he hadn't truly ruled out the possibility that it was all in his imagination, but he still felt a little better. Then he felt bad for feeling better because Ned was probably not happy to be dead.

Rather than continuing, he walked back to the body and pulled the afghan aside, not really knowing why he was doing so.

Dead body, dead body, dead body, he thought. *Not throwing up.*

He wasn't going to throw up again, which was important because heroes don't throw up, like ever.

"Keys!" he said aloud.

Ned had keys to the whole place on his belt. This was why he'd gone back, he decided. Not because he was a sick—or crazy —kid who enjoyed staring at bodies. He could find the keys, open the door, get the police...

But the key ring was missing. Ned kept his battalion of keys on a giant ring attached to a pull chain on his belt, and it wasn't there. Could be it was underneath Ned, but Corry would have to flip him to check that, and he wasn't willing to do any such thing. Besides, who wears a key ring on the back of their belt? Probably whoever killed him had taken the keys.

Corry felt his stomach grumble again and thought maybe it was a good idea to walk away from Ned now and get on with the hero stuff. So he covered up the guard and stepped into the hallway.

Going left from there, it occurred to him that he had now officially traveled deeper into the hospital than he'd ever been before. "Hero," he reminded himself, because that word made his hands stop shaking. "That's right, I'm a hero."

The problem was in coming up with a name. He'd already accomplished the hard part—having an actual superpower— but now he needed a good name. All the best superheroes had one. A bad name and you didn't even get your own book, no matter how cool your power was. The Batman, for instance, had no powers at all, just a really awesome name and a fairly cool costume.

So what will my name be?

The first few steps down the hall were uneventful. There were four doors to check, but as he was now prepared to forge ahead without an adult, he didn't see a great need to go door-to-door. He needed to get to the T- junction at the end and figure out where that led.

Something to do with time would be good, he thought. Time Boy, say, or the Clock Beater. Except maybe not either one of those because they were stupid. He had to do much better than that.

He reached the edge of the hallway. There, the corridor split to the left and the right with a door directly ahead that looked like most of the other doors in the hallway and was probably another Mildly Crazy ward room. He didn't know for sure which way to go, but he recalled on the one or two occasions when he happened to still be standing in the hall as Violet went off to work, she headed to the right.

He pressed up against the wall and, in the Secret Future, leaned around the corner to peek at what was down there. It looked as if there was a well-lit area about twenty feet away that wasn't just another part of the corridor. Looking to the left, he saw a long corridor of what appeared to be more patient rooms and no open space at the end. So he'd go right.

Best part—nobody took a shot at his Secret Future head.

He figured it was okay to step forward in real time, and so he did, looking both ways and then heading to the right.

The hospital had already proven to be a lot bigger than he ever realized, especially if the left turn part of the corridor really went as far as it looked like it did.

Where the heck is everybody? he wondered.

Then he decided not to wonder about that, because for all he knew, each of them looked like Ned now.

Chrono-Kid sprang to mind and then immediately sprang back out again. *Terrible name.*

The Time Tamer? That wasn't so bad. He instinctively liked any name that was supposed to have a "the" in front of it. But it wasn't really accurate because he didn't *tame* time, he just saw it differently.

That was the problem, he figured, as he reached the open space at the midpoint of the hallway. His powers were too difficult to describe in a name. He was going to have to come up with something that described what he did with the powers, rather than what his powers were.

The open space at the end of the hall was occupied by the Medium Security Nurse Station he'd tried to telephone. The station was a round desk area in the middle of a large square space. It had three chairs and a bunch of video monitors on a lower desk level. It was completely unoccupied. No nurses, no dead bodies of nurses, no anybody. Maybe they really were all dead.

No, can't be, he thought. He knew enough about guns to understand they had a limited supply of bullets in them.

"They can't *all* be dead," he said. His voice echoed in the open space, emphasizing his aloneness.

He sat down and examined the desk but found it about as useful as the desk near the front door, meaning not useful at all. So he checked out the monitors.

There were six of them, and each one was labeled via the sophisticated method of magic marker on a piece of masking tape stuck to the top of the plastic casing. The first four showed rotating views of patient rooms, and the other two were labeled "public" and "halls."

Corry decided it would be a good idea to look at all of them.

Maybe this way he could figure out where everyone was without leaving the comparative safety of the nurse station.

It took only a few seconds of watching to gain an excellent understanding of the difference between Mildly Crazy and Really Crazy. It seemed that about half of the Really Crazy patients were still in their rooms, and Corry sincerely hoped their rooms were locked, because—*wow*. One guy had his pants off and was doing things to his Private Place that Corry was pretty sure must hurt a lot. Another one was licking his padded wall, and a third was busily picking at the skin on his arm, causing a thin trickle of blood.

The most interesting was the guy on screen twenty-seven who kept screaming at the camera. Like the one he'd seen at the back door, it was weird watching him because there was no sound, but clearly the guy was making as much noise as he could. Corry stayed at that monitor for a while because it looked like he was trying to say something. It wasn't until the third pass that he figured out the word. *Medication.*

Oh God, he thought. *What time is it?*

He looked at the clock on the wall. The Mildly Crazy patients were supposed to get their meds after lunch, which was an hour ago. If the whole hospital was on the same schedule, that could mean the entire building was full of unmedicated crazies.

On the fourth pass, the screaming guy wasn't there anymore. Since it was basically impossible to not appear on camera— Corry could see the whole cell—it could only mean that the rooms were not, in fact, locked. Screaming guy was out in the halls somewhere.

His heart rate going right on up again, Corry switched over to the view of the corridors. The cameras there moved much more quickly, as apparently McClaren Hospital was *huge*. The stairwell he saw in one shot explained that; there was a second level, probably underground. Also—and it was difficult to tell because the cameras were showing poorly lit hallways—two or three times he could have sworn he saw more bodies. It was mostly just a leg here or there, and the system was moving from shot-to-shot very rapidly, but by the fourth cycle he was pretty positive about what he was looking at.

He found screaming guy. He was running down the corridor toward who knows what. Briefly, Corry considered that the man might be heading for *him*, as he was sitting at the nurse station. But he didn't hear any screaming.

Guy must be downstairs, he thought.

He could use the cameras to follow the man—every time he disappeared around a corner on one camera he'd appear on another one. It was a very useful way to map the basement, really.

But then something odd happened. It looked at first like the guy tripped, but when the camera found him again it was clear there wasn't anything to trip over.

He stood up and looked around. Just before the camera cut away it looked as if something struck him in the back of the head. The shot returned in time to show... nothing.

Screaming guy—no longer screaming, by the looks of it—was on his back and holding up his hands in self-defense. He thought somebody was hitting him, but there just wasn't anyone there. Except there was blood on his face, and he didn't get that beat up just from falling over.

Maybe someone *was* hitting him, but they weren't on camera. Which also didn't make any sense at all.

The camera cut away again, and when it returned, the screaming man was neither screaming nor moving.

A terrible thought came to Corry, the As-Yet-Unnamed Superhero. What if he ran into someone else who also had superpowers? Like someone who was so fast he didn't even appear on a video camera?

His eyes flitted over to the last monitor, hoping there he would get some good news. But while "public" had four cameras, just one of them was working. From the working camera angle, he could see only that it was a pretty big room, somewhat reminiscent of his school's cafeteria. Dozens of chairs were stacked up on top of one another, forming a barrier and almost completely blocking off the big window that took up most of the wall. Sunlight came in through that window, so the room had to be on the same floor he was, seeing as how the basement level was underground.

He caught the movement on the fifth camera pass. There were people behind the chairs and in front of the windows. Lots of people. And they weren't running around and screaming for their meds or otherwise acting outwardly crazy.

They're hiding! he thought. *That's where everyone went.*

Of course, because that's what sane people do when someone in the place has a gun. Hide.

It was impossible to tell who and how many there were, but it was a good guess that Violet was there, too.

He just had to figure out where *there* was. And maybe more importantly, where the person they were hiding from might be.

A ccess to the Really Crazy ward rooms and whatever lay beyond—like the public room, hopefully—was easily gained via a door behind the nurse station. Corry opened it and stood there for several deep breaths to review what he was about to walk down and to drum up the courage to do so.

Nothing jumped right out at him, literally or figuratively, as being dangerous. It looked pretty much like the other corridors he'd already been down, red-tinted from the spotlights, but with no apparent movement or visible bodies. Satisfied, he stepped over the threshold and started walking.

Then he heard the door behind him close and the lock trip into place. Stupidly, he'd just locked himself in. Again.

Idiot Boy, he thought. *Or Stupid Kid*. He was pretty sure those names weren't taken.

Sighing mightily, he headed down the hall, slowly at first, picking up speed as he went. It seemed the further away he got from the comparative safety of the nurse station, the faster he wanted to go.

Doors in the hallway were alternately open and not open, which he guessed corresponded to occupied and unoccupied. He could probably open one of the doors and find an adult, but that was no longer the most sensible plan, not in the Really Crazy wing.

Find a nurse, or an orderly, or a guard, or a doctor, or anyone not wearing the outfit of a patient.

Moving faster worked the same on foot as it did on his bike, extending the Secret Future because he got to places quicker. So as he came up to the first turn in the hallway—no T-junction here, just a right-angled left turn—he already knew he was going to find somebody there. The sight was so jarring, in fact, that he stopped short of the corner and temporarily altered his own future.

Corry stood just shy of the turn. What he'd seen was a patient, sitting down against the wall and crying. He could hear the man muttering something, but Corry couldn't make out what.

In the Secret Future, he turned the corner and saw what the man was looking at. He turned the corner for real and saw the same thing.

It was Carl.

He was lying up against the side of the wall, very still and probably dead, which was a conclusion Corry would probably never have jumped to about half an hour earlier.

Temporarily ignoring the other guy, he knelt beside his friend, with whom he would now never get the chance to discuss baseball. Unlike Ned, there didn't seem to be any obvious wounds on him. Just the same, he wasn't breathing.

Now he won't get to see the Sox win the Series, he thought, and the thought filled him with a tremendous sadness.

Trying to get his mind off that, he checked out the guy huddled against the opposite wall. He was a thin, little man who could have used a shave and a bath—and probably a whole gallon of medication. His head rocked back and forth; it looked like his eyes weren't focusing on much of anything, and he was actively chewing on his wrist. Blood was in his teeth and on his chin.

"Hey," Corry said. "Are you all right?"

The man didn't respond. Corry couldn't figure out what the guy was muttering, but he seemed pretty harmless. He returned his attention to Carl.

Corry had only a vague appreciation of what made one person alive and another person dead. On television shows they did stuff like putting fingers on necks or wrists to feel for something or other, and he would've tried that, too, but he didn't know what he was feeling for, so he skipped it.

"Carl?" he asked. Carl didn't say anything. His eyes were closed, though; might as well have been asleep.

He slapped the old guard's face a couple of times to see if that helped. It didn't.

"Guess you really are dead," Corry said.

"Duuuugh!" the patient against the wall declared loudly.

"What?" Corry asked. "Do you have something to say?"

He fell silent again.

"Because I could use some help here," Corry went on. "I'm just a kid, you know."

Nothing. The guy went back to being catatonic. First adult he runs into and he turns out to be useless.

"Mom couldn't work in the mall or something, could she? No, it had to be a mental hospital."

He started feeling around Carl's belt. He didn't know for sure whether Carl had the same kind of key ring as Ned, but it seemed worth a try. Unlike Ned, though, Carl was lying on his side, and after a few seconds of searching, he concluded that if there were keys, they were under the guard's body.

"Have'ta roll him over," he decided.

That meant touching an actual dead body.

The day was becoming a series of obstacles filled with things Corry never expected to have to do, and touching dead bodies was right up at the top of the list. But he had to pass each obstacle eventually, didn't he? Otherwise, he wasn't getting back out again.

"Hey," he said to the catatonic guy. "You wouldn't want to help me, would you?"

"Dunnut . . ." the man declared.

"Guy, you wanna say something, get your wrist outta your mouth, okay?"

Sure, bad idea to yell at crazy people. But he was a little crazy person, and Corry had decided he wasn't going to be scared of him. As much as it was possible to decide such a thing.

Yelling didn't change anything, though. The guy just sat there and stared back at Corry. At least he was recognizing there was another person. Maybe next he'd try speaking words.

Carl was a big guy, short but tubby. He wasn't going to be easy to move. Corry walked around him a couple of times looking for an angle or an idea how to do it while ignoring the voice in his head that kept crying *Carl's dead!* because that just wasn't helpful.

Finally, he decided on a plan. He grabbed onto one end of Carl's belt and started pulling. After no small amount of effort, Corry got him rolled onto his back.

"Sorry, Carl," he said quietly.

"Do not consort," said the man on the floor.

"What?" Corry asked.

"Donnut consssort," he repeated. His words were slushy again.

"Guy, I don't even know what that means." He stood over Carl and reached down to the other side of the belt. His hand came up wet. "Oh..." he muttered, jerking his hand back in surprise.

In the red emergency lighting, the color of the liquid now coating his hand looked black, like motor oil. But he knew what it was; it was blood. Carl's blood.

He tried to use Carl's white shirt to mop it up, but that only made matters worse, because he didn't want to see the blood at all, and instead he was spreading it.

"Don't throw up, don't throw up, don't throw up..."

"Monsters," said the crazy man.

"Shut up!" Corry snapped. He wiped his face with the not-bloody hand, realizing he was crying and perhaps had been crying for the last few minutes. "Superheroes don't cry!"

He closed his eyes and felt along the belt some more. It was all wet along that side of Carl's waist, as was the floor where Carl had been laying at rest. But as long as his eyes were still slammed shut he could pretend it was just water, even though he knew better.

He found a key ring.

"Monsters!" the crazy guy screamed again.

"Yeah, monsters," Corry agreed.

The ring was attached to the belt by the same kind of clip Ned had. He forced open his eyes to study the mechanism.

He needed to slide the clip up off the belt; the problem being Carl's pudgy middle was in the way. He had to push the guard's stomach in to clear space for the belt, and when he did so, it caused more blood to pour out of the body and over Corry's hands. He gagged reflexively.

"*Monsters!*"

The shout came from right behind him. In a few seconds the crazy man would be grabbing him from behind by the shoulders and shoving him hard into the wall while screaming his new favorite word.

He pushed harder at Carl's pudge. The blood made the clip all slippery, but... *there.* The key ring came free. And just in time.

He ducked and rolled to the side a half second before Mr. Monsters lunged forward. The crazy man fell comically atop poor Carl while Corry crab-walked some distance and got to his feet.

"Sorry, guy. I gotta go."

"Do not consort with monsters," the man repeated, still lying prone on top of Carl.

"Right. I'll remember that."

He stumbled away, backing down the hall and keeping an eye on this Grade A nut job.

Running Boy? He thought. *How about The Flee?*

Mr. Monsters found his footing, not caring that he'd gotten some of Carl's blood on him. His wrist was bleeding anyway, so there was plenty of blood to go around.

"Monnnnsters," he droned.

"I know!" Corry said. "Go . . . go back and sit down against the wall, would'ja?"

He didn't do that. Instead, he started walking down the corridor. Toward Corry.

"Fantastic," Corry said. Mr. Monsters wanted to beat him up for reasons that only made sense to Mr. Monsters. The guy didn't move all that quick, but searching with the very real possibility that if he lingered too long he'd be grabbed from behind by a crazy just wasn't going to make this go any easier.

"I don't need a sidekick!" Corry shouted.

CHAPTER SEVENTEEN

I n the middle of the corridor, only a few feet away from where Corry was standing, there was a man going to the bathroom.

Not the "ducking behind the bushes after pulling over on the side of the road" kind but the other kind. Number two. Poop. Dooty. Feces. Shit. Yes, Corry decided, there was a reason why that word was a Bad Word. Not for the polite kind of pooping one did quietly in the toilet, hoping the noise wasn't loud enough to inspire one of the ninth graders at the sinks to make a stupid joke. What he was doing was what the word "shit" had been invented to describe.

He had his pants down around his knees, his underwear just off his behind, and his behind sticking up in the air like those orangutans Corry's science teacher had showed them pictures of last term. Except this guy's behind was hairier than the orangutan's.

He was crouched in profile, his hand on the door to support the position, his ass aiming shit projectiles across the part of the corridor Corry had been hoping to pass through. He was grunting loudly and kept saying unkind things about his mother, who he seemed to think was standing behind him, perhaps with a catcher's mitt.

Corry had gotten used to a lot of things in the past hour. Like dead bodies. Since Ned and Carl, he'd seen at least three more, although he didn't stop to check any of them to see whether they were actually dead or just injured badly. Also unlike the two guards, it looked like they had been hit with something. A baseball bat maybe, or the end of a broom. And he'd had to get used to the sight of blood, which, thanks to the lighting, seemed to be the color of everything in the hospital. But a man rocketing diarrhea across a six-foot-wide corridor was something he never expected to get over.

Or get past. Which was the real problem. He wasn't about to walk through the shit storm in front of him, and going back meant having to get around the annoyingly persistent Mr. Monsters, who apparently still wanted to grab Corry for some unknowable reason.

It would have been great if one of the doors between Corry and the Shitstorm Guy ended up leading to the public room, but he could tell just by looking at them that they were all ward rooms, just like every other door he'd seen so far, except for one. That one led to a stairwell down. He didn't want to go down.

But Shitstorm Guy couldn't go on forever, could he? How much shit could one guy produce?

"Hey, you almost done?" Corry asked.

Shitstorm Guy looked over at Corry, his face red from exertion.

"Wait your turn, Bobby," he barked. "The kitchen's not done yet."

O-kay. "How about you take a break for a minute, just so I can... walk by? Cuz, you know, this really isn't a bathroom?"

"Dunnut . . ." Mr. Monsters declared.

He was only about ten feet away. If he felt like picking up his pace, he could reach Corry pretty fast. Fortunately, he was still stuck in some sort of Frankenstein walk.

"I know it's not a bathroom," Shitstorm Guy said. "You think I'm crazy?"

"Yeah, actually. How about you just stand up for a second, and I'll go between you and the wall over here. So I don't wreck your... shit art, or whatever it is you've got going there."

"It's for mother, Bobby," Shitstorm Guy explained.

"Yeah. She'll love it."

"Do you really think so?" He sounded touched, like he was going to start crying or something.

"Sure," Corry said. This seemed to have a positive effect on Shitstorm Guy. He stood up. Corry saw his chance and ran past him. The guy reached out to grab his arm, but Corry saw that coming and adjusted so that he was out of reach.

"Mommy loved you, Bobby," Shitstorm Guy declared as Corry continued right on running. "It was just an accident."

Corry wasn't listening anymore. He was trying too hard to pretend that none of that had happened, instead checking doors along the hallway. Patient room doors, all of them.

Where the hell is the public room? he wondered.

He turned the corner and found... Carl's body.

"Oh no," he said. "Oh hell, oh damn, oh *fuck*!"

How could he not have noticed he was traveling in a circle?

Looking down the corridor behind him he could see— barely—the door to the nurse station. He had somehow not noticed it when he went by. And he certainly was not up to going back in that direction again to get to it, not with both Shitstorm Guy and Mr. Monsters—walking through Shitstorm Guy's creative masterpiece at that very moment—in the way.

I could go around again, he thought. But that didn't strike him as the very best plan ever. Shitstorm Guy was not the only person he'd come across that he was both lucky to get past and hopeful that he'd never have to try doing so ever again. Like the guy with no shirt who was trying to dig through one of the walls and kept shouting the word "Sparrow" or the one who was crawling along the floor like an inchworm.

Neither one of them had seemed dangerous at first, but neither had Mr. Monsters. Who knew how they'd act when Rerun Kid—*stupid name*—walked past them again?

But that wasn't the real issue. The real issue was the obvious fact that he'd searched the entire floor and never found the public room.

Somehow, there was a room underground that got sunlight. It didn't seem possible, but he'd eliminated all the other possibilities, so...

"I'll take the stairs, then," he declared definitively.

He knew each time he made these little decisions he was moving further away from a quick and easy exit, but that wasn't the kind of thinking that would help him get to Violet, so instead he concentrated on running as fast as he could for the door to the stairs, which was only down the hall and around the corner. It was easy enough to identify, being the only door with a push bar on it.

Running hard felt good, and it put some distance between him and Mr. Monsters.

When he reached the door, he hit the bar with vigor. It gave easily, and he was soon standing in the stairwell. He pushed the door closed.

The stairs were cement, like the ones in his school, only without the raggedy carpeting. He took the steps two at a time until he reached the first landing and found himself facing... a door to the outside. He could see grass on the other side through a small rectangular peek-a-boo window.

The wiring on the side of the doorjamb was a good indication that this was the alarmed door Ned had been telling him about seemingly decades ago. It was the place he'd seen someone trying to escape.

So where's that guy now?

First question first. How could a door that was a flight of stairs below the ground level come out on grass? Corry thought about it for a few seconds before deciding he was a complete moron. The whole city of Belmont was one hill after another, so of *course* the hospital was built on one.

He peeked through the window and confirmed the downward slope of the lawn outside. And naturally, that explained how the public room got sunlight, too.

Idiot, he thought.

The second question was answered as soon as he turned around. There was someone lying on his back at the bottom of the stairs, near the door leading to the sublevel.

"Hey, you okay?" he asked.

The guy didn't answer, so Corry went down to check on him.

He was lying funny, with his head at an odd angle compared to the rest of his body, like he'd developed an elbow in the side of his neck.

With a shudder, Corry decided not to think about it any more than he had to. The guy was obviously dead, and that was that. How he'd gotten that way probably had something to do with going down the cement steps wrong after he'd gotten the door slammed in his face.

I should go out the side door, he thought. *Get the police.* It made the most sense. Besides which, he'd had plenty enough of crazy people for one day.

Just as he came to this conclusion, though, he heard the crash bar upstairs engage and the door swing open. He looked up, but seeing through concrete was not one of his powers, so he couldn't tell who was there. He could guess, though.

"Hello?" he asked.

"Monsterssss."

"Great," he said. Rather than try and reach the exit, he grabbed the handle on the basement door, because going away from Mr. Monsters by any means made more sense than heading toward him.

There was only one problem, the handle wouldn't turn. The door to the sublevel was locked.

Shit, shit, shit, he thought. He vaulted over the legs of the dead man and reached the third step up, hit it running, and dashed the rest of the way up the cement stairs to the landing. The exit to the outside had a push bar of its own, which Corry hit as hard as he could. The door gave a bit and then... pushed back.

It was so unexpected—for some reason he hadn't seen it coming—that he fell backward and right into the arms of Mr. Monsters.

"Monnnnsters," the man said loudly. His breath smelled sour, and the rest of him stank of shit—a combination that made Corry gag, which he had little time for as he was being lifted off the ground and tugged away from the door.

For just a half of a second, he thought he saw someone else looking in at him outside the door. Somebody who wanted to keep him in.

This would have been terrifying enough all by itself but then Mr. Monsters wrapped his left arm around Corry's shoulders, his right arm around Corry's waist, a blood-smeared hand reaching down to the Bad Touching area, and all Corry could think was to scream—so he did. And what came out of his mouth was, "Do not consort with monsters!"

Mr. Monsters, his hot breath curling the hairs on Corry's neck, hesitated. And then he loosened his grip.

Corry pushed himself free, nearly going headfirst down the stairs, where he would have ended up right next to the last guy who had done that and in a similar condition. He caught himself on the metal railing and stumbled the rest of the way down.

"Lest ye become a monster," Mr. Monsters said. Corry ignored him. He had remembered the key ring still gripped firmly in his left hand, and began shoving keys into the door lock one at a time. It was hard, as they were slippery with his sweat and with Carl's blood, and his heart was beating so quickly it was making his whole body move. He didn't want to be a superhero anymore. He just wanted to find his mother.

"That's the rest..." declared Mr. Monsters, who was coming down the stairs.

"Rest of what?" Corry said, almost under his breath.

"The . . . it's Nietzsche. They locked him up, too."

Mr. Monsters sounded so lucid, Corry chanced a look over his shoulder, and saw that he'd sat down on the bottom step and did not appear to be preparing to renew his interest in groping children. Corry kept trying keys.

"He here?" Corry asked. *Keep him talking.*

"Who?"

"This Nee-chuh guy."

"No. He's dead."

"Oh. Sorry."

Mr. Monsters fell silent. Corry looked over at him. He looked back.

"You shouldn't be here," Mr. Monsters said.

"No kidding," Corry said.

"Just a kid. You should go. There's something terrible here. It's going to kill everyone."

"Can't," he said without elaboration, as he was not ready to process what he'd seen through the window, and he had only a few keys left to try. If Carl didn't have a key for this door, he didn't know what he was going to do.

"I was trying to protect you," Mr. Monsters said.

"Funny way to do that," Corry said.

"You didn't see what I saw. You don't understand."

Corry looked at him. "What did you see?"

"Nobody," Mr. Monsters said. "I saw nobody, and he killed the guard."

"That's helpful."

"And then he put out the Cyclops' eye . . ."

"Really, that's great." Corry found the key. He jerked open the door.

"Don't," Mr. Monsters said. "Don't go through there. Stay here. Nobody isn't here."

"I said I can't," Corry said. "My mom's down here somewhere. I have to save her."

The sublevel of the Really Crazy section of the hospital was a lot like the floor Corry had just left, only more so. The lighting wasn't nearly as good, there were people screaming intermittently, and it smelled like something was burning somewhere.

He had this sense that going on everywhere around him was frantic activity, maybe just around the corner or two steps beyond the shelter of the nearest light, in the shallows of what seemed to be unnatural darkness. It felt like being dropped directly into the middle of a Halloween fun house, only this time the corpses weren't stuffed with cotton, and the scary people lunging out randomly would actually try and hurt him if he wasn't careful.

A half-remembered safety tip sprang to mind, something about crawling when there was a fire. That was to keep from breathing smoke, and there wasn't any, but he kind of liked the idea of making himself as small as possible. So he crouched down and started to crawl along the wall to his left.

He chose the left because he'd seen sunlight through the windows of the public room, and it was the afternoon, which put the sun on the side of the building where he was heading. He was kind of proud of himself for having figured this out.

Crawling turned out to be an excellent decision a few seconds later when a screaming man wearing absolutely no clothing whatsoever sprinted past. As the man was sticking to the center of the corridor, Corry didn't have to worry about the possibility of being touched by a naked man, something he anticipated never wanting to experience.

A little further along, he came across another body. This one looked to be a patient, and as he got closer—he was eye level with the body—he realized it was one he knew.

It was Mr. Conway. He was lying on his side, staring down the hall, looking like his last breath was spent screaming.

The back of his head was missing. Corry didn't know what might cause such a thing to happen, but thought that maybe if you hit someone real hard back there, the head could cave in and look something like what he was seeing.

As far as horrible things went, it was just about the horriblest thing he had ever looked at, or it would have been if he was still feeling anything. But by this point, whatever was inside of him that was meant to help him register and process shocking things had either fainted, or died from overuse. The lifeless expression on Mr. Conway, a person he happened to like a good deal, would come to haunt him in the coming days, but at that moment it meant nothing.

Nobody killed him was the only thought he could muster, hearkening back to Mr. Monsters's strange warning. Patting his friend on the shoulder, he crawled around him and kept moving.

He was still thinking about Mr. Conway as he crawled along at a brisk pace, not at all paying attention to the Secret Future —*stupid*—which was how the broken glass took him completely by surprise. He discovered it in the worst possible way, with a sharp pain in the palm of his left hand.

Letting out a little yelp, he jumped back against the wall, dropped the key ring, and pulled his hand off the ground. A half-inch-long shard of glass had been driven right through the middle.

"Oh God, oh God," he muttered, staring at the wound. The glass was thin and curved, and had a crosshatch pattern on the part of it that wasn't sticking into his hand. It was part of the spotlight. He had gone and crawled under one of the disabled lights and hadn't even taken into account what might have happened to the glass once it was shattered.

The Punctured Wonder, he thought, grimacing.

There was only one thing to do. He had to pull the glass out. Already, his blood was leaking out through the sides, and he was sure once the glass was removed, more would come out, but he also couldn't use the hand as long as the glass was in there. So he clenched his teeth, gripped the glass carefully between the thumb and forefinger of his right hand, and pulled.

It didn't hurt half as much as he thought it would. That was the good thing. The bad thing was that it bled even more than he expected, so much so that he was genuinely alarmed by the sheer quantity of it all. For a few seconds he just sat there watching it drip down his hand, past his wrist, and onto the floor.

Bandage. I need a bandage.

But there weren't any bandages anywhere. Corry didn't know what would happen if he let it just bleed—he'd never actually cut himself before but understood that bleeding nonstop led to something bad—so he pulled the bottom of his T-shirt out from his pants and tried to tear a strip off it. This turned out to be impossible to do with only one hand, and he succeeded only in getting his own blood all over his shirt.

"Dammit," he said quietly. He was crying. He barely even realized he was doing it, and once he did, rather than stopping, he moved into full-sob mode. Soon his shoulders were shaking, and he was gasping for air and trying not to make too much noise, and still he couldn't stop crying.

"Nnno," he grunted through the sobs. "Heroes don't cry..."

His hand hurt like hell, he smelled like shit, he didn't know where he was going, and he was going to bleed to death. And he still didn't know where his mom was or what in the world was going on in the hospital. He just wanted to go home.

His eyes, tear-streaked and blurred, drifted over to Mr. Conway, and then he got a brilliantly stupid idea. He pulled himself together a bit and proceeded to hop and crawl back to his dead friend, who loved to talk about science on good days and on bad days bore the marks of his psychosis.

After a couple of minutes of searching, he found what he was looking for, a thick wrap of gauze spun around Mr. Conway's left upper arm.

"Lucky it wasn't a Band-Aid today," he said as he unwound the gauze as fast as he could. At the bottom of it was a thin cotton pad that still smelled of alcohol and below that was a long thin cut that would never bleed again anyway.

Corry flipped the cotton pad over and folded it in half, and then he stuffed it into the palm of his left hand and held it there with his thumb while he wrapped it up in the gauze. When he was finished, his hand looked like a Mummy hand, but that was okay; at least he'd managed to stop the bleeding for a while.

Solving the problem of his hand made him feel much better. He didn't feel like crying anymore... it was time to move on.

He wiped his eyes clear and crawled back to the edge of the

glass, stopping when he reached the key ring. He picked it up and pulled himself to his feet—a little dizzy, but not too bad—took a couple of deep breaths, and jumped over the glass.

This caught somebody's attention.

"Hey. Boy."

Corry looked around, puzzled. His eyes were adjusted to the poor lighting, but despite that he couldn't see anybody around.

"Over here."

Mr. Conway was still dead behind him, and ahead of him there were two more apparently dead bodies along the opposite wall.

"Where are you?" Corry asked, his heart rate picking up and causing his hand to throb harder.

One of the bodies in front of him waved.

"Under Elton," he said.

Corry walked closer, squinting. "What are you doing under there?" he asked. It wasn't two dead bodies. It was one, with a living one underneath it.

"Keep your voice down!" he barked. "Lie on the floor, against the wall. Go on."

Picking a spot on the opposite wall, he did as he was told.

"How's this?"

"Not bad. But you should really find a body to hide under if you can. I think there's one over there." He pointed to Mr. Conway.

Distantly, someone was laughing. It was an unsettling sound, more like the Joker than the Carol Burnett studio audience.

"Why are we doing this?" Corry asked. He had fervently hoped that the person he was talking to was sane. He sounded like it at first, but the fact that he was wearing a dead person didn't help his cause.

"He won't hurt us if he thinks we're dead."

"Oh. Guess that makes sense." *Corpse Boy*. "Who won't hurt us?"

"Look out. Here comes Marty again." Marty, the screaming naked man ran past a few seconds later. This time Corry took note of the fact that his feet were bleeding; probably cut them on some of the same glass that got his hand.

"What happened to his clothes?" Corry asked.

"He hates clothing and he likes young boys, not necessarily in that order," said his new friend. "Don't let *him* see you either."

"Either?"

"Marty won't kill you, but he might hurt you. The other one, he'll probably just kill you."

"What other one is that?"

"The one who did all this."

"Well, who is it?"

"I don't know," he admitted. "I haven't seen him."

"I can't tell," Corry said. "Are you a patient?"

"So they tell me," he said. "Does that surprise you? Should I perhaps do something wildly insane so that you might be satisfied?"

"Sorry," Corry said, as he'd evidently offended the man. "Just saying, because you seem okay."

"Thank you. To be honest, I'm actually enjoying this. It's much easier being insane in a world equally so. Don't you think?"

"I wouldn't know," Corry said. He sniffled a couple of times; his nose was still running from the earlier bawl-fest.

I don't have time for this, he concluded.

"Listen, I'm thinking I'm gonna keep moving. D'you know where the public room is from here?"

"You'll be much better off if you just lie where you are until it's over."

"I want to find my mom and get home, mister," he said, climbing back to his feet. "That's why I'm here."

"Get down!" the man urged.

"But I can't find her if I just lie on the floor."

"She's probably dead already."

"Shut up!" Corry said, louder than he wanted.

"Don't—"

"No! This is stupid," Corry said. "You know what? I'm starting to think this is all over and nobody knows it yet."

"Keep your damn voice down!"

"Seriously, somebody's s'posed to have a gun, right? So where are they?"

"They're invisible."

"Oh, don't *you* start with that!" he snapped.

Corry had started off the day with a certain respect for the difficulties of the insane, but that understanding had been worn away to nothing over the past hour or two—or however long it had been. Now they believed in the boogeyman, which was fine for them, but he didn't have to if he didn't want to. And the boogeyman couldn't hurt you if you didn't believe in him.

"Quiet! Quiet! Quiet!" the man screamed. Someone, somewhere on the floor, echoed his words. A loud bang—the sound of glass shattering—soon followed.

"What was that?"

"*HIM!*" the man said.

"Tell me where the public room is," Corry said.

"He's coming!" the cowering man cried. And for a second, Corry started to think maybe there really was somebody coming.

No, he thought. *Not real.*

"Quickly, mister," he said. "The public room. Tell me or I'll shout some more."

"Down the hall and around the corner. It's the second door on your left. Hurry, before he gets you."

"Thanks," Corry said.

"Goodbye," he said. "It was nice to have known you."

C orry had to go past another possibly dead person and step aside for Marty the screaming naked guy's third circuit, but aside from that, the trip to the public room door was uneventful. It seemed—again, aside from Marty— that all of the Really Crazy people on the floor were acting more like the guy who had given him the directions. They were hiding somewhere, waiting for it all to end.

The way Corry figured it, if a twelve-year-old kid could make it from the emergency exit to the public room, then all the adults inside could easily make it from there to the exit. So he was feeling pretty good about himself, seeing as how he'd found a way to be heroic without doing much more than wandering past crazy people. Maybe that's all there was to being a hero— not being afraid to keep going.

Then he opened the door.

Mr. Nilsson was standing in the middle of the room on top of one of the tables, and at first, Corry was so happy to see a familiar face that he didn't even notice the gun in his hand.

He was spinning around in a slow circle with the gun pointed more or less all over the place, aiming at either nothing or everything, depending on one's perspective. His shirt was torn and stained with blood, his feet were bare, and his pants had drifted slightly south, revealing the top of his underwear. His expression was weirdly calm, like the face on someone reading an especially exciting book.

"Oh no," Corry said.

"Master Corry," he said, although he never, it seemed, actually looked at Corry. "Thank God you're here. I'm going to need your help."

Corry knew all too well that there was something slightly unhinged about Harvey Nilsson, but it never would have occurred to him that *he* was the one behind everything going on that day. It never occurred to him that it could be anybody he knew, actually, because everyone he knew was so nice.

Of course it was worse than that. Mr. Nilsson was the one person in the entire world he'd ever seen move in a way he couldn't foresee in the Secret Future. And he was waving a gun around.

Get out, get out, get out, he thought. His body turned and tried to do just that.

"Corry?" It was Violet's voice, and hearing it made him hesitate. "Oh, God, Corry get out of here!"

He heard the door close behind him, and the lock engage. *Oops.*

"Door's locked," he announced. He turned back around. Mr. Nilsson was still spinning slowly atop the table. Corry kept his eyes trained on him while speaking, as this seemed to be a wise thing to do. "I have a key, but... Mom, where are you?"

"Over here," she said. She was, as he'd thought, behind the chairs. There was a whole bunch of people back there with her, mostly along the floor beneath the windows.

"She's safe, Corry," said Mr. Nilsson. "Don't worry; I'll protect her."

"Um, okay," Corry said. He backed up until his butt was against the door, and then edged along the wall. Feeling the sturdy concrete behind him was a comfort at a time when his knees didn't want to hold him up. "Safe from who?"

"It's one of them," Mr. Nilsson said. "It came here for me."

"Harvey, let the boy come over here," said somebody from behind the chairs.

"Dr. Ames, I told you before to be quiet," said Mr. Nilsson. "I meant it."

Corry didn't know what to do but decided leaving was probably out of the question, as it would take him a long time to get the door open, and he didn't think Mr. Nilsson would want him to try. He could join Violet behind the chairs, but he was pretty sure once he got back there he wouldn't want to get out again, and being trapped like she was didn't strike him as all that exciting or necessarily all that safe. So he decided to pretend there was no gun and just talk.

"What do you want me to help you with?" he asked Mr. Nilsson, trying to sound like he wasn't about to wet himself.

"I need you to help me spot it. Only you and I can see him. I explained this to you."

"Y-yeah, okay. Is this why you shot all those people?"

"Don't be ridiculous. I didn't shoot anybody. It was *him*. He can manipulate things, don't you see? Make it look like somebody else. Do you think I alone could have done all of this? An old man and a handgun?"

He actually had a point. Carl, Ned, Mr. Conway, and all the others in the hallways... only some of them had been shot.

"Where do you want me to look?"

At least it's something to do, he thought. And so far Mr. Nilsson hadn't tried to shoot *him*, which was pretty good news. Maybe it was okay.

"No! Corry, come here right now!" Violet demanded.

"It's okay. I'm just gonna help Mr. Nilsson look for... what am I looking for?"

"You will know when you see."

"Right. Okay."

"Check under the tables."

And so Corry became Vision Boy, peering under tables and behind chairs, looking for a monster that only Mr. Nilsson could see. He could hear his mother crying in terror from behind the chairs. He sort of understood why she was so afraid and all, but still, it was embarrassing to have her making such a scene.

"I'm not having any luck," Corry said, after a few minutes.

His search had taken him pretty close to Mr. Nilsson, but he wasn't nearly strong enough to take the gun away, so he didn't try.

"Are you sure he's here?"

"Positive. I shot at him."

"Oh," Corry said. "Recently?"

"I don't know. The timeline is... I'm having trouble focusing, Corry. You understand how that can be sometimes."

"Yeah." He was having just that problem, because Mr. Nilsson kept moving in unanticipated ways. It made the whole Secret Future collapse when he looked in his direction, although sometimes it just blurred. It was an uneasy sensation, like trying to get your legs back under you right after getting off a roller coaster, except it wouldn't go away.

"Where was he then?" Corry asked. "When you last saw him. Where in the room?"

Mr. Nilsson lowered his gaze for just a second, long enough for Corry to note that this was an upsetting question for some reason.

"Near the chairs," he said.

Corry looked over at the chairs that were protecting everybody. One of the seat backs had a bullet hole in it. Behind the chair, on the ground, he saw blood. At least now he understood why Violet was so worried. There was a big difference between a guy waving a gun around and a guy waving a gun around and also shooting it at invisible monsters. He was starting to appreciate how unstable this situation really was. *Can't go back now.*

Staring at the bullet hole, he said matter-of-factly, "You missed him and hit somebody else instead."

"He moved!" Mr. Nilsson insisted.

"Who did? The invisible monster?"

"It's not . . . I *know* this sounds insane, Corry, but when you see—"

"Who did you shoot?" Corry said, his voice raised to a low yell.

"Now you're here, and you can help me fix it!"

"Who did you shoot, Mr. Nilsson? Who was behind the chair?"

"It's Osgood Pierce, Corry," his mother said.

Corry's heart, which had been drifting up his throat for the past few minutes, dropped right out the bottom of his stomach.

"Is he dead?" Corry shouted.

"No," said the doctor guy, Ames. "But he needs medical attention soon or he will be."

"How could you do that?" Corry asked Mr. Nilsson. "He didn't ever do anything to you. He's my friend!"

"We can fix this!"

"How? Are you going to go back in time and un-shoot him?"

Corry didn't even recognize the sound of his own voice at this point. The entire afternoon of horrors boiled down to a simple equation: Mr. Pierce was dying; Mr. Nilsson was going to let him; and Corry was going to have to stop him.

Mr. Nilsson looked taken aback by the burst of anger.

"Help me, and then we'll get him to a hospital. They won't see until I've killed—"

"Fuck you, you crazy old man! There's nothing here!" It was the first time he'd ever uttered a curse word around an adult, and he didn't even think about it.

"That's because he's *hiding*!" Mr. Nilsson insisted.

"Was he hiding behind Ned when you took his gun and shot him in the back?"

"I didn't *do* that! I told you—"

"Or how about Carl? Or Mr. Conway?"

"You have to—"

"You're a liar, Mr. Nilsson!"

"Don't move."

"You're crazy, and now my friend is dying, and—"

"I said *don't move*, Corry!" Mr. Nilsson barked.

Only then did Corry realize, first, that he was about ten feet away from the barrel of the gun, and second, that Mr. Nilsson was pointing it right at his head.

"Okay . . ." Corry said quietly.

Headless Teen. Brain-Dead Boy. The Faceless Wonder.

Mr. Nilsson took two calming breaths and steadied the gun. Corry looked right down the barrel and into the darkest place he'd ever seen.

"Corry," Mr. Nilsson whispered. "Listen to me. He's right behind you."

"Corry!" Violet called out.

"Harvey, don't...!" Dr. Ames said. There was a gaggle of half-choked off voices coming out from behind the chairs, all trying at once to talk Mr. Nilsson into not shooting, which Corry very much appreciated.

"Who's..." His voice caught on the rest of the words. He tried again. "Who's right behind me, Mr. Nilsson?"

"He's standing five feet behind you. He has the end of a mop in his hand. He's been sneaking up on people all afternoon, hitting them. It's... you were right. He's a monster."

"Guys . . . is there anybody standing behind me?"

"No, honey, there's nobody there!" Violet cried.

"See, Mr. Nilsson? Nobody there."

"They can't see him."

"Well, okay . . ." He had his hands out in front of him, palms up, shaking.

Calm down.

"How about this? How about I turn around, and if I don't see anybody either, you stop with the shooting and... and give me the gun or... give it to someone else if you want to."

"Trust me," Mr. Nilsson said. "I know what to do."

In the Secret Future, Corry saw Mr. Nilsson firing the gun. He saw himself move to get out of the way of the bullet, but then the future blurred when Mr. Nilsson adjusted to him moving and blinked out for a millisecond. Concentrating very hard, he saw himself trying out other possible futures, and wherever he dodged, Mr. Nilsson corrected. He was running out of time.

At the last possible moment, Corry did the one thing the future did *not* show him doing; he stood completely and utterly still. It was like Mr. Nilsson had described it when doing his secret talking—decide to do something and then, at the last moment, don't.

The gun fired, which was a ridiculously loud sound, but one for which—thanks to Charlie Bluff—Corry was somewhat prepared. Still, he winced at the sound and slammed his eyes shut without meaning to. When he opened them again, he discovered that he was still alive and didn't have any holes in him.

Mr. Nilsson was smiling.

"I got 'im. Finally. I got him." He fell to his knees on the table. "I'm so proud of you, young Corrigan."

In the Secret Future, Mr. Nilsson put the gun up to his temple and fired. But the gun was empty. Seeing this, and knowing Corry could see it as well, he just smiled, let the gun slide from his hands, and collapsed onto the table.

Corry walked over and picked up the gun.

"Corry, honey, no!" Violet shouted, still sounding desperately afraid, perhaps of what her son would do with a loaded gun in his hands. Hearing commotion behind him, Corry turned around and saw everyone swarming out from behind the chairs, more or less all at once.

"What are you doing?" Corry shouted at them. "Get an ambulance for Mr. Pierce!"

"We will," one of the lab coat guys said. "Just hand over the gun, son."

"Oh, right. It's not loaded. See?" He pointed it at the ceiling and pulled the trigger. The clicking noise confirmed for all of them that the gun was out of bullets.

For some reason—Corry couldn't imagine why—this caused his mom to faint.

A n hour later, after all the adults in the room finished freaking out and somebody contacted both an ambulance and every cop in the entire city of Belmont, Corry was sitting on a table in the public room next to Violet, who seemed unable to find a way to stop holding onto him.

"I'm all right, Violet, Jesus," he said, blushing.

"I'm sorry," she whispered. "I just thought—"

"I know what you thought. I'm sorry if I scared you, but…"

I was trying to rescue you, he wanted to say. And he *did*, which was why he really wished she'd quit babying him.

"You should have gone for help as *soon* as you saw something was wrong," she said, and now suddenly she was angry with him, which he completely did not get.

"I didn't think they'd believe me."

"You should have tried!"

"I thought I could help!" he snapped.

"You're just a child! What did you think—"

"Mom!" The unexpected use of her title in lieu of her given name stopped her in mid-lecture. He looked her in the eyes. "You know I'm not an ordinary twelve-year-old, don't you? I'm not like other kids."

"Of course. You're very special."

"Not special. Different," he said. "Like in Maine. You remember what happened in Maine."

"I..." She went back to being afraid again. He was beginning to wonder if maybe she should find some meds for herself.

"I didn't make the gun go off, Mom."

"I know, it's just—"

"No, you don't know. You won't let me talk about it, so you never get to hear what really happened. It wasn't my fault."

"Oh, Corry—"

"Charlie shot his own leg off. I heard it fire before you did, is all. I'm not some kinda devil child. I wanted to tell you..."

Violet began weeping just as soon as he started talking about Maine, and Corry had to stop talking because he was crying, too. She pulled him to her breast, hugging him tighter than he could ever remember being hugged.

"I never thought you were a devil child, baby," she whispered. "And I will always be proud of you."

This made him cry even more. So they sat there for a few minutes, getting one another wet.

"Well, there's the little hero," said someone from behind them. Violet loosened her grip, and Corry turned around to see that it was Dr. Ames.

Ames was a short guy, only a little taller than Corry, with long white hair that stood almost straight up and thick glasses that made him look like the Mole Man from the Fantastic Four comic books. As amusing as that comparison was, he had Osgood Pierce's blood on him, which was sobering.

"How's Mr. Pierce?" Corry asked.

"The paramedics think he'll pull through."

"Good. How about Mr. Nilsson?"

"Oh, don't worry about him. He won't be hurting anyone anymore."

Corry wasn't sure what that meant but was pretty positive it didn't mean they were going to kill him or anything like that only because he didn't think that sort of thing was done.

"Good," Corry said. "I guess."

Ames said, "Violet, is it? Is it all right if I talk to your son alone for a moment?"

She looked at him. "Corry?"

"It's okay," Corry said.

Violet glanced at Dr. Ames, then back at her son, as if gauging whether it was a prudent thing to leave her son in the company of anybody other than her any time soon.

"All right," she said finally. "But we have to get someone to look at this hand. The paramedics—"

"I'll be all right," he said, holding up the hand. His makeshift bandaging job was holding up well, and he wasn't looking forward to having it removed, as that would involve looking at the cut again. It could wait.

"I'll be right outside, then," she said.

"They're clearing the building, Violet," Dr. Ames said. "I'll bring him out back in a minute, and then we can get his hand tended to."

"Okay?" she asked, looking at Corry again.

"I know the way out, too," he said helpfully.

She smiled, staring at him for a few more seconds, and then walked out, escorted by one of the cops who were still pacing around the room, waiting for one of the chairs to do something illegal or whatever.

Dr. Ames stood in front of Corry and waited for Violet to be out of earshot.

"So how are you feeling, Corry?" Ames asked. He had his hands behind his back and kept rocking on the balls of his feet, which was the same thing Corry's fifth grade English teacher used to always do. It annoyed him.

"I'm fine."

"The hand?"

"Cut it on some glass," he said, fiddling absentmindedly with the bandage.

"Starting to throb now, is it?"

As soon as Ames said that, Corry realized yes, that was exactly what his hand was doing. It was a dull pain, but every time he flexed his hand it became a sharp one, so he stopped doing that.

"Yeah." He winced.

"That's the adrenaline," Ames said. "The adrenal gland's secretions tend to override the pain, and now that you've calmed down, it's going to start to hurt more, I'm afraid."

Corry didn't understand about half of what Ames had just said, so he only nodded.

Discussions of gland secretions were apparently what Ames considered small talk, and having gotten it out of the way, he moved on to the meat of the conversation.

"The reason I wanted to talk to you... Corry, you saw a lot of pretty terrible things today, didn't you?"

"I guess."

Ames sat next to him on the table. "Sometimes, when we see terrible things, we put them away for a while. In here." He tapped the side of his head. "Do you understand? It's not that we pretend they never happened. We just put them someplace in our heads where we don't have to think about them for a while."

"Sure," Corry said. "That happens to me in history class."

"History?"

"Yeah. I always forget the answers during the tests, but I remember them as soon as the test is over."

He nodded and patted Corry's knee in a sort of grandfatherly way. "It's almost like that." He smiled. "You seem to have dealt with all of this very well. Better than most of us, and that's a very rare thing."

"Oh," Corry said, surprised. It had seemed at first like he was heading for a lesson about some other glands, but this was okay. "Thanks."

"But... there may come a time when these terrible things you have put away come out when you don't want them to. And it will be difficult to put them back again. Do you understand?"

Corry nodded. "I think so. You're saying I'm gonna go crazy."

"No." He laughed. "Not crazy. Upset. Just upset. And I'm telling you now because I want you to know that when this happens, you may need to talk to someone. In fact, I think you should start talking to someone right away, just in case."

"I talk to people all the time," Corry said.

"I know. That isn't the kind of talking I mean. I mean more like the kind of talks we have here with the patients."

"So I *am* going to go crazy."

"No," he repeated slowly, like he was trying to train a puppy. "But you may become a bit confused. Corry, most adults would be seeking therapy after enduring what you survived today. Many of the ones here probably will. I'm suggesting you let me help you cope with all of this. Put it into perspective."

He looked about ready to put his hand on Corry's shoulder before deciding against it.

Ames continued. "When we leave here, I'm going to be speaking to your mother and recommending that you and I sit down once a week for at least a little while just to talk, like we are right now. But I'm telling you first—asking you, I should say

—because it strikes me that you are a young man who makes his own decisions about things. So how about it?"

"I wasn't planning to come back here again," Corry said. "Even before—"

"We don't have to come here," Ames said. "I have an office in Lexington. We can meet there."

Corry said, "I guess that'd be all right. I mean, for a little while."

"Good. And you know, if you'd rather talk to someone else, I would be happy to make the arrangements."

"Nah, you seem okay."

He smiled, taking it as a compliment. "That's set, then."

That should have been the end of their conversation, but Ames hesitated. He was looking down at his shoes for some reason.

"Can I leave now?" Corry asked.

"Yes, of course... is it all right if I ask you one more question? Before we go?"

"Sure."

"Harvey's reaction to you was... interesting."

"Well, he was kinda crazy."

"*Disassociated*, Corry. We prefer the term *disassociated*."

"Whatever."

"I was just wondering how often you interacted with him in the past. I know you've been visiting here for some time—"

"I dunno," Corry lied. "I didn't hardly know him at all."

"Curious. Because of all the people he could have chosen, you were the one he thought . . . never mind." He smiled. "I guess I'm a little rattled myself. He was my patient, you know." He slipped off the table and held out his hand for Corry. "Come on. Let's go find your mother."

Corry slid off the table without any help and headed for the door with Dr. Ames.

Around the room, police were still milling about, and a photographer was taking pictures, which Corry guessed was important, but he couldn't imagine why.

There was someone else there, too. Corry didn't spot him until he was nearly to the door. It was a short bald guy dressed in overalls. He didn't look like a cop, or like anybody Corry had ever seen in the hospital before.

The most curious thing about him was that he was sitting down against the wall and just... trying to breathe or something.

He had his hand—a funny hand, with really long fingers—over his stomach at first, but then he moved it, and Corry saw that he was wounded.

Having now seen a fair number of like wounds in his short lifetime, Corry could attest to the fact that it was from a gunshot. It looked really bad, like the guy was about to die. Nobody was helping him, and Corry was about to say something to that effect until he realized nobody else knew the man was there.

Don't let them know you can see them.

"Everything okay, Corry?" asked Dr. Ames, noting the young man's hesitation.

"Yeah," Corry said. "You know, I think talking will be good for me."

"I'm glad you feel that way."

"I don't want to end up like Mr. Nilsson."

"Don't worry," Ames said, putting a reassuring hand on Corry's shoulder. "That won't ever happen."

PART THREE

RED IN TOOTH AND CLAW

CHAPTER EIGHTEEN

Now

I t was five in the morning, the sun was not yet up, and Corrigan Bain stood naked before his wall map of the City of Boston, his hand extended, eyes closed, and lips prepared to utter the first location of the day.

He was trembling slightly, a direct consequence of having had almost no sleep for the past week, coupled with the beer he had the night before that had not entirely left his system.

The beer may have had something to do with why he was cold and sweating simultaneously and why his head had an entire percussion band inside of it slamming on the sides of his skull. But no, that was probably the vodka.

"You know you're not gonna get anything," said the boy from the hallway.

"Shut up. You're not here."

"Nope. Not here," the kid agreed.

He waited. There were flashes of heat but not in his hand, just his face and shoulders. He would have to go throw up soon.

Nothing. Nobody needed his help any more. It had been

nine days. He lowered his hand.

"Close program," he said. The computer chirruped.

"Told ya," the kid said.

Corrigan ignored the apparition, as there were other matters that needed his immediate attention. He took care of those matters by running to the bathroom and vomiting extensively, mostly into the toilet.

An hour later, he was camped on his overstuffed couch, chewing on a piece of dry toast and trying to decide if he should bother to put on any clothing today, while his gorgeous, big flat-screen television was showing him all the people he didn't save the day before. Most of them had died in a four-alarm fire in Allston he thought he probably could have done something about had he known ahead of time.

"Those poor people," Emily Jensen commented. She was an elderly woman who fell down the stairs in her apartment building on a snowy morning five winters ago while Corrigan was busy racing into the wrong building. She was sitting next to him on the couch. Except, of course, she wasn't.

"Yeah, breaks your heart, doesn't it? That's why I never watch the news."

"Oh, I never missed it."

"Figured you were more of a soap opera and game show-type."

"Maybe I was," she said, leaning back. Her head lolled to one side unnaturally, such that when she spoke to Corrigan she had to look up past her forehead. "I don't rightly remember."

"I could find out," he said. "Call your daughter or something. Would you like that? I'm not busy."

"You'd never do that," she said.

"No, you're probably right," he agreed, adding, "and now, the weather."

Corrigan said it a good three seconds before anybody on the

news did and used it to clarify where he was temporally. His voice was the only useful tool he had because his ghost companions were still absent any futures. It made living with them unsettling, but on the plus side, it was an excellent way to prove they weren't really there. Which, of course they weren't.

"This is what happened to you, isn't it, Harvey?" he asked. His words came back to him twice, which was bad.

"Who's Harvey?" the boy asked. He was sitting behind the chair and throwing a ball against the wall.

"That's that old crazy dude he used to know," answered Ndeki, formerly a dreadlocked, club-hopping biker with a bad habit of taking his bicycle on Storrow Drive, and now a somewhat amiable ghost lying on the coffee table of the guy who got hung up in traffic that day. The right side of his body was compressed toward the center of him, like a locked accordion.

Of the nine days Corrigan had gone without a work schedule, the last three had been spent dealing with the routine appearances of the ghosts during his waking hours. They had been appearing here and there even before his recent meltdown, but silently. Now they talked all the time, and no matter how much he yelled at them, they refused to leave.

He hated to admit it, but he was sort of enjoying the company. Plus, during the day they hardly ever gave him a hard time about not having saved them, reserving that horror show for when he tried to sleep. The only real drawback to having them all there was that he was pretty sure he'd gone mad.

He got up off the couch. He was still sitting on the couch thinking about getting up. He stepped around the pizza boxes and over the woman in the blue suit, who was sleeping on the floor. He got up off the couch.

Focus!

He stepped around the pizza boxes, over the blue suit, and into the kitchen.

"You look kinda pale," the boy noted.

"Can't find the present, kid," he said, and now his words were coming back to him three times, like he was standing in an echo chamber.

He opened the refrigerator and grabbed a beer. He didn't grab a beer. He grabbed a bottle of water. That was what he needed, not beer. No more beer. He drank the water, which tasted like beer until his decision to drink a beer vanished into the nonexistence of a future that didn't happen, going to wherever it was those hypothetical futures always went.

He closed the fridge door. He closed it again. He left the kitchen.

"I'm not Harvey Nilsson," he declared, closing his eyes. Finding the present was like trying to dock a boat on a fast-moving river.

"Of course you're not," said someone from his easy chair.

Corrigan walked back into the living room and noticed all the ghosts were gone. No, that wasn't right. Someone with no future had said something from the chair.

He stepped around the coffee table and got a good look.

"Harvey?" he asked.

"In the flesh," Harvey Nilsson said. "More or less. How good it is to see you again, young master Corry."

"Oh no," Corrigan whispered. He sat down on the edge of the couch— recently occupied by Emily—and stared at the face of a man who died more than twenty-five years ago.

Corrigan Bain has gone insane.

"You don't look happy to see me," Harvey said. "After all this time, do I still frighten you?"

"It's not that, Mr. Nilsson," Corrigan said, reverting without realizing it to the title he used for the old man back when he was twelve. "It's that . . . if you're here, then it's really true; I've lost my mind."

"Possibly so."

D r. Frederick Allan Ames, former assistant director of McClaren Hospital, former professor-in-residence at Boston University, former husband of the now-deceased Molly Ames *née* Blackwell, and current resident of the Norris Retirement Community, did not have B7.

He very much wanted to have B7, and stared longingly at the six Bingo cards on the table before him on the off chance one of the numbers he *did* have had transformed magically into B7, but this didn't work. To make matters worse, Estelle Wilson, two rows up and one chair to the right, did have B7. He knew this because whenever she had a match, she thanked Jesus for it, loudly and fervently, as if Jesus gave a flying fuck.

Ames chewed on the edge of the chip he'd been hoping for the past few minutes he'd get to put down somewhere, and waited for the next number to be called. This was what his life had become—waiting impatiently for a little spark of excitement. Only a little. Too much and his heart might just shrug and give up, something it had done twice in the past fourteen months before paramedics convinced it to get going again. Sometimes he caught himself just sitting still and feeling his heart beat in his chest to see if heightened scrutiny would cause it to stop again.

Unhealthy was what it was. He knew that as well as anyone. But, as he'd heard thousands of times before from people far worse off, he just couldn't help himself.

"Dr. Ames," said one of the young interns, whispering in his ear. She'd snuck right up on him while he was busy listening for the next number or for his heart to stop, whichever came first.

"Yes?" he asked. He turned and noted that when she leaned

forward, he could see right down the neck of her blouse. She was trying to kill him—that's what it was.

"There's an urgent phone call for you. From your nephew."

Ames stared blankly at the intern's breasts and said, "Nephew? Miss . . . " he glanced at the nametag, "Beverly, I don't believe I *have* a nephew."

She smiled the patronizing sort of smile one develops when working with the pathologically elderly.

"He said to tell you his name is Corrigan. I don't know if that's his first name or last, but..."

"Cor—Yes, yes of course. My nephew. How stupid of me." His mind succumbed to a lengthy flashback his body didn't have time for, and his stomach pirouetted, twice. He hoped none of this showed on his face. "What is it my nephew Corrigan wants?"

"He says there's been..." she leaned in closely for a whisper, "a death in the family."

One didn't say the *D* word too loudly in a place that was single-handedly raising the mortality rate of Newton Upper Falls by three percent.

"I should go take that call then, shouldn't I?"

He tossed the chip on the table as the caller onstage declared another combination Ames was pretty positive he didn't have on any of his boards. It was just as well he was quitting. Plus, this was easily the most excitement he'd had in a year, and he hadn't even answered the telephone yet.

Beverly helped him to his feet and handed him his cane, which was one of those damned metal ones with the four-pronged feet. The whole place was full of them, which meant everyone had the same sort of trouble pedestrians with open umbrellas have navigating sidewalks. Except most pedestrians don't fall over when you knock their umbrellas askew.

Without being asked, the intern took his arm at the elbow

and walked him patiently—i.e. slowly, as he was on his second hip and third knee—down the church pew-sized row to the side door. His departure in mid-Bingo caused a mild ripple of interest, which would surely turn into a tremendously complex bit of gossip by dinnertime—not that he particularly cared.

Ames was what one might call *maladjusted* to his current lot in life. Specifically, he hated being old and wished on more than one occasion that he had not outlived his wife—even though she divorced him two years before her own death due in large part to the aforementioned maladjustment. If he were to ever adopt a "physician, heal thyself" mentality, he might even conclude that he was in dire need of antidepressants. Sadly, he usually didn't care enough to show any interest in making himself less miserable, so that was out of the question.

The side door led to a wide corridor with the hall he'd just left on one side and large, tinted picture windows on the other. Through the window one could see the rotunda that stood before the visitors center and beyond that the brick walls and iron gates that marked the boundary of the gated community/elderly hospice/hell on Earth.

It was a place where older persons such as himself might move if they wanted all the disadvantages of an old age home combined with all of the disadvantages of living alone in a private condo *and* all the disadvantages of living in New England. And people wondered why he was grouchy.

The telephone took a few minutes to get to, as it was at the front desk and they had left by the least convenient door, but when they did get there the phone line was still lit up. Beverly helped him around to the back of the desk, sat him down, and handed him the receiver.

Corrigan Bain was already talking. "...to finally find you," he said.

"What? Corrigan? It's... uh, it's Uncle Fred. What were you saying?"

There was a pause.

"I'm sorry. I'm ahead."

"That's all right," he said. "I'm glad you found me, too. It's good to hear a friendly voice. You said there was a death?"

Pause.

"I had to say that. They wouldn't find you for me otherwise."

"Yes, of course. But something is the matter."

"Something is the matter," Corrigan agreed, and then added, "Harvey suggested I call you."

"Harvey? Not Harvey Nilsson. But he died back in—"

"I know. He's in my living room right now. I'm... I'm a little confused, Doctor. Haven't been able to sleep for, oh, nine or ten days now because of the ghosts and... and well, Harvey said I should do this, and I think he may be right."

"Corrigan, where are you?"

"It's what we were always afraid of, isn't it, Doc?"

"Where are you, Corrigan?"

"At home."

"Can you find a way to get to me?"

Pause.

"I'm kind of afraid to go out in public right now."

"Then I'll have to go to you. Can you tell me your address?"

Corrigan did. Ames scribbled it down on a notepad and then said, "I'll take a cab and be there as soon as I can, all right?"

"Okay. I should put on some clothes, huh?"

"I think that would be for the best."

Ames hung up and noticed that Beverly was still loitering around the desk. "Your friend Harvey died?" she asked.

"Yes, very sad. I wonder if you could have one of those golf carts take me to my condo for a couple of things. And then I'll need a cab."

CHAPTER NINETEEN

Now

Cold.

The whole case had gone cold. Maggie Trent hated to admit it, but it was the truth.

This happened a lot more often than anybody in the FBI would ever care to admit. Sometimes, there just wasn't enough evidence. Either the guilty party stopped doing whatever it was they had been doing and never got caught, or they kept going and eventually slipped up somewhere. What frightened her was that this might be one of those rare occasions when the bad guy had no intention of stopping, while at the same time the FBI had no hope of catching him.

It was, in short, the kind of case most agents spent their entire careers trying to avoid.

As she sat in her cubicle with the voluminous case file weighing down the center of her desk, the words Randall Hicks had spoken to her not ten minutes earlier still hung in the air like a rain cloud.

"Bury it," he ordered. "For the sake of your own career."

GENE DOUCETTE

While it killed her to admit it, he was right. All she had to do was declare the deaths to be an unusual mixture of accidents and suicides, plus one *unrelated* home invasion, and she could put it to bed and go back to the usual terrorism task forces and money laundering seminars. The best part—it was easily the most logical conclusion. It's what Randy and everyone else in the building would have done already.

But it was wrong. And five years from now, after she'd buried the case under piles of open cases, after another five or ten kids from MIT ended up dead because she thought of her career first? It would still be wrong.

She flipped the case file open for the umpteenth time and wandered through, either looking for a good excuse to put it to bed or for the one thing she missed that would make all the difference.

Her fingers stopped at a part of the case she only dimly understood. It was a handwritten brief of Archibald Calvin's big idea, penned by Calvin himself and handed over only under duress.

Much of the text was easy enough to understand, but it was followed by a dozen pages of mathematical calculations using a symbology that, if pressed, Maggie might have identified as Martian. She'd been led to conclude that were she to show the entire thing to anyone with an advanced math background, they were as likely as not to simply stroke out on the spot.

Maggie stood up and looked around. It was ten minutes before five and the office was nearly empty. Not because most of her coworkers quit early but because there was a big law enforcement gala going on across the street. Randy was speaking, and nobody wanted to be the one agent with nothing to say about his speech. Maggie even had a slinky black dress still in dry cleaners' plastic hanging on the side of her wall just above a matching pair of sling backs. She'd been waiting all day to slip

258

into that outfit. But that was before her boss had told her to ignore a murderer. Now she wasn't in the mood.

Satisfied there was nobody around who would rat her out if she was spotted still reviewing the Dead-End Case From Hell, she sat back down to go over Calvin's notes one more time.

Archie Calvin started off with three questions.

How did Corrigan Bain see the future?

Why did he see only a few seconds of it?

Where did the possible futures—the ones he'd altered out of existence—go?

For the second and third questions, he proposed a hypothesis. From a probabilistic standpoint, there were *very* likely futures and *less* likely futures. Starting from the present and moving one second ahead there were, macroscopically, a limited number of possible outcomes. One second after that, there were contingent outcomes based on what had happened in the first second. And so on.

He argued that up until five or six seconds passed—it got shorter as more variables were introduced—the most likely future, or as he called it, "the path of greatest likelihood," was predictably evident. After that, the number of contingent outcomes was too great for there to be a clearly defined path.

Corrigan couldn't pin down definitively how many seconds into the future he could see, and the reason was that it depended on where he was at the time and how many "objects" were in play. Hypothetically, in a room by himself, he would be able to see several minutes ahead, although he wouldn't know he was. But in a crowded room he might see only three or four seconds.

Whenever Corrigan altered the future substantially, he

complained that a brief period followed in which the future simply disappeared. She remembered him describing it as like temporarily losing sight in one eye. Calvin reasoned that the problem had nothing to do with Corrigan losing track of the future. Within the region in which Corrigan had acted, that future briefly ceased to exist. He was forcing it to reset.

Maggie was with Calvin for all of that. It made so much sense she wished Corrigan Bain were answering her phone calls so she could explain it to him. He might even find it useful in his work.

But when Calvin went about answering the first question— how it was possible to see the future at all—she got dizzy.

He reasoned that Corrigan's block of time might be eminently knowable precisely *because* of its invariant nature. He coined a term for it—*chronoton*—that borrowed from subatomic particle names. The *chronoton* was "a period of time bounded by the limit of contingent likelihood."

From this he suggested that as a practical matter, there was no reason why an ordinary soul such as himself should not be able to view more than just a point on the *chronoton*—the "point" being the very front tip of it, or, more urbanely, the present. Just because it hadn't happened yet, he argued, didn't mean it wasn't real. It simply existed further down the time line. He then embarked on a chain of reasoning that could be summarized as, *if it's real, it can be seen.*

This launched him into another several paragraphs on Corrigan, whom he described as "unbounded by the one-dimensional present on the arrow of time and thus not subject to its laws." But the big questions had less to do with what Corrigan was than with what happened as a consequence of his actions. *He* could change events taking place within the *chronoton*, and that, based on Calvin's own theorizing, should not be possible.

In altering the future, Corrigan must therefore be temporarily shortening the *chronoton*—severing the arrow of time, as it were—which was the real reason why the future disappeared briefly whenever a change was effected.

Calvin then drew an interesting conclusion. He said that while Corrigan could change the future, nobody else, being bound by time's laws, could do the same. He wrote, "It is only possible to view the entire *chronoton because* it is invariant. An explicit alteration of an event within the period would fore-shorten the *chronoton*, making it impossible for the viewer to *see* the event he seeks to alter: a paradox. Ergo, the viewer can only view that which is not only unchanged but that which is, by its nature, *unchangeable*."

Maggie was pretty sure she understood this all right, although it did make her head swim when she tried to follow the logic's circuitous path too carefully. But from there Calvin took a dive into ridiculous complexity, almost dropping the English language entirely in favor of lengthy mathematical equations. The gist of all the math, or so he assured her, was that it proved the existence of the *chronoton* and hypothesized that a method for accessing it was possible.

Taken from cover to cover, the whole thing read like a bunch of Star Trek science-fiction doublespeak, which was how Maggie might have taken it if it weren't for the fact that the team at MIT had apparently done it.

Great for them—except it was getting them killed, and she still didn't know why.

———

She flipped ahead and found the list of the postgrads who had participated in at least a part of the project. Before the deaths began there were thirty of them, plus Offey. Most of the surviving members of the list were still out of town, and over the past few days she'd spoken with every one of them by phone just to make sure they were still alive. Clearly they were.

The killer, it seemed, preferred to wait until they returned—provided he even intended to kill them all, which was an open question. Calvin's assumption was that there was only one aspect of the project's execution that was "causing" the deaths, which was reasonable insofar as Calvin himself was still alive. But until one of the postgrads spoke up, there was no telling what aspect it was and which of the remaining survivors were in danger.

The lab vandalism Erica told Tanya about had also ended up being a dead end, only because MIT was being institutionally pigheaded. What she needed to know was which lab it was, and who on her list of names had access to it. Hopefully, this would give her an idea of how many people were still at risk. But the university wasn't interested in promoting the notion that their students were in danger of being murdered by a phantom, and had resolved to be as unhelpful as possible. Like Randy, they'd just as soon wait until the whole matter went away.

"Maggie?" Karen said from behind her. She jumped at the sound of the voice. "Sorry, didn't mean to disturb you."

Maggie turned. "No, it's okay. My mind was elsewhere. What's up?"

Karen Taylor, dressed in a very smart-looking, albeit ill-fitting evening gown, looked ready to go and hit that bar across the street—hard.

"You coming?" Karen asked.

"Oh! What time is it?"

"Five-fifteen. Our boy is onstage in another twenty."

"Yeah, right, okay." She glanced at her own dress, which really desperately wanted to be worn. "You guys go on ahead. I have to change."

FIXER

"You sure?" she asked. "Because two or three of us walking in late looks a lot better than just one of us walking in late. Besides, I don't really want to hear the whole speech, do you?"

"Go," Maggie insisted. "I'll see you there."

"All right. I'll hold a drink for you."

"Thanks, hon. Think I'll need it."

"I bet you will."

Karen smiled. She, and probably everyone else in the place, knew exactly what the details of her afternoon meeting with Randy had been all about. It was hard not to know these things in this kind of office, populated as it was by federal employees whose expertise lay in detecting things.

Karen took off, joining a number of tuxedoed agents for the *en masse* exit. Maggie listened for the elevator chime and then counted to five.

"Hey," she called loudly, "anybody here?"

Silence.

"Good enough."

The women's room for the floor was down the hall, past the elevators, down another hall, and to the right. She figured by changing at her desk she could cut four or five minutes off her time, with the only possible drawback being someone from the staff or the cleaning crew—which usually didn't show until after seven—spotting her in a stage of undress. It was a moderate risk but worth taking, especially since she was already wearing the appropriate undergarments.

She had succeeded in stripping down to said undergarments when her line rang.

"No, not now, not now," she muttered. She picked up the line. "Agent Trent."

It was the hospital.

Erica Smalls was awake.

Erica's survival was one of the few things about the case that had gone right, but only barely so. The girl lost a ton of blood and narrowly escaped permanent damage to a number of vital organs. According to the paramedics, her heart stopped twice on the way to the hospital and then once more during the nearly twelve-hour surgery to clean up the damage.

And after that she was put into a medically-induced coma from which the hospital didn't fully expect her to wake.

Taking the doctors at their word, neither did Maggie.

Still, Maggie thought it would be prudent to keep Erica's battle for survival a secret while her killer was still loose. Outside of certain hospital staff and one or two people in the FBI office, nobody except for Tanya and Erica's parents knew.

And now she was awake.

It was her first decent break in the case, but it came at an especially bad time. Maggie needed to turn up for the gala, and if she didn't her absence would be noticed. More importantly, her boss would be incredibly pissed if she not only skipped his speech, but skipped his speech to follow up on a case he told her to bury. She was, in short, standing at the crossroads of a career decision.

"I'll be right there," she said, hanging up.

But not in her underwear. She glanced at the business suit and white blouse she'd just thrown off, now laying haphazardly across her chair, and then the dress.

"Screw it," she said, tearing the dry cleaning plastic off.

CHAPTER TWENTY

Now

It took somewhere in the neighborhood of three hours to get Dr. Frederick Ames from Newton to East Cambridge, thanks to a series of delays that started with the difficulty of locating a cab company that would get him there for a rate he considered less than obscene and ended with the fact that he didn't move too fast, even when he wanted to. So he was not in an altogether fantastic mood when, having finally made it to the proper building, the concierge at the front desk refused to let him get on the elevator.

"I'm sorry, sir, but if you are not an invited guest—"

"I *am* an invited guest, young man," he snapped. "Corrigan Bain is expecting me."

"Yes, sir, so you've said. But Mr. Bain didn't call down with any instructions."

Ames leaned over the desk. "Son, look at me. Do you think I'm planning to burgle anybody? You suppose there's some sort of weapon hidden in this cane?"

"I understand that, sir. But I've rung Mr. Bain twice, and he's not answering. So—"

"Ring him again, then."

"We have a policy—"

"Ring. Him. Again."

The concierge stared at him. "All right, one last time. But you understand that the policy—"

"I've heard your damn policy."

"Yes, sir. No need to be rude, sir."

Dr. Ames could think of a thousand reasons to be rude. But he kept quiet, as the fellow at the desk had picked up the phone again.

"Mr. Bain! Sorry to disturb you, but there's a gentleman... yes... right away." He hung up the phone. "You can go right up, sir. Take the second elevator to the seventh floor, then take a right."

"Thank you," Ames said, trying out his gracious voice. "So what was the problem?"

The concierge sighed. "As I said, the policy is—"

"No, no, no. I'm not senile, dammit. I mean, what was Corrigan's problem? Why didn't he answer before, did he say?"

The man looked embarrassed. "I'm not—"

"Come on, son. I'm his doctor, you can tell me."

"Well... he said he wasn't entirely sure the phone was really ringing the first two times he heard it."

"Ah. Of course. Happens to me all the time."

"Uh, yes..."

"Second elevator, you said?"

"Yes, sir."

"I thank you."

Two minutes later, after a ride on a lift so rapid it actually buckled his knees when it launched, Ames was standing outside the door to Corrigan's condominium. He reached out to knock but saw it was ajar, so he just pushed his way in.

"Corrigan?"

The door opened directly into a horizontal corridor, meaning he was facing a white wall that was just crying out for some kind of artwork.

"Corrigan, it's Dr. Ames. Are you here?"

"In here."

The call came from his left, so he hobbled over in that direction, past a small kitchen space and into a barely lit living room. Or dining room. It had a little of both.

The only light in the room came from a muted television hung on the wall, and since the windows faced the east, there wasn't much of the early evening sunlight to help things. But he could make out the figure on the couch all right.

"There you are," Ames said. "Put on some lights in here for chrissake."

"Sorry," Corrigan said. He pulled himself off the couch and tiptoed awkwardly across the room, like he was dodging land mines on the floor trying to get to Ames, whom he greeted with a handshake.

Ames looked up. He'd forgotten how tall the boy had grown.

"Glad you could come."

"That's all right," Ames said, the neediness in his host's voice disarming him to the degree that he'd almost entirely forgotten he was grouchy. "It sounded important."

"Shut up," Corrigan said.

"I'm . . . sorry?"

"No, not you. The kid. Will, I think his name was. He said you look... well, he said something unkind. Let me get that light."

Ames looked around the room as Corrigan adjusted the lighting. There was clearly nobody else there.

GENE DOUCETTE

"He's a ghost," Corrigan explained. Ames had been about to ask him which kid he was talking about. "Bit of a brat, but he's all right most times. At least when I'm awake he is. Oh. And Harvey says hello."

"Harvey's here," Ames said levelly.

"Yeah. In the chair."

"Then I won't be sitting there. Why don't you tell me which space is currently unoccupied?"

M aggie pulled into the parking garage of Mount Auburn Hospital at just before six, making what had to be a new rush hour land speed record. Parking in the lot adjacent to the main building, she half-jogged to the lobby entrance, her expensive little purse—which matched the dress and shoes very nicely—slapping up against her back thanks to the extra weight from the dangerous little handgun she'd shoved inside it at the last minute. She made a note to move the gun from the bag into the pocket of her jacket, an inexpensive knockoff of a London Fog that didn't go with anything, as soon as she was by herself long enough to do so.

She was busy reviewing the room and floor number on the scrap of paper in her hand when, heading through the lobby, she nearly bowled over a cameraman for a local news affiliate.

"Excuse me," she said, smiling. The cameraman scowled, having almost dropped a very expensive piece of equipment, and then thought better of it when he saw Maggie.

"Not a problem," he said, suddenly grinning. He appeared ready to say something else in an attempt to prolong the conversation at least long enough so that Maggie could take the coat off, but she was already past him by then and heading for the elevators.

"Please, please, please," she muttered while waiting for the elevator to arrive and pulling out her phone. "*Please* don't tell me they're here for the same reason I am."

As the first real human being Corrigan Bain had seen in about a week, Dr. Ames was something of a shock. He seemed to be occupying a full six seconds of time simultaneously, and the muscle, or whatever it was, Corrigan routinely exercised to distinguish the present and navigate his way through had apparently atrophied irreparably.

It was as though he was five years old again and throwing snowballs out behind Bluff Commune.

"Why don't you tell me why you haven't been sleeping, Corrigan?" Ames was saying, over and over again, from the couch. He was sitting right where Emily had been a few minutes earlier, before Corrigan asked her to move.

"It's complicated," Corrigan answered, hoping he'd waited long enough first for the question to have actually been asked out loud.

"I'm sure it is. How long has it been?"

"I don't know. Seven, eight days, maybe."

Ames leaned forward, leaned forward, leaned forward. "What happens when you try to sleep?"

"The ghosts keep me up."

"Hey, don't blame us," blue suit said. She was still on the floor, right near Corrigan's feet, as he was still standing near the light switch. In a moment or two he'd be walking over to the couch. He was still standing near the light switch.

"Yeah," said the kid. "We're not even here, remember?"

"Quiet, both of you," Corrigan said.

"Are the ghosts speaking to you right now?" Ames asked.

"Yes."

"Who are they?"

"Just people," Corrigan said. "The ones I didn't get to save."

"Ah. And have you always seen them?"

"I don't know. Not always. Probably not always. I've been seeing them during the day here and there but... it wasn't a big deal. Not like when they turned up at night. See, whenever I screwed up, I'd get a visit that evening, and it would be bad, but the next day I'd have new appointments, and things would work out, and they would go away again."

"Why didn't that happen this time?"

"I didn't have any appointments." He headed for the couch and sat down. He headed for the couch.

"And why do you suppose that was?"

"I don't know. Something happened at the last appointment that I don't understand."

"Yeah, he didn't save me," blue suit said.

"Shut up." He sat down. "The timeline diverged or something. I picked the wrong one to follow."

"Do you suppose that this . . . divergence is what's preventing you now from getting any new appointments?"

"I don't see how. It's not like I'm in control of that. You know how it works. I told you about it before."

"Yes," Ames said, smiling. "I remember it well. You said you were receiving messages from..."

"The universe," Harvey said.

"...the universe," Ames said. "That's what Harvey told you would happen. Am I remembering correctly?"

"Yes."

Corrigan glanced at Harvey, who was nodding knowingly. Harvey had barely spoken while they were waiting for Ames to show, and even appeared to doze off a couple of times, but now he looked engaged.

"Except," Ames said, "I think we both know that's not really the case, don't we?"

"Get me Masterson," Maggie barked as soon as she reached the door to Erica Smalls's private room in ICU. The cop at the door did a double take, as he was not accustomed to taking orders from runway models. Then he recognized her.

"Where were you?" he asked. "Fashion show?"

"I was at a function," she said. "And now I'm here. There are news teams downstairs from more than one station about to tape their preamble for the eleven o'clock broadcast. Wanna take a guess what they're reporting?"

He blinked. "Masterson. Right." He radioed into the station.

Maggie paced outside the door and reviewed the defenses. They were standing in a wide corridor right around the corner from the ICU reception desk. Points of entry were three elevators with four sets of doors—where the unusual fourth set belonged to the elevator that came up in the middle of a split corridor—and the stairwells. There were three of those: one opening right next to the elevators and two fire-exit-only ones at the near and far ends of the floor. The entire floor itself was a warren of doors and walls, signs and walkways. None of the doors locked.

"He's off duty," the uniform said.

"All right," she said. "I'll get him at home." She called his profile up on her phone.

"Miss, you're not supposed to be using that here," a helpful nurse said as she walked past, pointing even more helpfully at the sign on the wall that said the same thing in four colors and three languages.

"Arrest me," Maggie growled, fingering the auto-dial.

"I don't know where the messages come from," repeated Corrigan. "I just wake up knowing where to go."

"I'm aware that this is what you believe is happening. Let's examine that for a moment."

"This is getting interesting," Harvey said.

"Quiet," Corrigan shot back.

Ames, who was doing an admirable job ignoring the ghosts in the room, continued. "You got that letter from Harvey when you were twenty-one, yes?"

"Yeah. I showed it to you."

"You did. Do you still have it? I'm just curious."

"I don't remember," Corrigan lied.

It was locked up in a strongbox in the bottom drawer of his office, along with his bankbooks and a few clippings that were meant to someday become part of a scrapbook.

"Young Master Bain."

Harvey began to recite his own letter.

"I imagine this has all come as something of a shock, and for that I apologize."

"Will you stop that," Corrigan snapped.

"Is that Harvey now?" Ames asked.

"He's reading his own letter back to me. Third time today."

"Ah." Ames smiled.

"There were many times in the years since our last encounter when I considered attempting to contact you, but the truth is, I am not a brave enough man. I could not bring myself to face the likely prospect of your scorn. This letter, then, like much of my life, is the coward's way out."

"As I was saying," Ames said, "when you got that letter you were working as a fry cook in some god-awful place."

"As my lawyers have undoubtedly explained in painful detail, using dozens of unnecessarily large words, I have decided to give all of my money to you. This is a gift, but it does not come without a price."

Ames went on. "Suddenly, at twenty-one, you became one of the richest men in the city, but to keep that money, you had to swear an oath to a dead man."

"Understand that, much like yourself, I did not begin my life with great wealth. The money I am forwarding in your name was earned through many years of hard work and dutiful cheating. By that I mean I put the curse you and I share to good use—often shamefully so. It was not until many years later that I even knew to feel guilty about it."

Corrigan was having a hell of a time paying attention to both of them at once. It helped only a little that he could keep up with Ames by listening to him twice, and that he already knew what Harvey was saying by heart. Still, it was a lot to take in.

"I didn't *have* to do anything," Corrigan said. "The money was mine either way."

"True. But you felt obligated to, as Harvey well knew you would."

"And so, here is the price. I have given you enough money to ensure that you never want for the rest of your life. In return, I am asking you to do what I never could—help people. How you do that is up to you."

Ames said, "Despite being insane, Harvey was a good judge of people. He knew you would do what he wanted. But the question for you became, how?"

"This may sound to you like the foolish decision of an old man who is trying to get into heaven. But I am not a religious person, and if I were, I would know that no amount of last-second penitence would affect my ultimate destination. Having said that, I do think you and I were given this talent for a reason. Now, if you are asking yourself

how you can possibly apply your curse toward the greater good, I say the universe will provide a way."

"The universe will provide a way," Corrigan repeated.

"Just so," Ames agreed.

"I am taking quite a risk, giving you this money. I have no way of knowing if you have, in the intervening years since that awful day, grown into the man I saw you on the way to becoming. I can only hope you have."

"And when a way *was* provided," Ames said, "you didn't ask yourself how or why, you just followed along. You're still just following along, because you believe you must."

"Please, take seriously what I am asking of you. And if in the future, you find you've lost your way, think back to that young man and the day he tried to be a hero. That boy saw something wrong with his world and had to fix it, and he was braver than most adults could ever hope to be. Don't lose sight of your potential, young Corrigan. Even if you hate me, you can at least do me the honor of being a better man than I was."

Harvey finished his recitation and lowered his head, as if this had been his whole reason for being in the room. Ames, who Corrigan was nearly positive couldn't hear Harvey, picked up the conversation as if he had been tag teaming with the old ghost the whole time.

"But here is the question you should have been asking yourself, Corrigan: why did you not get these messages *before* Harvey gave you all of his money?"

"That's easy," Corrigan said. "It wasn't my job before then."

"All right…" Ames said, shifting in his seat. "A dodge, but all right. Try this then. Why do you suppose it is that the universe wishes you to save *these* people, and not some *other* people?"

"I dunno. Never thought about it."

"I imagine there are those worth saving who happen to come

under risk at, say, two in the morning. Do you get messages about them?"

"No."

"How about people who live outside the Commonwealth? Or ones who are murdered or die of natural causes? Why does the universe ignore them?"

"I don't see what you're getting at," Corrigan said.

"Yes, you do," Harvey said.

"Quiet, Harvey."

"My point is that everyone you save is within your limits. Physically, geographically, and temporally. You never have a scheduling conflict, you never have to travel great distances, and you never end up facing a situation that you cannot resolve."

"The ghosts would disagree with that last part," Corrigan said.

"The ghosts come from the same place your messages do. In here." He tapped his own head. "You, my boy, are a disaster area of misplaced guilt and misinterpreted cause and effect. You've convinced yourself that the only way to keep these manifestations of failure from haunting you is by working harder, and that conclusion has prevented you from dealing with your real problems. Now you're in a hell you've constructed for yourself, and the reason you cannot get out of it is that you refuse to recognize an important truth. Something happened to you nine days ago that upset your apple cart. Until you figure out what that was and why it had such an effect, you will continue to block the messages, the ghosts will continue to haunt you, and I will be calling my friends at McClaren to reserve a room."

Corrigan took all of that in a couple of times. Harvey, who was nodding through the whole thing, said in regards to the conclusion, "Stay the hell away from McClaren, boy. I was fine before they sent me there."

Corrigan ignored him. "That's a lot to absorb," he said.

"I know. I'm sorry. Under normal circumstances I would try and lead you to the point where you arrive at these conclusions on your own, but these are not normal circumstances."

"Meaning I'm a hair away from getting committed?"

"Meaning I'm old and expect to die soon."

CHAPTER TWENTY-ONE

Now

I t had been quite a strange day for Erica. It started with her waking up from a coma and discovering that (a) she was still alive, (b) she'd lost nine days, and (c) her parents were in town. (A) was probably the biggest shock of all, although (c) came close. One does not often survive the experience of being stabbed, as far as she knew, when there was nothing preventing her assailant from stabbing her a few more times—other than a screaming Tanya. And why would that have stopped him, really?

The coma was a weird experience. She had vague recollections of conversations taking place in her presence—of people speaking *to* her sometimes—but the details of those conversations were lost to her. Still, she recalled the confusion well. It had been as if someone had shut the world off but forgotten to hit the volume button.

At one point she decided everyone thought she was dead and these were people speaking at her own funeral. She kept trying to tell them it wasn't true, that she was still *in* herself somewhere and they had to try and find her, because someone had obviously made some sort of horrible mistake.

She was surprised to have woken up in a place other than a coffin.

When she came to, her mom and dad and Tanya were all there, looking alternately excited and on the verge of tears.

An Indian woman—her doctor, it turned out—who spoke to her as if they were old friends was by her side and asking her questions. Did she know where she was? Did she know *who* she was? She liked the sound of the doctor's voice and wondered if maybe they *did* know each other. Later she realized hers was one of the voices she had been listening to while in the coma.

After a question-and-answer session, in which it was established that Erica knew who she was and could infer that she was in a hospital, it was decided by all that it would be an excellent idea if she got some sleep. She had no objections to this decision, as breathing and talking turned out to be much harder than she remembered and besides, sleep was different from a coma, which she'd had quite enough of.

She dreamed of the others. In a way, this was an indication that her brain was well, because that's exactly what she did every night for a month leading up to the attack. It was a happy dream, with everybody celebrating again, except that each time she turned around to talk to one of her friends, they suddenly weren't there anymore.

When she woke up again a couple of hours later, she felt more like herself. Parts of her brain that hadn't been used for a long time stood up and stretched and began jogging lightly.

As a test, she ran through a couple of differential equations she'd memorized long ago, by way of a mnemonic technique. The equations were put to nursery rhyme tunes. By the time she opened her eyes again, she'd been humming the nursery rhymes for several minutes, which made the only other occupant of the room curious. Tanya was sitting where she had been earlier, gripping Erica's hand as if one of them was in danger of drowning.

"Where..." Erica tried. Speaking was harder with only one fully functioning lung. She gave it another shot. "Where is everybody?"

Tannie said, "Your mom and dad went back to their hotel. Something about Valium and mini-bars. It's been a long few days for them."

Erica nodded and found that to be no treat either.

Have all *my muscles decided to quit on me?*

She wasn't going to come out and say so, but she was glad her parents had left. Her father was a midlevel accountant who realized over a decade ago that his daughter was smarter than he was and had resented her for it ever since.

Her mom, while being much more supportive in general, was your basic WASP nightmare who had a habit of lobbing backhanded criticisms at her only daughter without realizing it and then either claimed she meant no offense or insisted she'd never said such a thing. Erica loved them both and all of that, but it was hard sometimes to get past the hostility to unearth that love and doing so now would just require too much energy.

Tanya caught the vibe from her friend. "Your parents are, um, interesting folks," she said.

"Spend a lot of time with them, did you?"

"Just the past week."

"Oh, I'm so sorry."

Tanya laughed. "S'all right. Hey, at least you had two of 'em growing up. That's hard to beat."

They smiled at one another for a time, and then Tanya turned serious.

"Do you remember much?" she asked.

Erica did, but didn't really want to. "A little," she said.

"Any chance you'd want to . . . explain it? Because I gotta tell you, Rickie, I don't understand. And I saw most of it."

"Another time," Erica said.

"Yeah. All right."

Light from the hallway crept across the room, and a woman Erica had never seen before poked her head in through the open doorway. The woman glanced at Tanya, who smiled and waved her in.

"Hey, hey, Rickie," Tanya said. "You should meet her. She's a friend. Kept me out of jail."

"Excuse me?" Erica said. She tried to slide onto her elbows in an attempt to sit up, but the muscles in her arms weren't responding well, either.

"Lemme get that," Tanya said. She fiddled with some buttons on a black remote and lifted the whole head of the bed.

"Thanks," Erica said. "Jail?"

"It was a misunderstanding," the woman said. She had long red hair and was wearing a fantastic black dress. Erica remembered coveting that very outfit in a downtown shop window not so long ago.

"The cops thought I'd done this to you," Tanya explained.

"Oh," Erica said. "Sure. That makes sense, doesn't it?"

"Maggie Trent," the woman said by way of introduction. "FBI. Can I...?" She gestured at the chair on the near side of the bed.

"Go ahead," Erica said.

"Thank you."

She sat down and then looked uncomfortably toward Tanya.

"I was wondering if I could talk to Erica alone for a few minutes. Would that be all right?"

"I could use some coffee," Tanya said. "You okay?"

"It's fine," Erica said, still looking at her new guest.

Maggie Trent didn't look anything like an FBI agent, and if

Tanya hadn't been there to confirm it, she'd be asking for credentials. She was also clearly worried about something.

Tanya released Erica's hand, patted it a couple of times, and then promised to be right back. As soon as the door was closed, Agent Trent leaned in.

"I need you to tell me everything you can about who attacked you," Maggie said, skipping the preamble. "And fast."

"I really don't feel like talking about it right now, Agent," she said, for essentially the same reason she wouldn't answer Tanya's questions. She wasn't ready yet.

"Yes, I'm sure you don't, and I'm sorry, but this is terribly important."

"I . . . couldn't see him," Erica said, which was true, but didn't sound as insane as it could have.

"We know that. Listen, let's skip ahead. He's invisible. I don't know how or why or if he's even a *he* and not some sort of... thing. You don't need to be worried about telling me something that sounds outlandish. We're way past that. I need to know how to stop him."

Erica's heart started to race, a fact that was betrayed by the heart monitor she was hooked up to.

"Stop him?" she asked.

"Here's the thing. After the attack, I kept your survival out of the press. Or rather, I thought I did. But there are TV reporters downstairs, and in a little while the entire city is going to know you pulled through. I can't stop them. I've tried. But maybe I can stop the one who did this to you before he shows up to finish the job."

Erica smiled, but it was a sad smile she didn't really stand behind.

"You can't stop him," she said. "But... oh God. Jamie. You should warn Jamie before he gets to him, too."

"Jamie Silverman?" Maggie asked. Just the way she said it sounded bad.

"He's not—"

"More than two weeks ago."

"Oh..." Erica's vision started to blur. She was crying. It would have been an all-out weep, but she was too spent to muster the energy for it. "Well, that's it, then."

"I don't understand."

"In a little while he'll take care of me, and then he'll be finished, and you won't have to worry about him any longer."

"You think he's going to stop?"

"He'll just be done." She took the deepest breath she could to keep her voice steady so that her next point was clearly understood. "I'm the only one left, Agent Trent."

"But why?" Maggie asked. "Why you and the others? Why is he doing this?"

"Because you're wrong. He's not invisible. We saw him. I think that's why he's killing us."

Twenty Months Past

Erica Smalls was standing before two video monitors and holding her breath. It was something she tended to do when she was excited, a biological factoid that didn't always work out all that well for her, especially when she was working on a calculation of some kind and had a need for a constant supply of air to keep her brain moving. In this case, her brain didn't have to do anything except interpret the signals sent to it from her eyes, so she allowed it.

The monitors were being fed images from two very different devices. One was a standard video camera borrowed from the

AV lab a couple of buildings away from where she was standing. The other was a bastardized mutation of a video camera. It had some of the component parts of a standard camera, but aside from the lenses, there was no telling where exactly those components were located. Also included in this apparatus were the heat coils from the back of a junkyard refrigerator and an ample supply of Freon—it took them months to get the proper permits for this—a dozen circuit boards that were built from scratch, a Pentium microprocessor ripped from a spare computer, three prisms, two low-grade industrial lasers, a dinner cart stolen from the Radisson, roughly two miles of cables and wires, and about fifty other random objects whose nature and purpose Erica only dimly understood. Which was okay. She only worked the theory and some of the math.

Once she'd proven it was possible without invoking anything the engineers in the group couldn't salvage or invent—a quantum singularity, say—she was done. Her responsibility to the project had thus been completed a few months ago, after a brutal two years that would have gone faster if it weren't for all the damned infinities.

The twin video monitors showed the same event from slightly different angles—Kelsey and Dina walking from opposite ends of the camera's optical range, meeting in the middle, shaking hands, and then walking off again.

As events went, it was wholly unremarkable. Equally unremarkable was the fact that it appeared one video monitor was on a five-second delay. That was misleading, because the monitor showing real time was the one that was five seconds behind. The other one had recorded the transaction before it had actually happened.

"It's beautiful," she gasped.

Everyone else in the room—Doc Decaf, Saj, Jimmy, El, and Jamie—were too stunned to say anything at all. Maybe it was

GENE DOUCETTE

because after two years of work by the seven of them, and by at least fifty others who had contributed time and expertise, nobody truly believed it would ever work. Even Erica, who could recite the physics so well she sometimes caught herself singing the necessary equations in the shower to the tune of *Mary Had a Little Lamb*.

"So?" Kelsey asked. He and Dina, having been the first two people to see their grand new toy work, were past the shocked-and-awed stage.

"Yeah," Dina said. "What d'ya think?"

Doc Decaf, still unable to speak, started clapping. And then everyone was hugging and cheering. Someone pulled out champagne.

Their lab was one of four large private spaces in the applied sciences building. Like all of the labs, it looked to have been decorated by a psychotic junkyard man, with random tubes, semi-assembled computers, loose wires, circuit boards, and an entire wall devoted to Tinkertoys. It was also the place where the first successful Advance Temporal Segment Viewing —or simply ATSV—test was run and where its designers elected to stay in order to properly celebrate.

There were exactly eight people at MIT who had a complete understanding of the Advance Temporal Segmentation Project, and seven of them were in that room to see it pay off.

The eighth, Professor Archibald Calvin, whom Erica had never even met, was the one who came up with the idea in the first place. It was rumored he got the idea after meeting someone who could see the future, but none of them seriously believed that.

They had each headed a team to work out various aspects of

the problem, breaking it into small enough pieces so that no one student who wasn't meant to see the whole picture would see the whole picture. This was Offey's idea. Nobody expected that to work out either.

"To Archie Calvin," toasted Doc Decaf, holding up one of the bottles of champagne.

"And his visitor from the future," Jamie added—to much laughter.

Erica grinned and drank straight from her own bottle. She was not one to drink in the middle of the afternoon, but this wasn't a normal day. A niggling voice in her head—her mom's voice, because the subject was alcohol—reminded her to be careful, as she tended to get a mite horny when drinking, and these were people she wanted to be able to look in the eye again tomorrow. Plus, she was bound to embarrass herself with Doc Decaf, who she'd only been crushing on for two solid years.

She ignored this admonition and gulped some more of the champagne. This made her dizzy, so she found the nearest chair, which happened to be occupied by Jimmy Ho. Fortunately, Jimmy came equipped with a fully functional lap.

"So now what?" she asked, ignoring Jimmy's hand around her waist. "I mean, are we rich yet?"

"Now we design a testing protocol," Offey said mildly. "So we can show off our new toy without anybody thinking we're pulling a stunt."

"Wait," Eleanor said. "Didn't we just do that? With the walking?"

"So you say," Offey countered. "But suppose Dina and Kel here secretly rigged it? They could have filmed themselves doing the exact same thing and put it on a loop to play before the live version."

"Would we do that?" Dina asked Kelsey, who had his arm around her shoulder.

"We migh'. We're a crafty pair."

"So you are," said Offey.

"C'mon," Erica said. "They're not *that* smart." Dina stuck a pierced tongue out at her.

Offey took another deep drink and then said, "The question I want all of you to ask yourselves is how do you prove this to a skeptic? Assume we're talking about someone who does not know what fine, honest, hardworking folks you happen to be. For while you may look at yourselves in the mirror and see Einstein, Bohr, and Feynman, keep in mind that there will be many who will see instead Pons and Fleischmann."

A silence fell over all of them as this sank in.

"Wow," Jimmy said eventually. "What a buzz kill."

"Hey," Dina said. "We have a window."

"Don't jump," El said—to laughter.

"No," Dina continued, "the optics aspect is actually pretty small. It's not really portable, but—"

"We're saving the portable one for the army contract," Kelsey quipped.

Sajjan said, "Set it up at the window, film whoever's out there."

"Why not?" Dina asked. "We just have to extend a couple cables."

"That might do it," Offey said, smiling.

"Oh, guys, we totally have to do that right now," Jimmy said.

"Absolutely," Erica agreed. Because while it was cool to see Kel and Dina walking around the room, trying it out on an unsuspecting civilization would be—and this might have been the champagne talking—fucking awesome.

Two hours—and the purchase of a number of pizzas and sodas—later, the still pretty drunk ATSP team had gotten the delicate optical piece moved twenty-five feet across the room to the edge of the frosted-glass window.

The window, when opened, afforded them a view of a minor side street and a small park that was, fortuitously, around the corner from a Starbucks. So even though it was cold out, there were a half dozen people who had opted to stop and sit in the park while they drank their coffee. Between the people and the cars, the team had the makings of a perfect test sampling.

"We're ready here," Dina said, holding the ATSV's optics steady. Jimmy stood next to her with the digital camera.

"Hold on," Kelsey said from the control board. He finished off the last of his champagne bottle. "Okay, ready now."

"Perhaps we should have done this before we started drinking," Offey said paternally.

"I can work this blindfolded," Kelsey said. "Now you have to keep in mind that the views are going to look a little different. Before, we had the camera and the ATSV showing almost the same angle. We haven't done that here."

"Why not?" Erica asked, standing next to Doc Decaf and bouncing on the balls of her feet from a combination of excitement, mild arousal, and a great need to pee.

"Takes too long," Dina said. "We're just doing this for fun, right?"

"Turn it on already," Jamie said.

"Alrighty," Kelsey said.

He flipped the switch, and both monitors came to life.

As before, the view from the ATSV showed events on the street happening before the regular camera did. Erica caught herself holding her breath again and wondering if there would ever come a day when she found this anything other than extraordinary.

The scene outside was that of a lightly populated public space. A mixture of students and employees of the office building down the street milled about, and occasionally a car drove by on its way to Mem Drive. It was, overall, only slightly more interesting than the handshake demonstration, except that there was no way to stage this sort of public interaction.

"There's your test, Doc," Kelsey said with a smile.

"We are so clever," El said.

"Damn straight," agreed Jamie.

They stood there and watched for what seemed like an hour. At one point Dina and Sajjan switched places so she could see the monitors, and then Jamie located a tripod to support the regular camera so Jimmy could join in with the staring.

"Hey," Erica said. "That's weird."

"What is?" Dina asked.

Erica had seen something that could conservatively be considered anomalous.

"Look over here," she said, pointing to the ATSV monitor. "See the guy in orange?"

Dina said, "With the... what is that, a prison uniform? What about him?"

"He's not on the other monitor."

Offey leaned forward. "That's strange."

The man was sitting on one of the benches by himself, looking down at his own feet. He had a bald head and worn sneakers, and didn't appear to be dressed well for the weather. The outfit he was wearing did indeed look a lot like a prison uniform, except it had no number or name insignia on it. Erica thought he looked eerily still—a poorly dressed statue.

"Are you recording this?" Offey asked.

"Yeah," Kelsey said.

"Hey, Saj," Erica said, "can you see a guy out there in a bright orange jumpsuit?"

Sajjan peered around the apparatus. "Where?"

"Second bench on the left."

"There's nobody there," he said.

"According to our device, there is," Offey said.

"Huh."

On the ATSV screen a woman holding a large coffee walked up to the where the bald man sat. She was about to sit right down on his lap, then changed her mind and picked a different bench instead.

"Someone almost sat on him," Erica said to Sajjan.

"I'm telling you, there isn't anybody there," he insisted.

"Well," Doc Offey said, "we have a new problem. If this is showing imaginary people..." he trailed off, as there was really no adequate answer to what it was they were all witnessing.

"Maybe he's really not there," Kelsey suggested. "And this is just some sort of crazy glitch."

"I can test for that," Sajjan said.

"Could this be showing us a possible future instead of the actual one?" Erica asked.

"I don't see how," Eleanor, the other pure theoretician in the room, said. If such a thing were possible, it would probably be she and Erica who figured out how.

The bald anomaly's head jerked upward, which caused Erica to gasp involuntarily. There was something deeply creepy about the way he did that. Like a bird almost, but more fundamentally predatory.

He was looking right at the window—and at them. She was holding her breath again, but this time excitement had nothing to do with it.

"Why did he do that?" she asked quietly.

"Hey!" Sajjan shouted out the window. A few of the people on the street looked up at the sound. "You in the orange outfit!"

The man had a large, pointed nose, perfectly black eyes, a mouth that seemed to be much too big, and no eyebrows or other facial hair of any kind. His head tilted to one side, and an expression of commingled fear and curiosity passed across his face.

"He's looking at you, Saj," Kelsey said.

He looked up before Sajjan spoke, Erica realized.

"Yeah," Sajjan said, still shouting out the window. "Yeah, we can see you."

The man opened his mouth and seemed to articulate something none of them could hear. Erica was too busy staring at his teeth to read his lips because his teeth were huge and coated in a thin layer of reddish gore.

Shark's teeth.

"What did he say?" Dina asked, sounding very small and scared.

"Honestly?" Jamie said, "I thought I saw the word 'kill' in there."

"Guys," Jimmy said, "I think we should turn off the ATSV. Now."

The bald thing stopped speaking and had moved on to howling, his mouth open wide and head tilted upward like a baying hound.

"Yeah," Jamie said. "Kel, turn it off."

"But..."

"Maybe you should," Offey agreed. "Until we figure out what's gone wrong with—"

"*Turn it off!*" Eleanor screamed.

"Okay, okay." Kelsey threw the necessary switches, and the ATSV image went dead.

At the window, Sajjan carefully lowered the optic piece to the floor, saying, "So what does this guy look like?"

"Close the window, Saj," Dina said. "Quickly."

"You afraid this boogeyman's gonna climb the wall and slip in through the window?" he asked.

"Yes," Dina said, completely serious. "That is exactly what I'm afraid of."

CHAPTER TWENTY-TWO

Now

Maggie sat back in her chair, still holding Erica's hand and wondering whether anything she just heard was even remotely possible.

"After the champagne wore off," Erica continued, "we all just sort of convinced ourselves that none of that happened. We started the work on our theses."

"This was what, twenty months ago?" Maggie asked. "Why didn't you go public with the machine? I mean, imagine the press."

"Pons and Fleischmann."

"I don't know who they are."

"You've heard of cold fusion? They thought they'd discovered a chemical process that could initiate a controlled fusion reaction on their tabletop. Rather than write it up and submit it for peer review, they went public right away. The problem is, they were mistaken. We *knew* we had something, but we didn't want to lose the scientific community right off the bat by not following the established channels. Plus, each of us had a doctorate on the line that was just as important as fame and fortune..."

At first Maggie thought she'd just become too tired to continue, so she let her be and quietly contemplated the cost-benefit relationship of a smoked cigarette in the middle of a hospital ward room.

"And then," Erica said. "People started dying."

Corrigan tried to understand the point Ames was making, but it wasn't registering. Of *course* the messages came from elsewhere, be it the universe or God or... whatever. How could Ames think otherwise? Likewise, Corrigan had no more control over the ghosts than he did the messages. If he could control them, he would.

"Let me ask you something," Ames said, trying to drive home his point. "What is it you fear the most?"

"Screwing up," he said immediately. "Not saving someone when I could have."

"No! That is a symptom of the fear, not the fear itself."

"Um, okay."

"Why is Harvey here right now?"

Harvey answered, "Because you need my help. You can't do this alone. We need each other."

"He says we need each other," Corrigan said. "Something about my not being able to do it alone."

"He said something very similar to you before, didn't he?" Ames asked.

"Yes, but—"

"Corrigan, Harvey Nilsson was insane. He saw things that weren't there. And now, here you are complaining about ghosts, and Harvey himself has come back to visit. You are looking down the maw at the one thing, above all other things, that truly frightens you."

Corrigan Bain is going insane.

"I'm not Harvey Nilsson," Corrigan said automatically.

"Yes! But deep down, you fear that that is *exactly* what you're becoming."

"Going crazy," Corrigan said. "Sure, I've always been afraid of that. That doesn't explain anything."

"It had a trigger. What happened to you nine days ago?"

"I didn't save someone. Something..."

He stopped.

"Yes?" Ames asked.

"I thought it was new. But this happened before. At McClaren."

"Now we're getting somewhere. What was it?"

"The future split in two."

"So you've said. But *why* did that affect you so?"

"Because Harvey used to be able to do that, too."

Ames looked down, and it occurred to Corrigan he'd hit on a tough subject for Dr. Ames.

Ames had been Harvey's doctor, and while it took Corrigan more than a year to convince Ames that he could see the future, the doctor did eventually come to accept it. But he had never believed Harvey.

The moment passed, and Ames continued. "I don't know what it's like for you when you see what you see, but I imagine it must be jarring to *not* see what's coming, like the rest of us do every day. Your reaction was to block the messages you've only been getting *because Harvey told you to get them*. It all comes back to him."

"Because I was right!" Harvey said.

"I . . ." He couldn't bring himself to take the next step.

"Go on, tell him the truth," Harvey yelled. "He deserves to know."

"Harvey says you're wrong," Corrigan said.

"Well." Ames smiled. "Harvey said that a lot in his day. Where might I have strayed? Does he say?"

Corrigan took a deep, calming breath. "Okay. The thing is, the messages Harvey told me to expect... that wasn't the only thing he got right. I never really wanted to admit it, which is maybe why I'm still a mess after all those years of therapy, but... those monsters only Harvey could see? They're real."

"At first, I figured the same thing everyone else did," Erica said. "Accidents and suicides. It wasn't until Doc Decaf that I really started to wonder if it had something to do with our project, specifically. El and I, we started talking, trying to figure out how someone could appear only in the ATSV and not in the real world. We were working out the math on it, until..."

"Until she fell off a bridge," Maggie finished.

"Yeah. She was on her way to my place when that happened. As terrible as that was, it put the pieces together for me. I knew for sure then that the thing we saw that day was killing us one by one."

Maggie gripped her hand tighter. "There's still time," she said. "We can stop him."

"No, you can't," Erica said.

She started crying once more, and Maggie didn't think she knew her quite well enough to provide a shoulder, so she offered a tissue instead and waited. After a minute or so, Erica got herself under control enough to answer questions again.

"Erica," Maggie said. "Did you ever figure it out? What it is?"

"I don't know what it is," she said quietly. "But I know when."

"I don't understand."

"The laws of physics don't really care about things like the present and the past and the future. Mathematically—believe me, I worked it out—the present has no objective value. His present is different than ours. The reason we can't see him, Agent Trent, is that he lives five seconds in the future. He can affect our future, but we can't ever affect his present. And that's why you can't stop him. If he wants to kill me, he will. He might even be in this room right now."

A mes was confused. Initially he thought his young friend was reaching for some sort of metaphorical or otherwise non-literal definition of the word *real*. Because one of the first things Corrigan Bain had said to him in therapy was, "I know Mr. Nilsson was seeing imaginary things. I don't want to see them. Can you help me?" It was the cornerstone of their ten years of work together.

"You mean 'real,' as in emotionally impactful, or…"

"No. 'Real' as in *real*," Corrigan said.

Corrigan's eyes were darting around the room, a clear indication he was still seeing the ghosts and perhaps also still "hearing" Harvey talk to him. That couldn't possibly help. All those figments did was feed him back what he already had in his head. The Harvey that was sitting in his chair could no more impart new information than the chair itself could.

"Corrigan, we spent a lot of time on this," he said. "Harvey lost his grip on reality, and you know that."

"He did. But that doesn't mean he was wrong. I saw it, too."

"Saw?"

"The invisible monster. Or whatever it was."

"When? In the hospital?"

"Yes. But I didn't want to admit it to myself." He looked away to the chair.

"What does Harvey have to say?" Ames asked.

"He's talking about the day in the public room. He wounded it. I think he even killed it. That was why he lowered the gun. He'd finished what he'd set out to do."

"He shot the gun at you and missed."

"No," Corrigan said. "He was never shooting it at me."

Ames sighed heavily. "We're not going to get anywhere if you opt out of reality. This is exactly the problem you and I—"

"I *saw* it dying. And I was so terrified, I asked you to help me convince myself I hadn't. *That* is what I've been repressing all this time."

Corrigan seemed upbeat and lively for the first time since Ames walked into the room, like a burden had been lifted. That was certainly the reaction one hoped for after a therapy session. But the conclusion he was drawing was definitely *not* healthy.

"All right," Ames said. "Let's work this through. I'm going to pretend for a moment that you are right, that thirty years ago Harvey Nilsson terrorized an entire hospital in order to kill an invisible monster. You saw it and tried to bury the truth in your own head, and now that truth has resurfaced and mucked up your whole life. What was the trigger? Was it still the anomalous event of nine days ago?"

"Yes, but it started before that. I was approached by... hang on."

Corrigan reached across the coffee table for a small black device with a panoply of buttons on it that Ames only gradually realized was the remote for the television set. The television had been on—muted—the entire time he'd been there.

He glanced up. The image on the screen showed a young, pretty blonde woman in what looked like a close-up of a class photograph. It was a news teaser. Corrigan took the television off mute.

"...what hospital officials are calling a miracle. Graduate student Erica Smalls, attacked nine days ago in her own apartment, has taken a turn for the better. We'll have a full report at eleven."

"Oh my God," Corrigan said.

"Is this... important?" Ames asked. This was all very confusing.

"Maggie, how could you not tell me?" Corrigan asked. Ames wondered which of the ghosts was this Maggie.

"Doctor, you've been a great help." Corrigan stood up, wobbly. "I have to go now."

"*Go?* Where?"

"There," he said, pointing to the television. "The girl is in danger."

"You're in no condition to go anywhere," Ames pointed out as his host proceeded to tiptoe through the living room, dodging phantoms. Ames got to his feet after multiple attempts—the couch appeared to have its own gravitational field—and followed Corrigan down the hall, into a room with a computer and a large wall map. Corrigan was rifling through his desk.

"Listen to me, please," the doctor said. "You are in no condition to go out in public much less attempt to save some girl you happen to think is in peril."

Corrigan pulled a lock box out of the bottom drawer and put it up on the desktop.

"It'd take too long to explain," he said. "But I know what I'm doing. Honestly." He started working the combination.

"You haven't slept soundly for almost nine days. At least get one night of sleep behind you." He reached into his pocket and pulled out a pill bottle.

"What are those?" Corrigan asked, without looking.

"Sleeping pills. They're mine, but I have plenty. Use them tonight, get some rest."

"I will, but not right now." He swung the box open and reached inside for something, pulled it out, and then closed the box again.

"Corrigan, please! You can't just declare some sort of deeper understanding and then expect it to all be better. It doesn't work like that. You are in crisis."

"I know," Corrigan said with a half-laugh. He walked to the doorway and shoved what turned out to be a large wad of money in Ames's hand. "But I have to try and help. I'm the only one who can."

"At least—"

"I'll try the pills. But not until after this is over. And don't argue about the money. I don't need to see the future to know that's the next thing out of your mouth. You've helped more than you realize."

"Really?" Ames said. "It seems as if I've made matters much, much worse."

Corrigan and Dr. Ames rode the elevator down together ten minutes later, after the former had changed into more appropriate outdoor clothing and called the front desk for two cabs.

Ames spent the entire ten minutes, including the ride down, talking about transference. It seemed he felt that was what Corrigan was doing with Erica. Specifically, the doctor thought that by creating an imaginary emergency, he was avoiding having to deal with his very real problems. Corrigan wanted to explain to Ames what was really going on, but he didn't think he had it in him. It was too hard just keeping reality in check long enough to make it to the lobby.

The doors opened, opened, opened. There were a dozen people in the entryway, dressed nicely and apparently waiting for a limo, and there was the concierge, and beyond that, the ghosts.

"Do you still see them?" Ames asked quietly. It was obvious something was wrong, as Corrigan had neglected to step off the elevator.

"I told them to stay upstairs."

"You can't possibly expect to go anywhere like this."

"I have to," he said, taking one shaky step toward the lobby.

Ghosts have no future, he reminded himself, *that's how you can tell.* But that was only nominally helpful, as the real people not only had futures, they were showing off those futures in their entirety. He couldn't focus on the present at all.

He walked to the front desk, Ames crutching along beside him.

"The cabs are here," Corrigan said to the concierge, who was about to say, "The cabs are here, Mr. Bain."

"Eh, yes," said the man at the desk, his future blinking out temporarily. "Will there—"

"Nothing else, thanks."

He turned around and assessed the lobby. Tuxedos and evening gowns stretched out in curls of forward-movement.

Caterpillars, he thought.

That was what he always thought they looked like when he was a kid. Multi- legged beasts that got longer when they ran. But even as a child he coped better.

And the *noise.* Everyone was talking all at once, entire paragraphs of dialogue pouring out of their mouths. How was he going to do this?

Harvey, now sitting in one of the lobby chairs, said, "Make me proud, my little fixer."

Ames grabbed him by the elbow. Corrigan nearly jumped away from the contact.

"You need rest," he repeated.

"Help me through this?" Corrigan asked. "Just to the curb."

Ames sighed. He wasn't going to win this argument.

"All right. But when this is over and you end up in a mental hospital because you've gone and done God knows what? Lose my number."

To one of the lobby occupants, it probably looked as if Corrigan Bain was helping frail old Fred Ames out to his cab. That is, unless the observer happened to listen to them as they walked. Then they would have heard Ames saying, "Step... step... step... that's good..."

Corrigan put Ames into a cab first, handing the driver a hundred-dollar bill and not bothering to worry about whether that was too much money. Ames's last words to him were, "Visit sometime, if you're not locked up somewhere."

Sliding into the back of his own cab, he instructed the driver to take him to Mount Auburn Hospital, and just in case he didn't really say it out loud, he said it one more time.

"I heard you, mon," the driver said, stepping on the gas and peeling out of the rotunda.

Harvey was sitting next to him. "Don't worry," he was saying. "We can do this."

"You're not even here. How can you help?" Corrigan asked.

"What's 'at?" the driver asked.

"Talking to myself," Corrigan said. "Just ignore me."

"A'right."

"We did this before and we can do it again," Harvey added.

Corrigan did his level best to ignore Harvey, staring out the window and trying to retain some semblance of a grip on the world.

Cars skated through their own likely futures, catching up to themselves only at stoplights, and only briefly. Pedestrians occupied entire sections of the sidewalk, becoming fuzzy whirlwinds when they started walking. None of the blurs ever ran into one another, which was remarkable.

Unbidden, his thoughts returned to the day in the public room when Harvey Nilsson nearly blew his head off.

Through some degree of conscious effort, Corrigan had succeeded in not thinking about that moment in detail for years. And when he did think about it, it was with Ames's help at a time when he was ready to accept any explanation the doctor would provide as the factual truth, even though deep down he knew better.

"He lives in the future," Harvey said. "You understand that, right? That's why only we can see him."

Corrigan nodded, rather than attempting a verbal reply that might screw up his driver. But how do you stop something that has five seconds or more to react to everything you do?

He remembered the way Harvey moved when he was up on that table with the gun. He was intentionally mucking up his own time stream to make himself a less predictable target.

But that hadn't been enough. It took two of them, both moving outside of the stream, to confuse it.

"He was behind me the whole time," he said. "Wasn't he?" The driver looked up in the mirror, but didn't say anything.

Harvey said, "That's right. He was trying to force me to shoot you. But he didn't know you could move like me until it was too late. Winged him good, I did."

So how do I do this alone? he wondered.

F rom the river side, Mount Auburn Hospital was an intimidating beast of a building—actually a number of smaller buildings that had, over time and seemingly via some sort of organic process, merged into a single structure.

Built on a rise overlooking the Charles River, the land had been tending to the sick and wounded since the Revolutionary War, when soldiers were laid out on the hill so that, should they soon meet their Maker, the first thing they might say to Him would be, "That was a nice view you gave me, there."

The only way to actually gain entrance to the hospital was on the Mount Auburn side, which was where the cab driver ended up. But rather than choosing the main entrance—actually the second floor of the building thanks to the hill—he came to a stop at the basement door to the emergency room.

"We here," he said, pushing the meter.

"Why this entrance?" Corrigan asked. He hadn't said the lobby specifically, but still.

"Mon, you havin' some kind of emergency, don't tell me you ain't."

"Fair enough," he said, tossing a fifty into the front seat. "Thanks."

Corrigan slid out of the cab, steadied himself with help from the cab's roof, tried walking, and then reached out and steadied himself on the roof again.

Oh, this is bad, he thought.

He'd been all right in the car, but independent bipedal motion was much more difficult, especially since the world, in addition to not being interested in sticking to a single time frame, had also begun to spin.

Dizzy, he concluded and then wondered, *Did I eat anything today?*

The revolving door entrance was a few feet away but may as well have been a mile. Disengaging again from the top of the cab, he staggered toward it, freeing the driver to take off before Corrigan changed his mind.

Standing next to the door was the boy.

"Geez," the kid said. "You look awful. You sure you're up to this?"

"Shut up."

"Seriously, maybe that old guy was right. You need some sleep."

"Food would've been good, too."

"Yeah, definitely. Wanna get some pizza? I love pizza."

"Shut up, I said."

Corrigan half-fell, half-pushed his way through the door, which was a nightmarish experience in and of itself because the thing spun automatically and thus appeared to be a solid mass or something that spun so quickly he had no hope of getting through unhurt. In the end he just closed his eyes and trusted that the hospital, being a hospital, wouldn't install a door that spun eighty miles an hour.

His ghost didn't even bother with the door, reappearing on the inside as if there were nothing special about that. Which there wasn't, seeing as how he wasn't even there.

"Can I help you, sir?"

The nurse at the emergency room desk was looking up helpfully, her words echoing through time at him. How long had he been standing there?

"ICU," he muttered.

She smiled, smiled, smiled. "Down the down the down the hall red line to the follow the elevator floor first floor to the follow the red line corridor down the corridor to the set of second set of elevators elev seventh floor seventh floor."

Oh God.

"I'm sorry," Corrigan said. "Could you repeat that?"

"There has to be a way we can move her," Maggie was saying to the doctor on call, a severe-looking woman named Nair. They were standing at the desk near the entrance to the ICU, twenty steps from Erica's room.

"To another hospital? No, ma'am," the doctor insisted. "Another room perhaps, but I would not advise it. Out of the ICU—absolutely out of the question."

"Well, I'm happy that you're thinking of the patient's health, but so am I."

"As you've said. Yet you have provided me with no compelling argument beyond that. You have also had a policeman outside of her room since the day she arrived, and in that time she has not suffered any manner of misfortune. I fail to see how the issue is any different now that she is awake."

"How about, every news station in town just announced that she's still alive because your hospital couldn't keep a secret?" Maggie snapped. "How's that?"

"Again, you have an armed guard outside her door. Please tell me why that will not suffice, and then we can discuss jeopardizing her recovery."

Because the killer is invisible, Maggie wanted to say. But she somehow doubted that would improve the situation any. "Fine," she said instead. "Just make her better as soon as you can."

"The body heals when it heals."

"Yeah, yeah." Maggie turned in her very expensive heels and stormed back to the policeman outside the door.

"Any luck?" the cop asked. His name was Clancey, and he was due to be replaced in another twenty minutes, but not, unfortunately, by an entire SWAT team.

"Course not," she answered. "Good Christ, I need a cigarette. How's she doing?"

"Her friend's in there with her."

"Did you check on them?"

"You think the friend is going to do her in?"

"No." She cracked open the door enough to see Erica sleeping and Tanya sitting alertly by her side. She shut the door. "I'm worried about something else entirely doing her in."

Clancey nodded. "The boogeyman," he said.

"Is that what you guys are calling him?"

"It's better'n Kilroy."

"Not very imaginative, though."

"Sir, you can't go down there!" somebody shouted. It sounded like Dr. Nair.

Maggie said, "That doesn't sound good, does it? Stay here, Clancey. Nobody goes in or out."

"I know what I'm doing," he said.

With her hand on the service revolver in her handbag, Maggie hurried back to the front desk.

"Smalls!" a man yelled.

"If you are not a friend or a family—"

"Shut up."

"Sir, I'm calling security."

"No, not you. I wasn't telling you to shut up. I was telling the boy."

"Corrigan?" Maggie said, turning the corner. She'd pulled the gun out upon reaching the desk and had to slip it into the pocket of her jacket quickly before it caused a scene all its own.

"Sir, what boy are you referring to?" the doctor asked.

"Maggie?" Corrigan said, turning to an empty space to his right, empty because Maggie hadn't gotten there yet. "Wow. You look great."

"Thank you," she said, walking around to the front of the desk.

"You know this man?" Nair asked.

"Do I?" Corrigan said. "Haven't slept much lately."

"He's with me, Dr. Nair. Special consultant."

"Yes, let's," Corrigan said.

"Then he's your problem. But when he yells, he is my problem. I don't want any problems."

"I understand," Maggie said. She walked over to Corrigan and took him by the elbow.

"Jesus," she whispered, "you look terrible."

"Didn't we just go through this?" he asked.

"Let's get you out of the middle here."

"Yes, let's," he agreed, now looking very confused.

"Focus, Corrigan," she said, leading him down the hall.

He didn't answer for a few seconds before saying, "I'm trying. No, I haven't been drinking today, to answer your next question, and yes, I think I am losing my mind."

"You just need some coffee," she said, but he'd stopped dead in his tracks.

"A bald man in orange overalls."

"What?" A chill went down her back. It was the second time she'd heard that description in the past hour.

"I saw him before, before at the apartment, I saw... *Hey!*"

Everyone on the floor turned to stare at the insane shouting man. Maggie resisted the urge to slap her hand over his mouth. "Corrigan, will you—"

"Down here?" he asked, pointing.

"Slow down!" She grabbed him by the ears and forced him to look her in the eye, which was no small feat as he was more than a head taller. "You're running ahead, Corrigan. What's going on?"

"I saw him."

"At her apartment, nine days ago," she said. "You saw a bald man with orange overalls. That was what we were looking for. Only you can see him, do you understand?"

"Yes, I understand that. I saw him."

"Nine days ago."

"A few seconds ago."

"What?"

"Walking down this hallway and right past us. Where is her room? It's down here?"

CHAPTER TWENTY-THREE

Now

Corrigan was only dimly aware that the cop at the door very nearly shot him as he barreled down the hallway.

"Let him pass!" Maggie was yelling, either before or after the cop drew his gun. It was impossible to tell.

"Excuse me! Excuse me!" Corrigan shouted, hoping that would get the blurs of people out of his way.

"That door there!" Maggie said, which meant nothing to him as he had no real notion of where he was in respect to her timeline. But there was only one door with a policeman standing in front of it, so he went on the assumption that it was the one she meant.

He hit the door with his shoulder, nearly falling over when it swung far more easily on its hinges than he'd been expecting. Tanya screamed and almost fell backward in her chair at the sight.

"Not here, not here," he muttered, sweeping the room. Tanya was still screaming, and he couldn't tell whether it was because she had continued to scream after he'd burst in or if he was just hearing the initial scream on a loop.

"Try the bathroom," the boy said helpfully. Corrigan did, and found it to be small, clean, and empty. The closet was equally unoccupied.

The man in orange wasn't there.

"It's okay," Maggie was saying to Tanya, at roughly the same time Erica woke up and started asking what was going on.

"Not here," Corrigan said again.

"He's not here?" Maggie repeated. "Corrigan."

"Not here."

"What the hell is going on?" the cop asked, coming in behind Maggie.

"Let him pass!" Maggie shouted, except she couldn't be shouting that because she shouted that earlier in the hall, and it didn't make sense in any other context.

The hell? His knees buckled, and the room swayed. Someone caught him.

"...over..."

"...chair..."

"...heavy..."

He was sitting. Someone blurry was talking to him.

Maggie was shouting, "Let him pass!" again.

He was looking at the man in orange, walking past him in the corridor.

Tanya was screaming.

"Slow down," Corrigan said weakly.

"...drink..."

"..."

There was a drink in his hand.

"Slow down," he said again.

"Drink the coffee," the blur said again. Or perhaps this was the first time, repeating itself. It sounded like Maggie.

He sipped the drink. Coffee, all right. Shitty, black coffee, but hot. He blinked.

The world started to clarify itself. He saw Maggie sitting on the edge of the bed and looking worriedly at him. She was dressed like an expensive call girl, which made him wonder if this was real or one of his better dreams. The friend—Tanya something—was sitting beside the bed, looking at him like he had horns. The cop at the door was in a quiet argument with a hospital staffer over something or other. He kept rubbing his lower back. Maybe he was the one who'd gotten Corrigan into the chair. And sitting up, studying him closely, was Erica Smalls.

"Hi," he said. His words echoed. That hadn't gone away. *So much for the miracle of caffeine.* "I faint?"

"Yeah," Maggie said. "When's the last time you ate?"

"Dunno," he answered, speaking over her question. "I was wondering the same thing a little while ago."

"You should listen to me," the boy said. He was still around, hanging by the sliding doors of the closet.

"I told you not to follow me."

Everyone else in the room stared at the closet door Corrigan was talking to.

"Is he here now?" Maggie asked quietly.

"That's just one of my ghosts," Corrigan explained, skipping ahead in the conversation a couple of steps. "Thinks he's special because he helped me get up here. I couldn't follow the directions. Compound sentences are a problem right now."

"If you just listen to me, I'll tell you when to talk," the kid said. "I know where the present is."

"You do?"

"Corrigan, what's happened to you?" Maggie asked. He looked over to the boy, who nodded.

"Haven't slept for a while is all. My head's a bit of a mess."

"Ghosts?"

Nod.

"People I didn't save. Long story. Hey, kid, this'll work."

"Told you," the kid said, smiling. Having a hallucination that was not only offering to help, but was successfully doing so, was certainly weird, but no weirder than anything else he'd had to deal with lately. He decided not to overthink it.

"You're him."

The voice was a quiet one, and it came from the bed. Erica Smalls was boring holes into him.

"Hi," he said. "Corrigan Bain, fixer, raving madman. Nice to meet you."

"I met this guy before," Tanya said/was saying/was about to say. "After you were attacked. Some kinda—"

"Can you really see the future?" Erica asked.

He nodded.

"Right now I can't *not*, which is a problem. But yeah. I'm sorry, I'm usually much more charming. It's just been a long week. Hey. Lemme ask you something. Were you in Downtown Crossing, a little before five in the afternoon, day you were attacked?"

"You're doing good," the kid said near the closet door. "Didn't think you could say that much at once."

"Thanks," he said to the kid. "Trick is to just keep talking, I guess."

Erica glanced back over at the empty space where Corrigan's ghost companion was standing. Upon reflection, he realized this was probably disconcerting for everyone else.

"You're freaking them out," agreed the ghost.

"Um... Tanya?" Erica asked, looking at her friend, who was still staring at Corrigan and wondering if he was going to tear off his clothing and announce he was the King of Prussia or something. "Downtown Crossing? I can't remember."

"Yeah, we were there," Tanya said. To Corrigan she said,

"Why d'you ask?"

"He must have been stalking you all day," Corrigan said, shooting a look at Maggie, who was nodding. "He can alter the future, like I can. Like Harvey could."

"Harvey?" Maggie asked. "Who's Harvey?"

"Not important. My point—"

"That woman you couldn't save," Maggie said, filling in the rest.

"Yeah."

"Go ahead, tell her who I am," Harvey said. He and a chair had just appeared next to the kid. Corrigan thought it was good thinking, him bringing his own chair.

"She doesn't need to know that, Harvey," Corrigan said.

Erica, her curiosity overwhelming any outstanding concerns she might be holding about his ongoing conversations with nonexistent people, asked, "So how does it work? Do you see an entire *chronoton* at once, or—"

"Chrono what?" Corrigan asked.

"That's what we called it. The period of virtual certain future time, up to the border of manifestly equivalent probabilities."

"The hell is she talking about?" Harvey asked.

"Too many big words," the boy agreed.

"You're going to have to use smaller words," Corrigan said. "We can't... I can't understand you."

Erica explained. "The arrow of time moves down the most likely path, statistically, but the further away it gets from the present, the less likely it becomes. There was an uncertainty border we couldn't see beyond."

"They figured out how to do what I can do?" Corrigan asked Maggie.

"Would've told you about it if you'd answered your phone," she said.

"And how far ahead was this border?" he asked Erica.

"Depended on how much was going on. I bet it's the same for you."

"What's she mean?" Harvey asked. "This is interesting."

"Yes, it is," Corrigan said. "What do you mean, 'depended'?"

"Do you have a harder time in crowds?" she asked.

"Yeah. The future gets all mucked up."

"That's because the *chronoton* is smaller the more variables there are, so you can't see as far ahead as you're accustomed to. That must make you very anxious."

"Did you see the whole . . . *chronoton*, is it? Did you see it all at once with this machine of yours?" Corrigan asked.

"No, just the end of it. We had some problems with infinities whenever we tried working out the numbers for a period of less than one *chronoton*. At first we thought it was a flaw in our methodology, but when I redid the calculations, I realized it's because there's a qualitative difference between the points at the end of it and the period in the middle. The present and the lead edge of the *chronoton*... resonate. Kind of. I think of them as octaves. Anyway, that's probably more than you wanted to know."

"S'okay," Corrigan said. "Sounds interesting."

"That's why we looked at the other end of the *chronoton*. It was the only place we *could* look."

"I guess Archie Calvin was onto something after all. Almost makes me wish I had paid more attention to him."

Tanya, who looked confused by the whole conversation, asked, "So now what happens? Are you here to protect her or something?"

"Unless she can wheel that machine of hers in here, I'm the only one who can see him."

"It's broken," Erica said. "And it wasn't portable, anyway. But how are you going to stop him if you're stuck in the same end of the *chronoton* as the rest of us?"

"No idea."

Time passed. Sustenance was located for Corrigan in the form of a few Snickers bars from the commissary. Maggie, after finding time to sneak outside for a desperately needed cigarette, took up a spot on the chair on the other side of Erica's bed.

Erica's parents checked in via telephone from their hotel room a few miles down the road. Tanya left a few minutes after the call, having been assured that Maggie wouldn't go anywhere and that Corrigan was motivated by good intentions and wasn't usually insane.

Corrigan stayed right where he was—in the quite comfortable reclining chair in the corner of the room—and watched for Kilroy to darken the door. Since, for the past week, he'd been unable to get any sleep at all, now that he had a solid reason for staying awake, he was quite sure he would. Then, of course, he fell asleep.

He woke up back in his bedroom, which was the first indication he wasn't awake at all. This was another of his hauntings. Still, it seemed real enough to have him questioning whether the entire trip to Erica Smalls's hospital room was the dream.

"She's coming," the kid said. He was standing at the foot of the bed again. There was a different quality to the ghosts when they showed up in his dreams than when they turned up as hallucinations. He couldn't quite pin down what it was, other than that they tended to be less helpful.

"She can't come now. I have to be someplace," Corrigan said.

"She's coming. Because you've been bad. You need to be punished."

"Christ," he said, rubbing his own forehead. "Enough already."

"Who're we expecting?"

Corrigan turned and discovered Harvey sitting in the bed next to him.

"Oh wonderful," he said. "I bet Ames would love to hear about this."

"Wasn't my idea. Now who's coming?"

"It's... ah..."

"The first," answered Steve. He was a construction worker who fell to his death because Corrigan couldn't get past the foreman in time to warn him. He was lying on the floor next to the bed in much the same position in which he died.

"Her name was Diane," Corrigan said. "First message I ever got."

"Corrrrrigan..." Her voice felt like a hand around his throat.

He lay back in the bed and tried to pull up the covers, hoping he would wake up sometime soon.

I can't do this now, he thought. *I have to be awake... for something...*

"You screwed up your first appointment?" Harvey asked. He didn't look frightened at all.

"Didn't know it was an appointment. I'd just gotten your money, and—"

"What did you do?" Diane roared from everywhere at once.

"And all I knew was I was supposed to show up someplace. I watched her die."

"Well, this is not at all what I expected from you, boy. Frightened by a loud voice? Honestly. I thought you were made of tougher stuff."

"It gets worse."

"*What did you do?*"

"She was crossing the street to pick up her children when

someone blew through a red light," Corrigan said quietly. "The kids... they were standing right there when—"

The bed started to shake. It felt like it was on the back of something large and awful and that large and awful thing was trying to buck it free.

Corrigan held onto the bed sheets for dear life. Harvey still didn't seem bothered, like a man sipping tea on a boat in high seas.

"What a coward," Harvey spat. "You were braver when you were twelve, young man."

"What do you expect me to do?" Corrigan asked. "It's my fault. I can't change that."

An arm burst through the middle of the mattress and grabbed Corrigan by the ankle. He let out a scream. *Wake up, wake up, wake up!*

"You didn't kill her."

Corrigan was being pulled down through the middle of his bed. He reached up and grabbed the bedpost. He didn't know what would happen if he got sucked down because he always woke up before it happened. But he was never this tired before.

"I let her die, isn't that close enough?" he shouted to Harvey. The disemboweling of his bed was making a horrendous noise, like a dump truck being torn in half.

"*Join us down here!*"

"Oh quiet, woman," Harvey barked. "And no, Corry, it is certainly not close enough. I killed Osgood Pierce, remember? It took six months and a bout of sepsis to finally do him in, but I pulled the trigger. *That* is killing someone. You neglected to save her, and that's completely different. You didn't know any better at the time."

"Tell *her* that," Corrigan said.

He was losing his grip on the bedpost. A second hand reached up and grabbed his other leg, and he couldn't wake up

—and he was pretty sure he had just wet himself. Violet would yell at him for that.

"All right," Harvey said. He leaned forward and grabbed one of Diane's wrists, pulling her hand loose from Corrigan's leg with about as much trouble as one might remove an ant from a picnic table.

"Go haunt the guy who was driving the car!" he shouted into the widening hole in the middle of the bed.

Corrigan pulled harder on the bedpost and somehow freed his other leg himself.

"*Join us!*" Diane wailed.

"No," Corrigan said quietly, but firmly. "I have to be someplace."

"He's here," the boy said.

"What?" Corrigan asked. The kid had moved from the foot of the bed to the side, and was staring Corrigan in the face.

"*He's here.*"

Corrigan woke with a start. He was back in the hospital again, still sitting in the chair. The lights in the room had been dimmed, probably by some helpful nurse. He could see Erica lying in her bed, breathing steadily. Maggie was in the chair next to the bed, still in her fabulous evening gown, which was probably being ruined. She'd rested her head on the side of the mattress and fallen asleep that way.

And standing at the door, staring right at him, was Kilroy.

———

D*on't let them know you can see them.*
Harvey's words came back like a splash of ice water in the face. It was pleasantly surprising that Harvey wasn't there saying it to him, meaning perhaps the short amount of sleep he'd just gotten was enough to clear his head.

The creature—Kilroy—looked to have more in common with a species of bird than with a human being. His bald head was slightly oblong, perched atop a long buzzard neck. His nose, which came to a very precise point, seemed beak-like, and his eyes were black and without pupils.

But there were other aspects that bespoke of entirely different species of animal. His head was cocked, which seemed nearly canine. The sides of his mouth curled up almost past his ears, and his lips didn't completely cover a row of teeth that looked shark-like. His body—which appeared almost too skinny to support the weight of his head—came with arms that were too long, like an ape.

That was, Corrigan realized, just an illusion. It wasn't the arms that were long, it was the fingers. They extended so far from the wrist, there had to be an extra joint involved. In one of those hands the creature had a wooden bat, the end of which dragged along the floor.

The overall picture was of something only nearly human. It was the thing you see at the edge of your vision but which disappears when you turn your head. It was the thing that went bump in the night. It was the boogeyman. And it was really there.

Corrigan looked away quickly, mindful of Harvey's warning and the general lessons McClaren had taught him. Kilroy hated to be noticed, and once he got a taste for mayhem he seem to enjoy it.

Is this the same one Harvey shot?

"Maggie," Corrigan said. "Maggie, wake up."

Kilroy turned his gaze to Maggie's still form. She stirred a few seconds later.

"Whu... Corrigan, what is it?" Maggie asked. "Is it—"

"Shh."

He had to operate on the assumption that whatever Kilroy was, he understood the English language.

Maggie sat up and looked around. Kilroy moved to the open space near the closet, but Maggie's eyes didn't track that because she couldn't see him. She instead looked over at Corrigan again. He nodded almost imperceptibly.

"You sure?" she asked.

"Positive."

"Okay. Okay. Now what do we do?"

"Someone's coming."

The door to the room swung open, causing Maggie to jump and let out a little yelp that, in a different context, might have been amusing. One of the floor nurses walked in.

"Hi!" she whispered, moving with the quiet grace of someone who was used to maneuvering around sleeping people on a daily basis. "Just doing my rounds, don't mind me."

"Sure..." Maggie said, rubbing her eyes. "Fine."

Corrigan involuntarily found himself holding his breath as the future version of the nurse stepped right in front of Kilroy and around the end of the bed.

"What time is it?" Corrigan asked.

"It's about one in the morning, dear," she said. The nurse was at an age where she could call anybody *dear* and get away with it. "And what good folks you all are, staying with her like this."

She went to work checking the IV drip and recording Erica's pulse rate with her watch. "Yes," she went on, "this one is a miracle, isn't she? Steady as she goes." She put down Erica's wrist. "I think she's going to be all right."

"Is there still an officer outside the door?" Maggie asked.

"Yes, ma'am. Wide-awake and bored silly. You know, you two might want to retire for the night yourselves. I'm sure she'll be just fine until sun-up."

"I think we better stay here," Corrigan said.

"Well then, at least make yourselves comfortable." She was

heading for the closet, which both Corrigan and Kilroy could see about to happen. Kilroy stepped to the side, well before the nurse reached the closet door and slid it open. "Hang up your coats."

There is a demented semi-human killer standing ten inches away from you, Corrigan thought. *And you don't even know he's there.*

It occurred to Corrigan at that moment that he had no idea how a creature stuck in the future could do damage to people stuck in the present. Kilroy existed with their future selves, but by the time their future became their present, he'd already moved on, because he was always ahead.

The bat, he thought. *He'd have to use the bat.*

The dead in McClaren had been beaten with a mop-handle or shot with a gun or, in one case, slammed by a door. But if the Kilroy who'd been there that day was like the one before him now, he could just as easily have choked someone with those long fingers or done something comparatively gruesome.

Likewise, Erica was stabbed with a kitchen knife and hit in the head with a baseball bat. Objects, it seemed, were not subject to the same restrictions as the one who held them.

"Thanks," Maggie said to the nurse. "That's a good idea."

"Coffee's down the hall," the nurse pointed out, adding, "we're always happy to help the FBI."

"Glad to hear it," Maggie said.

The nurse left the room with a smile.

"Corrigan," Maggie said, a bit louder with the nurse gone. "What now?" She looked ready to wake up Erica, even though she was clearly not ready to be moved.

"Don't know," he said, although he sort of did.

When Harvey was put into a similar situation, he did the only thing he knew how to do: try and kill the Kilroy before it hurt anybody. Unfortunately, in Harvey's case he also terrorized an entire hospital, accidentally killing a number of the people he was trying to save. It made for an excellent cautionary tale, but it also held an important point. The thing went to the hospital to kill Harvey and went through anybody who got in the way, which meant Corrigan and Maggie were hardly safe, provided this Kilroy had similar character traits—and given his track record, that seemed like a good bet.

But what Corrigan also knew was that if these things didn't like to be seen—were, perhaps, afraid to be seen—the only way to keep Erica safe was to offer up a different target.

If Harvey were still there, he'd tell Corrigan he was crazy for even considering such a thing.

He got out of the chair, the blood rush causing the world to go squiggly for a second or two. It felt as though he'd been sitting there for days.

"What are you doing?" Maggie asked, or was about to ask. It looked like he wasn't quite perfect with his identification of the present, as he heard her say it a couple of times. And the boy wasn't around anymore to tip him off on when to speak.

"Just stretching," he said casually. He kept Kilroy in view, out of the corner of his eye. He still wasn't moving. Corrigan stretched, just as he said he would.

"Going for a jog?" she asked.

"Maybe."

Maggie stood as well. And whether she knew it or not, she ended up positioning herself right between Kilroy and the still-sleeping Erica Smalls.

"Did I tell you how much I like that dress?"

"Designer," she said. "Probably ruined."

Kilroy moved. It was an odd thing to watch, because unlike everyone else, the bald man didn't have a past and a future, just a present *in* the future.

Thinking about it made Corrigan's head ache.

He can't stand around forever.

That seemed to be the same conclusion the killer reached as he decided, right then, to take care of all three of them, starting with Maggie.

In the future, Kilroy's bat connected with the back of her head.

"Maggie," Corrigan said, "don't move."

At the last possible moment, Corrigan stepped between them and blocked the bat with his hand.

From Maggie's point of view, it must have looked like Corrigan was defending himself against empty air, even though the impact of the bat on the palm of his hand made a loud *PAP!*

Kilroy jumped back and shook his head, looking like a dog that'd been slapped across the nose with a rolled-up newspaper. Then he took a swing at Corrigan.

He saw in his own future how the bat impacted him flush across the nose. It was so real he could taste the blood and feel the solid shock of impact travel through his body and wobble his knees. He could even see the floor coming up to greet him. But then he dodged, and the bat whistled through empty space.

Again, Kilroy stepped back and looked about, confused.

"Corrigan, what's—"

"He's putting it together," he said. "Guess he's never met someone like me before."

Kilroy looked him in the eye and displayed a new expression for him—fear.

"That's right, asshole," Corrigan said. "I can see you."

And then, to his surprise, Kilroy turned and ran.

Corrigan saw him doing it and dove at where his legs were going to be, but of course they were already gone. He saw the creature exit the room while lying on the floor.

"You stopped him!" Maggie said happily.

Corrigan pulled himself to his feet and headed for the door.

"Where are you going?" Maggie asked.

Officer Harry Kupchak hated working the night shift, hated even more working the night shift when the assignment in question required him to be attentive the entire time, and absolutely despised beyond all words any assignment that stuck him on a chair in the hospital for the night.

It was even worse than working as a security guard—something he did for five years before he was accepted to the force—because at least in the mall, there were perks. Especially in the summer, when half the young women in the city of Cambridge dressed like off-duty hookers, or so it sometimes seemed. Here, he had nurses to look at, but it appeared that all the attractive nurses in the hospital were elsewhere, possibly worked only days, and maybe not even in this hospital.

The girl he was guarding was pretty cute, but he'd only gotten one glimpse of her a couple of nights ago when she was still in a coma, and, well, being attracted to someone in a coma meant there was probably something wrong with you, so he didn't dawdle in that regard.

He didn't even fully understand why he was there. When he checked in with Clancey, he was told that the FBI chick and some other *consultant* were in the room and he wasn't to disturb them. It seemed to Harry if they were inside, there was no reason for him to be out in the hallway at all. Granted, Clancey's description of how the FBI chick was dressed whetted Harry's interest, but as she had not stepped out at all since his arrival, he wasn't holding out on the hope that she would any time soon.

It was well into his fourth hour in the chair when he heard some sounds coming from the room.

It was early morning and the floor was quiet, so noises weren't difficult to pick up on. He'd already heard two of the nurses discussing psoriasis in embarrassing detail from the front desk a good thirty feet away and around a corner. This noise was somewhat like the sound of a foul ball on a bare hand.

Harry stood and faced the door, debating whether to open it. He looked down the hallway in both directions—he was there, ostensibly, to make sure nobody entered, rather than worry about someone exiting—and then listened some more to see if the noise repeated. There was talking in the room, but Harry couldn't pick up what was being said.

He unclipped the holster for his handgun, possibly more because the coffee he'd been drinking for the past couple of hours was making him edgy than because of any real danger.

Then something hit him in the chest. His first thought was that he'd been shot, except that he'd heard no gunshot ring out, which one should rightly expect to happen first under these circumstances.

Still, the blow felt an awful lot like he always imagined it might feel to take a load in the chest while wearing his vest. Basically, his whole ribcage was shoved toward his backbone.

He hit the wall gasping for breath and was facedown on the floor before he fully realized it.

Clutching his chest and feeling around for a bullet hole—there *had* to be one—he managed to crawl up onto his knees when someone came barreling out of the room: a big dude Harry never met before. The guy stumbled over him, and Harry ended up on his back with the guy on his knees on top.

Having no breath to speak of, Harry didn't have anything to say to the big guy, who looked down at him, apologized, and then stood up and sprinted down the hall toward the elevators.

"Corrigan!" someone shouted from in the room.

The FBI chick flew out—Clancey's description didn't do her justice—and saw Harry lying on the floor. She knelt down beside him.

"Are you hurt?" she asked.

"M'okay . . ." he rasped. His lungs seemed to be developing a rhythm again, which was good. But he thought maybe one of his ribs was busted. This was bad, as he still didn't know what had hit him, and that would make for one very embarrassing incident report.

"Nurse!" she shouted. "This man needs assistance!" To Harry she asked, "Where'd Corrigan go?"

He pointed. She nodded. "Call for backup. I think you got nailed pretty good there, officer; you need to get someone else down here as soon as you can. She cannot remain unattended. Understand?"

He nodded and started fumbling around for his radio, which was attached to his belt beside the butt of his gun... which, he suddenly realized, was no longer there.

"Gun," he whispered.

She was getting to her feet and about to walk away. She couldn't hear him.

"Hey!" he said, louder and, *oh, that hurt*.

"What?" she asked.

"That guy who tripped over me... took my gun."

She stared at him for a second. "He didn't trip," she said. "He couldn't have."

"Then..."

"He did it on purpose."

She ran off, muttering something as she went. Harry couldn't quite catch all of it. Something about McClaren.

———

Corrigan checked the safety with his thumb as he ran down the hospital corridor toward the elevators.

It was a slow night in the ICU, which was a very good thing as he had quickly discovered that he wasn't nearly himself yet, despite the short nap and the ingestion of a number of candy bars.

The faster he ran, the more there was to take in, until he had a serious overabundance of input, and his ability to filter out the future in favor of the present was quite clearly still broken. He wouldn't have been surprised to see the back of his own head running in front of him.

Just keep going, he thought, shoving the gun into his pocket.

Ahead of him—temporally and spatially—the front end of his hypothetical Corrigan centipede caught sight of Kilroy rounding the corner of the central elevator and ducking into the stairwell. Corrigan hit the door for the stairs shortly thereafter. No, that wasn't right. He hadn't even reached the door yet.

"Wait, dammit!" he heard Maggie shout. He looked back to see her running, running, running even as he reached the door, while on the other side of the door he was already trying to figure out which way Kilroy had gone.

Too much going on.

Since the ICU was on one of the hospital's middle floors, the stairs went both up and down. He was nearly positive Kilroy would have gone down, as he looked hell-bent on getting away from Corrigan. But he wouldn't put it past the thing to head up a couple flights, find a different stairwell, then double back down and take out Erica while Corrigan was somewhere below. So rather than choose, Corrigan decided to go both up and down.

This turned out to be easier than one might have imagined. By favoring neither direction, he ended up choosing both. Had he been well rested, this approach would have never occurred to him, but his head was so muddled and his sense of reality so bent, it seemed like a perfectly reasonable option. And it worked, so he was not about to question how he was doing it.

His going-down self spotted the Kilroy a flight below, while his going-up version found only an empty landing. He abandoned the latter future and continued down.

Downstairs, the very edge of his future self spotted his quarry exiting onto the second floor of the building, while at the same time he heard Maggie enter the stairwell and shout his name again. She seemed to be extremely agitated. He couldn't imagine why.

Reaching the door and jerking it open, Corrigan discovered the main hospital lobby, which confused him for a second until he recalled that the lobby was *supposed* to be on that floor. It was a long, thin expanse centered on a vast desk area manned by exactly one person, for whom at least a dozen people were waiting. A few looked over at him, surprised, as adults only rarely run through buildings without a good reason, and he had clearly arrived at that point after a fair amount of running.

Corrigan was fortunate in that nobody was moving much, so the future distortions were slight and easy enough to parse. It also helped that he had stopped running long enough to figure out where Kilroy went.

That didn't turn out to be too hard.

The creature was standing still behind the queue near a man in a suit. It was an odd effect, seeing him hover behind a row of blurry people because with no future blur of his own, Kilroy was the only one in focus. It was like seeing a black and white movie with one character artificially colorized.

Noting that he had Corrigan's full attention, Kilroy smiled and raised his bat into the air, meaning to club the fellow in the suit with it.

Corrigan knew it would come down to this. The consequence of chasing Kilroy was that it put everyone nearby at risk.

But that was why he'd taken the gun.

Dropping to one knee, Corrigan drew the handgun from his

pocket and took aim. Behind him Maggie was screaming something, but he ignored her; he knew what he was doing. He fired.

Corrigan was always a pretty good shot. It was one of the things he prided himself on. He even owned two guns and on weekends liked to drive out to a private shooting range in Medford for target practice. A couple of times this proficiency came in handy, most spectacularly in the bank robbery he helped foil the first time he worked with Maggie Trent.

It didn't help this time. He watched in horror as the head of the man in the suit disappeared in a cloud of pink dust. The woman behind him in line shrieked in horror, even as the remnants of a human head coated the front of her face and clothing.

Kilroy—who used the bat to bump the dead man into the path of the bullet—smiled satisfyingly.

What have I done? Harvey, I understand now.

"Corrigan, no!" Maggie screamed. He looked down and realized he was still kneeling, the gun was just coming to bear, and he was about to take aim.

I'm in the future, he realized. *I haven't done this yet.*

He lowered the gun, and the death of the man in the suit vanished, as did the rest of the future. This was jarring for Corrigan, but considerably more so for Kilroy, as when the future vision reinstated itself, Corrigan could see that Kilroy was clutching his head in pain.

"It hurts him," Corrigan realized.

"Give me the gun!" Maggie screamed.

The people waiting in line noticed for the first time that Corrigan was waving a firearm. This caused a mild panic, not nearly as bad as when one of them had had his head vaporized, but still. Everyone scattered, and Corrigan's sense of the present went all to hell again.

"Give me the gun!" Maggie screamed.

"You said that, didn't you?"

She leaned down to swat the gun free from his hand, but Corrigan saw it coming and moved his arm out of the way.

"Fine," he said, "I'm fine. He's getting away."

And he was. Kilroy recovered quickly from the shock of having his present pulled out from under him, altered, and shoved back into place. He was making for the side exit, which led to the top floor of the parking garage.

Maggie was still shouting at him. "...shoot you," she had just finished saying.

"What?" he asked.

Kilroy stepped out through the sliding doors, preceded by the future version of a young pregnant woman who looked terrified of Corrigan. He wondered what could possibly have dragged her to the hospital at one thirty in the morning that didn't involve the emergency room, but his speculation was cut short by the fact that Maggie was pointing her gun at him.

"I said you have to let go of the gun, Corrigan. I don't want to shoot you."

He stared at her. "You're not going to," he said.

Corrigan was out through the sliding door before Maggie could properly ruminate on her actually having to shoot him, deciding that if she really had to think about it, she obviously didn't have it in her. She hated him for knowing this before she did.

"FBI," she declared loudly, for at that moment everyone who was still in the lobby had seen her gun. She held up her badge for emphasis. It would have been better overall if she looked like a professional law enforcement officer instead of like another type of professional, but she'd been saying a variant of that for most of the evening, especially the parts of the evening that had her running in three-inch heels.

"Everything's okay. We're... uh... we're chasing down a fugitive."

This sounded mad, but whatever.

Let them figure it out for themselves.

She followed Corrigan out the door.

He was already at the far end of the garage, heading down the ramp to the ground level and probably toward the street, where he would surely find more civilians to accidentally terrorize. Not knowing what else to do, she headed in the same direction.

It was insanity, thinking she could help him bring down an assailant she could neither see nor affect in any real way, but it seemed equally wrong to let him run off alone and hope for the best.

There has to be some way I can help, she thought. And just then, she thought of one such way.

The front corner of the parking garage afforded her a view of Mount Auburn Street a good quarter of a mile in both directions. Directly below her was the outlet through which anybody —on foot or driving—would ultimately have to emerge if they wanted to exit the garage without also breaking a leg. It was a twenty-foot drop onto a steep hill on the other side.

From there, she should be able to see where Corrigan was heading.

She slipped the gun into her jacket pocket and then pulled a much more useful device from the same pocket—a cell phone.

"C'mon, c'mon," she muttered, listening to the ring.

Finally, he picked up.

"Professor Calvin? It's Agent Trent. Listen, I don't have much time..."

CHAPTER TWENTY-FOUR

Now

Sir Isaac Newton appeared to be ringing. This was certainly odd, but it was not the very oddest thing about Newton. The very oddest thing about Newton was that he was roughly fifty feet tall and appeared to be wearing a trout on his head in lieu of a powdered wig.

The fish was making a disturbing sucking noise in order to remain atop Newton's head—for he was mouth-first—and that noise had been distracting them both throughout the entire conversation. Newton had apologized a couple of times already for this.

"Terribly sorry about the fish, good sir," he said. "But if I took him off, I'd never finish with the recoinage. You understand." Archie did not understand but had the good sense not to ask for an elaboration.

Archie Calvin, who was—as far as one could tell such things —still completely normal sized, sipped his tea and tried not to think about the fact that he was sitting at the same table as Newton and that the table accommodated both of them handily, despite being a normal table, and despite Newton's gargantuan size.

"What did you say?" he asked Newton politely. One must always be polite to Newton.

"Ring," Newton repeated.

Sir Isaac had been in the middle of a lengthy treatise on the nature of time as a thing independent of observation and perspective—a viewpoint that no longer aligned with the modern understanding— and *ring* did not fit in well with the rest of his argument.

"I see your point," Archie said. Which seemed like the thing to say, really.

"Ring," Newton said again. His nose trembled slightly.

"Um..."

"It's the phone," said the fish, who had removed Newton's head from his mouth and was now perched sideways, danger-ously close to sliding off Newton's head and onto the table. "Wake up and answer it before Ronnie has to."

"Ah. Thank you."

"No problem."

Archie lunged for the nightstand in the dark, the remnants of the fifty-foot Newton and his talking-fish wig still darting about his unconscious like fireflies under a porch light: there, but lost in the background. He could still taste the tea in his mouth. *Darjeeling.*

The phone was to the right of the alarm clock, which had a red LED display that was annoying when trying to sleep but extremely useful when looking for the phone. He picked up the receiver. It was wireless, so he didn't concern himself with the possibility that the cord might knock over something he may wish to keep.

"Hello?"

"Professor Calvin?" said a woman on the other end of the line. "It's Agent Trent. Listen, I don't have much time—"

"Agent Trent?" He rummaged through his brain for a one-to-one match but found only more of Newton's *Principia Mathematica*.

"Look, I'm kind of in a bind here. It's about Corrigan."

This name he recognized. And having made that connection, he knew who was on the phone. "Yes, Agent Trent. Of course."

Ronnie rolled over and snorted. She had been a loud snorer for every day of their married life, and he'd never found a way to tell her, preferring instead to swaddle his head in pillows in order to muffle the sound. Interestingly, through a down pillow, the snoring noise sounded very much like a trout might if sucking upon a head.

He climbed out of bed a tad unsteadily and walked to the hallway, closing the bedroom door behind him.

"What's wrong?" he asked.

"We found out why these people have been dying," Maggie said. "There's a... well, I don't know what he is. A being. He lives in the future."

"I'm sorry," he said, wondering if he was still dreaming. "Did you say, 'lives in the future'?"

"Yeah. That's what Erica—*Oww*!"

"Are you all right?"

"Just twisted my ankle. I'm running in heels."

"Oh. Right."

Archie started heading down the stairs toward his study. He kept expecting a talking fish to pop up and tell him he hadn't answered the phone yet.

"Erica—you mean Erica Smalls. The student you led me to believe had been killed."

"We led everyone to believe that. Look, this guy lives at the other end of the chrono-thingie. They saw him by accident—he got pissed off about it and started killing people one at a time. Are you with me?"

"Sure," he said, although his mind was still trying to catch up.

"Corrigan, who *can* see him, is chasing him down, and I'm running after Corrigan and completely ruining a great pair of Manolo Blahniks in the process."

He reached his office and sat down in his desk chair, wondered what the heck a Manolo Blahnik was, and decided it was probably not important.

"There is a sentient being living in the future, is that what you're saying?"

"Professor, I need to know how to kill it before Corrigan hurts somebody and we're looking at another McClaren situation. Do you understand?"

"No, I'm afraid I don't just yet. You might have to give me a minute."

K ilroy wasn't the best of runners. He had an odd gait that made him look like someone who was trying to move quickly while holding a ball between his knees, and his arms flailed about arrhythmically, as if he couldn't quite figure out just exactly how to keep them from getting tangled up in his legs. He still had the bat in his hand, but didn't seem to know what to do with it any more than he did his arms, so it swung wildly from side to side, rapping into telephone poles and parking meters as he passed them by.

Corrigan, who started off more than a block behind, was having little trouble gaining. It helped enormously that there was hardly a soul in sight for Kilroy to threaten, as it was approaching two in the morning. This also meant fewer moving parts in general, which was frankly a godsend for Corrigan, who had not only lost track of his present, he had given up trying to look for it.

And then a car came down the street and offered him a cue. The sight was so alarming he actually stopped and stared at it as the front end of the car's future sped past.

What he saw first was the headlight beam, which was uncommonly visible thanks to an early-morning mist. The beam seemed to stretch for hundreds of feet, terminating suddenly at the front of the hood and the beginning of a car that looked as though it were as long as a football field. Used to be he could distinguish between the present and the hypothetical future somewhat easily because the future was ever so slightly indistinct, but there was nothing ghostly about any part of this car.

He knew perfectly well the car was really car-sized. But what he knew and what he saw diverged so dramatically that he was inclined to believe his eyes.

I am so not prepared for this, he thought.

"You're doing fine," Harvey said. He was sitting on the hood of a parked car. Another bad sign. Surely the rest of the menagerie was on its way. "Now keep going. He's getting away."

"No, he's not," Corrigan said.

Kilroy had stopped running at around the same time Corrigan had and for approximately the same reason; he saw the car, too.

"He's going to do something."

"Looks like," Harvey agreed.

"Go away, Harvey."

"Corrigangangangangàwaitititttttt," said someone from behind him. He looked back and saw a Maggie-like shape moving in his direction. He ignored her.

Kilroy stepped out into the middle of the street.

He's going to wreck the car, Corrigan realized.

The superlong car's superlong hood continued past Corrigan as he ran in a vain effort to reach Kilroy before the car did. In another few seconds the hood reached Kilroy, at which time Kilroy swung the baseball bat into the driver's side of the windshield. The formerly streamlined giant vehicle's front jerked around like the head of an electrified snake and came to a jarring termination at a telephone pole.

"No!" Corrigan shouted.

"You have time," Harvey said calmly. He'd been taking up sitting positions at various points along the route.

"It's too late," Corrigan said. "It already happened."

"No, it hasn't. That was the future. You know it."

"Yeah..." Corrigan said. "You're right."

"Course I am."

I'm not going to like this, Corrigan thought as he realized exactly what he had to do next.

"Of course. That would make sense," Calvin said, having woken up enough to wrap his mind around the concept. "He could... well, this thing could get to anyone, couldn't he? No one would be the wiser for it."

"Exactly the problem," Maggie said, a bit out of breath.

"Always ahead. He would have to be vibrating at a different frequency, figuratively speaking. Like Pythagoras's harp strings, yes..."

"Professor—"

"But if that's the case—"

"Professor, just tell me how to kill it, please?"

"Oh, you can't," he said. "You're on different planes of reality, my dear."

"Then how does he hurt *us*?"

"Object permanence. A thing, like a knife or a bullet, might not be subject to the same constraints. It's complicated, but essentially it comes down to the question of whether time is an objective or subjective—"

"Professor, I—Corrigan, wait!" she shouted. "Sorry, he stopped. I almost caught up."

"Ah. As I was—"

"Just skip ahead. Why can't I hurt him with objects just like he can hurt me?"

"Because of his position in time, he will always know what you're about to do. He'd have to be suicidal, very confused, or simply not paying attention to allow himself to be harmed by someone in our present."

"So there's nothing we can do to stop him, that's what you're telling me?"

"There's nothing *you* can do. Corrigan Bain is another story entirely."

"Why... oh, God, *no!*"

———

Having spent some of the early parts of his life surrounded by the kind of people who meditated regularly, Corrigan was intimately familiar with the idea of a mantra.

He never fully appreciated the calming influence the repetition of one might have, though, until he had to hurl himself from a curb and directly into the path of an oncoming vehicle, at which time he discovered his own personal mantra: "Please don't be drunk, please don't be drunk, please don't be drunk..."

His senses told him the sobriety of the driver was not nearly as large a concern as the fact that he was about to thrust his head and shoulders through the side of the car, which still looked perfectly solid. But intellectually, he understood the vehicle couldn't really be a quarter of a mile long, so instead he focused on the driver's competence.

Astonishingly, he did not slam face-first into solid metal. Instead, the car moved away from him, a feat seemingly as likely as a river instantaneously jumping its own streambed.

The future got wobbly from the change, and for just a second Corrigan stood entirely in the present. Even Kilroy disappeared from view.

Corrigan watched the now normal-sized car swerve madly into the opposite lane and around him. There was a thump, but not the thump of the car hitting him: it hit something else.

He blinked, and the future reasserted itself. Kilroy was lying on the pavement a few yards away, on his back.

"The car hit him," he said with undisguised amazement.

"You changed the future," Harvey said. He was sitting in a chair on the median strip and looking very full of himself. "Kilroy didn't have time to react to the change. That's how I bagged mine, remember?"

"I remember. But it can't have been that easy."

It wasn't. The Kilroy was already sitting up, rubbing his shoulder.

"Whatarewhatdoingareyoudoing?" he heard several Maggies ask. "Streetgetofbeforetheoutofstreetbefore..."

"Still alive," Corrigan said. "Resilient little bastard, aren't you?"

Kilroy climbed to his feet, staring at Corrigan like a cornered animal. Then he opened his mouth and let out the most god-awful howl Corrigan ever heard in his life. He clapped his hands over his ears and let out a scream of his own.

Maggie really thought she was keeping her shit pretty well together under the circumstances.

She'd gotten over the whole "killer who cannot be seen" issue, and she'd come to grips with the idea that she was running after a fight she had no hope of contributing to in a positive way. She even tapped her only scientific resource in a desperate attempt to problem-solve her way to a contribution. But when Corrigan Bain, a man she would never use the word *love* in describing but whom she nonetheless liked a great deal, inexplicably threw himself into the path of an oncoming car... well, that was it. Clearly, she had no hope of controlling or even understanding what was happening in front of her, and she never would. Especially if Corrigan didn't survive long enough to explain all of it to her.

The car, which swerved to avoid Corrigan, ended up on the wrong side of the road for a good block before jerking back into the correct lane and then accelerating away madly, leaving Corrigan in a genuflecting and unharmed state right in the middle of the street. And then he just stayed there.

"What are you doing?" she screamed at him.

"Still alive," Corrigan said. He was speaking—not to Maggie, but to an unoccupied spot on the median strip. "Resilient little bastard, aren't you?"

"Get out of the street," Maggie shouted. "Before—"

And then Corrigan fell to his knees, put his hand over his ears, and started screaming, apparently in acute pain.

"Alrighty," Maggie said. "Dunno what the hell is—"

"Agent Trent?" said someone in her ear. She'd completely forgotten she still had Professor Calvin on the phone. *What was he saying before?*

"Hang on," she said.

"What is that awful racket?"

"Corrigan. I don't know why he's doing that, but if he keeps it up, we'll have to contend with the cops soon."

After a time, Corrigan realized he was the only one screaming, so he stopped. He opened his eyes and looked around. Kilroy was no longer in the middle of the road, and for just a moment, Corrigan thought he'd been given the slip. But then he spotted the creature about half a block away, limping and still holding his right shoulder.

Kilroy hadn't lost his bat, which made him dangerous to anyone who might stray too close. Fortunately, with the car gone, the only such beings around were Corrigan and Maggie, and possibly a few waterfowl, if Kilroy's direction stayed true. He was heading for the bank of the river.

"Stay away," he said to Maggie before picking up his pace and heading after Kilroy. Even though what came out of his mouth sounded more like *stayayayawayastayway*, he trusted that for her it was clear enough. He didn't expect her to follow his advice, but it felt good to have at least tried. It was only a matter of time before Kilroy decided to demonstrate his displeasure with Corrigan by taking it out on her.

They were a good six blocks from the hospital now, to a point at which Mount Auburn Street veered closer to Memorial Drive and the Charles River, and also where the line of buildings between both roads disappeared, to be replaced by a small grassy island that—in an overpopulated city— qualified it as a park. Kilroy reached a gathering of trees and slowed considerably, giving Corrigan all the time he needed to catch up.

"Okay, ugly," he said, as Kilroy turned to face him, "what do we do now?"

The creature smiled, once again showing off his strangely huge mouth and rows of jagged teeth.

"Kilroy," he said through the smile.

"Yeah. Whatever."

Kilroy raised the bat in his right hand and took a swing at the spot Corrigan would be standing if he didn't know any better. Corrigan did, and stepped aside. Then Corrigan drew the gun, aimed carefully at Kilroy's head, and fired. Kilroy stepped to one side at the last second, the bullet heading toward the river beyond.

"Huh," Corrigan said. "Guess we have a problem, don't we?"

Rather than responding conversationally, Kilroy performed something approximating a curtsey, his arms gesturing wide with the flourish of a Shakespearian actor acknowledging the applause of the crowd. Corrigan felt as if he should bow in return, as if this were some sort of pre-battle sumo ritual. But Kilroy was actually communicating a simple message. *Here are my friends.*

Stepping into view from behind trees on either side of Corrigan were two other Kilroys. He'd walked right into a trap.

Archie switched the phone to speaker mode and dove into the contents of his marginally organized desk for his notes, of which there were plenty.

On many occasions in the past ten years, he'd had members of the student body in this study. Without fail every one of them, upon looking around, would ask the same question: where's the computer? But to Archie, a computer was a large thing, possibly even a large thing attached to a larger thing that ran to an even larger thing—a warren of computational outposts that were connected by a series of cables and always,

always, in a building to which one traveled. One did not have such a thing in one's home, nor would one wish to any more than one would wish to have one's coworkers sharing one's house.

Not to say that Archie wasn't up-to-date on the revolution in personal computing, at least conceptually. Emotionally, his ideas weren't real until he saw them written down on a piece of paper in his own handwriting. A computer file was too ephemeral, too nonphysical for him to digest.

The drawback was that he had the organizational sense of a blind pack rat. So it took a minute or two to find the right pages. As was the case for much of the top layer of paperwork on his desk, they were about Corrigan Bain.

On the phone, he could hear a variety of strange noises in the background, including the screeching of car tires and a lot of gasping and panting. Agent Trent had momentarily forgotten she was on the phone, which was fine as he needed a few seconds to gather his thoughts, and he thought best when he had—*there they are*.

"Agent Trent?" he called loudly, reading his notes at the same time.

Someone had started howling on her end of the line. It sounded like that primal screaming therapy that was so popular in the Eighties.

"Hang on," she said.

"What is that awful racket?"

"Corrigan. I don't know why he's doing that, but if he keeps it up we'll have to contend with the cops soon."

"He sounds in pain."

"I think he is. Hold on, okay?"

"Holding."

The notes were a summarization of a drawer full of research into Corrigan's background, research he had to compromise a number of his personal ethics to obtain. But it was, he constantly told himself, important.

He figured out fairly early on how it was possible to *see* the future on a short-term basis much in the same way his fixer friend could, but that was only one component of the whole. What he learned from his extra research was that Corrigan Bain didn't just see the future. He heard it, smelled it, tasted it, and touched it as well. In other words, Corrigan didn't just see, he *experienced*.

Michael's team could approximate the visual aspect fairly simply—it was really just a matter of light, or more rightly, optics—but not the entire package. Not until they understood how such a thing was even possible.

The answer to that wasn't in Corrigan's history. But it *was* in Archie's notes.

"Where are you... Hey!" Maggie was shouting again.

"What's going on now?" Archie asked.

"He's run off again. It looked like he was saying something, but I couldn't hear him. So what were we talking about?"

"I was saying that while you could never find a way to do harm to this being, Corrigan should be able to."

"Why is that?"

It sounded as if she'd begun to run again, which caused the hands-free speaker in her ear to jostle against the side of her head and make an annoying fuzzy scratching noise that roughly matched her gait.

"I don't know if it's anything he's seriously thought about before . He never struck me as much of a deep thinker..."

"No kidding," she remarked.

"...but there is really no reason for him to remain in the same present which we currently occupy."

"Come again?"

"The reason Corrigan knows the future is that he experiences it, and the reason he experiences it is that he exists in all phases."

"What?"

Archie sighed and tried again.

"Agent Trent, in order to hurt this... future being, one must first travel into the future, to the same plane of existence he occupies. But our fixer friend doesn't need to do any traveling. He's already there."

CHAPTER TWENTY-FIVE

Now +

Kora-gan of the Echo People expressed a funny/scared look that made the Kilroy Prime of the River Tribe Kilroys laugh. Seeing Kora-gan so confused/frightened made the Prime feel good/happy for figuring out that Kora-gan was the See and for not being afraid.

The Kilroy Prime had been told the old legend/myth of the See as a child-thing over a hundred cold-cycles past. The See of legend/myth was the bringer of darkness/pain, who with mighty hands would rend the world in two until there was no world to rend. Through him would the Void Beyond be given voice and form. The See was the destroyer of all.

Or so it went.

It wasn't supposed to be real/true, only something to tell the child-thing at dark-time to frighten it into behaving. But then was the time word/rumor came from the Hill Tribe Kilroys that their Prime had been slain in a great battle with the See.

This word/rumor spread through the Fourteen Tribes faster than a hundred gathering screeches. When the Prime heard it, much of the tale was already draped in legend/myth that the Menials of his Tribe swallowed whole, but as the Prime, he knew there was an essence of non-myth in its core.

With effort, he chewed away at the falsehoods and got to the truth/fact inside. The See was real, and he hid/traveled among the Echo People.

So on the great/horrible day two cold cycles past, the Kilroy Prime of the River Tribe Kilroys knew/understood what it meant when one of the Echo People spoke to him.

They were trying to turn themselves into Sees with one of their Echo machine/devices. He knew/understood what he had to do.

The killing of Echo People was an idea/notion the Prime never entertained before that day. Everyone in the Tribes knew the Echo People were best left alone. They were Primitives and worthy of no more than pity/scorn. But sometimes, when they acted foolish and forgot their place/role in things, they needed to be punished.

What the Kilroy Prime never imagined/thought was how much he would enjoy this. The Echo People were stupid, more stupid then the lowest of the Menials, and so easy to frighten/terrorize. In fulfilling his duty/oath to the Tribes, he stumbled/discovered a greatness. He, Kilroy Prime of the River Tribe Kilroys, was the bringer of death himself, a god-thing to the lowly Echo People. So he gave them his name that they might know who smote/punished them.

For his arrogance, Kilroy Prime of the River Tribe Kilroys was himself punished when the *true* See, bringer of darkness/pain, revealed himself in the well-making room of the final Echo.

The Prime should have known when he first saw Kora-gan that he was different. Others of the Echo People appeared fuzzy/rough, but Kora-gan looked crisp/solid. And then the Prime saw how Kora-gan could move.

When the Kilroy Prime swung his great stick at Kora-gan, he saw/felt the stick hit Kora-gan's face. And then in blink-time Kora-gan was not there anymore. Nothing but the See could have done such a thing.

To his shame and the shame of his ancestors, Kilroy Prime of the River Tribe Kilroys became afraid.

He ran.

But then he realized that as much as the legend/myth/story of the death of the Kilroy Prime of the Hill Tribe Kilroys needed to be chewed upon for the truth to be divined/understood, so, too, did the legend/myth of the See itself.

Kora-gan, Seer of all, the destroyer from the Void Beyond was still only an Echo. And Echo People could die.

Yes, it was true that Kora-gan had the power of the See. The Prime saw/felt what happened when the See called forth the horror of the Void Beyond, but while it was truly horrible/painful, it was not permanent/fatal, as he had been led to understand/fear it would be. Getting struck by the Echo machine/device in the road almost hurt more, and he was nearly recovered from that blow.

No, Kora-gan the See was no more worthy of his fear than any of the Echo People. He could be killed/defeated. And when that happened, the legend of the Kilroy Prime of the River Tribe Kilroys would be greater than that of any of the heroes of old.

The Prime smiled some more.

Now

"Didn't I tell you they always travel in packs?" Harvey was saying.

"No, Harvey," Corrigan said. "You never mentioned it."

"How do you suppose they did all that damage in the hospital? Those things were all over the place."

"But you only shot one of them. Why didn't they keep attacking?"

"I shot the leader," Harvey said.

"The one in the overalls," Corrigan said. "So, I take care of him, maybe the other two leave me alone?"

"I don't know. Maybe."

The other two looked nearly identical to the first, except for their clothing. One had on jeans and a torn brown sweater, and the other a navy blue suit and a T-shirt. Both looked like they did their shopping at the Salvation Army, which was probably exactly the case.

More important than their clothing, was that both had weapons. The sweater guy had what looked like a policeman's nightstick, while the one in the suit had a *sword*.

"A sword?" Corrigan said. "Are you fucking kidding me? Where did you get a sword?"

"Seemustdie," the first Kilroy—*the Alpha Kilroy*—said, still smiling.

They closed in on Corrigan, showing a coordination that indicated this wasn't the first time they'd worked together. The Alpha appeared to have generalship over the other two, as he communicated positioning to them via a series of short chirps and head bobs. Corrigan did his best to keep all three in sight without having to turn his head, but the closer they got, the harder that became.

Now, he thought.

In the future, he felt the nightstick—from his left—crash

down on the side of his head. He ducked away from that and right into the swing of the sword, which was coming in low. His only safe dodge was to fall to the ground and roll, which took him right into the path of the baseball bat.

He swatted the bat away at the last second with his forearm, but this opened him up to a vicious shot in the ribcage from the nightstick. Still on the ground, he rolled away from that and managed to regain his feet outside the circle of attack.

Rib's busted, he thought. *Might be time for me to run.*

The three Kilroys repositioned themselves with impressive speed and precision—or so it seemed given they were still ahead of him in the timeline—and in another second he was surrounded once more and facing the sword, which was whistling at his face.

Above all else, avoid the sword, he reminded himself.

It was the most dangerous of the three weapons, for while blunt-force trauma was no picnic, at least the bat couldn't chop him in half. It seemed the Kilroys understood this, too, for as he stepped to the side before the sword hit home, he found himself occupied avoiding swings from the night stick and the bat. That gave the one with the sword a chance to swing at him again, and this time he had no chance to avoid it, unless he went *through* the swordsman.

It made perfect sense and probably should have occurred to him earlier. They weren't in his present, even if the things they were swinging were. Corrigan couldn't hope to understand why that was, but he didn't need to. He just had to know it to be the case.

His present-tense self dove through the future-tense swordsman. In one of his futures, this resulted in him passing directly through the unmoving sword-wielder—diving through his midsection like a linebacker executing a tackle—and getting a mouthful of suit. It was like running through somebody's closet.

In the other future—the one that stuck—the Kilroy with the sword reacted and stepped aside. And that was all he had time to do. Corrigan landed safely outside of their attack circle.

Corrigan should have had time to get to his feet after that, but by the time he got his bearings, the Alpha Kilroy was already upon him, swinging the bat.

That was much too fast, he thought, just as the bat connected. The side of his face exploded in a shower of flashing lights and thudding pain.

What's going on?

He rolled away awkwardly, and then tried again to get to his feet, but found that this was not a simple matter; the shot to the head had messed up his equilibrium. He fell back over. Then nightstick guy hit him in the arm, and the Alpha took another swing at his head, which he was now covering with his hands.

More swings followed, to the chest and legs. And the one with the sword was coming around to deliver what would probably be a deathblow.

Corrigan, reduced to ducking and covering, couldn't understand what was happening. It was like all three of them had suddenly started moving in fast-forward, and he had no idea where the rewind was. *Are they really this fast?*

He was going to have to do something about the sword first and worry about the rest of it later, even if it meant being brained.

In the temporary lull—the others had stepped back so the swordsman could administer the fatal blow—Corrigan slid his hand into his pocket and pulled out the gun. He knew the Kilroy would dodge it before it did any damage, but maybe, if he was supremely lucky, he could hit the sword.

He took aim and fired at right around the same time the Kilroy raised the sword over his head. Corrigan meant to hit the handle, but none of his attendant body parts—hand, arm, head, eyes—were entirely up to the task thanks to a sound pummeling. The gunshot missed low and hit his attacker squarely in his gargantuan forehead.

He didn't dodge it? Corrigan thought. *I can't be that lucky.*

The Alpha Kilroy knocked the gun from Corrigan's hand before he could try another shot, but that was okay; the damage had been done. Mr. Blue Suit staggered backward, dazed, possibly wondering where the bullet hole above his eyes had come from and how he hadn't expected it. He made a noise that sounded a little like a disappointed kitten, then fell to his knees, and collapsed awkwardly onto his back. The sword fell to his side.

Okay, I think I get it, Corrigan thought.

Breaking his silence, the Alpha shrieked madly and swung at Corrigan's face with the bat, but Corrigan anticipated the move. He rolled to his right so that the head of the bat struck the ground harmlessly. Then, once the head of the bat was grounded, he rolled left and pinned the bat under his left arm and torso. This brought the Alpha's face closer to the ground— he didn't want to let go of the bat—and within striking range.

Corrigan swung his right fist at the creature's nose with as much force as he could muster. There was a loud crack from the impact. The Alpha squealed in pain and jerked backward, upending Corrigan and releasing the bat from its temporary confinement.

"Hah!" Corrigan said, ignoring the significant pain in his knuckles. "Guess who just arrived for the party?"

Now

Something weird was going on with Corrigan. Maggie noticed it when he stopped in the grassy park a stone's throw from the river and fired the gun. There was absolutely no question whatsoever that he had fired it because the gun lit up the night with its discharge, and she'd been around enough handguns in her lifetime to know there was nothing else a gun could do that might be mistaken for it.

Yet, it didn't make a sound.

And that wasn't possible. Even silenced guns make a little noise when they fire, and there was no way the service revolver was silenced. All the laws of physics with which she was personally familiar required that there be a loud *BANG!* involved. As there was not, she was forced to conclude that perhaps there were some laws with which she wasn't entirely familiar.

"How would he go about doing that?" Maggie asked Archie Calvin. "Go ahead in time, like you said."

"I suspect he has always done so in small increments and not realized it," he said. "All of the people I spoke to who are familiar with him explained that there are occasions in which it seems he's not really there. They described it as a lack of concentration on his part, which is about how I would expect it to happen. It's not that he loses track of the present. He quite literally *drifts out* of the present."

"But I've seen that happen," she said. "And he doesn't disappear or anything."

In front of her, Corrigan had begun a complicated dance, looking as if he were avoiding attacks from a number of invisible assailants.

What is he doing to you, Corrigan?

She knelt down behind a shrub that divided a small children's play area from the space Corrigan and Kilroy occupied, hoping to go unnoticed.

"He wouldn't disappear," Archie said. "Part of him still occupies the present; it's only that the driver is missing. Look at it as a mind-body problem. Where does the mind end and the body begin?"

"Isn't the brain part of the body?"

"Not the brain. The mind. The part of us that is *us*, that thinks and reasons and is self-aware. In most of us it's located in the same temporal space as our body, which is also stuck in that one space. In Corrigan, the mind can be anywhere along his future timeline."

Corrigan dove, fell on the ground and covered up. His head got rocked hard to one side. Kilroy was absolutely whaling on him.

"Can I still communicate with him?"

"Well, yes. He still occupies a space in our present. He should also hear your words spoken in the future."

Looking pretty ragged, Corrigan drew the gun from his pants and fired a desperation shot. Maggie was only a couple dozen feet away. *Still no sound.*

"He just shot a gun, and I didn't hear it. Explain."

"He's gone ahead, then!" Calvin said.

"Shouldn't I hear the gunshot when I catch up to it?"

"This is where it gets somewhat complicated. In a sense, there are two kinds of 'now' in play here. There is your 'now,' which has caught up with Corrigan's former 'now.' And there is the 'now' that he and the creature occupy. The two are not the same, as should be apparent since we cannot ever see the creature. He fired the gun in the other 'now,' and every non- object-related thing associated with that act—like the sound of the gunshot—is gone by the time your 'now' catches up to it, for the same reason the creature and the sound he might make are gone by then. This is a non-symmetrical arrangement. The sounds you make will be heard in their present, but the sounds they make will not be heard in yours. It gets even more complicated from there, but—"

"Skip it," she said. "How come I can still see him when I can't see the thing he's fighting?"

"The creature has no presence in our 'now.' Corrigan does. It's what makes him unique."

Maggie had more questions but her phone had just beeped loudly, curtailing a more extensive discussion that would probably have not brought her any closer to a full understanding anyway.

"My battery's low," she said. "Tell me, does Corrigan even know he's been jumping ahead?"

"I imagine not. His grip on the present is usually very firm, from what I've been led to understand."

"Yeah, unless he hasn't gotten a lot of sleep."

"What was that?" Calvin asked. The beeping had gotten more persistent and was affecting the audio.

"Nothing. I'm losing you, Professor. I'll have to call you later, when it's over."

Provided, she thought, *we're still alive.*

Now +

Kilroy Prime of the River Tribe Kilroys squealed from the shock/pain of the See's unexpected attack on his nose.

Not possible!

The Prime backpedaled from Kora-gan and tried to shake away the shock/pain. He needed to think/chew this through because obviously he had underestimated the See's true power.

No, he is still just an Echo.

But when he looked up, he saw the Minion had similar

misgivings and appeared ready to dash/scream away. The Prime hissed a command.

"See must die."

It was far too late for them to back off now.

While the Alpha Kilroy stepped back and dropped his bat, staring the way one might look at a squirrel who'd suddenly gained the power of speech, Corrigan got to his feet. He chanced a look at the other one, who appeared no less confused.

"Seemustdie," the Alpha said, but he didn't sound all that sure of himself anymore.

"Do you say anything else?" Corrigan asked.

He swung his fist into the creature's stomach, doubling him over.

"Ooow," it said.

"There you go." He smiled. "How about 'I'm gonna kick your ass now.' "

Corrigan was—he would reflect moments later—a tad cocky. He had no idea what mechanism allowed him to jump forward into the realm of the Kilroys, nor did he particularly care to know. What he did care about was that his wish had come true.

Although not a violent man by nature, these creatures had pushed him to the limit, and he was not just ready to kill the both of them with his bare hands if need be; he was looking forward to it.

"Kickyourassnow," the Kilroy mimicked.

"Good!"

Corrigan risked another look at the second Kilroy. He was still standing well away, uncertain as to whether he should be fleeing or attacking.

I take care of the Alpha, the other one will run off, he reminded himself. Harvey would have said it for him, but he seemed to have disappeared. Things were looking up all around.

"Corrigan," the Alpha Kilroy said. Corrigan had been about to kick the guy, but hearing his own name caused him to hesitate. "Corrigandie."

"Um…"

The Alpha Kilroy swung his arm up and right at Corrigan's face, faster and harder than Corrigan expected him to be able to. He also thought he'd positioned himself outside of the Kilroy's wheelhouse, forgetting this was a being with unnaturally long hands. The triple-knuckled open palm slap across his face broke his nose on impact, rocked his head backward, and actually caused him to lose his footing.

When he landed and looked up again he was a good two yards away from where he'd been standing a second ago.

"Wow," he said, spitting out some blood and part of a tooth. "You guys are a lot stronger than you look."

There was a downside to being able to hit them, Corrigan realized: they could hit him too, without needing a weapon. And as far as hand-to-hand combat went, their hands were a lot bigger than his.

"Gun," he muttered. "Where's the gun?" He looked at the spot where he'd dropped it, but the gun wasn't there anymore.

Maggie was holding it.

Now

Once her call with Calvin ended, Maggie was left with a choice to either sit out the rest of it and hope for the best, or find some way to insert herself into Corrigan's fight. Her thinking, in choosing the latter, was keyed on something Calvin said, about how she could only hurt this Kilroy if he wasn't paying attention to her. Corrigan was keeping him pretty well occupied; maybe she could get off a lucky shot if she could figure out where he was—which shouldn't be all that hard as long as he kept hitting Corrigan.

So she left the haven of the bushes, walked into the midst of the battleground, and was about to draw her own weapon when she spotted officer Kupchak's gun.

It was just sitting there on the ground. Her initial impression was that it was something she wouldn't be able to touch, as Corrigan had carried it into the future with him. But when she leaned over and picked it up, it was as solid as ever.

Object permanence, she remembered. *This is what he meant.*

Corrigan picked that moment to fly across the lawn, landing only ten feet or so away from her. His nose gushed blood and he spat more out of his mouth when he sat up to speak.

You guys are a lot stronger than you look, he said.

She couldn't hear him, but she could read his lips well enough, and gave a quiet thanks to the FBI for teaching lip-reading as part of their surveillance training.

"Keep talking," she said loudly, as if volume could somehow allow her words to bridge the temporal gap more quickly. "Maybe I can figure out what the hell is going on."

Now +

"Keep talking. Maybe I can figure out what the hell is going on," Maggie said, or would say shortly, depending on one's perspective. She waved the gun around in the vicinity of where the Alpha was standing, calculating his position based on where Corrigan had been standing when he was struck. But she didn't know there was more than one Kilroy.

The second Kilroy also heard her. Having just gone from terrified of Corrigan to pleasantly surprised that Corrigan might be relatively easy to beat up, he now looked extremely happy to find a less dangerous victim in the area to prey upon. He was directly in front of Maggie, maybe fifteen feet away, and she didn't even know it.

"Great," Corrigan said. "I told you to stay away, dammit."

The Alpha Kilroy picked up his bat again, but he looked so shaky it was obvious he wasn't going to be a threat for a few more seconds. The problem was the second Kilroy.

I need the gun, he thought again and then wondered why Maggie had to go and grab his gun at all when she had one of her own.

The Kilroy was walking up to Maggie and brandishing his nightstick while she was still quite oblivious.

Getting back up off the ground, Corrigan's hand fell on the only weapon left—the sword.

"Hey!" he shouted, swinging the sword around wildly and trying to look like he knew how to use it. "Stay away from her!"

But the Kilroy was too interested in Maggie to be distracted and Corrigan had no chance of getting to him in time.

The creature swung his nightstick right at her face.

"Duck!" Corrigan shouted.

Now

Corrigan had picked up, of all things, a sword. She was afraid to even guess where it came from. Perhaps now he was fighting a medieval knight?

He was looking right at her. She saw him shout, *Stay away from her!* and all at once realized she'd made a mistake.

You guys are a lot stronger than you look, he said earlier.

Plural.

There's more than one.

She thought she had a good idea where one Kilroy was, but hadn't factored in the possibility of multiples. Now, one of the extra combatants was about to take a free shot at her.

Duck! Corrigan shouted. So she did. Something whooshed in the air above her head.

Now +

E ven prior to ducking, the physical presence of Maggie Trent in the future-verse occupied by Corrigan and both his sparring partners was oddly indistinct. The Kilroys and Corrigan were solid and clear and as evidently real as anybody in the commonly agreed-upon present would appear to anybody else in the commonly agreed-upon present. Maggie—even when standing still—was fuzzy, as if a poorly focused camera had captured her.

Had Archie Calvin and Erica Smalls been standing next to Corrigan, they might have been able to explain to him that this was because no matter how close to accurate this future path was, there were always going to be minor uncertainties. As they were not there, the best Corrigan could muster by way of explanation was, *how odd.*

And then Maggie ducked, which was an explicit alteration of her future. The timing was correct because while Corrigan said it to the future Maggie, the blow she was ducking was being inflicted upon the future Maggie, so that when she caught up to this future and it became her present, the warning and the attack happened more or less in the same order in which they should have.

Corrigan didn't think of this either; he was just hoping it would work.

In one version of events, Maggie stayed where she was and took a nasty blow to the face, caving in her nose and right cheekbone. But now there was a second Maggie, one that lowered her head at just the right moment. She split from the injured version, and when her future changed, the entire world—the ground, the trees, the air—wiggled, spun sideways, and was temporarily rent in two. There was a sound that came from this rending that was somewhat like a tremendous steel door being fed through a gigantic wood chipper.

This sound had a physical impact on Corrigan and equally so on the Kilroys. It rattled his teeth and shrank his genitals and punched him in the stomach. He screamed—silently for lack of air—then fell to his knees and seriously considered running himself through with the sword. It was worse than the shriek of the Kilroy he'd heard earlier—worse than anything he'd ever heard or felt in his life.

And it lasted barely half a second.

When it was over he understood a little bit about the motives of the Kilroys. Someone who saw them could also do this to the future. *He* could do this to the future, and already had. Although it didn't appear to be the case when he altered his *own* future. It only happened when he—or Harvey, or someone like them—changed the future of someone else whose destiny was otherwise set.

It was so painful that if Corrigan was destined to remain stuck in the future—and who was to say he wasn't at this point —he might consider acting the same way the Kilroys did, if only to prevent that horrible sound from ever happening again.

The beneficial result of Maggie having ducked was that she didn't end up with her face smashed in, and her attacker was temporarily incapacitated.

Corrigan, as shaky as he was, saw this as an opportunity to close the distance between him and the Kilroy.

He staggered forward as best he could, holding the sword over his head like an axe. It must have looked comical—he moved the way a person who had been spinning in place for several minutes might—but with the Kilroy still focused on Maggie, he didn't notice that he had a sword coming at his head until too late.

With a loud *clang*, the blade bounced off the Kilroy's skull, and the weapon nearly vibrated right out of Corrigan's hand. He actually fell over backward with the ricochet. The Kilroy, although decidedly wounded after being struck by a long piece of metal, did not suffer death by cleaved cranium, as one would expect. He did fall down, however.

Getting up again, Corrigan ran his hand along the blade's edge. It was dull.

Decorative, he thought. *Naturally.*

He examined the point and found that it was slightly rounded, which was also a major disappointment. But it was still a heavy, flat piece of metal that tapered at the end. He figured he could drive it through someone if he had to.

But the gun made a lot more sense. He tossed aside the sword and grabbed the gun from Maggie's hand. Her future self jumped back in surprise.

The Kilroy got to his feet and emitted a whiny screech. It was nothing like the one the Alpha Kilroy had let out earlier in the street. More like something a miffed parakeet might utter. He charged.

Corrigan shot him twice in the chest and then, when he fell over, a third time in the face, just to be sure. A headshot had worked on the first one, and he couldn't be sure these things had a heart in which to put a bullet. Then, rather than dallying any longer, he spun around to take care of the Alpha Kilroy. Unfortunately, the Alpha happened to be right behind him at that time, such that when Corrigan turned, he brought the gun right into the creature's swing.

The bat knocked the gun at least thirty feet and also, not incidentally, broke two of Corrigan's fingers.

Without thinking of much beyond how very painful that was, Corrigan grabbed his broken fingers with his good hand, which, of course, left his head unprotected for the next swing of the bat.

At the last second he turned his shoulder enough to absorb most of that blow, but it still hurt like hell and nearly knocked him to the ground.

"Corrigandie," the last remaining Kilroy declared once again.

He swatted at Corrigan with the bat, but this time Corrigan was prepared. He grabbed it with his uninjured hand, planted a boot into Kilroy's chest, and jerked the bat free. It was a maneuver that would have worked a lot better if, after completing it, he'd managed to hang onto the bat, but it ended up flying over his head and far enough away that it may as well have landed in the river for all the good it did him.

The Kilroy continued to press the advantage, lunging forward and wrapping his tremendously huge hands around Corrigan's windpipe. In a second, the Alpha had Corrigan pressed up against the trunk of a tree, their faces inches apart. Corrigan couldn't breathe or move.

Kilroy opened his mouth, his gigantic yellow teeth glistening. His jaw seemed to have no hinge to it. Like a snake, it looked as though he could have eaten Corrigan's head whole. And as the creature leaned closer it occurred to Corrigan that might just be what he was planning to do.

Now

The nonstop entertainment that was the Corrigan Bain Pantomime Theater had Maggie so entranced she almost completely forgot she was in mortal danger. There was the Mystery of the Sword, in which Corrigan swung hard at something that was not there, hit it, and then almost recoiled his way across Memorial Drive. This was preceded by the Dance of Agony, which seemed to involve the lead actor grasping his head tightly in an apparent effort to get his eyeballs to pop out.

Then there was the Grabbing of the Gun. She didn't like that piece. Corrigan went from standing beside her to ripping the gun from her hand without his hand actually traversing the necessary distance in between first. It was spooky.

The performance got much more serious after the Firing of the Gun with the climactic Breaking of the Fingers and The Choking. Maggie realized then that she was watching Corrigan die but didn't know what she could possibly do about it.

"How do I help?" she shouted. "Tell me what to do!"

He was mouthing something.

He was looking right at her and mouthing something.

She edged closer—expecting any second to get attacked by another invisible Kilroy—to figure out what it was.

What are you saying?

It was harder to read his lips because he was busy being strangled and seemed to be losing some motor control. But eventually she got it.

Shoot me.

GENE DOUCETTE

Hoping quite fervently that she'd gotten that right, she pulled her gun from her coat pocket, said a quick prayer, and aimed at his chest.

"Hope you know what you're doing," she muttered.

Now +

"Hope you know what you're doing," the Echo said.

Caught up in his bloodlust, Kilroy Prime of the River Tribe Kilroys had almost forgotten there was another Echo in the area.

He'd forgotten because Kilroys only rarely thought of Echoes at all. The sounds they made were just a part of the cacophony of background noise/buzz that each Kilroy as far back as when they were child-things just learned to ignore. But this Echo said something that Kora-gan thought was important. The Prime could tell, because Kora-Gan had stopped struggling.

The Prime looked over his shoulder and saw. The Echo was holding a gun machine/device.

"No," he muttered.

"Yes," Kora-gan said.

The Alpha Kilroy realized he'd fallen into a trap and was trying to pull free, which would not do—not with Maggie taking aim at Corrigan.

To keep the Kilroy still, Corrigan slapped his hands on either side of the Alpha's head, pulled him as close as he could, and held on for dear life.

They were easily close enough now for the creature to try

368

taking a bite out of Corrigan, but Kilroy wasn't thinking about that any more. His motions got increasingly frantic, and as Corrigan was fighting to hold him still with the help of two broken fingers, it hurt like hell.

"You're not going anywhere," he whispered.

"Seemust... mercy," Kilroy said, his eyes widening. He knew he'd run out of time.

"Not a chance," Corrigan said.

In her own present, Maggie Trent fired the gun, and then something strange and a little awful happened.

Corrigan felt the bullet hit him in the chest. It happened to the version of him that occupied her present, but he had little understanding of that distinction given he'd just been shot. The bullet impacted his breastbone and fragmented, hitting various internal organs, including at least one lung. He gasped and fell backward against the tree, but perhaps quixotically at this point, still held onto Kilroy's head.

Maybe she'll try again, he thought, *before I die.*

Then her future self caught up with the present he and the Kilroy shared, and the gun was fired a second time.

Two things happened at once. First, Kilroy shrieked, his back arching as if he'd touched a live wire. Second, the blackness came, and for just a second Corrigan thought *this is me dying.*

But it wasn't that. It was the same world-shattering, reality-tearing agony he went through earlier when Maggie had ducked. Added to the pain from the gunshot, Corrigan fervently hoped it would all be over soon, because death would hurt less.

And then the darkness receded, and the pain went away. All of the pain.

He patted his chest where the round had struck him and found no damage. A deep breath confirmed that all was well, internally.

What the hell just happened?

"Seebringvoid," Kilroy said.

Corrigan realized he was lying on the ground next to the tree, so he sat up and looked around until he found the Kilroy on the ground nearby. Corrigan crawled over to him, not altogether certain what he would do if the creature wasn't mortally wounded.

He needn't have worried. The bullet that hit Corrigan's past self dead center had instead struck the Kilroy around where his heart should have been.

"Void," the Kilroy repeated. "Hailbringer..."

His head sagged over.

Corrigan sat still, holding his breath and waiting for the creature to spring back to life. He didn't.

"Well," he said. "Thank goodness for that."

"Corrigan, are you okay?" Maggie asked. She was kneeling next to him.

"Yeah," he said, looking at her. "Nice shot."

Then, not knowing what else to do, he lay back down.

Aside from the two broken fingers, broken nose, broken ribs, and the gigantic bruise his body had become overall, he had no idea how to get back to Maggie's time. But that could wait. What he really wanted was to get some sleep.

"Well done, my little fixer," he heard Harvey say.

"Thanks, Harvey."

He closed his eyes.

EPILOGUE

The street itself seemed solid enough, but everything that moved around on it was fuzzy.

No, that wasn't quite the right word for it.

Foggy, he thought. People who were only partly there walked along the sidewalk, some well-focused, but most only lightly represented misty ghost-figures. The whole effect was jarring, like slipping on a pair of 3-D glasses halfway through the movie. Probability had been introduced as a dimension.

Corrigan looked around for street signs and other identifiers and found he was standing on an island in the middle of Commonwealth Avenue, having just stepped off a subway train that was blurred to slight indistinctness by several possible arrival and departure times in its future.

It was pulling away from the aboveground landing beneath his feet. Various phantom representations that meandered off the train stood waiting for a walk signal.

Okay, now I know where I am. Why am I here?

Not seeing anything obvious, he joined the crowd and

crossed the street to the waiting sidewalk. Everybody there was too ghostly—or in Calvin's words, *temporally uncertain*—to be the subject of his appointment. But he was close.

He started walking uphill, alongside a block of tall red brick buildings that tended, more often than not, to house students, as they were within walking distance of Boston College.

In the summer, the apartments were largely unoccupied, and it was still a couple of weeks too early for the caravan of moving trucks that heralded the commencement of the fall semester. So it seemed unlikely that Corrigan was looking in the right place.

But it *felt* right. And this was one of those times when feel was all he had to work with.

He came to a stop at building 317. An indistinct woman walked an indistinct dog on an indistinct leash past him, and a honking imbroglio had broken out on the street, where someone who nearly ran a red light almost ran into someone who jumped the green light.

Both cars came to a blurry stop inches from their faint bumpers. Corrigan studied their interaction, could see no layers of future-fog wherein the two cars collided, and decided to ignore them. It would be, at worst, a minor fender-bender.

Corrigan looked at his own hand. When he got off the train he was nearly solid, but now he was much fainter. This told him he was very likely to come this far, but less likely to stand on the street like this. Somewhere, he had diverged.

There was a loud *clang*. It was louder than the honking or anything else going on around him. This wasn't because it was *actually* a louder noise. It was a more *certain* noise, and so took place in almost all of the time-possibles Corrigan was standing in the midst of.

He turned to locate the source and spotted a window screen

falling to the street, closely followed by the animated body of a young man.

The young man screamed. He looked almost perfectly solid, and his cry of shock was piercingly loud. The scream was prematurely appended by his violent impact with the ground. Corrigan looked at his watch. It was 4:02 in the afternoon.

Various foggy people ran up to his partly smeared body lying dead on the sidewalk. Corrigan ignored all of them—and the semi-noises they made—even when a few brushed past him. This was an odd sensation, like running the back of your hand over a bowl of cold oatmeal. He looked up instead.

Okay, where'd he come from?

There was only one window in the path of descent that was open and had no screen. It was on the fourth floor.

Running up the steps inside, he soon reached apartment seven, which looked to be the right floor on the correct side of the building. The door was ajar—a big time-saver—so he just pushed his way in.

The window through which the kid had gone was in the living room. A young woman was standing at it and screaming.

"What happened?" he asked.

"FellGodjustfellheleanedwhoarewhatcallhelp?" she said.

Fuzzy people, he'd learned, almost never spoke in logical sentences. What he was getting was pieces of an untold number of possible sentences she might speak. But he'd gotten pretty good at piecing these together.

He leaned on the screen, he thought.

Stepping up to the window, he examined the groove where the screen had rested. It didn't look damaged or bent, so he checked the window next to it.

Screens are the wrong size, he thought. *That's the problem.*

Leaving the confused and still shouting fuzzy woman in the

living room, he went to the victim's bedroom and rifled through some of his things until he came across a pile of opened mail.

Tom Harrison, he read. *Tom Harrison in building three seventeen, opposite the T-stop on Comm Ave. 4:02.*

Mark it down.

Now

Corrigan awoke with a start, sat straight up, and let out a little yelp.

Bedroom, he thought. *I'm still in bed, I'm still in bed...*

Repeating this, he got his heart rate to slow down to something like normal and convinced himself he was where he thought he was.

In a lot of ways, the old method was easier. The waking up part, for instance, never used to be so disorienting. It also felt like he'd gone through a whole day already, even though he'd been asleep the entire time.

But, no more hauntings. It was hard to beat that.

He reached for the notepad on the nightstand and jotted a page worth of notes before he forgot all of it, then climbed out of bed.

It looked like it was going to be another hot, sunny day. He resolved to find some time in the week for a trip to the beach.

It was a small step, but he had to do this in small steps. His hope was to be able to work in an entire vacation week sometime, maybe to go down to the Cape to visit Violet and her new husband. He had never been down there. She'd like that.

Heading down the hall to the bathroom, he passed his office, which no longer had a map on the wall, and where the computer hadn't been turned on for almost a month. He was thinking of turning the space into a guest bedroom if he found the time and a guest or two who might like it. That would involve developing a more nuanced social life, but he was confident that such a thing was within his grasp, for perhaps the first time ever. Again, small steps.

Back from the bathroom a few minutes later he found Maggie awake and looking over the top page of his notepad.

She'd been staying over more often of late. He wasn't sure exactly why that was but was reluctant to broach the subject for fear it would cause her to stop coming over.

"Busy day," she said.

"Not so bad," he said, slipping into a pair of sweats. "And the last one's not too time-sensitive."

"Tom Harrison?" she asked, struggling to read his handwriting. Two of his fingers were still taped together, and his penmanship suffered for it.

"Yeah. He's scheduled to fall out of his window at 4:02. I'll show up early, tell him to stay away from the window. That should do it."

"Yecch," she grimaced, making a face. She put the list back down on the nightstand and stretched out in the bed, managing to do so in the most erotic way possible.

"I still don't really get it," she admitted, ignorant of his ogling.

"What?"

"This, with the notes."

"I'm going into my own future," he said. "It's complicated."

This was a phrase he was getting used to hearing from Calvin and one which he found himself repeating on occasion.

After he passed out in the park near the hospital, Maggie fetched an ambulance and got him a bed at Mount Auburn. He woke up bandaged, rested, and otherwise well ministered to, almost two days later.

Shortly after that, once he checked out and returned to his ghost-free life, he began having very interesting dreams. As the dreams appeared to be conveying to him the same information he used to wake up with before—only now in a much more accessible format—he was understandably confused. He knew of only two people he could talk to in the interest of an explanation.

Erica Smalls was whom he'd gone to first. Unfortunately, Erica wasn't quite conversant enough on the subject of Corrigan Bain to offer any solid theories—although she was glad to see him, and he promised to keep in touch. She recommended he speak to Calvin.

Archie Calvin was up to the task.

According to him, Corrigan had "breached the wall beyond the limits of the *chronoton*." In English, it meant that in his sleep he was occupying his future self.

Years ago, Harvey said he could go further into his own future if he wanted to, provided he was very relaxed. Corrigan thought at the time that Harvey was just bragging. Now he understood.

When Corrigan explained this to Ames, who he was seeing regularly now, the doctor added that this was something Corrigan had probably been doing from the outset, but he had unconsciously blocked most of. This was why he had always gotten only partial information before. For whatever reason, that block was gone, and Corrigan couldn't be happier about it.

"I *know* it's complicated," Maggie said. "But, okay, look. You're going to visit Tom Harrison this afternoon and save his life, right?"

"Plan to, yeah."

"But the only reason you're going to be there is because you dreamed you would be there, and you only dreamed you would be there because you are actually planning on being there. So where does the information start? What process put you on Commonwealth Ave in your dream in order to witness this accident?"

"Dunno," Corrigan admitted, sitting back down onto the bed. "Maybe part of my future me wanders throughout the city every day looking for accidents. Or maybe I'm just naturally drawn to them. I try not to think about these things too much."

"That's your answer for everything."

He smiled. "It's gotten me this far, hasn't it?"

ABOUT THE AUTHOR

Gene Doucette is a hybrid author, albeit in a somewhat round-about way. From 2010 through 2014, Gene published four full-length novels (*Immortal*, *Hellenic Immortal*, *Fixer*, and *Immortal at the Edge of the World*) with a small indie publisher. Then, in 2014, Gene started self-publishing novellas that were set in the same universe as the *Immortal* series, at which point he was a hybrid.

When the novellas proved more lucrative than the novels, Gene tried self-publishing a full novel, *The Spaceship Next Door*, in 2015. This went well. So well, that in 2016, Gene reacquired the rights to the earlier four novels from the publisher, and re-released them, at which point he wasn't a hybrid any longer.

Additional self-published novels followed: *Immortal and the Island of Impossible Things* (2016); *Unfiction* (2017); and *The Frequency of Aliens* (2017).

In 2018, John Joseph Adams Books (an imprint of Houghton Mifflin Harcourt) acquired the rights to *The Spaceship Next Door*. The reprint was published in September of that year, at which point Gene was once again a hybrid author.

Since then, a number of things have happened. Gene published three more novels—*Immortal From Hell* (2018), *Fixer Redux* (2019), and *Immortal: Last Call* (2020)—and wrote a new novel called *The Apocalypse Seven* that he did not self-publish; it was acquired by JJA/HMH in September of 2019. Publication date is May 25, 2021.

Gene lives in Cambridge, MA.

For the latest on Gene Doucette, follow him online
genedoucette.me
genedoucette@me.com

ALSO BY GENE DOUCETTE

SCI-FI

The Spaceship Next Door

The world changed on a Tuesday.

When a spaceship landed in an open field in the quiet mill town of Sorrow Falls, Massachusetts, everyone realized humankind was not alone in the universe. With that realization, everyone freaked out for a little while.

Or, almost everyone. The residents of Sorrow Falls took the news pretty well. This could have been due to a certain local quality of unflappability, or it could have been that in three years, the ship did exactly nothing other than sit quietly in that field, and nobody understood the full extent of this nothing the ship was doing better than the people who lived right next door.

Sixteen-year old Annie Collins is one of the ship's closest neighbors. Once upon a time she took every last theory about the ship seriously, whether it was advanced by an adult ,or by a peer. Surely one of the theories would be proven true eventually—if not several of them—the very minute the ship decided to do something. Annie is starting to think this will never happen.

One late August morning, a little over three years since the ship landed, Edgar Somerville arrived in town. Ed's a government operative posing as a journalist, which is obvious to Annie—and pretty much everyone else he meets—almost immediately. He has a lot of questions that need answers, because he thinks everyone is wrong: the ship is doing something, and he needs Annie's help to figure out what that is.

Annie is a good choice for tour guide. She already knows everyone in town and when Ed's theory is proven correct—something is apocalyptically wrong in Sorrow Falls—she's a pretty good person to have around.

As a matter of fact, Annie Collins might be the most important person on the planet. She just doesn't know it.

The Frequency of Aliens

Annie Collins is back!

Becoming an overnight celebrity at age sixteen should have been a lot more fun. Yes, there were times when it was extremely cool, but when the newness of it all wore off, Annie Collins was left with a permanent security detail and the kind of constant scrutiny that makes the college experience especially awkward.

Not helping matters: she's the only kid in school with her own pet spaceship.

She would love it if things found some kind of normal, but as long as she has control of the most lethal—and only—interstellar vehicle in existence, that isn't going to happen. Worse, things appear to be going in the other direction. Instead of everyone getting used to the idea of the ship, the complaints are getting louder. Public opinion is turning, and the demands that Annie turn over the ship are becoming more frequent. It doesn't help that everyone seems to think Annie is giving them nightmares.

Nightmares aren't the only weird things going on lately. A government telescope in California has been abandoned, and nobody seems to know why.

The man called on to investigate—Edgar Somerville—has become the go-to guy whenever there's something odd going on, which has been pretty common lately. So far, nothing has panned out: no aliens or zombies or anything else that might be deemed legitimately peculiar… but now may be different, and not just because Ed can't find an easy explanation. This isn't the only telescope where people have gone missing, and the clues left behind lead back to Annie.

It all adds up to a new threat that the world may just need saving from, requiring the help of all the Sorrow Falls survivors. The question is: are they saving the world with Annie Collins, or are they saving it from her?

The Frequency of Aliens is the exciting sequel to *The Spaceship Next Door*.

———

Unfiction

When Oliver Naughton joins the Tenth Avenue Writers Underground, headed by literary wunderkind Wilson Knight, Oliver figures he'll finally get some of the wild imaginings out of his head and onto paper.

But when Wilson takes an intense interest in Oliver's writing and his genre stories of dragons, aliens, and spies, things get weird. Oliver's stories don't just need to be finished: they insist on it.

With the help of Minerva, Wilson's girlfriend, Oliver has to find the connection between reality, fiction, the mythical Cydonian Kingdom, and the non-mythical nightclub called M Pallas. That is, if he can survive the alien invasion, the ghosts, and the fact that he thinks he might be in love with Minerva.

Unfiction is a wild ride through the collision of science fiction, fantasy, thriller, horror and romance. It's what happens when one writer's fiction interferes with everyone's reality.

———

Fixer

What would you do if you could see into the future?

As a child, he dreamed of being a superhero. Most people never get to realize their childhood dreams, but Corrigan Bain has come close. He is a fixer. His job is to prevent accidents—to see the future and "fix" things before people get hurt. But the ability to see into the future, however limited, isn't always so simple. Sometimes not everyone can be saved.

"Don't let them know you can see them."

Graduate students from a local university are dying, and former lover and FBI agent Maggie Trent is the only person who believes their deaths aren't as accidental as they appear. But the truth can only be found in something from Corrigan Bain's past, and he's not interested in sharing that past, not even with Maggie.

To stop the deaths, Corrigan will have to face up to some old horrors, confront the possibility that he may be going mad, and find a way to stop a killer no one can see.

Corrigan Bain is going insane ... or is he?

Because there's something in the future that doesn't want to be seen. It isn't human. It's got a taste for mayhem. And it is very, very angry.

Fixer Redux

Someone's altering the future, and it isn't Corrigan Bain

Corrigan Bain was retired.

It wasn't something he ever thought he'd be able to do. The problem was that the *job* he wanted to retire from wasn't actually a job at all: nobody paid him to do it, and nobody else did it. With very few exceptions, nobody even knew he was doing it.

Corrigan called himself a fixer, because he fixed accidents that were about to happen. It was complicated and unrewarding, and even though doing it right meant saving someone, he didn't enjoy it. He couldn't stop—he thought—because there would always be accidents, and he would never find someone to take over as fixer. Anyone trying would have to be capable of seeing the future, like he did, and that kind of person was hard to find.

Still, he did it. He's never been happier.

His girlfriend, Maggie Trent of the FBI, has not retired. Her task force just shut down the most dangerous domestic terrorist cell in the country, and she's up for an award, and a big promotion.

Everything's going their way now, and the future looks even brighter.

Unfortunately, that future is about to blow up in their faces...literally. And somehow, Corrigan Bain, fixer, the man who can see the future, is taken completely by surprise.

Fixer Redux is the long-awaited sequel to *Fixer*. Catch up with Corrigan, as he tries to understand a future that no longer makes sense.

FANTASY

The Immortal Novel Series

Immortal

"I don't know how old I am. My earliest memory is something along the lines of fire good, ice bad, so I think I predate written history, but I don't know by how much. I like to brag that I've been there from the beginning, and while this may very well be true, I generally just say it to pick up girls."

Surviving sixty thousand years takes cunning and more than a little luck. But in the twenty-first century, Adam confronts new dangers— someone has found out what he is, a demon is after him, and he has run out of places to hide. Worst of all, he has had entirely too much to drink.

Immortal is a first person confessional penned by a man who is immortal, but not invincible. In an artful blending of sci-fi, adventure, fantasy, and humor, IMMORTAL introduces us to a world with vampires, demons and other "magical" creatures, yet a world without actual magic.

At the center of the book is Adam.

Adam is a sixty thousand year old man. (Approximately.) He doesn't age or get sick, but is otherwise entirely capable of being killed. His survival has hinged on an innate ability to adapt, his wits, and a fairly large dollop of luck. He makes for an excellent guide through history ... when he's sober.

Immortal is a contemporary fantasy for non-fantasy readers and fantasy enthusiasts alike.

———

Hellenic Immortal

"Very occasionally, I will pop up in the historical record. Most of the time I'm not at all easy to spot, because most of the time I'm just a guy who does a thing and then disappears again into the background behind someone-or-other who's busy doing something much more important. But there are a couple of rare occasions when I get a starring role."

An oracle has predicted the sojourner's end, which is a problem for Adam insofar as he has never encountered an oracular prediction that didn't come true ... and he is the sojourner. To survive, he's going to have to figure out what a beautiful ex-government analyst, an eco-terrorist, a rogue FBI agent, and the world's oldest religious cult all want with him, and fast.

And all he wanted when he came to Vegas was to forget about a girl. And maybe have a drink or two.

The second book in the Immortal series, Hellenic Immortal follows the continuing adventures of Adam, a sixty-thousand-year-old man with a wry sense of humor, a flair for storytelling, and a knack for staying alive. Hellenic Immortal is a clever blend of history, mythology, sci-fi, fantasy, adventure, mystery and romance. A little something, in other words, for every reader.

Immortal at the Edge of the World

"What I was currently doing with my time and money ... didn't really deserve anyone else's attention. If I was feeling romantic about it, I'd call it a quest, but all I was really doing was trying to answer a question I'd been ignoring for a thousand years."

In his very long life, Adam had encountered only one person who appeared to share his longevity: the mysterious red-haired woman. She appeared throughout history, usually from a distance, nearly always vanishing before he could speak to her.

In his last encounter, she actually did vanish—into thin air, right in front of him. The question was how did she do it? To answer, Adam will have to complete a quest he gave up on a thousand years earlier, for an object that may no longer exist.

If he can find it, he might be able to do what the red-haired woman did, and if he can do that, maybe he can find her again and ask her who she is ... and why she seems to hate him.

But Adam isn't the only one who wants the red-haired woman. There are other forces at work, and after a warning from one of the few men he trusts, Adam realizes how much danger everyone is in. To save his friends and finish his quest he may be forced to bankrupt himself, call in every favor he can, and ultimately trade the one thing he'd never been able to give up before: his life.

Immortal and the island of Impossible Things

"I thought I'd miss the world."

Adam is on vacation in an island paradise, with nothing to do and plenty of time to do nothing.

It's exactly what he needed: beautiful weather, beautiful girlfriend, plenty of books to read, and alcohol to drink. Most importantly, either nobody on the island knows who he is, or, nobody cares.

"This probably sounds boring, and maybe it is. It's possible I have no compass to help determine boring, or maybe I have a different threshold than most people. From my perspective, though, the vast majority of human history has been boring, by which I mean nothing happened, and sure, that can be dull. On the other hand, nothing happening includes nobody trying to kill anybody, and specifically, nobody trying to kill me. That's the kind of boring a guy can get behind."

Nothing last forever, though, and that includes the opportunity to *do* nothing. One day, unwelcome visitors arrive in secret, with impossible knowledge of impossible events, and then the impossible things arrive: a new species.

It's *all* impossible, especially to the immortal man who thought he'd seen all there was to see in the world. Now, Adam is going to have to figure out what's happening and make things right before he and everyone he loves ends up dead in the hot sun of this island paradise.

Immortal From Hell

Not all of Adam's stories have happy endings

"Paris is romantic and quests are cool. But the threat of a global pandemic kind of sours the whole thing. The good news was, if all life on Earth were felled by a plague, it looked like this one could take me out too. It'd be pretty lonely otherwise."

--Adam the immortal

When Adam decides to leave the safety of the island, it's for a good reason: Eve, the only other immortal on the planet, appears to be dying, and nobody seems to understand why. But when Adam—with his extremely capable girlfriend Mirella—tries to retrace Eve's steps, he discovers a world that's a whole lot deadlier than he remembered.

Adam is supposed to be dead. He went through a lot of trouble to fake that death, but now that he's back it's clear someone remains unconvinced. That wouldn't be so terrible, except that whoever it is, they have a great deal of influence, and an abiding interest in ensuring that his death sticks this time around.

Adam and Mirella will have to figure out how to travel halfway across the world in secret, with almost no resources or friends. The good news is, Adam solved the travel problem a thousand years earlier. The bad news is, one of his oldest assumptions will turn out to be untrue.

Immortal From Hell is the darkest entry in the Immortal series.

Immortal: Last Call

"I'm something like sixty-thousand years old, and I've probably thought more about my own death than any living being has thought about any subject, ever. I used to be unduly preoccupied with what might constitute a "good death", although interestingly, this has always been an after-the-fact analysis. What I mean is, following a near-death experience, I'll generally perform a quiet review of the circumstances and judge whether that death would have been objectively good, by whatever metric one uses for that kind of thing. I'm not nearly that self-reflective while in the midst of said near-death experience. Facing death, the predominant thought is always not like this.*"*

A disease threatening the lives of everyone—human and non-human —has been loosed upon the world, by an arch-enemy Adam didn't even know he had.

That's just the first of his problems. Adam's also in jail, facing multiple counts of murder, at least a few of which are accurate. He may never see the inside of a courtroom, because there remains a bounty on his head—put there by the aforementioned arch-enemy—that someone is bound to try to collect while he's stuck behind bars.

Meanwhile, Adam's sitting on some tantalizing evidence that there might be a cure, but to find it, he's going to have to get out of jail, get out of the country, and track down the man responsible. He can't do any of that alone, but he also can't rely on any of his non-human friends for help, not when they're all getting sick.

What he needs is a particularly gifted human, who can do things no other human is capable of. He knows one such person. He calls himself a fixer, and he's Adam's—and possibly the world's—last hope. That's provided he believes any of it.

Immortal: Last Call is the sixth book in the *Immortal Novel Series*, and also the end of a long journey for one immortal man.

Immortal Stories

Eve

"…if your next question is, what could that possibly make me, if I'm not an angel or a god? The answer is the same as what I said before: many have considered me a god, and probably a few have thought of me as an angel. I'm neither, if those positions are defined by any kind of supernormal magical power. True magic of that kind doesn't exist, but I can do things that may appear magic to someone slightly more tethered to their mortality. I'm a woman, and that's all. What may make me different from the next woman is that it's possible I'm the very first one…"

For most of humankind, the woman calling herself Eve has been nothing more than a shock of red hair glimpsed out of the corner of the eye, in a crowd, or from a great distance. She's been worshipped, feared, and hunted, but perhaps never understood. Now, she's trying to reconnect with the world, and finding that more challenging than anticipated.

Can the oldest human on Earth rediscover her own humanity? Or will she decide the world isn't worth it?

The Immortal Chronicles

Immortal at Sea (volume 1)

Adam's adventures on the high seas have taken him from the Mediterranean to the Barbary Coast, and if there's one thing he learned, it's that maybe the sea is trying to tell him to stay on dry land.

Hard-Boiled Immortal (volume 2)

The year was 1942, there was a war on, and Adam was having a lot of trouble avoiding the attention of some important people. The kind of people with guns, and ways to make a fella disappear. He was caught somewhere between the mob and the government, and the only way out involved a red-haired dame he was pretty sure he couldn't trust.

Immortal and the Madman (volume 3)

On a nice quiet trip to the English countryside to cope with the likelihood that he has gone a little insane, Adam meets a man who definitely has. The madman's name is John Corrigan, and he is convinced he's going to die soon.

He could be right. Because there's trouble coming, and unless Adam can get his own head together in time, they may die together.

Yuletide Immortal (volume 4)

When he's in a funk, Adam the immortal man mostly just wants a place to drink and the occasional drinking buddy. When that buddy turns out to be Santa Claus, Adam is forced to face one of the biggest challenges of extremely long life: Christmas cheer. Will Santa break him out of his bad mood? Or will he be responsible for depressing the most positive man on the planet?

Regency Immortal (volume 5)

Adam has accidentally stumbled upon an important period in history: Vienna in 1814. Mostly, he'd just like to continue to enjoy the local pubs, but that becomes impossible when he meets Anna, an intriguing woman with an unreasonable number of secrets and sharp objects.

Anna is hunting down a man who isn't exactly a man, and if Adam doesn't help her, all of Europe will suffer. If Adam *does* help, the cost may be his own life. It's not a fantastic set of options. Also, he's probably fallen in love with her, which just complicates everything.